THE CORRIDOR

THE CORRIDOR

N D CHAVDA

Ordering Information:

 BookTrail Agency
8838 Sleepy Hollow Rd.
Kansas City, MO 64114

Printed in the United States of America

PROLOGUE

2002 Andes, Argentina

Anthony Frenkel knew that his life was going to change drastically. He knew it a month ago when he was first asked to consider this project. He knew it when, after careful consideration, he accepted the challenge. He knew it when he left his wife and child at the airport and turned away as the sickening feeling arose inside him. He knows it today as he climbs his way up the Andes with his expedition. Just like he has always known when a crisis, however major, was going to cause waves in his life. As an eleven-year-old, he stood at the front door waving goodbye to his father, knowing that he was never to see him again. Fifteen hours later his father lay on a mortuary slab after a horrific car crash. Years later he had a gut feeling that his sister would do something which would affect the whole family. Two weeks later she eloped and married a drug dealer. He was in San Francisco rummaging through a wreckage of a small plane when he knew his wife was in pain. Hundreds of miles away, his wife was suffering a miscarriage. He could never quite say what was to occur, or how serious. But he was never wrong when it came to his own gut feeling.

As a child these feelings of his were mild, so mild that he thought they were a normal part of his mind. The normal way his brain worked. As he grew, he realised that not only was it something separate from his other abilities, but that he was alone. Nobody else had this ability. He had always regarded this special ability much in the same way as he did his arm, or his leg. An attachment which was essential but one which you hardly ever thought about, or even appreciated until it was damaged in some way and ceased to function quite in the way that it was meant to. He used this ability until he realised that he was different. It was not normal. He was not normal. He came to hate it and decided to cease using it. He tried hard to suppress it and after years of practise, he had it down as an art form. Only during times of crisis, he found the power hard to crush. He needed all his concentration twenty-four hours a day to suppress it. It was a constant battle in his head, one he normally lost. He just began to accept it with an air of resignation. It was there and always would be and control it he must.

It was a warm July morning about six weeks ago when he woke with a small niggling feeling. Jake was jumping on top of him and Jennifer was screaming at him from the kitchen. She wanted him to get up, shower and help her get Jake ready for school. But his heart sank when he sat up in bed and felt *it*. Like an irritating cut on a finger. He ignored it all the way through his shower, all the way through the nagging of Jennifer and the tantrums of Jake. His eyes kept resting on the phone, the ring of which he dreaded but which he also knew was inevitable.

Anthony Frenkel was an aviation crash expert by profession. He travelled all over the world assessing crashes. His main expertise lay in military crashes and he worked directly for the American Government. He loved his job, and every trip was looked upon as a challenge. But this morning, his entire existence was overshadowed by a cloud. With every minute, the niggling grew. The cut on the finger had grown to a gash in the arm. Whatever fate had in store for him, he was to find out very soon. He pushed breakfast away and sat, watching the phone. Jennifer still nagged and Jake still screamed. And Anthony just watched.

When it finally came, the gash in the arm had grown to partial amputation as he listened. There was never any question of him refusing the job and he knew it. Like most things in his life, he was just resigned to accept the fact that this job was to change his entire life, and that there was nothing he could do about it. It was a two- week assignment which was to start as soon as possible, and it meant that he was saying goodbye to Jennifer and Jake five weeks after he received the phone call. It was a blur which took him to his plane, which saw him through the journey. The only thing that he had managed to do with any great success was read the details of the assignment.

It was a mission of recovery and the incident itself was one of the most puzzling and fascinating stories to have rocked the aviation world. In fact, it became a hugely controversial mystery which puzzled experts for over 50 years. The event started back in 1947, in Buenos Aires. Stardust, a passenger plane, a British Lancaster Bomber which had been converted for civilian service took off for its destination across the Andes to Santiago. There were a handful of passengers on board and the flight was to be routine and at first, all seemed to go exactly as planned. The control tower at Santiago airport received a message from the plane to say that it was literally just approaching the airport and was preparing to land. Two more rather strange, incoherent messages were heard as the control tower prepared to receive the plane. It was then that the plane disappeared clean off the radar and radio contact was ceased. Several attempts were made to contact the plane but nothing more was heard.

A search was carried out of the immediate area around Santiago airport, but nothing was found. The search was extended across the Andes, but it was all in vain. Hours of searching led to nowhere. The search was extended to cover almost the entire flight path of the Stardust. They found nothing. No plane. No wreckage. No message. A plane that was apparently minutes from landing at Santiago airport disappeared clean off the face of the earth.

It became a huge mystery and gave way too many theories ranging from Government conspiracies to murder and even alien abduction. The latter seemed to have stemmed from the rather strange message sent from the captain of the plane: S.T.E.N.D.E.C. When no normal meaning could be found to this strange collection of letters, it was suggested that aliens must have sent the message and abducted the plane! The mystery remained for fifty-three years.

Until the year 2000. As the world woke up to the new millennium and debated whether the real millennium started with 2000 or 2001, the early part of the year saw the mysterious appearance of a plane, or what seemed to be part of a plane, high up on a glacier in the Andes. The discovery was made by climbers who reported it. The Argentine government arranged for an expedition which was a collaboration between the Argentines, the Americans and the British. The expedition itself included crash experts, climbing experts and forensic scientist. There were many questions to be answered, the main one being what had happened to the plane.

The expedition took about eleven days to reach the glacier in question and the journey included trucks, mules and gruelling leg work. Indeed, parts of a plane wreckage were found and positively identified as those belonging to the doomed Lancastrian, Stardust. How did a plane which completely disappeared in 1947, re- appear in the year 2000? Why was ninety percent of the wreckage still missing? To add to the puzzle, how come it was found 50 miles away from Santiago airport when the pilot in 1947 had radioed in that they were about to land at that airport? In short, months of investigation led the experts involved to a plausible theory as to what had happened to this plane.

In 1947 very few planes could fly above the clouds, the Lancastrian being one of the few that could. Due to this the pilots and air traffic controllers of the day were ignorant of a phenomenon we know today as the jet-stream, a powerful weather condition that forms above the clouds and can have speeds of about 100mph. Flying into the jet-stream can severely slow a plane down and technology today considers this so that flying speeds can be accordingly adjusted. However, in 1947, pilots had to rely on vision. They relied on what they could see. If a plane flew above the clouds, there was no way of knowing exactly where the plane was other than estimation. According to the facts of the time, the captain of the Stardust decided to fly over the clouds across the Andes to avoid bad weather below. The control tower at Santiago airport knew of his intentions. As the plane rose above the clouds, it encountered a severe jet-stream. According to the weather data at the time, there *was* a jet-stream effect at that time of day, which meant that Stardust was flying directly into it. The result was that the plane's progress was slowed down considerably. When the pilot thought that they had cleared the Andes mountain range, they were still on the wrong side of the mountains. Thinking that he was almost over Santiago airport, the pilot began his descent. This proved to be a fatal descent, for directly in their path was a glacier. The plane hit the glacier killing all on board instantly. The impact of the crash into the glacier caused an avalanche, which totally covered the plane with snow within seconds. The rescue teams had no chance of finding the wreckage. It lay buried inside the glacier for 53 years.

The plane must have been buried high at the top of the glacier. Over the years layer upon layer of fresh ice covered it whereas towards the bottom of the glacier, old ice was melting as the temperature was warmer further down the mountain. It seems the plane wreckage travelled through the glacier, being covered by more ice from the top, and moving down towards warmer climate. Early in 2000, the first parts of the wreckage finally melted out with the ice and emerged, out into the open. This was the theory which was widely accepted. If it was true, then the rest of the plane which was still buried in the ice would emerge over several years.

Which is exactly what happened. In 2002, two years after the wreckage was first discovered, new parts had been found by climbers and reported. The Argentine government organised another expedition. Which brings us back to Anthony Frenkel.

This was his mission, to help recover the new parts found, to confirm the present theory and to help recover the remains of the dead so that they could be identified and returned to their relatives. An expedition as famous as this would have been the highlight of his career, the pinnacle of his life and it would normally have been difficult to drag him down to earth from cloud nine. However, every step that took them closer to the glacier also sent a chill down Anthony's back. The aches and pains his colleagues felt was nothing compared to the pounding which he felt in his head, the churning in his stomach and the ever growing feeling of despair over hanging him.

They had been travelling for days and all seemed to be well to begin with. The trucks took them up as far as the path existed, and beyond that, the climbers had to rely on footwork and mules. Mules are resilient creatures but even they struggled on the rocks and the adverse weather. In fact, it was this adverse weather which almost spelt the end of the whole expedition. They had long reached a point where the mules were also abandoned, and the party continued on foot. They were tired and weary, and the day was almost drawing to a close. In hindsight, they should have stopped. But there was a shortage of time with supplies running out. They had to take the gamble, which in the end went against them. The weather suddenly turned. The chilling wind brought with it sleet and poor visibility. They were unprepared since there was no expectation of bad weather. For half an hour they were almost blind, and progress was nil. They decided to wait until it calmed down, only to find that clear skies showed them to be way off course. They could not at first figure out very well where they were, and it took another hour before they realised their position. It was rather odd that at the time the storm hit, they were on course and yet now, they were very badly-off course, even though the storm made it impossible for them to travel very far. The shock of this sent panic among the climbers. There was a difference of opinion among them where some wanted to abandon the climb and the rest wanted to continue. They were still in radio contact with base, so it was not as if they were totally isolated. They then decided to get themselves back to the point they were at when the storm hit before reviewing the situation.

Throughout this crisis, Anthony Frenkel said nothing. He thought maybe the storm was the 'crisis' that he was waiting for, but it did not *feel* right. The pounding should have soared, and he would have *known* that it was time. But he felt nothing. No. That was not the crisis that he was waiting for. His crisis was yet to come. He found himself lagging behind his climbing partner and could feel the tension growing among the others in the group.

They collected their scattered belongings and continued their journey. Anthony began to follow his partner but just a few paces later, *it* happened. He had been expecting it for over a month with despair but now that he knew the moment had come panic and fear raged through his mind and sent shockwaves to his body. He began to tremble while trying to control acute nausea. His legs felt like lead pipes while the ringing in his head increased to levels, he found unbearable. He had totally misunderstood the severity of his impending 'crisis'. He had never had a feeling as sickening and as acute as this one. This was not a 'crisis'. This was death. He could almost feel the claws of death creeping about his shoulders, pushing him, coaxing him, guiding him in the right direction. To fight this would have been futile. He put up no resistance as he moved to his left. He knew the direction he was to go in and he walked. The climate was certainly chilly, but the breath of the Devil was even chillier, and it was running in circles around his body. He would have given anything for the nagging of Jennifer and the tantrums of Jake. He was the last in the group, the furthest behind so that his climbing partner did not even notice the change in direction taken by the man behind him. By the time he realised, Frenkel was already many paces in the wrong direction. He called after him but there was no response, so he called for the group to stop. They all shouted and swore and thought that Frenkel must have lost his mind. Two of them began to follow him.

Frenkel moved with surprising ease through the snow and swiftly walked towards a huge rock-like feature at the foot of the glacier. At first, it seemed like he was walking straight into the rock, but as he approached it, he realised that round the left of it, was an opening. He did not even pause and ignored the frantic shouting of his climbing partner. This was to be, and nothing could or should even be attempted to stop him. He disappeared into the opening.

His climbing partner dashed as quickly to the opening of the cave as he could and was just in time to see a sight which shocked his very soul. His brain had no time to register the huge, rectangular blue haze that took up most of the cave. It emanated from the floor of the cave and rose towards the ceiling, flickering and radiating intense heat. There were sparks flying out of it at intervals and although such a phenomenon looked like it should have an electric buzz, it was silent. It just existed there, in the middle of the cave like a huge hazy door. But the concerned climbing partner did not even notice any of the finer details of this 'door'. He just stood there, frozen, rooted to the spot, just in time to see the shadowy figure of Anthony Frenkel disappear into the blue haze.

All that remained was the sharp, piercing scream which echoed in the cave, chilling the bones of all who heard it.

CHAPTER 1

2007, Argentina

A new day was beginning as dawn broke high above the ice-covered mountains. It warmed the chilly breeze and threw huge shadows into the valleys and rocks below. The sky changed colour from purple to a light, clear blue. The mountains were gradually uncovered from the darkness so that every detailed crevice was visible, from rock formations to valleys. One of the most natural and remote parts of the world, full of natural minerals, animal life and strange, rare and unusual flora. A place so unique and isolated, one could have been forgiven for thinking they were close to their Creator. Peace, tranquillity and purity. All the ingredients for transcendental meditation and spiritual harmony.

However, look closely and even here one can find Homo-Sapiens infection. Look deeper into those ice-peaked mountains and one could just make out the signs. Like ants travelling through the house, looking and invading and working. Little rows dutifully carrying out in-built orders. Even here man has managed to live, work and spread like a rapidly growing fungus, growing and destroying as he moves. The mountains look beautiful as they stand there but they hide the vermin that works and destroys from inside.

If one wants to know where the ants invade from, one has only to follow the line as they travel with their loot. They will eventually disappear down a tiny hole that one did not even know existed. Dig that hole and the community is instantly seen. Look closely at the base of one of these divine mountains and one may spot people moving about, getting out of jeeps and moving into an opening at the foot of the mountain. Close inspection would reveal a building. Even here, civilisation has installed itself in the name of research and development. For the good of the Earth. For nature.

This is the Blue Haze Corporation. A new institution built, financed and controlled by the major powers of the world. A joint organisation established solely to research nature. The ozone layer, air pollution, water purity, harmful gases in the air just to name a few. Some of the world's most intelligent scientist were proud to work for such an organisation for the good of the Earth. Saving the planet! Thousands of workers, from scientists, mathematicians, cooks and cleaners willingly agreed to work in this isolated community where many lived in accommodation provided by the Corporation. Social life was limited. The main prestige lay just in being able to say that they worked for The Blue Haze Corporation which was widely known around the world.

Look deeper into this tumour and a sharp eye may actually see the real malignancy which lay behind the smokescreen. The true nature of the work carried out by the Corporation was known only to a mere ten percent of the workforce. The rest played an unwitting part in acting as a front. Of course, some really good work was being carried out but was just a bonus for the men at the top. For the powerful team that was being shielded by the rest.

Susan Preston was fortunate for she belonged to the small minority who knew what was really going on. She belonged to the group that were lying to the rest rather than being lied to. Susan, like most of the staff working at the Corporation, lived in the accommodation provided for her. She was quite an 'important' person with no time for menial tasks, so she had a cleaner, who like the rest, was immensely proud to be working for the Corporation. The cleaner thought that although Susan had a nice job and a lovely place to live in, what she really needed was a nice man. Someone to spend the evenings with. Someone that can take her out to the many restaurants and bowling alleys provided for by the Corporation for social purposes. They thought of everything the Corporation. She was in her late thirties and at one stage would probably have desired a husband and children. She came from a wealthy family. Her father and mother were both in the medical profession and her path to Harvard was sealed long before she grew out of brightly coloured toys. Academically, she was not particularly gifted, but she was a quick learner and showed keen interest. Her father's career was particularly important making Susan's name important without her having to do anything.

Her father was one of the people who was involved in the construction of the Corporation and the logistics of the planning. It was inevitable that Susan would have a role to play. Although she had a nice face and a pleasant manner, Susan always under-estimated the influence that her father had on her career. She overestimated her own 'brilliance'. She could never really help herself when it came to other scientists and never missed an opportunity to remind people what an advanced lady she was. She was a woman, and a brilliant one at that.

Despite the cleaner's efforts, Susan had decided that she would sacrifice a 'normal' life for this one that she led now. Her desires and needs centred around her job. The best job in the world. Her parents were ever so proud of her and though the world did not know it, she was an important person, and her skill was essential for the Corporation. They need her expertise, and she was happy to serve them, here, in this isolation, for the rest of her life. She had the odd fling every now and again but decided that wife and mother was too primitive for her. She was above all that. She had no need for primitive romance. She had all she wanted. She was Susan Preston and someday her name would go down in history.

She walked majestically into the building passing the various offices. She took a quick peak into each room to see what the staff were doing. Poor people she thought. They thought they were important. She could not help but laugh at them in their ignorance. From the outside it took her a full ten minutes to walk into the building and make her way up the lift to her office. She got into the lift and looked at the board. She fumbled about in her pocket and was highly irritated when someone entered the lift. Surely, with all this organisation, the Corporation could have provided different lifts for the 'special' staff. The person pressed the button for 15th floor and Susan stood there waiting. When the floor arrived, Susan was ready. As soon as the person got out, she pressed the button to close the door and took out her special key. She fitted it into the lock and opened a small door. Inside were the buttons for the seven floors at the top of building that nobody but the privileged knew about. She pressed the second one.

Today was important. There was an update, but she knew that this one would be heated. She knew that the agenda would be thrown out of the window. She knew that now was the time to decide what should be done. They must move forward and now was the time to do this. She entered her office hoping that her secretary would be there. Finding the desk empty she made two coffees herself and left the room with them.

CHAPTER 2

The real work of the Corporation was carried out on seven floors only. The entire structure was built inside a mountain, so it was difficult to see it from outside. There were twenty floors below the seven secret levels above. The main reception, canteen and lobby areas were on the first secret level. The second level housed all the offices for the staff. The third level was where the laboratories were. As Susan entered this floor via the stairs the smell was the first to hit her. She hated this smell. It was a mixture of chemicals, animals and that awful smell of incinerated materials. It almost ponged like a hospital, only much worse. It seemed ironic that a whole department existed within the smokescreen below which contributed to air pollution and radioactive dumping and yet the rest of the organisation was blissfully unaware of the environmentally unfriendly activities carried out here.

She knocked on one of the doors and entered without waiting for a reply. The place was well lit and had massive bench areas full of equipment which bleeped and hummed and ticked. Some of the equipment took up a whole bench while some benches housed centrifuges, cells washers and vortexes. There were several cell mixers with vacutainers attached to them happily mixing away. On the far side were two computers chucking out piles and piles of computer paper. Obviously, nobody here had the interests of the rain forests foremost on their minds! Susan walked in trying to find empty bench space to put the coffee cups down on. She moved further into the laboratory to the right side.

'Ed. Where are you?' she called.

'Here.' He called from the far side of the laboratory. Susan walked in that direction and found him standing at the fume cupboard with his head stuck inside, hovering over something. He made no attempt to stop what he was doing so she went and hovered there with him while he worked.

'What are you up to? she enquired. 'I'll give you three guesses.'

Heaven knows why she asked him such a dumb question. She knew exactly what he was doing. He was doing what he always did. Dissect animals. Most people she knew smoked to relax or drank tea or went for a stroll or even watched Argentinean T.V. But not Ed. He relaxed himself by dissecting animals. She again looked around the laboratory walls which were filled with jars. Some containing whole animals, some containing animal parts all happily pickling away in formaldehyde. There were some new additions to the collection from what she could see. Hearts, kidneys, muscles, eyes, pituitary glands, thyroid glands, whole arms, the collection seemed endless.

'You always seem more interested in what's inside an animal than in the animal itself,' she said trying to prompt him into conversation.

'You don't discover anything new unless you look!' he grinned, still not stopping what he was doing.

'But what's there to discover?'

'The Soul, Susie, the *Soul!*'

'The soul is not an organ.'

'How do you know it isn't. Maybe its waiting to be discovered!'

He's taking the mickey, she thought. He has a nerve talking to her like that. He had no respect for her. God only knows the name of the insignificant institute that he graduated from in some poky little English city. She was tortured by the fact that he was regarded a genius among their colleagues and yet, she is the only one to graduate from Harvard University. Blatant sexism that was. Of course, any other unbiased person looking at her would have guessed that her irritation was also stemming from the fact that he had never once tried to talk to her about anything other than work. She would never admit it, but she did regard herself as irresistible. Of course, there is only one thing that men want. She could not believe that in all the time they had worked together, Ed had never tried it on with her. 'People have been doing this for centuries,' she said. 'We *know* all this. It's such a primitive science! You are on the threshold of a major discovery and you insist on burying your head in this mortuary! What can be more interesting than what you're officially involved in now?'

'You may be slightly more intelligent than your average person but you're not beyond nagging, are you?' he said calmly, hoping to inflict as much insult as possible.

'*Slightly* more intelligent! *Slightly?*' she yelled.

Yes, he thought, the insult had been well received. Maybe she would just go away and leave him alone now. Her ego and her superior attitude were beginning to get on his nerves recently. He was certain that underneath that brilliant scientist facade was a really nice, charming person who would be far better company if she just relaxed and tried to say and do what came naturally. As far as he was concerned, Susan's abilities were fed into her, almost programmed into her. Nothing came naturally and she tried far too much to be a genius. Everyone has limitations and the art was to know what they were. 'Look Susan. I'm just in the middle of something. Can you let me just finish it?'

'We've got a meeting this morning,' she said stiffly. 'Oh damn! I forgot about that.'

'How are the latest tests?'

'Well,' he said as he started to clear up around himself. 'The latest one to go through as you know was Harry. Now for a chimp, Harry was already overweight. Not by much. By human standards, I think you would describe him as a bit plump. He was gone for 3 days. Seventy hours and eighteen minutes to be precise. He has been back now a week and weighs in at double what he was when we put him through.'

'Double!'

'It seems his appetite knows no bounds and has been affected.'

'Can you help him control it?' she asked.

'I've been trying but he shows uncharacteristic violent tendencies if I try too hard. He does not have an increase in any hormones in the blood but does have the same increase in antibody levels in his serum. Behaviour seems to be exactly the same as before. He still is normal in every respect except that he gets violent if he does not get extra portions with his meals. Which ain't such a bad thing really. Many human males seem to act the same way!'

'What are you going to do?' she asked.

'With Harry? Nothing. He has served his purpose. I'll keep him happy and monitor him for as long he lives. Which may not be too long as it happens. His obesity, sudden as it was, is causing him breathing and circulation difficulties. He needs to exercise but is really not up to it. If he carries on like this, he may well suffer a heart attack. I've also almost finished the latest tests on that probable antigen structure that the antibody is being raised against. It should be sort of accurate and at least that way we will have something to look for. But I think progress is slow with animals.'

'What's the next step?'

He looked at her full in the face but made no reply. 'Let's go,' she said.

'Right. There is just one thing I have to do before I get to the meeting.'

'Here's your coffee,' she said, handing him one of the cups she was holding. 'Thanks Susie.'

'Please Ed, can't you call me Susan,' she pleaded as they left the laboratory.

CHAPTER 3

The floor directly above the laboratories was the 'animal' floor. There were a huge number of animals housed here from small rodents to chimpanzees. The place was looked after by two animal handlers although Ed had over-all responsibility. There was an area which resembled London Zoo, where the animals could be seen in cages which in some way or another tried to mimic the natural habitat of the animals. Making them feel "at home". Then there was the laboratory area where the caged creatures could be found in small cubicles. These were very clinical, and no attempt was made to make the animals feel relaxed. They could be visualised through a glass barrier and directly in front of these was a clip board with the name, description and treatment of the animal. A detailed account of behaviour notes was made mostly by Ed. This is where he was. On his way to the meeting on the management floor above he sent Susan ahead while he quickly popped in to record Harry's hourly observation details. The animal was quietly asleep in the corner of the cage sleeping off a huge meal which was given to him an hour before. Ed scribbled down a few notes. As he dashed out of the animal area and made his way up the stairs, he became aware of a slight 'tingling' feeling in his head. He had been ignoring it almost all day and in fact could not remember when it started. Did he wake up with it? It was just an annoying feeling that was not painful, just irritating. He could not let that get in the way. He had important business to attend to now and he meant to get his own way.

Edward Hamilton always tried hard to get his own way. He was born in London and as a child lived in Aldgate with his parents and sister. He had a brilliant brain and could have passed any exam he needed for Oxbridge, but at that time all he wanted was a pretty little thing called Nicole. She was small, cute, quiet and pure. Pharmacology and physiology were her chosen options, and she had no time for distractions. Her education came first, and she could not figure out what Ed wanted from her. From Ed's point of view her attractiveness lay solely in the fact that she was untainted in body and mind. He knew that she was the perfect female which at that time was difficult. Most young girls of the day were more experienced than he was! That was disgusting as far as he was concerned. Nicole was a rare breed. She was as God had made her. It was this very fact that drove him mad with desire and distracted him away from reason. Nobody could have convinced him not to throw away his talents at Liverpool University studying psychology. He had wanted to study the same as Nicole, but he thought that her options would be far too much work! He wanted an easy degree. He was driven almost crazy with passion for Nicole and at one stage he feared for himself. He studied for three years at the same university hoping that she would find him just as irresistible as he found her. He fully expected his patience to be rewarded and was totally gutted and humiliated when he saw her holding hands one day with a spotty- faced, nerd-like creature who looked like he belonged in a science convention! His humiliation only lasted about ten seconds to be quickly replaced by rage. An awful rage that knocked all the sense out of him. He knew that if he ever came close to that spotty-face nerd, he was likely to acquire a nice little spell in prison. Although he never intended to harm Nicole his thoughts turned to hatred and the shock of these events meant the difference between a 2:1 with Honours and a 2:2 with Honours.

At 23 years of age, Edward was faced with the loss of his mother. He was an adult, but without her, he was no more than a child. He felt like someone had taken away his right arm. She was everything to him. She taught him everything with a patience that he himself did not have. She never put him down or magnified his weaknesses. Even when he was a real obnoxious teenager she never once put him down. He was never really very concerned about his future prospects as a scientist for he knew his mother would always look out for him. He had a reasonable relationship with his father, but although his father never directly said anything to him, Edward knew that in his father's eyes he was an idler who almost drifted from one thing to another rather aimlessly. Which, in a way, was absolutely true. Edward inherited from his mother a small flat and a small fortune which meant that "getting a good job" was not really an issue. He moved from one research institute to another studying animal and human psychology and somehow always managed to associate himself with reputable scientists. He always thought that his was an easy path to brilliance and although he was not religious, he always thought his mother was looking out for him from wherever she was.

Religion was not important to him, but he did believe in the Soul and was fascinated with the Hindu idea of reincarnation of the Soul. The Soul was the real essence of a person, the thing that made a person. He read somewhere that many Hindus believed that certain birds and rodents where actually the Souls of humans waiting to be reborn. He found a book of ancient Indian arts and noticed that many Hindu Gods were painted with little mice or pigeons at their feet and these represented Souls. He believed that there were good Souls, bad Souls and those Souls forever cursed with suffering. Of course, he also believed in the idle Soul because he was one. One thing he knew for certain. The beautiful, calm and gentle Soul of his mother was looking down on him and protecting him.

Years of working "with the right people" eventually brought him to Maximillian Braun. There were many rumours of Professor Braun not actually being a professor at all but a secret agent who had defected from somewhere or another and was now working for the United States government. As a figure he did resemble something out of a James Bond movie! Before he met Braun, Edward's career was entirely based in London, but he was associated with scientist from America and France and was often head-hunted by those whom he had impressed. He had no intention of leaving London but then an opportunity came to work in Braun's team in the States. He could think of no place he hated more than America with its fast foods, its deformed English and its obsession with superficial beauty but Professor Braun was an important and clever man. His work on the human brain was exceptional and just to be in the same room with the man was some kind of an honour. Edward rose above the dislike of all things American and decided to join the Professor's team along with another London based colleague in Florida.

He had no ties at home except London itself, a city which was his birthplace and which he loved with a passion. It was never going to be easy, but Edward had no mother to guide him now. He had to take care of himself and he decided for his own career, he needed to accept Professor Braun's offer. The man was a genius and associating himself with such greatness did wonders for Edward's ego. He worked in Florida for two years on trauma and severe mental illness induced by trauma. At the tender age of 32, Edward had made an impression not only on Professor Braun but had shown signs of genius himself. He broadened his expertise to biochemistry, physiology and immunology. He had great passion for learning and for the first time in his life, actually used the intelligence that he was gifted with. Maximillian Braun himself had been head-hunted by the American and Argentinean governments to put his expertise into the development of The Blue Haze Corporation. The Corporation at that stage was no more than money and a few ideas about how to physically build the complex. Professor Braun needed staff who were good and loyal. He knew the truth behind the Corporation and because of this, secrecy and trust were important. Whatever else impressed him about Edward Hamilton, the professor knew he could trust him. The Professor not only asked Edward to accompany him to Argentina but told him the truth. The whole truth.

At first, Edward was convinced he was being taken for a ride, but the Professor was not the type to do this, so Edward decided someone was taking his mentor for a ride. But he eventually met with some of the Government officials and accompanied the Professor to some of the discussions and felt that nobody was treating this as if it was a wind-up. A *time corridor!* Something that took you to another time zone!

The people in charge were slightly unhappy about Edward knowing everything but they had no choice, the Professor was threatening to pull out. It took the team a year to prepare the equipment they would need and actually move into the Corporation deep into the Andes mountain range. The next four to five years were the most fascinating of Edward's entire life. His job was to assist the Professor. Animals were sent through the 'Corridor' which apparently sent them through time. They eventually returned and it was up to Edward and the Professor to carry out extensive tests on them. This included extensive physical and mental tests. The animals were closely monitored to see what effects the journey had had on them. One thing that did puzzle Edward was how did anybody know that it was a *time* corridor? The animals could not tell them where they had been. Professor Braun always had the same answer for him. 'Trust me, Edward, trust me.' And so, he did. Two years later Maximillian Braun died suddenly. The members on the board were totally stunned. They had lost a major asset. They were reluctant to bring in another 'outsider' since there were few they could trust. On the other hand, Edward Hamilton was the only scientist who was closely involved with the Professor's work. He already knew everything. They were reluctant to accept him on the project when it first began and now, they reluctantly accepted him as the Professor's replacement. Edward clearly had signs of genius that they could not ignore. Also, they could not risk him being sufficiently annoyed enough to blow the lid on the Corporation. So, for political reasons, the clever, but idle drifter who blew his education following the young and pure Nicole all over Liverpool ended up heading a section in the most secret and to date, fascinating project the world had ever seen. Now Edward Hamilton really took his work and himself seriously. Now he had grown up and he only wished his mother had been around to see him.

Today, as he rushed to the meeting, Edward had been sole leader of his section for two years. He was at a crucial point in his work and no tingling headache was going to stop him.

As usual, he was the last to crash through the door and everyone looked at him. It was not a particularly large board room mainly due to the fact that building inside a mountain had its limitations on space. Also, there were a small group of VIPs who actually knew what was really going on. The main players were George Lucas from New York and Manuel Perez from Santiago. Susan ran the radioactive section and Michael Rodriguez was in charge of finance and was directly in contact with both the American and Argentine governments. In addition to these there were the direct government representatives from Argentina, America, Britain and France. They answered directly to their head of government. These were normally the people who sat around this table but today there was an extra body. Nobody had actually seen him before, but they all knew he existed. His posture alone was enough to chill even the most warm-hearted. Ruthlessness seemed etched in the lines of his face. Well dressed and formidable, he sat and watched proceeding from tinted glasses. This the was the man at the top. He probably had a name, but it must have been years since anybody used it. Here, at this meeting, he was referred to simply as the President. George Lucas waited for Edward to sit down and then started.

'Thank you for all attending this update meeting. You all have heard of our President. Today we are honoured to have him attending this meeting,' he said as he waved his hand towards the man in question. There was a small collective gasp from the others around the table.

'Mr. President, would you like to start the meeting?'

'No.'

'Well… er. Well, let us begin.' He started fumbling about with his papers and eventually settled down. 'Mr Rodriguez, I think we ended the last meeting with a view to audit the distribution of finance within the Corporation. I think we can start with that today.'

Michael Rodriguez, dark tanned and articulate then proceeded to give a detailed account of the financial structure. Of course, lack of money was not an issue, but the point was that the Corporation was not making money. The money ploughed into it was never coming back. Everybody concerned had agreed that the Corridor had to be investigated but a huge amount of money was going into the project, just to ensure secrecy. This discovery getting into the wrong hands could be dangerous. Progress was slow on the actual research itself and there was the problem of trying to decide what to do with this Corridor. Certainly, the public can never know what they had found. This Corridor would always be dangerous.

'So,' concluded Mr Rodriquez, 'we are channelling a little more money into protection of this institute and trying to wind down some of the functions of the environment departments below.

'But surely that would arouse suspicion,' declared the American official.

'How do you mean?' enquired Mr Rodriguez.

'Well according to the world, the Blue Haze Corporation is learning how to protect the environment. It's still new. If we wind down certain areas now the public will start to ask questions. That will bring more publicity. Surely, its publicity we want to avoid.'

'It is just a matter of time before the world has something else to talk about. Then we will be left in peace. But as you know, we have a hugely difficult task here. We have to balance secrecy with ability'.

'Mr Rodriguez,' the American was changing his tone now, 'my Government and I'm sure the governments of all those involved have an equally difficult task. There are people out there who are trying to infiltrate the complex. We are battling security risks all the time. We need to scale down this world-wide attention. There are already questions being asked about productivity, and what the Corporation actually does. Yes, we publish papers and Governments listen to the research that come out of this group, but questions are now being asked about the extra floors. The cost of the secret floors. Everyone knows there is something different going on here. We are attracting the wrong type of attention.'

'Yes,' scowled Mr Rodriguez. 'Security is important. But where would it leave us if the financial commitment of your government dried up? We have been here five years and we still know very little about anything and yet we expect huge amounts of money just to maintain the complex! We have to have results soon and we are not going to get them at this rate. We need to invest more to the top levels. You do not seem to understand that two-thirds of our capital is being squandered on the 'environmental' studies below.'

During this time, the tingling in Ed's head began to increase. He was tempted at this stage to interfere, but something held him back.

'I think,' interrupted Mr Perez, who was concerned about the President being present, 'that both these issues are important, and we will discuss them at length later. For the time being I think we ought to hear from the ground reports.' There was a small lull before Mr Perez addressed Susan Preston. 'Miss Preston we are pretty up to date on your work, but for the benefit of the President, could you please give us a small summary to date?'

'Of course,' replied Susan. She was her usual confident self. 'It has been established that a huge amount of radiation is involved in this process. This includes alpha, beta and gamma rays in quantities about 10-40 times normal. The exposure to the animals is huge. So far only one animal seems to have died as a result of radiation. The others should have had some signs of illness but seem to be in good health. On one of the animals, we found traces of wood, which, according to our information, originates only on the remote Island we refer to as Easter Island. This particular type of wood was from a tree that was a rare species which died out in the early 1900s. We can only imagine what that animal had seen!' she added rather dramatically.

'What about the latest case,' asked Mr Lucas.

'The latest is Harry. The main line of study here is small traces of a compound which we cannot identify. The closest we have is ink. The sort we use in Bic pens. But the compound found on Harry is totally alien to us. We think is could be well maybe an improved version of the ink we know today.'

There was a small pause as they all soaked up what was being said.

'Am I to understand Miss Preston,' asked Mr Perez, 'that this compound does not exist?'

'We can find no evidence of such a compound existing at this present time.'

'Are you suggesting that this animal has been '

'Yes Sir, I think this animal did not travel back in time, but *forward.*' There was another collective gasp from those around the table. Everyone seemed fascinated except Edward, whose tingling feeling was still rising. He felt like a little insect was inside his head, running around the crevices of his brain. He wanted to open up his head and have a good scratch.

'That is fascinating Miss Preston,' said Mr Lucas. 'Mr Hamilton, we know that the journey the animals are making is having an adverse effect on them. Can you elaborate for the benefit of the President? Thank you.'

As Edward prepared to speak, the feeling in his head suddenly accelerated. It was at a point too difficult to ignore. 'Whether or not the effects are adverse remains to be seen. There is no doubt that the animals are different. The first one we sent through had a total personality transformation. It was a small chimp, Ziggy. He was a happy, lively creature, very affectionate and warm. Always seeking affection and comfort and was fond of physical exercise. He also loved music. Edward trailed off while the others stared at him. He was not normally a rambler. He usually gave a succinct account of things, but the tingling was raging in his head. 'I'm sorry. I'll stick to the point. Well anyway... Ziggy was put through and was away just 11 hours and something minutes. He... well, it seemed like Ziggy's body but a total personality implant! He was moody, sat in the corner of his cubicle, refused exercise, music, communication. Everything was gone. Like he had lost the will to do anything.'

For the first time the President leaned forward and spoke. 'What about the next one?' George Lucas was puzzled. All the work carried out here was translated in report form to the President.

'Jonah was the next. Another chimp. He was a leader and in the wild he would have been the head male. He was away 38 hours and 5 minutes. He came back and appeared to be normal in every respect except that he was unable to live together with any other chimps or indeed...' his head was throbbing terribly, 'any animal at all. He had an abnormal sex drive and a desire to attack other animals.'

Now Edward was sweating. His pulse was racing, and he felt he heard echoes in his head. 'Saffron was next. A female. Can't remember how long she was away. She came back normal in every respect except she developed a fondness for tearing paper. She would do it tirelessly, for hours,'

'Fascinating, 'murmured the President. 'Is there a pattern in the way these fetishes occur? A link?' Edward just shook his head. He was trying to shake off the pounding in his brain.

'Are there any other facts that may explain things?' persisted the President.

'Well, I have carried out extensive physiological and immunological tests. Dr Braun always insisted on doing everything possible. The only thing that we have found is that the animals have a huge increase in the production of a particular type of antibody, IgG1. Their immune system produced this in huge quantities, but we have so far been unable to track down the antigen that triggered this response in the first place. The type of IgG1 in each animal is very similar suggesting that they had all been exposed to the same antigen. There is a process common to all the cases. In short it means that the stimulant must have been encountered in the actual Corridor itself. The only other thing is some of the animals had high levels of corticosteriods in their blood. Structure and function of the organs seems normal.'

'Could it be the radiation, Miss Preston?'

Susan began to relate her opinion and the conclusion was that no explanation could be offered. The others began to talk and throw ideas backwards and forwards and certain other details began to emerge, but Edward remained quiet. He looked like he was in pain and all the time, he could feel this tidal wave of sensation in his head. He knew he wanted to speak but he was almost paralytic. Eventually he heard the one trigger that he needed. He heard George Lucas's voice ask, 'Where do we go from here?'

Immediately, Edward rose and banged his fist on the desk and before anyone could breathe another word he shouted, 'HUMANS! For God's sake, HUMANS!' Before he had finished blurting this out the pain in his head vanished. Gone. He could think again. He looked round at his stunned, almost frightened audience. 'Let's stop arsing, about shall we? I think five years is long enough to prat about with chimps and rats and tests and things. We need to send a human being who could talk, feed-back their experience, *tell* us where they had been, what they had seen! For goodness sake! Don't any of you see the way ahead?' He looked round at each and every face to see their reaction. He really expected some to be nodding in agreement, but they all just looked at him like he had a tree growing out of his head. The President immediately looked at Mr Perez and Mr Lucas in a puzzled manner. Mr Lucas, Susan and Mr Rodrigues all just looked away, almost in embarrassment as if they were trying to make things easy for Edward.

Eventually, the President broke the silence.

'Gentlemen,' he said addressing Mr Lucas and Mr Perez, 'it seems to me that Mr Hamilton is not aware of everything. I think now is the time to bring him up to date.'

CHAPTER 4

Crystal Moon was the rather unusual name of a bar situated halfway between the Corporation accommodation and the actual company building itself. It was meant to be a posh wine bar for the employees to socialise in and everyone here were either employed by the Corporation or had business to attend to. Susan Preston was here with a few colleagues. The chattering was, of course, very work orientated which usually meant, animal behaviour, tests, results and the like.

Susan had spent most of the day trying to avoid Ed, but it was not too difficult. Ed was keeping himself hidden on purpose. He had locked himself in his laboratory and spent the entire day dissecting animals. He was so used to it that he did it without even thinking. He was fairly calm and relaxed by the time he decided to head for home. It was obvious to him that someone knew something, and nobody was telling him what it was. He knew that they all knew. Eye contact was difficult with any of them and he was angry. He knew that the only person who could tell him was Lucas. But George Lucas had been busy all day with the President and it was impossible to see him. He had to do it the next morning. He had to spend the whole day and now, probably the whole night wondering what it was they had kept him out of. He decided to keep to himself during the day for fear of losing his temper and yelling. Tomorrow he would know.

On his way back to his flat he had a brainwave and decided to try and find some answers at the Crystal Moon. He walked in and made eye contact with Sergio at the bar. Sergio immediately started to mix a gin and tonic. Ed looked round and found Susan's head. She had of course seen him coming in but pretended she did not notice.

She tried to feign surprise when he sat down with her and the others. Sergio came over and handed the gin and tonic to Ed and then stood there having a small, menial conversation with him. Sergio then went back to work, and Ed joined a small group that Susan was talking to. The main conversation was centred around two other people in the group, so Ed just listened and sipped his drink. He was not sure what exactly he wanted there but eventually he began to relax. They had a few laughs and then some of the group began to leave and Susan saw her chance to escape.

'Where are you going?' Ed asked.

'It's been a long day Ed. I have to get an early night.'

'You! An early night? I thought you stay up into the small hours reading science journals.' He was in mocking mode as usual. 'I do actually sleep you know.'

'Look Susan. Just sit down for a second.' She did so but was cringing. 'Tell me what is going on.'

'Ed, I think......'

'Susan,' he interrupted, 'I think you know something more than I do and I want you to be honest with me.'

'Ed, I receive my information from George and Manuel. I think you ought to talk to them.'

'Susan!' he was getting impatient, 'you are my colleague. You are meant to be on my side.'

'There are no sides Ed. There is only the job you do. I do my job and you do yours. I really do have to go Ed.'

He was never going to get anything out of her. He let her go. He must have been a real fool if he thought that she would tell him anything. She was probably loving every minute of it. Being part of an important scientific team and being elite was stopping her from confiding anything in him. Susan Preston the great scientist. She really believed that she was an elite intellectual who should not have to even breathe the same air as other mere mortals. It never even crossed her mind that her education was sealed even before she had started it. Her father had seen to that. Edward knew all about the American education system where who you knew was everything. Many sportsmen had graduated solely on their sporting ability rather than academic. Susan's father probably meant the difference between a pass and a failure. It was not that Ed was jealous. He had nothing to be jealous of, but he was annoyed by the fact that Susan always threw her education at everyone. Harvard was a well-worn name with her. She never mentioned her father, but she always mentioned her sex. She was a *female*. And a brilliant one at that, talented, educated and beautiful. She rode on her father's influence and never showed an ounce of modesty or gratitude. She never waited for others to tell her how good she was. And here she was now working on the most important discovery of modern times, forever nurturing her already inflated ego. She always described his work as primitive. It was not that Ed was sexist either. Ed believed in the Soul and he believed that the Soul had no sex. People were people. Every man and woman lived and worked as they chose, and their very being depended on their soul. A female soul was just as capable of high intelligence as a male one. No, he was not sexist. Kerry was a scientist. Kerry was the best immunologist that he knew, and she was incredibly intelligent. She was smart not only in her work but had good general knowledge. Susan on the other hand thought that Ho Chi Min was a Chinese dish! Ed learnt a lot from Kerry and he never had a problem with that. But Susan relied on other people's intelligence. Her current team was the backbone of her section. They carried her, guided her and then stood back and let her take the credit. That is what he hated so much about Susan. The girl who had sacrificed a conventional female existence for an elite one! The girl who was forever telling everyone that she had given up normal function of her *womb*. Which was her way of saying she was never going to have children. That was after all, primitive. Yes, he had made a mistake there hoping for something from the elite Ms Preston. He stayed there and drank a little more. He then made his way to his flat and spent a terribly restless night tossing and turning in bed. He tried reading, television and drink. He must have dozed for a couple of hours but when he awoke, he could feel that annoying tingling in his head. It was not as bad as it had been the previous day. He had his tea and then made his way to the Corporation.

George Lucas was in his office. He also had had a restless night. It was his idea to supress certain details from Ed but why exactly he felt it necessary to do this he could not justify. He was struggling all night to try and prepare some words that would not only explain things but would pacify Ed. It worried him so much he was unable to satisfy his young gold-digging wife that night! It was one of those things that just got out of hand. He was to co-ordinate the whole project with Manuel Perez. It was difficult enough to handle this alone, but their lives were made even more complicated by the secrecy issue. It was bad enough trying to stave off attention from other countries but when it was your own that you had to hide things from. The whole company was false, and the idea of this super eco-sensitive organisation had to be sold to everyone. Secrecy was the word. When it came to vetting the staff, who should know everything Ed was not on the list. In fact, Ed was never on their list of employees at all. He was a man shrouded in secrecy himself and all he had going for him was Maximillian Braun. Nobody knew anything about Ed except that he was of above average intelligence. It did not seem right that the Professor insisted on Ed accompanying him and it was totally unacceptable that this shadow of a man should know the whole truth. Snobbery played its part and Lucas knew this. He was as guilty as was the next man. Lucas himself had got where he was by being the best. He was in the navy as a young man and eventually turned to politics. He was a shining star of the George Bush Senior era. As an advisor he made many contacts and always managed to give the correct advice to the right people. It was his years with Bill Clinton that really turned him into a VIP. He had power. There was nothing about American defence that he did not know that he did not play a role in. He was always a key figure and a very personal friend of the Clintons. He was one of the closest friends advising the unfortunate President when he fell into trouble with the Lewinsky affair. He had played host to the Clintons many times and was sorry when the eight years of Bill Clinton's term of office came to an end. Although Lucas made his name with Bush Senior, he found relations with this man's offspring difficult. He thought Bush Junior was an ass. An ass riding on the reputation of his father. Lucas quickly had to make other friends within the government since he did not want to be part of the new government. He, George Lucas had worked, played and dined with the best. The most important people in the world and the most important job in the world. He had been offered this huge operation because of this. Now here he was, having to work alongside the likes of Edward Hamilton. Having to work with Ed was bad enough but now, having to admit that Edward needed to know the nature of this important project left a bitter feeling in his throat. He knew he should have updated Ed ages ago. His chance came when Braun died. If ever there was an opportunity to make amends and make sure that Ed did not fly into a justified rage, then Braun's death was it. But Lucas still did not trust Edward Hamilton. What if he were a spy who was instructed to wait for as long as it took to get to the secret. Of course, American Intelligence also considered the possibility that Edward, being a spy, had somehow caused the death of the Professor, thereby making it possible for him to step into the Professor's shoes. This was seriously investigated without Edward even knowing that he was under suspicion. The only reason why this was eventually thrown out was the fact that the Professor died under strange circumstances which Ed could not have played a part in. There were many feasible reasons he could give but George was not a man to shy away from the truth. He did have a problem with Ed and if really pressed, he would tell the truth. He had just made up his mind to do this when Ed walked in without knocking.

'You had better tell me what's going on Lucas.'

'Sit down Ed.'

'OK.' He sat down and waited patiently.

'Edward, you know the animals that you have sent through intimately. You know that each one came back with some strange fetish or behaviour problem. Unless we can understand what is causing this, it is not possible to send humans through.'

'But these are only animals. You cannot talk to them to tell them where they will be going. They cannot mentally prepare for it. They do not have *intellect!* A human knows what is going on and a journey like that would not mentally shock them.'

'That is all supposition.'

'Oh, bloody hell, George!' He got off his chair with this and started pacing the room. 'It is still a big risk!' yelled Lucas. 'And who do you suppose we elect to take a risk like that?'

'I know it is a risk. We did not get this far in science and technology without taking risks! In order to test out the smallpox vaccine Jenner injected it into a little boy! He had to take that risk. Somebody had to take the risk of being the first man in space! Somebody had to have the first heart transplant! George, we are at a stand-still now. We have reached a plateau with this. We are no longer finding out anything new.'

'Yes, we are. Susan found that the latest animal probably went forward rather that backwards.'

'Bollocks to that! Her testing is incorrect! It's about time someone noticed how daft she is!'

'Edward calms down.'

'We are here now, George.' He thumped his fist on the table. 'We have reached the stage we all feared. We have to think about sending someone through. There are hundreds of people on death row who would willingly volunteer. There are an equal number of nutters out there who want their name going down in history. I, myself would volunteer!'

'Susan Preston may be a poor scientist but you're not. We need you here. You cannot go risking anything. There is no way we would be able to bring in someone else so don't you even think about it.'

'Forget Susan! There are a hundred more tests we could do. Hundreds of observations we could carry out. A human would talk back, explain, describe!' persisted Ed.

'You agree there is a high exposure to radiation,' said Lucas. 'You agree that the immune system has been stimulated by an unknown antigen. There are strange mental problems in almost all the creatures that you sent through. We cannot explain any of this.'

'Yes, but none of the animals died!'

'Animals have been known to react differently from humans. Say the process exposes the humans to something we have not found? Say in humans, the process is more damaging?'

'But that is all supposition! Lucas, you have to see, we are going nowhere!'

'Who do we send? What guarantees can you give to the individual?' Lucas rose from his chair, paced a bit and sat back down again.

'That they won't *die!*' yelled Edward.

'Do we pay them compensation? What about their families?'

'Fuck the bloody families! Is that all you have to say? Is that all that is standing in our way? Compensation and families! Like I said, there are hundreds of volunteers if you really want them!'

Ed was so busy arguing his point that the headache he had just seemed to creep up on him. He tried to calm down and relax but the tingling was back. Then he suddenly remembered why he was here in the first place.

'Oh…' he slowed his pace and wagged a finger at Lucas. 'Very clever George! Oh, what a clever sly fox you are! Keeping me arguing with you so I forget the real reason why I am here? Nice one mate!'

'Edward, please '

'What did he mean, George? The President said something about me not *knowing everything.* What is it I don't know?' He was talking quietly now and leaning over onto Lucas' desk waiting for his answer.

Lucas was silent as he sat there, playing with his thumbs. He had to handle this carefully.

'The President does not think the time is right to send humans. The governments of all concerned will listen to his opinion at this moment in time. The President will not give permission.'

'I don't understand what the great risk is! A few fetishes. Some strange behaviour patterns. What's the big deal? We have not lost one single animal! They all came back!'

Lucas lowered his eyes and stared at his desk. There was silence.

Then the penny dropped. Boy! Did it drop! A massive, huge 10 feet tall penny dropped causing a massive earthquake in Ed's head.

Edward Hamilton's whole body went numb. *They all came back!*

His own words echoed in his head. *They all came back.* In a single moment, Edward understood everything. He could not believe how stupid he had been. He prided himself on being a scientist and yet he failed in the last five years to see that which was as obvious as the nose on his face. He realised he had not only been daft but deceived by those he had trusted. *They all came back!* He sunk into the chair and held his head in his hands.

'I've got to hand it to you, you fucking bastard,' he said quietly without looking up. 'You really made a fool of me there.'

'Edward, we were in a difficult '

'Shut the fuck up, Lucas!' he yelled as he flew off the chair and leapt out in front of Lucas. Lucas pushed himself back in fright.

He began to pace the room again. Up and down. Lucas just sat there. 'So,' said Ed, calmly. 'Who knows?'

'Rodriguez and Susan. And the heads of all the governments involved.'

'Susan! Sodding Susan knows and you kept me in the dark?' he gritted his teeth as he spoke. 'Why, Lucas, why? Why the bloody hell did you keep this from me?

'Well Braun '

'Sodding Braun! He knew and he did not tell me?' Ed was beyond reason now. 'It was not his fault. We made him hold that part from you!'

'Why?' Ed was red in the face as he shouted.

'Edward. We were under strict orders for God's sake. We had to get the best but were also sworn to secrecy. We had to carry out checks on everyone. Everybody had a solid past except you!'

'What! Solid past? What the hell did you want to know? I would have told you!'

'We could not understand how you came to the Professor. Your background, your education was all a bit vague.'

'Vague? What? Because I don't come from fucking *Harvard?*'

'We wanted to check you out fully but needed more time. Then when Braun died...... well... I suppose we should have taken the step then. '

'YES! You should have fucking told me then you bastard!' He then leapt to the desk again and with one fell swoop pushed everything off the desk. 'You should have told me because now I'm going to wreck you! You shit-head!' He picked up the chair and flung that at the wall. At that stage, the secretary walked in to find out what was going on. 'Get out! Get the fuck out!' The poor woman screamed and ran back out leaving the door open. 'And that BITCH Preston knew all along,' he kicked the door shut, 'and she couldn't even say anything last night! The bitch! It's all a big joke! You made a bloody laughing stock out of me. I'm no more than those bloody monkeys that I work with. All my work, it all means NOTHING! It's all a big joke. I have wasted the last five years of my fucking life! *Five years!*' Somewhere from his sub-conscience came a song: *Five Years, my brain hurts a lot.* And boy! Was his head aching now!

'Please, Edward. Please. We made a mistake. We considered you a security hazard.'

'A bloody security hazard! Boy, this gets better and better! What the fuck did you think I would do? Tell the world? Let him out? Parade him around to the vultures? What did you think I would do?'

During the pause that followed Ed punched the filing cabinet and could feel the pain searing into his wrist. The phone rang and he leapt to it before Lucas could and yelled down it, 'He's busy so piss off!'

He then tried hard to calm down. He paced around a little and kept trying to block out thoughts of that bitch who knew everything. He now understood it all. He always kept asking how did they know it was a *time* corridor? He was forever asking the Professor and was constantly told to 'trust me'. Oh yes, and he did. He trusted the Professor. He trusted everyone! That was how they knew! He then sat down opposite Lucas again. He kept telling himself to calm down.

'Where is he?' he said quietly.

'On the sixth level.'

'SIXTH! Just three floors above me all this time! I'll not forget this George. Not this!'

'What are you going to do?'

'I want to know everything. All the files. The whole sodding lot of it. I want the details. The tests, the paperwork, the analysis. EVERYTHING! Then, when I have read it, I want to *see* him.'

'Of course.'

'You piss me about again and I'm going to kill you!'

'I don't think that will be necessary.'

'*I'll* tell you what is necessary.' He turned around as if to walk out and then stopped and made his way back to Lucas who was now standing next to the filing cabinet.

'Oh George, I almost forgot!' and with that he landed a full, heavy punch on the side of the face which totally floored Lucas. Then he stormed out. As he did so, he left the door open. Lucas was sighing heavily and getting up off his feet just as his bewildered secretary quietly creeped in and looked at the mess.

'Well,' said Lucas, 'that turned out better than I thought!'

CHAPTER 5

E dward Hamilton was livid. He was angry with the Corporation for treating him like an outsider and also angry with himself for being so stupid. All the facts were in front of him and had been for years. He should have been able to figure it out himself. All those years the truth was staring him in the face. He knew that the Corridor was discovered when a man fell into it. Although there were many rumours as to what happened to this man, he had always assumed that this unfortunate had never come back. How come he could have been so stupid as to never really pursue this? Why did he never question the details of this part of events? If all his animals came back, then why not the man who unwittingly discovered the Corridor? He trusted the Professor so much that all these natural questions never occurred to him. He trusted everyone. He never even thought that there may be something that he did not know. They all bloody knew. Even the Professor betrayed Edward. But the one thing that really riled Ed was that Susan 'I'm a great scientist' Preston *knew*. He could almost see her smug face laughing at him, almost sneering at the extra points she thought she had earned. Of all the people that had betrayed him he found her the most difficult to stomach. All this time, she *knew*. Five years she worked alongside him and knew the intimate details of his work, how he spent almost every hour of the day. Reading all his reports, making suggestions to his work, all this time. Five years. *Five years!* The *bitch!* His head raged now, and he could feel his teeth clenching just at the thought of the bitch's face. He wanted to smash her head against a brick wall and found himself having to control his thoughts.

He was racing through the corridors of the seventh floor with clenched fists hoping to find some comfort from the sick feeling that was rising in him. He had all the keys, and he made his way through door after door, showing all the necessary passes and making all the security checks as required. There were ten stages at which he had to either use a key or handprint to open the door. Each stage was guarded by two security guards and there were cameras at each door. At the final stage, an additional requisition order was needed which had to be given by either George Lucas or Manuel Perez. Ed always felt like a child being given permission by the teacher to open the tuck shop door! But on this occasion, it was random urge which brought Ed here. He had no requisition order and had not thought about it until he reached door number ten. Henry and Paul, the men guarding this door exchanged the normal pleasantries with Ed and then waited patiently for the order. Then Ed, already very agitated, realised.

'Oh damned!' he exclaimed. 'Problem, Sir? asked Henry.

'I don't have a requisition order. I was in a bit of a hurry.'

'I'm sorry, Sir, but we do need permission.'

'Well of course you do,' said Ed a touch wryly. 'We can't have you getting into trouble with the headmaster, now can we?'

'I think you jest with us Mr. Hamilton!' said Paul.

'I'm sorry guys. Please tell me I don't have to walk back through nine doors to get the master's permission!'

'Let's see what we can do,' said Paul quickly typing something into the computer of his. He then picked up the phone and dialled a series of codes and eventually gave a number of verbal passwords before the screen in front of him came up with Manuel Perez' face.

'Mr Perez, sorry to bother you. Mr Hamilton wants access here. Do you agree to it?'

'What exactly does he want to do?' Manuel Perez had just been enlightened to the conversation that had taken place between Lucas and Ed and so he was well aware of the fact that he was treading on eggshells now. He had seen Lucas' fat lip! He could not upset Ed any more than he already was. He knew this was not normal procedure but could see no reason why he should not give his permission. After all, if Ed had put in a written request, he would not have been refused.

'Tell him I have to think.' Ed looked straight faced back at the two guards. Paul relayed this and was told to let him in.

'There you go, Sir' said Henry.

There was a final palm print procedure Ed had to go through and then the door hissed as it opened. He nodded to the guards and went in.

Immediately, he could feel the change in atmosphere. The door closed behind him as he walked in. There was a huge control panel which stretched the length of the room. The whole panel was protected by thick tinted glass. There were temperature control panels, humidity panels, radiation panels and communications panels all buzzing away. Ed walked right into the centre of this small room and looked into the glass. There it was. Right in front of him. Bright, brilliant and blue. It shimmered and sparkled, and Ed's jaw dropped every time he looked at it. The Blue Haze. The *real* Blue Haze. Sparkling away, teasing him, almost inviting him in. It must have been superb craftsmanship for them to build around the actual Haze. The immediate area surrounding the Corridor was left untouched. You could still see the walls of the cave and the ice on the ground. From this side of the window, you could not smell anything, but Ed knew that the atmosphere was exactly the same as they had found it. The temperature had been unaltered. Nobody was certain whether the conditions in which the Corridor existed were vital to its existence or not so the area around it had been untampered. It must have been a huge building project to try and build the Corporation around this phenomenon without actually altering its existence. Ed stood there and stared. His own face looked strange as the light from the phenomenon reflected off his face. He stared hard and within seconds, he was off to other worlds. His brain was suddenly catapulted through time. How far was it possible to travel? Visions of cavemen, short, fat and hairy with raw meat stuck in their large, black teeth suddenly came to him. From that he moved to Byzantine times. The herb and spice trades. He could almost smell the pungent odours. He could stand and watch that which up to now he had only imagined. He could witness the building of the Pyramids and finally kill the question as to how the Egyptians went about erecting them. He could find out so many things that puzzled man today. Exactly what was Stonehenge all about? Talking of strange figures, who on Earth created the figures on Easter Island? No sooner was he imagining this than he found himself in the Tower of London the moment Anne Boleyn was becoming a martyr. Was Catherine Parr as ugly as history has described her? Was Queen Elizabeth I really a virgin? What if he ended up part of Alexander the Great's army travelling and conquering most of Europe? Would not that be magnificent! Was the Bible real? Did Moses really part the sea and did Jesus really exist? Was he really the great miracle performing Son of God or just a long haired, unemployed hippy who happened to be in the right place at the right time and who could perform a few great tricks? Talking of great mysteries, who the hell was standing on the grassy knoll about to change the course of American history forever? Would it not be fantastic to watch the fungus actually growing in Alexander Fleming's laboratory? He could witness Watson and Crick's building block discovery and read Salk and Sabin's notes on immune vaccines. His head was truly wandering madly through the centuries. The possibilities seemed endless. What if jumping through time actually altered history? If he found himself on the Titanic, would he mention the iceberg to anyone? Would he try to prevent the Enola Gay from carrying out her deadly mission? Where would the world be today if he had? He travelled backwards and forwards in a fevered rush, visions coming and going. He could almost smell the changes. His mind ran wildly about and eventually he began to think of the Corporation. Where exactly did the Professor come from? Who is the President? Would he, if he could, stop that bitch from graduating from her beloved Harvard? His eyes just stared at this Corridor of possibilities for what seemed ages. This was the Corridor. The *time* Corridor that had taken up the last five years of his life. The wasted years. The empty research. He could not help feeling like he had wasted all that time. He had an overwhelming curiosity to know exactly what lay behind this. What was beyond the Corridor? For a few minutes, the rage inside him had subsided as he looked hard at the Haze, almost hoping to see something inside it.

'What *are* you? He whispered under his breath. 'What the hell lies beyond you?'

Manuel Perez put the handset down after giving his permission to Ed and sighed heavily as he looked at Lucas and the President who were both in his office. The President had almost finished his visit and was giving final instructions before leaving the Corporation. Ironically, Edward Hamilton was one of the last subjects that they were discussing. The President could not and did not hide his dissatisfaction with the way this problem had been handled. He held both Lucas and Perez responsible and wasted no time in making this quite clear.

'Well gentlemen,' he said looking at them both through his dark glasses. 'We are meant to be controlling the security risks that face this Corporation. But with this case I think you have caused a major one.' He paused while he waited for a response. He got none so he carried on. 'Whatever your reasons for handling Edward Hamilton the way you did may have been justified. They certainly sound justified. However, I think the young man has every right to be severely annoyed, don't you think? It surely could not have taken you two years to carry out security checks on this man and if after all that time, you did not find anything suspicious, then you should have taken appropriate steps to keep him in line.'

There was a short pause before Lucas spoke. 'I take full responsibility, Sir.'

'I know you will,' said the President rather severely. 'You have in your lack of action created what we call 'an angry young man'. He is angry and on the war path not only with you, but with the whole Corporation. He is ripe pickings for undesirables. How do we know that his anger will wither away? How do we know that he is not now a loose cannon? One conversation with the press is all that it takes.'

'He certainly is angry, but he is not disloyal,' said Perez.

'Then why did you not take him fully on board?' asked the President. Perez shot fierce glances at Lucas. He knew that he was taking the blame for this mismanagement when all along, he was in favour of taking Ed into their confidence. He knew that it was Lucas who had a problem with Ed. His only mistake was that he let Lucas have the final say. Almost let him take full responsibility knowing that on paper he would also be held responsible as he was now. The way that they shared out responsibility seemed reasonable enough. Lucas took full control of Edward Hamilton and Susan Preston while Perez took the others. It seemed logical but now it seemed that both of them should have organised it differently. Lucas avoided eye contact with Perez, but he could almost feel the stare. He had to soothe the situation somehow.

'Mr. President, I think it is only fair to clear the air. On the subject of Mr Hamilton, I have to take the blame. Mr Perez left the decision to me because I insisted on it.'

'It makes no difference now,' said the President. 'What do you suggest we do to alleviate the situation? Mr Hamilton is now a major security hazard.'

They sat there for a while in silence. Although the President did not shout, rant and rave, his presence was awesome, and his audience had to think very carefully before replying. Stupid suggestions thrown down without an ounce of thought would be fiercely dealt with. The President was a well-dressed, highly groomed person. His skin was dark and worn with age, but his body was rather slim and fit. He had dark hair with bits of grey and a clean-shaven face. His eyes were never seen. He always wore dark glasses even when the room was dark. It was difficult to guess his background or even his nationality. He could pass off as Italian, Greek or Middle Eastern due to his swarthy complexion but then he spoke the most perfect English that even the Queen would have been proud of. Although George Lucas had worked and played with American presidents, he was not important enough to have been told the background of this judge-mentor who sat in front of him today. He was harsh, this President. But he was not ruthless without motive. On this occasion, he himself accepted that pointing fingers would get them nowhere. They had to move forward.

'I think it is safe to say that an error of judgement has been made. Now that we know that it is better to try and find a way to solve it. By what you have told me, Mr. Hamilton is not too happy, is that right?'

'No, he is not,' replied Lucas.

'I guess that he is more angry with you than anybody else,' said the President to Lucas. Lucas nodded. 'Then I suggest that we try to mollify him. I want future dealings with Mr Hamilton to be dealt with by either both of you together or with just Mr Perez. Usually, the presence of a second person acts to defuse an explosive situation. But do not let him know that there has been a change. Just try and act naturally.'

'I think that is probably for the best,' conceded Lucas. 'How do you get on with him, Mr Perez?'

'We have a pleasant understanding of each other although I have to admit, I have not had to deal with him on anything important.'

'Well try and ease yourself into his confidence. If you have to do this by criticising Mr Lucas' actions, then I suggest you do it. He already dislikes Mr Lucas anyway and it is more important for you to get him back into your control. Is that a problem with you Mr Lucas?'

'No. Not at all,' whispered the dejected Lucas. He somehow felt a bollocking would have been better than this quiet punishment that he was suffering now.

'How do you think we should approach him?' This question was open for either of them to answer.

'Well,' said Lucas, 'the last thing that he said was that he wanted to know everything. He wanted to read the files and update himself on everything and then actually carry out a personal interview himself.'

'Well, I think that should keep him busy and then hopefully, as he becomes more involved, he may...... well...... forgive. He probably won't forget.' It was Mr Perez that came up with this and was pleased that the President was nodding in agreement.

'Fine. That sounds reasonable. It means that he is still interested in the project. It seems a good place to start. We have to monitor him carefully and make sure we do not refuse him anything. Within reason of course. We may need to get someone from security to closely monitor him outside the Corporation grounds,' said the President.

'Are we still monitoring the flats of the scientific staff on a 24-hour basis?'

'Yes,' replied Mr Perez.

'Is that still audio?'

'Well, audio is standard, but Mr Hamilton's flat has visual,' said Mr Perez meekly. 'Oh? Why?' enquired the President. Mr Perez said nothing but glanced towards Lucas.

The President looked sternly at Lucas but eventually let a slight smile cross his lips. 'Mr Lucas, you really do not trust this man, do you? I wonder why you dislike him so much.' This was not really meant as a question, so Lucas made no attempt to answer it. He just sat there and waited for more quiet torture.

'Well since Mr Hamilton is already on 24-hour surveillance, I suggest we play this gently. Keep an eye on him at all times and inform me immediately if he speaks to anybody that does not work for the Corporation. Monitor all calls made outside and all visitors that he has.'

'He is usually totally dedicated to the Corporation and spends very little time outside work. He has a few friends whom he speaks to every now again and occasionally his father. But nothing else. He very occasionally talks to his sister. He keeps in touch with her through e-mail mainly,' said Lucas.

'Orwell would have been proud!' grinned the President. Both men just looked at this rare show of humour from the President. There then followed a small pause before the President concluded the meeting. 'I think the last step will be for me to talk to Mr Hamilton myself.'

Lucas looked up sharply. 'Do you think that is...' He stalled his sentence at the last minute on seeing the stern look on the face of the other man.

'Mr Lucas, in your career, when you were unhappy with White House policies, did you consult other employees, or did you go straight to the President? If Mr Hamilton's wrath has to be quelled, certainly for him to know that his grievance has reached the top and is being dealt with by those at the top is going to help our cause.' There was no reply from Lucas. 'I am surprised Mr Lucas,' added the President sarcastically, 'that you think you should have an opinion at all on this matter. I am further amused that you think you can question any attempt I make to correct your mistakes!' Somehow a reply to this did not seem appropriate either.

'I think gentlemen that we can close this meeting.' He stood up and collected all his belongings. 'I shall leave as soon as I have spoken to Mr Hamilton. I think we should let him calm down today. I shall see him first thing tomorrow and then leave. Please keep me closely informed on your progress. I want to know immediately if you think the situation may get out of control. We have to control Mr Hamilton at all costs. Is that understood?' Both men nodded like obedient children. As the President left, both men let out huge sighs.

CHAPTER 6

S usan Preston had had a quiet evening by herself. She went to her yoga class for some stretching and meditation and treated herself to a hot soak and a glass of wine before reading and turning in for the night. It should have helped her relax and calm her mind. However, no amount of meditation was going to ease the feeling of guilt. She has a restless night and could not deny that she woke with a certain amount of reluctance. Her favourite healthy oats, yogurt, banana and honey breakfast was not enough to lighten the burden she now felt on her shoulders. She knew all along that she should have told Ed everything. He was to find out the next morning anyway. She was angry and annoyed with herself because she knew that the *real* Susan Preston was a compassionate person who was in desperate need of friends and she had missed a golden opportunity. She was also angry with herself for not being able to control the *bitch* Susan Preston. Her image as a ruthless scientist were all very well but at times, she longed to be her natural self. She was aware of the fact that almost everything about her was a pretence, but it seemed to be like a disease within her. Every time she tried to be herself, the arrogant, insensitive and egotistical part of her surfaced and the *real* Susan Preston had to walk away in humiliation. *You are the missing link, goodbye!* Every chance she had, she always put other down. Always criticised others and always gave her opinion knowing that it was someone else's opinion that she had heard. She knew that she was not academically gifted but all her life she had to grow up in the shadow of her hugely intelligent and famous father. She spent most of her childhood trying to please him, trying to collect praise and appreciation. She could not remember whether this was a self-imposed burden or whether her father was a strict demanding man. It seemed so natural to her to concentrate all her abilities in pleasing him that it all became second nature to a point where she never did anything unless she knew that her father would approve. Even today. Being herself was far more difficult that being the person she thought her father wanted her to be. Sadly, the truth of the matter was that if she actually looked deeply into the soul of her father; she would find a man continuously battling with himself. A normal man trying to escape from the shadow of the genius that he was.

Susan had to make an effort to correct the awkward situation that she had got herself into. She still had to work with Ed and would prefer to have him as a friend. She decided for the first time to be completely natural and to do whatever comes naturally to make it up to Ed. She thought the one to one, honest approach would be the best, the one that Ed would understand. She managed to get to the Corporation a little earlier than usual and made two cups of fresh coffee. She then went to Ed's laboratory and waited for him to arrive. She was apprehensive and kept practising what she was going to say. How she was going to get out of this. It would be all over by the time she went home this evening and that's what she looked forward to. For the first time ever, she would appeal to Ed's better nature. What frightened her most was that she thought she may have to admit certain faults in herself. She may have to be really true to him and admit that she was not all that she pretended to be. She had to wait and test the ground. She must have waited for about half an hour, constantly looking at her watch and wondering why Ed was not on time. He was normally punctual. It was highly unlikely that he would not turn up at all and even more unlikely that he ran out of the Corporation in disgust. She knew enough about the Corporation to know that they would never allow that to happen. It was also likely that Ed knew this himself. In fact, they all knew this, but it was an unwritten law. In many ways, the Corporation was no better than the Mafia. Once in, there's no getting out. She was looking at all the jars lining the shelves all around the room. All the creatures that were once alive and breathing, running around. All ended up here. All a bit gruesome she thought. At this point she heard the sound of the laboratory doors swishing open. Somebody had just entered. She hopped off the bench and waited. She expected to see Ed but when he came round the corner, she was shocked. His appearance was totally changed. It was unlikely that he had slept at all. His face was unshaven, and his clothes were still the same ones he was wearing yesterday. There was a slight look of anger on his face as he came in. When he spotted her, he froze. She said nothing. She just looked at him. Words did not come to her. All the lines she has practised had left her. Her voice seemed to have left her along with her courage. In an instant, she wanted to get out. To leave the lab. He looked like he was about to fly into a rage. He stood there and stared at her.

'*Bitch*' this was a very low, almost inaudible whisper that escaped his lips, but it was loud enough to reach her ears. Oh God, she thought, please help me out of this one. 'Edward, I'm sorry. Really honestly. I'm …'

He took a step towards her and she stepped back. 'Bitch! What do you want here? Snooping around as usual', he growled. He looked into her face and was astounded by the look of terror in her eyes. He was delighted. She was human after all. He walked away from her with a chuckle when he noticed that she was looking over his shoulder with an equal look of terror. He glanced behind him and was a bit shocked himself. He turned around to face the figure that stood behind him. He wore a crisp navy-blue shirt with a white shirt and a red tie. Very standard, though he looked anything but standard. The hair was well groomed, and the glasses looked even darker than the previous day. He was in the process of lighting a cigarette when he paused and looked at Ed. Ed was a bit concerned about all the flammable solvents, he had lying around on the benches, but he was not going to ask him to stop.

'Don't mind if I smoke do you?' Perfect English. Ed made no comment, so the cigarette was lit. 'Delighted to see you Miss Preston. Have you seen your father recently?'

'Er no. I've not been able to get away recently. I speak to him on the phone.'

'Well give him my regards, won't you?' Susan was a little surprised. She has no idea that the President knew her father. She could almost see the strings which kept her career together. 'I'm sorry to ask this of you Miss Preston, but I need to see Mr Hamilton alone. Would you mind?' She was annoyed with herself for waiting until she was asked to leave but his presence numbed her. She apologised and left the laboratory. The President moved and leaned back on one of the benches but said nothing. Ed now crossed his arms and looked defiantly at the President. He knew exactly what the visit was all about.

'I see your anger has not totally subsided,' the President finally remarked. 'That's what you're here for isn't it? To pacify me?'

'Mr Hamilton, I will not waste your time. Yes, I am here to make sure vengeance is not on your mind. I am also trying to evaluate whether there is a possibility that you may be angry enough to blow the lid. Finally, I have to find a way of controlling you since you are now a volatile problem waiting to go off.' Ed was thrown off course by this level of honesty. He expected soothe talking and manipulation. This approach served only to quench his anger. 'I know that you have been badly managed. I cannot do anything about that which has already failed you, but I can correct your future role within the Corporation. I cannot afford to have you watched all the time and I need to be able to trust you. At the same time, you need to regain the confidence you have lost in us.'

'I hate to be rude but you're not seriously telling me that you did not know how Lucas was running the project? Don't tell me that you don't know everything that goes on here? You must have known what he was doing and maybe even endorsed it.' His voice was slightly raised, and the President was aware of this.

'Mr Hamilton, did you ever tell Mr Lucas in advance of any tests you were going to do? What next steps you were going to take? How you planned your research? Did you ever discuss with him how you should do your job?'

Edward made no answer, but he knew where this was going.

'Yes, I do know everything. My employees know what is expected of them. But they are also highly skilled individuals who know their jobs. It would be highly irregular for me to tell them how to do things. In your case, I knew what was going on but left it to Mr Lucas's judgement. His mistake was that he did not manage the situation very well. He seems to have... well a certain...'

'Dislike of me?' interrupted Ed.

'Well, yes. My mistake was that I should have seen the problem before and should have acted to prevent it. I do not know what else to say to you.'

'I have wasted *five years* of my life in this isolated pit! How am I supposed to get that time back? You think just coming here in person to apologise is enough? What exactly did you come here for anyway?'

'Mr Hamilton, I can only help you in the way forward. I cannot change anything that has already occurred. If you want to be helped.'

'And what if I don't?'

The President lowered his head. If one could have seen his eyes they would have been staring straight at the floor. He was not going to lie. 'That would put us in a very delicate position. I want you to remember that the Corporation has to be shielded at all costs.'

Edward stared at him. He, of course, knew that there was no way out once you were in. He knew too much to be able to walk away now. But to hear the implications from the horse's mouth was chilling. All he could think of was Patrick McGoogan's face when he opened the blinds of his bedroom and found himself in The Village. *I am not a number! I am a free man!* Free man? Bollocks. He was a prisoner to the Corporation the minute the Professor told him the truth behind it. Now he fully understood the truth behind the President's words. He was speechless.

'Look, I'm not crazy,' Said Ed. 'I know there's no way out. I still have work to do. Now more than ever. I am not going to do anything stupid because my curiosity won't let me. I have to see Mr Frenkel. I don't fancy a bullet in my head administered by my own side, so you need not worry. I do wish to be given a free hand to further my work.'

'You are an insightful man Mr Hamilton. I know you feel like your hands have been tied but I will try and loosen the grip for you. You may progress as you wish with your work. Any problems and you can ask to contact me.'

I just want you to know, I am not happy and will never trust the Corporation again,' added Ed. 'But I will carry on as before. I want to be kept fully informed.'

'I understand,' said the President. 'I hope you do not feel too threatened. ' 'Gives a whole new meaning to the term 'job for life'', grinned Ed.

'Please do not take it personally. Your employment conditions apply to us all!' Ed started at him in amazement. 'Yes, Mr Hamilton, even to me.' With that the President began to stroll towards the door.

'Who are you?' Ed asked. 'Where do you come from? What the hell is your name?'

The President stopped but did not turn around. The curiosity of the other man delighted him. He eventually spoke, without turning around. 'I work for many Governments; I came here in a Helicopter I borrowed from United States Air Force and my name... is The President.' He left.

Smart arse, thought Ed.

Edward had early in the day put in a request with Mr Perez to see all of Anthony Frenkel's notes. It was a thick, heavy file which he collected soon after lunchtime. He had much work to do. He had to update himself totally before he actually approached the man. Almost from the time he collected the notes to the time he took them back to his flat, he could feel the strange feeling in his head. He was considering seeing the doctor. He was not one to go running to the doctor, but this headache was odd and persistent. He could do without it. He managed to grab a pizza from Pablo's Hut. Some of his work colleagues were there having a sit-down meal and he went over for a quick chat while he waited for his order. They were a little curious as to what had happened to Susan Preston. She has apparently taken the afternoon off sick and that was definitely a first. When her name came up, Edward's thoughts began to turn to anger. He was still more than annoyed with her. He then headed to his flat.

He had a shower after eating, grabbed a cold beer and then planted himself on his comfortable sofa underneath the uplifted light. Then for the next two hours he was lost in Anthony Frenkel's life. He read rapidly. It read like a work of science fiction.

The notes started with Frenkel's shock return. The various Government agencies and intelligence experts had already established themselves at the site of the Haze shortly after Frenkel's disappeared into it. They had been carrying out tests solidly for four days when on the fifth, they watched in horror as the screams started coming from within the Haze. These were loud and chilling like an animal in last throes of death. As they watched a figure emerged. His hair was burnt and there were patches of scorched skin. Parts of his clothes appeared to be smoking and his face was bleeding. He fell onto the snowy ground and continued to scream as the shocked men around him struggled to believe what they had seen. Before they could act the man found enough energy to scramble to his feet, still screaming and wailing like a child. He ran. He seemed to run aimlessly. He looked at the men with fright, his scared eyes almost popping out of his head. One of the men tried to calm him down but it was no good. The unfortunate man seemed not to understand a word. When another official moved towards Frenkel, the latter suddenly shot a glance towards him. At the same instant, the recovery team watched in horror as their man seemed to fly backwards, almost as if pushed to the ground by an unseen force. Another two men ran up to Frenkel, but he shielded his face and head with his hand, almost in defence, at the same time the two men were catapulted clear off the ground and landed heavily on the icy ground. All verbal communication had failed, and physical help was impossible. The recovery team were too frightened to approach the madman and were totally confused as to what was going on. They could not explain what was happening to them, but they had no doubt that Frenkel was somehow using some unseen force for protection. He was not deemed dangerous as he was clearly frightened. Frenkel eventually stopped screaming and ran to a rock and sat there, catching his breath and watching the men. If any of them approached him he only had to look at them to send them flying. It was a stalemate and the men just sat there, both sides watching the other. The men watched but made no more sudden movements. Frenkel ran no more. He seemed exhausted. So exhausted, that eventually, he fell asleep. The men waited for a long time, before moving in. They approached quietly but it was plain he was too exhausted to wake. He could even be dead, as they poked and prodded him. He did not wake. It was then that they moved him and brought him back to base. The man had been kept heavily sedated for days while they took samples from him and worked round the clock to build a secure room to put him into. They still had no idea what forces served him and what he was capable of. There was something very strange about this man. Some of the medical team working around him were sure they kept hearing a voice trying to communicate with them while Frenkel was sedated. Others felt nausea and headaches when in his presence. The records also described the many wounds on the man's body. These range from small cuts to large burn marks. He had slashes across his face and his right arm was broken at the wrist. Most bodily hair had been scorched and he was severely malnourished. When his cubicle had been completed they put him inside and waited for him to wake up. That took five days during which time he was put on a drip.

Up to this point the notes had been typed and there was no indication as to who had written them and when. No indication of who had carried out the tests. It was not really a very scientific was of making notes and logging events. After this point all the notes had been written by hand and Ed instantly recognised the Professor's untidy scrawl. The writing resembles and flowing river, slanting first this way and then the other way. Some parts were clearly legible, and others were a mere excited scrawl making the notes difficult for Ed to read.

The Professor's notes from this point onwards describe the patient as being dangerously psychic but there were no tests or results described to prove this. Frenkel in his conscience state was intelligent and to a degree quite co-operative. However, he had sudden bouts of anger which resulted several times in the damaging of property around him. He seemed to shatter glass and throw stationary around by thought. When he asked about his wife and child, he was told that as far as his family were concerned, he was dead. They had been told that he had died in the expedition after an avalanche buried his body deep in snow. His wife was told that recovery of his body was impossible. She had accepted this, and he was given a memorial service. On hearing this, Frenkel was distraught to such an extent that his sorrow manifested itself in the form of violence. His room that had been specially built for him was totally trashed without Frenkel himself raising a finger. But the man himself was writhing in pain. The Professor's notes described it as a scene from a special effects' movie. The person who had told Frenkel about his family felt his throat was burning. He later described it like a severe burning sensation like there was a fire inside his mouth. He was unable to breathe properly and began to choke. He ended up on the floor in pain as an attempt was made to enter Frenkel's chamber and to try to sedate him. Both the medics who attempted this were battered about by invisible fists and ended up unconscious and bleeding.

In order to contain Frenkel, it was necessary to build a flat which was comfortable and homely, but which was designed with Frenkel's needs taken into consideration. Extra thick glass was used and almost all the furniture and cupboards were made of metal. Frenkel was not very good at manipulating metal. The flat also had a feature which was reminiscent of the Nazi gas chambers. There were four gas outlets all around the flat. At the touch of a button, these would spew out chloroform in gas form. It was to be used in an emergency whenever Frenkel lost control.

However, the notes made no reference to Frenkel's character. What they did not know was that Frenkel was a clever and astute man. He knew that although he felt like an animal in a freak show, there was little the Corporation could do with him. He knew he could not control himself yet. He also knew that this dreaded *gift* was over a hundred times stronger than it was before. He was never able to move objects. And he was able to read thoughts, maybe even manipulate thoughts. He just could not control anything. He felt like losing control out there would be fatal, either for him or to someone else. He had to remain with those who could help him. He had to co-operate. He could not control his thoughts, his desires and his powers and for this reason he accepted that he was dead to the world. He accepted that Jennifer and Jake considered him dead. The most eerie part of it was that he knew exactly what was happening in the outside world. He could see almost everything. If he wanted to know what Jennifer and Jake were doing, he only had to close his eyes and look! He knew everything they did, every move they made, what they said, how they felt. Their sorrow was his sorrow, their happiness was his happiness. However, much as he needed the Corporation, he felt no need to tell them everything. The Professor could not even have guessed the full extent of Frenkel's powers. That much, Frenkel had kept to himself. As far as the Professor was concerned, the man could move objects by thought. That was all Frenkel gave away.

Of course, all this was not in the notes so that the actual state of Frenkel's mind was still a mystery to Ed. There were details of the apartment that housed Frenkel. He was visually monitored 24 hours continuously and the audio was only switched on when required. Although he had television and radio from around the world and all the reading material that he could wish for, it was still a dull life. He had limited access to the internet. Almost everything was blocked and monitored. Frenkel made no request to take a stroll outside and the option was never put to him. He took part in all the tests and was as co-operative as he could be. As he learned over the years to control his mind, the violent outbursts were few and far between. He did, however, take up the Corporation's offer of further education. Over the years he studies Archaeology and Modern History. He had taste for food and learned how to cook. He could certainly teach Gordon Ramsey a thing or two!

Despite reading for two hours, Ed felt the notes were lacking a great deal in substance. There seemed to be no proper tests to evaluate Frenkel's powers. There was not a section anywhere which explained where Frenkel had travelled to when he fell into the Corridor. Where had he been? What had he seen? Why did he have a gash on his face when he came back? What had caused the madness which took him a good couple of months to recover from? The notes describe him as dangerous but did not explain why. There also seemed to be pages missing from the report. The numbering was all wrong and it seemed almost as if chunks of the report had been doctored. Ed began to wonder whether Lucas was still holding out on him. He made it plain that he wanted to see all the notes but there were bits missing. Would Lucas be daft enough to try and con him again? At this stage, the little bugs in his head started to run riot again and he felt he needed to stop reading. What *was* that tingling? He had to sleep. He would have to find out what is going on tomorrow. A quick flick through the rest of the notes told him there was very little else to read which would tell him more about the unfortunate man who was now the Corporation's secret prisoner for the rest of his life.

CHAPTER 7

'If he's holding out on me, I swear I'll floor him again Manuel.' Ed was in Manuel Perez' office. The latter man was fingering through the report on Frenkel. He had a frown on his face and as he examined the documents, he was praying that Lucas was not responsible for this. His job was difficult enough as it was, but this was really going too far.

'Edward, I do not know what to say. I read all the reports regarding Frenkel. This is not even half the notes. There were extensive tests, physical and mental that the Professor carried out. He gave details of everything and even made suggestions of his own as to Frenkel's real state of mind. There were also scores of incidents where Frenkel could not be controlled for one reason or another and drastic steps had to be taken. The gas had to be used several times but that is missing from these notes. The pages that are missing have been cleverly removed in a way that is not obvious. I would like to tell you that this was not Lucas' doing but I have to make sure first.'

'Why would he do this? What can he gain now? He's still taking the piss!' Ed was angry but he controlled it very well.

'Please, don't get angry. There must a reasonable explanation.'

'Reasonable explanation my *arse!*'

'Let me find out before you jump to conclusions. This report is top secret confidential property which belongs to a number of Governments. Whatever you think of Lucas, he is not so warped that he would risk his neck just to get back at you. His job is the most important thing in his life. There must be another reason.'

As much as Ed wanted to believe it was Lucas, deep down, he knew it was impossible. Lucas was many things, but he did most things by the book and ruining confidential material was not one of them. He began to wonder who really did remove those notes and why. His mind went back to the Professor. He tried to blank out any ill thoughts, but he was considering the possibility that it was the Professor. He must have had almost unlimited access to the notes and maybe he felt like Frenkel was his subject and nobody else could know everything about him. It was all rather strange, and Ed felt that this time Lucas was not responsible.

'Well, I suppose I'll go through some of the other work that Professor Braun carried out. He must have had a copy of all this for himself. He must have had something on a computer disk.'

'He always annoyingly insisted on hand-written reports. He refused to touch a computer and the nature of the report meant it was not safe to get someone else to type up his notes,' said Perez.

'That sounds like Max!' Ed paused a little before asking his next question. 'Manuel, if you read the original report, you must remember certain facts. Where had he been? What did Frenkel experience? What time zone did he go to? How did he know that it was a time Corridor?'

Perez hesitated as if trying to find the right words. Ed was certain that he remembered everything that was in the report. He was trying to delay answering so as not to give too much away. 'It was almost three months after he returned that he was able to communicate verbally. Before that we thought he was insane. We questioned him under varying conditions. At one point we had a monitor which was attached to his brain, reading brain activity. Being a man with special abilities his brain showed highly advanced pattern of waves and impulses. This seemed logical. But the odd thing was what happened when we questioned him about his experience in the Corridor. He was quite calm and collected on the outside, but his brain pattern was increased ten-fold and the scatter plots almost went off scale. He said it was a *time* corridor but refused to say where he had been. He laughed crazily when questioned further and kept referring to it as the Devil's Corridor. When further interrogation was attempted, he reacted by *mentally* attacking everyone in the room. He was still traumatised by it all but that is all he would say. He then fell to the floor and started screaming with his head in his hands. His pulse shot up and he suffered clinical trauma like a person would in a car accident. It took a week for him to recover from this. The whole thing was repeated every time we tried to question him. One of those attacks was enough to kill him and we were frightened of putting him under too much pressure.'

'Devil's Corridor! It's all a bit dramatic isn't it?'

'That's how he has always referred to it.'

'Who has been monitoring him since the Professor died?'

'Well…,' Manuel Perez was now embarrassed, 'he has regular medical check-ups and sessions with the therapist but.'

'Nobody! That's what you're saying. He has just been left there to do his own thing in his little prison.'

'Edward, we do not know what to do with him. He has powers we cannot control. He has so far co-operated with us, but we cannot get much more information from him without him having a fit! We want to fully test him but there is not one person here that he trusts. We thought he trusted the Professor but even that relationship came to an end. We may have conquered the moon and have technology that would destroy nations and at the same time create life in the laboratory, but we do not know how to handle Mr Frenkel. We are lost.'

Ed stared at Perez. He was slouching on one of the swivel chairs and remained like this for a short while before straightening up. 'Right. We've pissed about long enough! I don't care what happened to the blasted notes. It's time I saw him! I want to see him, now! Don't try to stall this or I'll cause waves.'

'Okay. I have already given security the relevant details and you will be registered to see him this afternoon.'

Ed was completely taken aback by this. He expected resistance but this was totally unexpected. 'You have already granted the pass? How did you know I wanted to see him today?'

'I didn't. He wants to see you.'

Ed was totally mystified. Up until now, Anthony Frenkel was just a file. A series of weird events. He had not actually given too much thought to the man. He thought he was at an advantage because he had read the files and the medical reports, and he knew the names of Frenkel's wife and son. He thought he was in control. But to be told that Frenkel apparently knew Ed by name and had predicted the actual day that Ed would see him sent a shiver through his body. Ed was the person being investigated. Anthony Frenkel obviously was in total control and the thought of being at a disadvantage worried Ed. He was at a loss as to what he would say to the man. An introduction would be futile. In fact, what was he going to do? Talk? Carry out more tests? Investigate the troubled mind? He had not thought of anything at all. He had no idea what to say or do. All this time, he could feel that bloody headache which was now more than just tingling. It was a dull thud. He also noticed that in the last few days, the pain would be worse when he was trying to relax. He always went to bed in peace but awoke with the pain. Sometimes he would wake up in the night with the pain. Damned that pain. He worried that it could be something serious, but he was at a crucial stage with his work. He could not let anything come in the way. All he was interested in now was talking to Frenkel. That was the priority he had on his mind now. All would be fine once he saw the man in the flesh. He would look at him and instantly know what to say! At any rate, Ed had very little time to think what to say. Within hours he was escorted by security guards to the sixth level. There were just as many doors and passwords to negotiate which increased the anxiety that Ed felt. The pain in his head was throbbing, thumping away and he could barely focus his thoughts as he followed his guides. At one stage he had to stop when a sudden feeling of nausea gripped him, and he thought he was about to be sick. He made his way to one of the rest rooms which could be found all over the building. He calmed himself and drank some water. The pain in his head did not ease at all but the nausea did. He must do something about this as soon as he could. For now, he collected himself and joined his little army of guides. After an eternity, they arrived at this huge door. It was heavily guarded and the procedure for getting in was long and irritating. The ache in Ed's head was like a train racing through it. Once the door was opened, there was a pause. All his guards turned towards him and waited. He assumed that some of them would come in with him, but he was surprised. One of them motioned him to enter and he hesitated. His hesitation lasted many seconds and for a brief moment, he thought he would change his mind. The coward inside him was growing and now he really thought that this was not what he wanted to do. Sweat was beginning to form around his head and just as he fought to find his courage again, he heard a voice deep in the passages of his aching head. *I'm waiting Mr Hamilton. Please come in.* He was shocked but there was no time to hesitate any longer as the guards were getting suspicious. He took a deep breath and launched his body forward.

It took some time for Edward Hamilton's eyes to focus on the room that he now stood in it. He just stood and soaked everything in. He found himself in a small three-sided cubicle. There was a bench in front of him, a chair and some buttons. There was a green and red light on the panel in front and the whole cubicle was in the dark. The only light that he saw was from the other side of the huge glass window directly in front of him. It reminded him of Harry's cubicle. He peered in but saw no one. He was shocked. He was not prepared for this. The thing behind the cage was a man, yet he was looking around this structure and thinking how demeaning it was. The man behind the glass could not feel like anything other than an animal. Watched. Observed. Caged. Always being analysed. Trapped in this tiny little corner of the world. Occupying this tiny space. Totally isolated from everyone and everything. A life that was not a life at all. He suddenly felt intense pity. Pity for this man who up until now was no more than a top-secret file. Just a bunch of reports and papers bundled into a folder. Even the notes were not typed out properly. Ed never normally felt pity for anyone. But he could not control his feelings now. *There's no need for pity!* What was that? Whose voice was that? Did he hear it, or had he imagined it? He then noticed his headache was gone. Marvellous! After hours of pounding, his head was silent. No pain, no thudding. He had definitely felt the pain when he stood outside the door but now, he felt nothing. How could a pain disappear so instantly?

'I'm sorry for the headache.'

That was definitely no imagination! That was a voice! He actually heard that. 'Yes, Mr Hamilton. That was a voice you heard.'

Shit! Now he was scared. All his thoughts were being *scanned*. Sure, there was a window in front of him where he could view the man locked inside, but he felt like the real animal was in the cubicle outside. The real animal was Edward Hamilton. The window in his mind was being violated. All the warning signs were coming up in his head. The lights were flashing, and he felt exposed like never before. He was being watched from *inside* as well as from outside. The sweat was trickling down the side of his face. He almost wished the pain in his head would come back so that he could have an excuse to bang his way out of the door he had just come in from.

'Now Mr Hamilton. You don't really want that headache to come back, do you?'

'Stop that! *Stop doing that!*' shouted Ed. He now peered inside the window. It seemed to be a neat little flat. What he saw was a living room. It was tidy and well decorated. There were plenty of pictures on the walls of planes, faces and a woman with a child. The furniture was modern. In the centre of the room was a single sofa and directly in front of that was a television. There was also a complex looking hi-fi system and many mini-CD's scattered all over the floor. Just beyond the living room was a partition with a rectangle into which Ed could see the kitchen. Like the living quarters, it was a modern kitchen and very tidy too. There were four other doors on the right-hand side which were all closed so Ed could not see inside but from the notes he knew that one was an office and library, one was the bathroom, one was a gym and the last was his bedroom. The whole flat was rather airy and spacious and would have been perfect if there had been windows in it!

Ed took in the details of the flat as he searched frantically for the man inside. The sofa in front of the television was empty. The part of the kitchen that he could see was empty. He did not seem to be in the actual room itself. Maybe he was behind one of the closed doors. Ed knew that the panel in front of him monitored the man's every move. If he was out of sight, the panel could show where he was. However, Ed was rooted to the spot. He could not move no matter how much he wanted to. He wanted to call out to the man but this uncertainty of what he would find was troubling him. But most of all, Ed was frightened of Anthony Frenkel. Was it him sending those messages in his head? How much of his thought patterns could he pick up? He decided to wait until the man showed himself willingly. It was not too long before he saw a slight movement on the left side of the room. It was well lit and, in the corner, stood a huge plant with huge giant fronds sticking out in all directions. It was amazing that the plant could survive without sunlight in a place like this, he thought. Suddenly, there he was. He came into view like a projected figure created solely from light.

There was a picture of Anthony Frenkel in his notes. Dark hair, dark eyes, a tanned, rugged face. He was a handsome man of about 35 years old when he disappeared. Very fit and healthy. This was the picture in Ed's head. What he saw in front of him was a man 10 years older although only five years had elapsed. He was still fit and healthy looking as far his body was concerned. But his hair was, dishevelled and grey. The face was the same shape, but the tan was gone, and the skin looked wrinkled. He had a long scar down the side of his face and parts of his forehead had blotches on it which looked like scars from burn wounds. It was difficult to imagine that this was the same man. The only part of him that looked young and alive were the eyes! They were still dark, but the light shone brightly in them making them twinkle and shine out. Like two huge sapphire stones sparkling away. He was standing right next to the plant and Ed wondered why he had not noticed him before. He was sure he looked at the whole room carefully and could not possibly have missed him standing there. Had he been standing there all that time?

'Yes. I'm sorry Mr Hamilton for making such a dramatic entrance. But as you can see, I don't get out much!' He then started to walk towards the sofa in the centre of the room. He turned around to face the glass and moved the sofa closer. Then he seated himself down and looked Ed full in the face.

'I'm Anthony Frenkel, at your service.' Ed had to snap out of his mental block. He had to act calm. He could not appear weak in front of this man. He had to block negative thoughts out of his head. 'Mr Hamilton. Relax. Take in a few deep breaths and sit down. I cannot understand why you are so tense.'

'Tense?' How the voice managed to escape his throat he would never know. 'Tense?

You have *read my thoughts* and sent messages back to me in my head and you wonder why I am so *tense?*'

'Oh, come now. You know of my ability. Why are you surprised?'

'Everyone knows what would happen to them if they attempted a few rounds in the boxing ring with the heavyweight champion of the world! But it's still a shock if you found yourself in the ring with him!' Frenkel let out a deep, loud, throaty laugh.

'I see what you mean, Mr Hamilton. Please accept my apologies. I'm afraid I used you for my own amusement.' He was smiling throughout this whole sentence, but Ed could see that the smile was hiding deep pain inside. The man was troubled, and you did not need to read his mind to be able to come to that conclusion. He had lines of worry on his face that should never appear on a face that young. For the first time it occurred to Ed that they were roughly both the same age. Yet the man in the room seemed to be carrying the woes of the world on his shoulders. He fought to introduce himself and explain exactly who he was. He sat down on the chair in front of the glass. He knew that he could actually enter the flat, but he decided to wait until he was invited in. It was Frenkel's home and it seemed indecent to barge in without being asked.

'I have to apologise to you in advance,' said Ed. 'It may seem odd, but I have to cover old ground with you. I will explain all… that is… if you do not already know all.'

Frenkel hesitated. 'I do know all. And a whole lot more that you do not know.'

'So, you know that your files are incomplete. I have to make an attempt to replace them with your help.'

'You can replace them if you want. But it's going to have to be without my help.'

'Why?'

'I used up a lot of energy in partly destroying them. Why would I want to help you replace them?'

'Run that by me one more time.' Ed was confused.

'I would like Lucas to get the blame. He's a sly bastard. I was also prepared to have the blame rest on Ms Preston since she is a selfish piece of work. The only thing was that she is a troubled person deep down inside. If you replace the notes, I will destroy them again.'

Ed was shocked. He was confused and at a total loss as to how to continue the conversation. 'Let me get this straight. You destroyed the notes? How?'

'I caused them to melt. To dissolve into nothing.'

'Impossible!'

'As you please.' Frenkel waved his arm in the air as he said this. 'Why?'

'I know you have animals in your laboratory. Your latest interest is Harry, yes?' Ed made no reply. 'Tell me Mr Hamilton, once you have finished observing and making notes and learning, once you have totally acquired all the information you can possibly get, what do you do?' Ed still made no reply. 'Is it not true that you destroy them?'

'I don't kill all of them. I hate killing them. But sometimes I need space and I have to destroy some'.

'Whatever the reason, you do not get rid of the important ones, do you? It's always the ones that you have finished with.'

'What do you think we are? Do you really think that you are the same as the lab animals? We're not barbarians you know.'

Frenkel looked hard into Ed's face. It was a while before he leaned forward and spoke in almost a whisper. 'I don't *think* I know anything. I *do* know. I know everything. I see everything. I know you; I know Lucas, I know the Corporation. I know about people I have never met! I know things without ever leaving this bubble. Don't try and fool me. You have no idea what sort of an organisation you are dealing with!'

There were hundreds of questions raging through Ed's brain. Which one to start with was a major problem. So far, he did not think the interview was going well. Ed was not in control of anything and he felt his thoughts were being read like a book. He felt like Frenkel knew exactly what he was thinking. How strong were his powers? He felt he had to start somewhere. He decided to ask the question that was most burning in his head. 'What happened to you?'

Frenkel's smile disappeared. His total body posture changed from laid back to tense. He shifted uneasily in his chair to the point where he suddenly jumped up and started pacing his room. Every now and again he would stop and stare at a single object in the room. Ed watched him with amazement. There was definitely turmoil in that head. The man was agitated in a big way.

'Look. You told us it was a *time* corridor,' persisted Ed.

'So? What more do you want?' This was almost spat out in anger.

'Where did you go? What happened to you.' At that stage, the man held his head and bent his body forward as if in intense pain. At the same time Ed could feel a burning sensation in his head. It was not a tingling now. It was pain. It moved about in his head like an animal running around. The pain rose to such a level that Ed also held his head in his hands. *Go away! Leave me!* He knew this was Frenkel. It was not a voice but a thought. But even the thought was in Frenkel's voice. He did not know how he knew it, but he was aware of the fact that Frenkel was not being hostile here. If it was hostility, then why would he inflict pain upon himself? It was uncontrolled confusion. Frenkel still did not know how to control his power. Ed was struggling to regain his mind as he moved from the chair and turned around. The idea was to try and reach the door. Just at that point the door swung open and the guards came running with the medic who was in charge of Frenkel.

'I'm sorry Mr Hamilton, but you had better leave. You can wait outside. He may be OK in a few minutes, but you have to wait outside while we deal with him.' He was then almost pushed outside, still holding his burning head. How long he had been waiting outside was anybody's guess. There were people around him and a medic attending him. The pain suddenly eased, and he was left shaken and feeling rather numb. His whole body was trembling, and his vision was blurred by uncontrolled streaming of the eyes. He could feel his heart racing inside him, the increased pulse he could almost hear in his head. He was eventually given a chair to sit on while the medic checked his pulse and blood pressure and passed the mini scanner all around his head. Any major damage in the brain could be indicated by the mini scanner. He waited for the alarm on it to start sounding but the doctor had passed the scanner over his head several times and there was no sound. Thank God! Although he felt like his head was melting with heat, obviously there was no permanent damage. He began to recover. Eventually the team that pushed him out of the cubicle came back out. They began conversing with the medic who was attending to him.

'What's going on?' he managed to whisper. They ignored him and continued to talk. 'What the bloody hell is going on?' This was said with a bit more force as he regained himself. They stopped and looked at him.

'Mr Hamilton, you have read his files?'

'Well, kind of.'

'Then you will know that there is a certain amount of delicacy to be attached to the questions put to him. He flies off the handle quickly.'

'He was *not* flying off the handle as you put it. He was losing control. He was in pain.'

'He was unmanageable, and you have to be careful when talking to him.'

'I was just asking questions!' yelled Ed.

'You must have read the notes Mr Hamilton. They specifically tell '

'What have you done with him? When can I see him?' Ed interrupted. 'You will have to let him calm down. He will still be groggy for a while.'

'Groggy? What have you done to him?' The medic made to walk away when Ed yanked him back by the arm. 'What the hell have you done to him? He's not beyond reason. He's not an animal!'

'You will be able to see him again in about half an hour. You can wait in the rest room.'

Bastards! What did they do to him? If this is the way they had been handling him since the Professor died, then Ed surely had much work to do. He staggered to one of the rest rooms and lay down on the couch while his head returned back to normal. He was sweating profusely, and his stomach ached, though he thought the latter was most likely hunger. He had not eaten properly all day. He could not forget Frenkel. Was he standing by that plant all along? How come he did not see him? Does that mean that as well as thought transmissions, Frenkel was also capable of blocking thoughts? Or blocking images. Maybe he could put an image into the mind of others. Make others see something that is not there. What on Earth can he do? Was he always a psychic? Was it the Corridor that did this to him? None of his animals showed signs like this. Or maybe they did. How would he know? The medics attending him seemed to have the idea that Frenkel was being confrontational, but Ed knew he was genuinely in pain. It looked like he had no control over his mind and something Ed said triggered off the reaction. This was a very troubled mind indeed. It must be an awesome effort for Frenkel to project a normal image of himself. Ed was trying to think how best to approach him next. Clearly, no more questions about the Corridor. He had to try and find out more about the power that Frenkel had. How much he could control it and how much he could actually do? Could he see the future? At this moment in time Frenkel was the most important man in the world. Also, the most fragile. Ed had no idea how long he lay there for but eventually sleep came and he disappeared into a world of Romans and warriors and wars. It was only when his head slipped sideways in an uncomfortable position that he woke up. It took some time for him to realise where he was. He then remembered. It could not have been too long otherwise the Chief Medic would have called him and removed him from the rest room. After all, he was a security hazard. He stretched himself and then made his way outside Frenkel's prison. The guards seemed to be expecting him. One rose to meet him at the door.

'I'm afraid you cannot see him again today, Sir.'

'Why not?'

'The Chief Medic left instructions that you have to wait until tomorrow, Sir.'

'Why?'

'I was instructed just to give you this message, Sir.'

'Where is the Medic?'

'He is no longer on this floor, Sir.'

'Call him! I want to see him, *now!*'

'I have to send out a system wide message.'

'Do whatever the hell you have to! I want to..' At this stage he heard a creek and a hiss. The door was opening! He looked round and there, slowly the door to Frenkel's cubicle was opening and an attendant was coming out holding a small tray on which Ed could see a needle and a vial. Within seconds, the attendant was shoved to one side and the guards were shouting after Ed. He made a dash into the cubicle and stood in front of the glass. His eyes stared in disbelief. In the centre of the room was the sofa. Frenkel himself had put it there facing the glass when Ed first saw him. Slumped in it was Frenkel. His hair looked even greyer and his skin was wrinkled and blotchy. There was saliva dribbling out from the corner of his mouth and his eyes were semi shut. He had been drugged. Of that there was no doubt. A small noise escaped his lips like a tiny cry.

'Frenkel! Frenkel! Can you hear me? Look at me!' He checked the panel in front of him and found that the communication system was on. Frenkel should be able to hear him. 'Frenkel! Can you hear me?' There was a slight movement of the head. Frenkel could hear him! However, he feebly looked up through slitty eyes and tried to utter something. In the end he managed to raise his hand curled up into a fist with the thumb sticking upwards. It was obvious that Frenkel had to rest. 'Look, I'll be back tomorrow, first thing in the morning. I like English breakfast tea with two eggs fried both sides and lightly toasted bread! Got that?' He was about to walk out the door when a feeble voice came into his head. *Got it!*

CHAPTER 8

E d had every intention of visiting Frenkel the next day. Things were delayed, however, by a serious complaint coming through from the Chief Medic as to Ed's conduct the previous day. He was in hot water but both Lucas and Perez were under orders to watch him carefully. This was a breach of security. Unable to come to an adequate response from Ed, they decided this was a good reason to consult the President. Ed was summoned to Perez's office and the President contacted remotely via Skype. Perez related the incident to the President but before anything else could be said, Ed reached out for the screen and turned the monitor to face him. The familiar dark glasses were now looking at him.

'Look, Frenkel is being neglected! Seriously neglected! He is being mishandled by your staff because nobody has told them *how* to handle him. What is the point of me being given access to him only when he is well? I have to examine him when he is ill. He needed help yesterday, not sedation.! If you want me to go about my normal business then you have to grant me access whenever *I* want, not whenever suits the head Medic!' Both Perez and Lucas were shocked that he could speak to the President in such a manner.

The President stared at Ed for what seemed ages. Then he lowered his head as if in thought. It seemed an age to Ed and he was contemplating adding to his appeal. Before he could think of anything else to say the President raised his head. 'Very well, Mr Hamilton. You have a free hand. Goodbye.' With that the transmission was cut off from the President's end. Ed did not want to turn round and gloat to Lucas and Perez, but he did! The smug grin remained on his face while he spoke. He only wished the Chief Medic could have seen.

'Well, gentlemen. I do not expect to have to call you every time I want to see Frenkel. I want access whenever I turn up there. Be seeing you!' He then smugly left the room and made the long journey to Frenkel's room. By the time he reached the door, he could see the guard was already communicating with Perez on the internal videophone. He could not hear what was said but he knew access had been granted when he heard the creaking and the hissing of the door. It was opened to let him in.

As he walked into the cubicle, he looked hard around the room to spot Frenkel. He saw nobody but could hear cluttering noises and he guessed that they were coming from the kitchen. He was looking through the little hatch when the huge metal door to his right made a clicking sound and he saw it open as if by remote control. Ed waited. He could smell something. Fried eggs! Then he saw Frenkel's head through the hatch.

'Come in Mr Hamilton, come in please! The breakfast is almost ready!'

Ed made his way into the flat. It looked rather more spacious than from the cubicle outside. Ed sat down on one of the chairs at the dining table and waited. Frenkel eventually appeared with two plates and placed one in front of Ed. There were two large fried mushrooms, two eggs fried both ways and very lightly toasted bread. The eggs had been placed on top of the toast and there was a small portion of baked beans. Frenkel then placed the salt and pepper next to Ed and ran into the kitchen and came back with a bottle of tabasco sauce. Ed smiled faintly.

'All perfect. Right down to the chilli sauce! One could say you read my mind!'

Now Frenkel grinned. 'I feel that we both got off on the wrong foot yesterday. I was on my guard and wanted to apologise. The smart-arse act was unnecessary.' He sat opposite Ed with his bacon and toast.

'Hey look, it was nobody's fault. Though next time you decide to destroy your notes, make sure you leave the important ones in!'

'Point taken.' Frenkel gave out a small laugh as he said this. For a while they were both silent as they tucked into their breakfast. Ed wondered if they were being watched. He wondered if they were being listened to. *Every word!* Frenkel's voice. Ed stared at him for a few seconds and understood.

'You know, I was joking about the breakfast. I didn't mean for you to go to all this trouble. But it's great, thanks.'

'Believe me, the pleasure is all mine. I don't have company often. You saw the type I normally get!'.

'What happened to you yesterday? I mean when you… well.'

'There are still many things I cannot control; I can't fully explain it. I do not have full control and certain things bring back memories and flashes that I cannot handle. I cannot control the pain either.'

'But what did they do to you?'

'Have you not read the files?'

'Like I said, leave the important bits in next time you destroy things!'

'I'm sorry.' He laughed again. 'When I lose myself like that, they use the gas. When I am somewhat legless, then they enter the flat and sedate me with drugs. I don't blame them really. I suppose they have no choice.'

'Surely there has to be a more humane way of dealing with it. There has to be another way to help you.'

'Sure. But it's time consuming and nobody has the patience. The Professor tried but I was not so charming then as I am now. I was not co-operative either.'

'Why not?'

Frenkel made no answer. In fact, he looked like he had not heard the question at all, and Ed felt that maybe he should not push it. He had to tread carefully. His breakfast was excellent. They now entered small talk. Frenkel asked about the outside world. Ed told him all he wanted to know. He asked questions about world politics. Many questions about American politics and world affairs. He then asked about Ed's background and career. Ed was surprised that he did not already know these facts, or did he? He asked questions but acted like he already knew the answers. But Ed was at ease and spoke freely. He did not feel that Frenkel was probing his mind, invading his Soul. They finished breakfast and then sat on the sofa opposite one another. Frenkel switched the television on and proceeded to watch the flickering pictures with the sound off. He continued his conversation with Ed.

'Tell me,' said Ed, 'is there anything you feel you need to make this place more comfortable for you?' Is there anything you want to improve your conditions here?'

'As you can see, I have all I want. I have TV, music, books, access to internat. They monitor everything of course so I can communicate with people in chat rooms, but I know someone is always watching and listening.'

'Does that not bother you?'

'Why should it? I have no intention of telling anyone who I am,' concluded Frenkel. 'But to be constantly watched and monitored. That must be restricting.'

'Mr Hamilton, the only thing that I find restricting is my *brain*. And that I have had all my life.'

'What? You've been psychic all your life?'

'It was mild at first. As a child I was able to read minds by thought. Nobody knew. I never even mentioned it to my parents. As I grew older, I had more control over it, and I found that there were a range of thought patterns I could read. I used them mainly to attract girls! Eventually I came to hate it. There were times I looked at someone's face, strangers in the street and know that something terrible was going to happen to them. I could see good and bad at first, but eventually I only saw disasters.'

'What do you mean by disasters?' probed Ed.

'One morning, I woke up and saw my father. I instantly knew that it was for the last time. I could not figure out why. But I knew I would not see him again. He left for work as usual, and I waited. It was not long before the phone rang, and I knew that was it. My mum collapsed before putting the receiver down and my sister freaked out. But I knew. He had been involved in a car crash and had died instantly.'

'What do you mean when you say you learned to control it?'

'Well, if I had not learned to control it, I would have been constantly tormented. I would look at people's faces and know what they were about to say. I would know people's thought patterns, but they would come at me one after another and if there were more than one person in the room, the thoughts would come at me from every angle and I would have a panic attack. My head would burn with other people's thoughts and I would have to leave the room. Sometimes, like at a wedding if I could not leave the room, I would collapse. I had to find a way of controlling this. I learnt how to block a person's thoughts out of my mind. Eventually I learnt to sort out the thoughts and put them in order. However, as I grew older, I was able to control them totally. The only thing that I still had a problem with was personal disaster. I could never be free from that. I always knew when something was about to happen to someone close to me.'

'Were you able to read other people's minds when they were not in sight?'

'Yes!'

'What about making people do things?'

'No. I was a psychic, not a freak! Now I'm a freak! But not back then.' He was smiling when he said this.

'I'm sorry, but to me all this is fascinating.' There were a hundred questions that Ed could think of. He did not know how to ask the next one. 'To me, it seems that you are capable of a lot more.' He paused to see Frenkel's reaction. The other man sat flicking channels with the remote control without actually registering what had been said. Ed decided to wait. He looked at Frenkel's profile as the television light flickered in the other man's eyes. Even now, the most alive part of Frenkel seems to be the eyes! Like fires burning inside them. Ed noticed a huge vein sticking out of Frenkel's temple. It curved and pumped away like a huge worm inside his head. The size of it was definitely abnormal. Ed wondered whether Frenkel would let him take a brain scan to see which areas were abnormally developed. If the *normal* person only used a fifth of their brain capacity, it would be interesting to see how much Frenkel used.

'Fourth fifths,' said Frenkel, quietly, still looking at the TV. 'Pardon?' said Ed, rather bashfully.

'You were wondering what my brain capacity was. Four fifths.'

'Four fifths? *Four fifths?*' He was shocked but did not want to sound as if he doubted the other man's words. 'That's impossible! I mean, incredible! How? What?' he stopped himself. Frenkel stopped flicking channels and was staring at the ground. Then he closed his eyes and sweat began to form on his forehead. He was struggling from within. The vein in the side of his temple was blue and pumping away madly. Frenkel's whole body trembled. Ed had to come up with something. He did not speak. He could feel a tingling and he knew Frenkel was in his head. Ed tried to clear his mind and thought of a brick wall. Just a wall. All other thoughts were blocked, and he projected an image of a grey, old brick wall. He then projected a man coming along and painting the wall yellow. A yellow wall. Bright and yellow. A cheerful man, whistling and painting wall yellow. Ed himself began to sweat as he struggled with his cerebral painter. He had to block all thought from his head and hoped that Frenkel picked up the wall and concentrated on it. He concentrated on what seemed to be an absolute age and was about to give in to exhaustion when suddenly another man appeared on the scene and started to paint the wall purple. That was not him! That was Frenkel! Frenkel had put the second painter in the frame. It had to be. He began to laugh. The yellow painter had to exit the scene as the purple one finished the job. When that was done, Ed opened his eyes and saw a calm and relaxed Frenkel, chuckling away to himself. From the corner of his eye, Ed noticed at the cubicle window the Chief Medic was already there, poised to come in and take action. The Medic glared at Ed.

'Sorry Doc, seems like we did not need the SS today!' mocked Ed. He then waited until the Medic and his team left the cubicle. 'You OK?' he asked Frenkel.

'Yellow was way too bright! What were you thinking?' They both laughed. It took both of them some time to recover. Frenkel, in particular, looked exhausted and slightly older than before. They collected themselves and eventually Frenkel switched off the TV.

'Something happened in the Devil's Corridor. I cannot say what. But when I came back, I was unable to control anything. Physically I am the same, only older. Mentally I can do things far beyond a human brain's abilities. I can now not only read a mind of another person but put thoughts into it. I can move objects, make fires, destroy things that are miles away. I can make you see things that are not there, or maybe block your vision so that you cannot see something that is there. The worst part is that I can see almost the whole World from this room. I can see Jennifer.' He paused for a full minute. 'At this moment she has dropped Jake off to school and has arrived to work. She is wearing a black skirt and jacket with a shiny orange blouse. She is hoping that Derek will notice her and ask her out, so she brushed her hair and re-applied her make-up. Jake is being bullied at school, one of the reasons being that he does not have a dad. He also has a temper which he finds hard to control and has fights all the time. At this moment he has been called to the headmaster's office for something he did yesterday. He did not tell his mother about that incident. But she will go to the school next week and they will move Jake to another school.'

Ed listened in fascination. 'Can you change things with him? Can you communicate with them?'

'Yes, to both questions, but I don't. I do not interfere with the world. I only watch. Like a pervert! I only watch. I can if I want, control the World and become a kind of God! Can you imagine what would happen to the World if the wrong person went through the Corridor, and came back with powers like mine? Disaster! I do not control things from here. It would be wrong. I only watch.'

'Did you block yourself from me the other day when I came here the first time? Were you standing by the plant all along?'

Frenkel grinned, 'I'm sorry, yes I was by the plant the whole time.'

'Are you never tempted to contact your wife? Or maybe, help Jake out if he is experiencing difficulties.'

'On whose authority? God's? Just because I'm a freak with superhuman powers does not give me the right to interfere with the natural course of events.' He paused as if in thought. 'Of course, there are those who believe in Guardian Angels. At a push, I would help Jake out if he really ended up in hot water. Just a little guiding hand.'

'When it comes to objects, do you have to be in the same room with the things in order to move or destroy them?'

'Obviously not! Otherwise, how could I have destroyed the notes?'

'You never really explained why you did that.'

'I think I did.'

'That was not the real reason. It could not have been otherwise why would you be so co-operative now? There has to be another reason that you are keeping from me.'

Frenkel got up and walked around the room. He eventually went to the sound system and started rummaging through CDs. He picked up one and placed it in the CD player. A few seconds later, and the introduction starts. A quiet drum beat. Low at first. Then, slowly getting louder, and sounding like it was skipping a beat.

Edwards recognised the intro and grinned. 'Do you have great taste in music, or is that for my benefit?'

'A bit of both. Vintage Bowie is hard to beat, but I know you are an admirer.' Edward listened.

Five years
Stuck on my eyes
Five years
What a surprise
We've got five years
My brain hurts a lot
Five years
That's all we got.

'Five years. That's how long I've wasted.' Ed said this in a whisper but Frenkel heard him. 'All that time I thought I had the best job in the World. But they held out on me in a big way. Five years down the drain. Five years of work that means nothing. It's like starting all over again. Like waking up and finding a whole chunk of your life that did not exist. How long would they have carried on without telling me?' Ed was aware of the fact that they were being watched but he thought he had said nothing that they did not already know. Frenkel probably knew as well, but he kept silent. He just listened. 'You know *she* knew?' Ed eventually said.

'The delightful Miss Preston? Yes, I know. She frequently visited with the Professor. She used to sit and listen to all that went on. I had to eventually ask her not to come.'

'Why?'

'I could read her thoughts. She has sickness in her mind. She is not in control.'

'What do you mean sickness?'

Frenkel sat down again. He made no attempt to answer the question, so Ed did not press the issue. *My brain hurts a lot.*

'Talking of the brain hurting, what exactly is happening to my head? Is that anything to do with you?' asked Ed.

'Again, I'm afraid I have to own up to that as well.'

'What the hell was that all about?' Ed was a bit annoyed considering he had a terrible time with it. 'What were you doing?'

'It was important that we met. I was trying to learn things about you. You had my file; I had your brain. I was walking in your head.'

'You were what?'

'That's the easiest way to describe it. I was literally walking in your head. That is why you could feel the tingling. I was moving from one corridor to another. When the feeling turned into a kind of itching... I was running through your head.'

'Why were you... walking... as you put it, through my head when I was at that meeting two days ago? What did you want there?'

'It was time you were made aware of me. It was time we met. I had to make sure you were getting your point through. If you were passionate enough about the next step, they would have to tell you about me. I also knew the President was not totally aware of the situation and he would make them tell you. I had to make sure that you made a noise. I apologise if that was a nuisance.'

'A bloody pawn! That's all I was! A fucking pawn!'

'Mr Hamilton, I am sorry. But I had to bring you to me. My only motive was that you should know about me.'

Ed calmed down. 'Edward. Call me Edward. Or even Ed. But not Ted. I can't stand the name Ted.'

'Anthony. But not Tony. Never Tony.' They both laughed and felt silent.

'Look. It's been a long morning. I think I ought to leave you to rest,' Ed said to Frenkel. 'You make me sound like an invalid!'

'Well. We ought to take a break anyway. I have to go and check my animals.'

'Sure. You are welcome back, anytime.'

'Tell me, what lies behind the odd behaviour of the animals that went through? They all came back odd in some way,' asked Ed.

'Somehow, the Corridor enhances certain features of their personality or ability. Your latest one loved to eat. After he came back, he could not control his eating. It distorted his abnormality. I cannot control mine either,'

'Do you want to come and visit my lab?'

Frenkel looked horrified. The fear in his face was unmistakable and Ed thought that he was about to have another attack.

'Visit? You mean… leave this… room?' he looked terrified.

'It was only a suggestion, take it easy. You are so isolated here. I could help you if you run into trouble. Think about it. Shall I come this evening?'

'Yes. Do. But dinners on you.'

'You got it.'

CHAPTER 9

Edward was on a high. For the first time in ages, he felt his work had meaning again. He had an aim and felt that he was actually moving forward. He was astonished with Frenkel. The man seemed to have accepted his fate with dignity and composure that he was sure many would not have had. He was co-operative and calm. It also frightened Ed when he thought how things could have been if Frenkel was not so decent. A mad person would have tried to destroy the world already. That much mind control in the wrong head would be a world domination type of temptation. It would make a James Bond movie more like The Muppets. There were still many things that he had to know but he was not in any hurry. There was plenty of time. Frenkel could be controlled. Using the mind, he could be controlled. He felt like he knew exactly where the next five years were going. They may even make up for the last five years! He was in the laboratory. It was tempting to abandon the animals now that he had a human subject, but he knew that would be unfair. They also needed his attention so there he was, observing and recording. He thought he would go to his flat for the afternoon and type up some notes on Frenkel. A couple of hours of that and then he would go and see him again. He was deep into his work when the door of the laboratory opened, and he recognised the steps. He knew who it was, but he had no idea what she wanted. Probably now that he had unlimited access to Frenkel, she wanted to be part of the work. She wanted to give him advice and tell him what to do next. He could feel the anger rising in him but what helped to stem it was the memory he had of her face when he had his hands around her neck! Those huge frightened bland eyes! She was not invincible! Now it was her chance to be left in the dark.

He carried recording his data on the animals and she stood a few feet away. 'What do you want? I'm busy,' he said sternly.

'I have a right mind to complain about you. What you did the other day was assault!' She now hated herself. This is not what she came here for. The Meek Susan came to apologise but as soon as Ed spoke the arrogant Bitch Susan from within came running forward, pushing the Meek one away, claws and teeth at the ready. She could not control the arrogant Bitch Susan and so the Meek Susan again retreated into the background.

'That's rich! You cheated me for five years! You think I'm scared of you? Do what you want. I've got the upper hand now.'

'Yes. I've heard. Unlimited access, eh?'

'I must say, he's not a great fan of yours either. You never mentioned that you worked together with the Professor. All these years. Working with him behind my back!'

'Frenkel was a handful. He needed help.'

'And it never occurred to anyone that being a psychologist, I would be useful?' There was a short pause. Ed just wanted her to go away. He carried on working.

'So, did he say anything?' she said. 'Frenkel? Of course, he said many things.'

'Yes. But did he say anything about... well'. 'About what?'

'About ' words seemed to fail her.

'Look, I know you're fishing for something. What exactly do you want to know?'

There was a long pause now during which time he stopped his work and looked at her. What on earth did she want? *Ask her about project 19.* That was Frenkel's voice! In his head. *INSIDE* his head! He must be watching! Project 19? What was that all about?

'So, do you want to tell me about Project 19?' he said, looking intently at her face for a reaction. She suddenly cursed a few words under her breath and stormed out of the laboratory. He listened for Frenkel's voice but there were no more mind thoughts. Project 19. There was nothing in the notes about that. There were many projects, but not Project 19. He must find out about that. He was also a little disturbed about Frenkel. He was not sure whether he liked to be *watched* all the time, if at all. He had to try and ask Frenkel not to do that. On the other hand, Frenkel's world was so limited. It may just be his way to have company. He typed up some of the notes that he had made and then showered. He had every intention of cooking but in the end, he did not have the will. He ended up with a takeaway. Then he made the long journey to Frenkel's flat. When he got there, the door again was opened without any hassle and he grinned slightly at the Chief Medic who had obviously just been in to see Frenkel. Ed went straight in and looked through the window. He immediately saw Frenkel lying on the couch and he instantly ran to the door to the flat, pushed it open and ran in almost yelling.

'Frenkel! Wake up!'

Frenkel jumped up in terror and shouted, 'Shit! What's wrong? What the fuck is wrong!'

Ed stopped dead in the centre of the room, stunned. He stared with somewhat embarrassment. 'Oh! You're O.K?'

'Well, no! You scared the shit out of me! What was that all about?' yelled Frenkel. 'Well… I saw the Chief Asshole leave your apartment. I came in to find you slumped on the couch.'

'You mean *napping* of the couch!'

'I thought you had been drugged again! What did you expect me to think?'

'It never occurred to you that I was asleep?' said Frenkel, annoyed.

'I'm sorry. I over reacted!'

'You have to be careful before you over-react with me! I do not always have control! I could have accidentally hurt you.'

Ed realised what he was saying. 'I really am sorry.'

Frenkel calmed down. 'Yeah well. I'm starving. What have you got?'

'The local takeaway! Lumps of assorted grilled meat! Hope you like it.'

'Believe me, anything outside this kitchen is exotic to me!'

'Let's tuck in.' Frenkel went and got plates for the two of them and they settled down to their meal. At first, they ate. Eventually, Ed spoke first.

'You were *watching* me today. How often do you do that?'

Frenkel paused a little but he knew the question was going to come up, so he answered it. 'Well. Every now and again, I go places. Like window shopping. I am confined to this room, but to keep my sanity I visit certain places. At that time, I was not actually watching you. I was scanning the place generally and found abnormal brain patterns coming from Miss Preston. She was up to something. So, I was watching *her*. She has watched me enough times for me to justify spying on her. She first went into your office and tried your drawers and read the files on your desk. She was looking for information about me. What you had been doing here. She could not find much joy there so she decided to try and see what she could find in your laboratory. She was hoping to find you there and she had every intention to come clean and to confess all her failures. She wanted her true self to talk to you. When she saw you, she lost control and carried on in her aggressive and rude manner. She really wants to be friends. I was watching her, not you.'

'I see. What do you mean her true self?'

'She is a bitter and twisted woman who has a person within her trying to escape. A person that is terribly suppressed by the Preston that you know.'

'What did she want? She looked like she wanted something.'

'She doesn't want you to find out about Project 19.'

'Yeah. I was wondering what that was all about.' Ed expected Frenkel to elaborate on this matter. But the other man remained silent. He just ate in silence. Burning to ask the question again, Ed had to hold himself back with great effort. He had decided not to push any issue. 'Tell me how you scan. How do you decide what to look at?'

'Well, I start from the Corporation. Then I work myself to other areas. I regularly visit my family. My mother is elderly and needs constant help and attention. She has mentally never got over my 'death'. My sister has children and I drop in on them. I like to see how my sister is and watch my nieces grow up. She is separated from that asshole she was married to. She lives near my mother and they are happy enough. My sister thinks my 'death' is some sort of conspiracy. She believes I am still alive somewhere. But no one takes any notice of her. Jennifer is a little too far to help my mother but with a little guidance from her guardian angel, she is coming to the conclusion that she ought to move closer to her and my sister. It's difficult really. I love her but I sometimes see her dating other men. What else is she to do? She thinks I'm dead. She goes out with some real assholes. The last one was a rich fucker, but he was married. I was hoping she would see the signs, but she didn't. So, I helped her. She will move closer to my mum. Her mother and father are nearby too. Jakie is alone where he is. He needs to change school and maybe a move closer to his cousins will be good for him. They all get on well together.'

'I thought you try not to interfere. Surely, if she's with a fucker, you can't interfere. That's not right. Changing someone's life. Controlling that which you have no business doing?'

'I do. I try not to. But when I feel it's really necessary, I can't help it. My mother needs help. My sister and wife are both alone and need each other. I just assist. I don't want assholes in my wife's life.'

'It must be difficult for you to know what they are doing and not being able to be with them.'

'Yeah.' He looked sadly at his plate. 'But really, there is no other way. Can you imagine what their lives would be like if they were aware of me? Jenny would not be able to have a normal life. All she wanted was to be a good wife and mother. She would not be able to marry anybody else if she knew about me. Jakie would be more disturbed than he is now. It's bad enough to lose your father, but at that age to try and tell him that daddy is unwell and has to live away from home. What on earth would they do? And as for that. What on earth would I do? I can't leave here. I can't see them at home. They would have to come and see me. It would be impossible to live like that. Impossible! Things are better this way.'

'You have been here so long! What keeps you together? How come you haven't lost it?'

Frenkel just smiled and rose to put his plate away. He came back with a beer for Ed and a soft drink for himself.

'Are you not having a drink?' asked Edward.

'I would love to. As you know, it does funny things to the mind. I cannot control anything when I drink. It's better left alone.'

'What exactly did the Professor do? We know we can control things to a certain extent because we did it this morning. Did the Professor try something similar? He must have come to some conclusion about how to take some of your restrictions away.'

'Well. He was a genius, that is for sure,' said Frenkel. 'But he had a different approach to you. He had other ideas about what should be done. His path of scientific testing was different from yours.'

'Well, he was a very intelligent man. I owe my whole career to him, almost. I was a bit of a drifter until he came along. I, at first, was not too keen to move away from London. Someday, I hope to live there again. But the Professor was desperate to take me with him to the States. But then again, I suppose you know all that already.' Frenkel nodded. 'It's difficult, talking to a stranger and finding they know everything! I only wish I could enter your head and learn everything in one go!'

'No! That would be a mistake! You do not want that.'

'Well, it would save work.' He chuckled.

'It would probably kill you. And if did not, then you would surely kill someone yourself!'

'What does that mean?'

'Well, I know things that would make you mad. That anger of your is hard to control,' said Frenkel. 'If you learnt everything that I know in one go, you surely would go away, raging and fuming and looking to take it out on someone. Also, my brain is not really human. If you acquired my powers, you would die. Your body is not designed for my brain. Neither is mine really. It's like putting one of tomorrow's advanced computer memories into the computers of the 1970's! They just blow up.'

'So how come you're... well you're not OK. But you are not dead.'

'The Corridor strengthened the body to a certain extent. Not enough to make it pain free! I still have to control things constantly, 24 hours a day. Even when I rest. If I give up, the pain takes over and it is unbearable. I also have to try and stop all the thoughts that are coming my way. If I went out there, into the world, I would pick up all kinds of transmissions. From the radio and video waves to people's communications. They would all fly at me and enter my head. I would not have the capacity to unscramble them and control them. I would die. It's like standing on the rail and waiting for a train. Certain death.'

'And the Professor knew all this?' asked Ed.

Frenkel clamed up again. He knew he had to discuss things with Ed, but the memory of what happened was still alive in him now. He could almost feel the pain and the image came back like a dream. He had much to explain to Ed. The problem was that he knew Ed was treading warily to question him, but the truth of the matter was that Frenkel would also have to inform Ed of certain things carefully himself. It would be too much of a shock for Ed to learn everything too quickly. Frenkel knew what his aim was. He had a mission, and he knew that his life at that moment had a purpose. This is what he could not explain to Ed. Frenkel believed in God and he believed that what had happened to him was meant to be. It was God's will. However, this was not the end of his life. He still had a major duty to perform. The only thing stopping him from destroying himself was the fact that his work was not complete. The purpose of him being born was still to be realised. The reason why he was given these powers had much to do with the future and his life was destined to be this way. His path was destined to cross Ed's and all this he had to explain to this man. He had to say the right thing and he had to take his time. Time was not in short supply.

''Like I said, the Professor was fascinated by me from a different angle,' he said. 'What sort of tests did he carry out?'

'Parlour tricks! He made me smash things and read his mind and look at other people outside this flat and tell him what they were doing. He wanted me to spy on certain people and then project the images into his head. He wanted to know the future and when he was going to die. That sort of thing.'

'You must be mistaken! Professor Braun was a professional. He would have carried out more scientific tests! What you are saying describes Preston.'

'Yeah well. She was not far either. She helped him a lot.'

'Look. I'm trying not to tax you too much. But you aren't holding out on me, are you? The Professor worked with you for three years. He must have done more than parlour tricks! He was a professional. And you avoided my question about Project 19.' Edward spoke sternly.

Frenkel got up and started pacing the room. He was in a considerable amount of distress. He was not an expert on the human brain and had no idea how on earth to bring up the subject. He had no idea how to handle Ed. By reading Ed's mind, he at least had some guidance but at this moment in time, Ed's brain was showing abnormal activity. Ed was troubled and he still was angry about the earlier meeting with Susan. Frenkel was trying to dig deeper when Ed interrupted.

'You're in my *head* aren't you! What for? What the hell are you there for? I can tell you what you want to know! Get out of my head! I can feel you.' He rose out of the sofa as he said this. Frenkel immediately held up his hands in front of his chest in surrender.

'Edward, I have delicate knowledge of things. But am not an expert on how to handle delicate matters with a volatile person. I was just trying to assess how calm your brain activity was. Right now, I would guess is a bad time.'

'Look. I'm here to help *you*! Do *you* a favour. You are not doing me one. You're talking as if you have to teach me a thing or two!'

'I think it would be better if you came back tomorrow morning. Early. We both need to be fresh. I cannot handle any of this right now.'

'No! It's a waste of time. I want to talk *now!*'

'A waste of time?' said Frenkel angrily. 'Where do you have to go? Who do you have to see? I'm certainly not going anywhere.' There was a pause. Ed could see the agitated look on the other man's face, and he realised that Frenkel was tired and troubled. His hand was shaking, and he sat down on the sofa again and seemed to be hyperventilating. Frenkel was right. His brain was far too powerful and the feeble, primitive body was finding it difficult to cope with it.

Ed calmed down. 'Look. I'm sorry. You're right. I think things are best left to the morning,' he said. He rose to leave.

'Hey, thanks for the dinner.'

'That's OK. Get some rest.

It was as he was taking the long walk out of the building that he remembered that they were being watched at all times. Every word, every move was captured. If anything, suspicious came up he was sure the videophone outside the cubicle would be booted up and messages would start a huge chain reaction. Images and sound from the room would be sent to Lucas and Perez and maybe even the President. Maybe this was what Frenkel was hesitating for. What could Frenkel want to say that they did not already know? Surely the Professor's progress was monitored as well. He needed to think of a way round the Evil Eye that constantly watched them.

CHAPTER 10

At about 10.00pm that evening, an urgent meeting had been called by Lucas and Perez. It consisted only of them, Susan Preston and Rodrigues. It was obvious to them that new facts were emerging about Anthony Frenkel. The Professor's notes were unclear about many of the things that Frenkel was able to do. However, Frenkel's own candid conversation with Ed had brought certain issues at the forefront. They were confused and felt they had to get everyone together, but at an hour that was unexpected so as not to cause tongues wagging. They could not let Ed know that they were meeting.

'Susan,' began Perez, 'you were, at one stage quite close to the Professor. You knew the work he carried out. The actual extent of Frenkel's powers. Is that correct?'

'Yes,' she replied cautiously. 'You already know that.'

'Yes, we do. We want you to look at this.' Perez then pressed a few buttons on the panel in front of him. The large mega television on the opposite side of the room turned itself on and flickered. Everyone turned their heads towards it. Perez then pressed another button only when everyone settled down. Lucas kept his eyes firmly planted on Susan.

The screen then came to life. The familiar scene of Frenkel's living room. They had all seen this on many occasions. This time, they saw Ed in the room with Frenkel. They were both eating. The time and date at the bottom of the screen showed Susan that it was footage taken earlier that day. The picture came before the sound. Eventually the voices of the two men came through, loud and clear. Frenkel's voice could be heard saying, *'Believe me, anything outside this kitchen is exotic to me!'* Ed then replied, *'Let's tuck in.'* There was a small pause after which Ed said, *'You were watching me today. How often do you do that?'* Susan then sat and listened to the answer. Her mouth had dropped, and she was burning inside with embarrassment. She heard Frenkel's words about picking up her abnormal brain activity, going through Ed's files in his office, about the short, curt conversation in the laboratory with Ed. Then the dreaded words that she knew would finish the conversation off: *Project 19! Project 19.* The words echoed in her head and she closed her eyes and wished she was elsewhere. Things were now going pair-shaped and the vision she had of a lovely, charming wife with a couple babies in her arms and a couple of toddlers at her feet in a lovely house came to her. That is what she should have been.

'It seems plain from this conversation that Frenkel has the ability not only to read minds, but to be able to do this without his subject being anywhere near him!' said Perez. 'And yet the notes never mentioned anything of the type. The Professor suspected that he could probably read their minds, but could not be sure? Did you know exactly what his capacity was?'

'No, I did not,' she answered sternly. The Meek Susan was hiding behind the Bitch. She quietly cowered behind a wall watching her dominant self, putting on a brave face. 'We had no idea. He never mentioned it.'

'He seemed to know things that only you could have known?'

'From what I could remember, he was not half as co-operative as he is in that video. He hardly said anything. Charm was not one of his strong points.'

'You and the Professor spent a huge amount of Corporation time and equipment on this man. Did you not gain any of his confidence? From the video, Frenkel did not seem to like you much,' persisted Perez.

'Manuel, just say what's on your mind,' she said, trying to get the upper hand. 'Susan. What he is trying to say,' interrupted Lucas, 'is that Hamilton is learning more about Frenkel in two days than you and the Professor did in three years. He can read minds. He can put thoughts into other people's heads. He can influence people that are miles and miles away. He can send thoughts to his wife from South to North America! He has awesome power and is literally the most dangerous man in the world! Right here in this complex! And you, along with the Professor, could not extract this information from him!'

'That was not our fault! We had no way of knowing what he was capable of without him telling us! How could we? You are being unfair. He refused to talk to us most of the time. He was drugged for a large part of that time.'

'Why does he dislike you so much?'

'I don't know!'

'Susan. What is Project 19?'

'I don't know! What do you want?' She wailed.

'Miss Preston,' said Rodrigues, 'it has come to our attention that half the notes on the three years research involving Frenkel have been removed. These are the notes made by you and the Professor. There was only one proper copy.'

'What do you mean missing? Where are they?' she asked genuinely perplexed.

'We were hoping that you could tell us,' said Rodrigues.

Now Susan was not too bright, but she had an idea of what was being suggested here. She took a few seconds to get it all straight in her head. They knew that the work that had been carried out was unfinished. She knew that the Professor did not carry out proper tests on Frenkel. They suggested that the Professor, along with her help, had carried out unofficial work not sanctioned by the Corporation. All this was true. What they were also suggesting was that she had destroyed the notes in order to hide this unofficial work. That was not true. She had no idea what had happened to the notes. She had not touched them for months. She had her own projects in the last two years and had not even seen Frenkel face to face since the Professor died. How could she say this without admitting that she and the Professor were carrying out unethical work on Frenkel? The Bitch Susan turned around and looked for the Meek Susan. She saw the Meek one crouching behind her, with her hands up to her face as if someone was about to punch her. The Meek one was half the size of the Bitch one and she cowered there in a pitiful manner while the

Bitch approached her. The Bitch wanted the Meek one to take the stage and put on a girlie, tearful act for these nice gentlemen. When the Meek one hesitated, the Bitch screamed at her. The Meek one came to the forefront but all she could do was cry.

Now, the men looked at Susan Preston saw an astonishing sight. The whole face had changed. The harsh lines, the stern features, the aggression was gone. Here in the chair before them sat a sad and lonely girl, weeping quietly. She did not say anything but then, she did not have to. They were all speechless at the sight of this wreck. For the first time in years, since she was a child, the Meek Susan had centre stage while the Bitch stood behind her. This was the *real* Susan Preston Imprisoned by her own weakness. Tormented by her jailer.

'The Professor was a great scientist. I never was, or… will be.' Her voice was quiet. 'I wanted to be involved in his work. I was proud to be associated with him. I worked with him and did what he asked me to do. We worked with Frenkel, yes. But we did not know the full extent of his powers. We could have won his confidence and we did try, but he never let us near him. Now… it all makes sense. He knew what we were up to.' She paused for a quiet sob. 'He could read our minds! But we did not know that. The work we did was always destroyed. We thought there was a spy! Destroying all our work. Maybe, it was *him* using that Devil brain of his!'

'This work. Project 19?' asked Lucas.

'Yes. Project 19. It seemed like a good idea to the Professor. He was obsessed with it. I just went along with it because he was a genius. Nobody should question a genius!'

'Miss Preston,' said Rodrigues, 'are you ready to tell us what Project 19 was all about?'

The Bitch at this point stepped forward and was about to relegate Meek Susan to the background again when suddenly, Susan Preston, the *real* Susan Preston turned around and hissed *sit down, bitch!* At that instance, the Bitch suddenly deflated in size like a punctured balloon while the *real* Susan Preston towered over her.

Susan Preston looked into their faces and said simply, 'Yes. I'm ready.'

Ed was slumped on his couch vaguely watching some old American made for TV series and chewing some currents when suddenly his head began to ache. He then heard Frenkel's voice. *Ed, there is something that you have to listen to right now! Switch the TV off.* He obeyed. *Lie down on the couch and blank your mind. Do not fight it.* Again, he did as he was told. *This conversation is taking place in Perez's office right now. Listen. I will not transmit images, just sound.* Ed relaxed his body and prepared to listen in this bizarre manner.

The *real* Susan Preston was in control. She had emerged from the wilderness and had found enough courage to fight back. She had done some terrible things and now was the time to confess. She cared little about what would happen to her. She wanted her Soul back. She took a deep breath and started to talk.

'Anthony Frenkel was a diamond! Not even that, he was a treasure! We could not understand it, but he had come back to this world with a super brain! He was able to... do things by thought. He pushed people and broke things and had tantrums all by thought! He never moved or ran about madly himself. It was terrible at first to control him and the notes on that are all accurate. By the way, I have done many stupid things in my life, but I did not and had no reason to destroy these notes! The Professor became obsessed with Frenkel but in an abnormal way. It was meant to be the Corridor that we were investigating but the Professor was obsessed only with Frenkel. Instead of learning from him and trying to control him, the Professor, well... he had other ideas.' She paused. She did not cry again. But her voice did quiver as she tried to put things in the best possible words. 'You see, the animals all came back with a different personality trait. I wanted to know why Frenkel came back psychic. I never had a genuinely good question of my own to ask, but this was a good one. What made him like this? Was he always a clairvoyant? The Professor seemed disinterested in this. He was not interested in that aspect of things. He was interested in something else. He wanted to know if Frenkel would... or could... if his brain was... er. well, a genetic thing. You know, like a genetic abnormality. He figured that

a genetic abnormality meant that the chromosomal defect could be…
well maybe it could be passed on!'

'Passed on?' asked Rodriguez.

'Passed on?' whispered Ed from his couch.

'Passed on,' repeated the real Susan Preston. 'He became obsessed
with trying to pass on the genes. He wanted to see if Frenkel could
pass on his powers. The Professor wanted to recreate a new human. A
brand-new human that could be controlled and one that would make
Frenkel useless. The Professor wanted to make babies with that power.
Super babies. All controlled by him. He talked to Frenkel and asked
for his sperm sample under false pretence. He said it was necessary
for experiments. Frenkel did not object. He was too out of it and was
used to being prodded and tampered with. He did not seem to care.
There were two parts to Project 19. One was procreation in the normal
way. The other was to go against scientific ethics altogether and to
clone Frenkel. Although, as you all know, the process has been banned
world-wide, it is possible. The Professor was serious. He wanted to
clone Anthony Frenkel using his cells. He regularly visited Frenkel
and again, under the pretence of regular tests, he took samples. He
took blood and tissue samples. Frenkel never asked or objected.'

'How far did he get with the process?' asked Rodriquez in disgust.

'We had managed to smuggle in special equipment for the
cloning process. Nobody checked his work at all. Nobody asked
about anything he ordered. All the expense, the organisation. He
always said it was for Frenkel. Over the years, the Professor managed
to successfully get Frenkel's cells to grow. They grew in the laboratory.
They were doing really well and formed strongly. He had numerous
eggs fertilised with Frenkel's sperm. He also had many eggs infused
with Frenkel's DNA. All waiting to be implanted. Just at the time that
they were ready for implantation, they died. In each case, three in all,
suddenly the clones died. In four cases, when a normal fertilized egg
was ready to be placed into the womb, the cells died. Totally bizarre.
The Professor was gutted. He acted like a man who had lost his own
children. He was devastated. He checked and re-checked. There
was no explanation. No reason for the project to fail. If anything
should have worked, it would have been *in vitro* fertilisation. Again,

all went well for ages. Four of the embryos survived and were ready for implanting but at the last minute, they all died. No reason. Heaven only knows whether he would have succeeded. God knows.' She stopped.

They all stared at her. All this going on right under their noses and nobody had the slightest whiff of what was going on. They thought about her words and for a time there was no sound. Then Rodriguez suddenly jerked his head up.

'Implantation? Procreate in the normal way? Womb?' he said. 'Sorry?' Susan asked.

'You said 'Procreate in the normal way.' In the *normal way?* Implantation?' Susan lowered her head. This was the real crunch. 'Miss Preston. *In the normal way* means… well, there had to be a *female.* Where was he going to implant these cells? Who was he going to implant the embryos into?' There was a long pause. They thought they would not get an answer when suddenly, Susan Preston blurted it out.

'Me! Me! I was the female! I was to give birth to Frenkel's monster superbaby!'

Edward jumped up from his couch and kicked the table next to him while screaming 'Bitch! Bitch! Sodding bitch!' He smashed the glass of beer and threw the genuine Portmeirion vase into the TV. He was livid! He thought about the Professor. His hero. His Idol. 'Bastard! Fucking unethical sodding Judas!' He mini-trashed his flat and then threw himself back on the couch, exhausted.

Frenkel also jumped up. But he was trying to protect himself from Edward's anger. He held his head and stopped contact with Edward's mind. Half of his work had been done for him.

CHAPTER 11

Susan Preston was happy. She had not been truly happy for years now. Right now, as she lay her bed and watched the dawn break from her window, she was happy. For the first time in years, she was her true self. The *real* Susan Preston looked round to see where the Bitch was. She saw a very tiny figure crouching behind that wall that she herself used to crouch behind. The Bitch could not touch her now. She had too much confidence in herself to let that happen. She liked the person that emerged the evening before. There were new plans in her head, new ideas and new wishes. She had a lot to achieve, and she was not going to waste a day. She had wasted so many years and had caused trouble to so many. Her plans were going about in her head and at no stage did she even think about her father. She thought she may visit her parents, but she thought of them as parents rather than influential rich people with good connections. She had many things to do before leaving the Corporation. Of course, the main questions were, would they allow her to leave. Leave? With all that information in her head? Of course, she could not just walk away. She no longer wished to stay so there was a problem about how she would go about this. Maybe, just this last time, she may need her father to pull a few strings, or rather, cut them altogether. She hated it here. She was already late, but she did not care. All these thoughts were running around in her head and she had a strange tingling feeling that she had noticed yesterday, when she was going through Ed's office. She could feel it now. Not a headache, just a tingling like her head needed a good scratch from inside. She almost jumped up at the sound of loud banging on her door. Her maid was preparing her breakfast and opened the door. She could here Ed's voice shouting at the maid. Well, she had to face the music. She got out of bed and was putting on her gown when her door was suddenly thrown open.

'You *bitch!* What the hell did you think you were doing?' he yelled, all his anger building up over the night. 'He is not a blood laboratory animal.'

She turned round to face him. He stopped and looked at her. She was different. The look on her face stopped his anger and he was speechless. There was something wrong. This was not Susan Preston the 'great' scientist. Not the one he knew. This was a pale, tired and sad face. No sparkle in the eyes, no evil streak, just a sad person who had had a rough time sleeping. There was no expression of anything on her face. She did not even tell him to get the hell out of her bedroom!

'I don't know what I was doing,' she whispered quietly. 'That's the problem, I never know what I am doing. Never have. I have no ability and had to sponge off someone else. I worshipped the Professor and was so blinded by a need to be greater than my father, I would have believed anything he told me. I would have done anything in the name of science. I could not control the Devil inside me. Or maybe I did not want to. At the time, it all seemed logical. Just the way it should have been. But now… now I want to apologise. It's not much good, I know. But I have nothing else to offer. So, you can leave now. I want to get dressed.' She turned away and without waiting, she began to peel off her night clothes, forcing Ed out of the room whether he wanted to or not.

'We all have our weaknesses, Edward. Some of us never realise what they are, ever. At least she does,' said Frenkel. Ed was slouched on the sofa in front of Frenkel's TV. He tried to remain adamant that she was a conniving bitch, but the transformed person he saw this morning was someone else, entirely. He could not maintain anger against a stranger.

'So that's Project 19! I guess it was you…' Frenkel interrupted him with his hand and made a face. *Remember, we are always being watched,* he warned. There was a short pause before Frenkel sent him another message. *Yes, it was me who destroyed the embryos and the cells.*

They were mine. I had a right to destroy them. It was her eggs full of MY DNA! I had every right to destroy them!

Then, in matter-of-fact way, he continued a proper conversation as it did not matter who was listening to his opinion. 'It is for the best that the work did not succeed. We have no idea what the consequences would have been. We would have been breeding a whole generation of humans with a mental capacity far superior to our own. We would have been the weaker race. Darwinian Laws would apply to us and survival of the fittest would spell the end of us, our children and our kind. Evolution would be controlled by a race not naturally made, but man-made. Man, already destroys as he goes, but that would have been the end. God would no longer be needed. Homo-Sapiens would have 'out-grown their use', we would have had to 'make way for the Homo-Superior.' The quote brought a slight smile on Ed's face.

Ed opened up his small black bag and started to prepare for samples to be taken from Frenkel. 'Look, I want to take some samples from you. Would you agree? Some blood, swabs, urine… number 2 if you're up for it?'

'Well, as long as you don't want my sperm!'

'No, to be honest, don't particularly want a number 2 either!' He placed a tourniquet round Frenkel's arm and drew blood with a syringe before placing it into several different topped vacutainers.

'All this modern technology and we still have not found a pain free way of getting blood from the veins,' said Frenkel.

'Don't be such girl! Anyway, the second one will be more painful. It's a radioactive substance called FGD-18. It's basically radioactive glucose. I need to do a PET-CT scan of your body and the radioactive material is a tracer.'

'Talking of doctors, why do you call yourself mister? You are a doctor, aren't you?' asked Frenkel.

'Titles are not important. What difference does it make what people call you? You are what you are. Calling me mister does not take away the doctor in me.'

'But it's a reward for all those years of study and achievement. It's prestige. That must account for something?'

'You must know a lot about me, yes?' asked Ed as he placed the plaster on Frenkel's arm. 'I felt that feeling in my head for weeks. That means you were watching me and reading my brain for weeks. Possibly years. You must have learnt a lot about me. You must know all about my life.'

'Yes,' Frenkel was almost embarrassed when admitting this.

'Well let's not pretend that I was motivated by science! Now, yes. I know have something that motivates me. But in years gone by, my early years, I was motivated by nothing! I was interested in little. I was driven by little. I just happened to meet influential people who liked me. I had natural ability, but it was people around me that made me use it. I relied on my mother, then on friends. Then work colleagues. Like that Judas bastard, The Professor! I just went with the flow. I was drifting along until…well… about… I would say…' he trailed off in thought.

'Until about 5 years ago when you came here,' said Frenkel.

'Well. Yes. I suppose. That is what is so galling. A man as intelligent and gifted as the Professor, turned out to be a liar and unethical! Why? Why did he do such a thing?'

'For some, the chance to play God is too tempting.'

'How could I have got it so wrong? I would have trusted him with my life.'

'Quite. We are not all as we seem,' Frenkel went quiet then. The door of the cubicle opened, and the Chief Medic came in. He sternly addressed Ed as if Frenkel was not even in the room.

'You requested the PET scanner? It's here. Do you want me to wheel it in?'

'Yeah,' replied Ed. 'I'll give you a hand.' He rushed out of the door and into the cubicle. Then he went totally out of the cubicle as Frenkel watched. He came back with the Chief Medic and the pair of them where wheeling in a strange apparatus. It looked like a bed but at one end there was a huge grey block with a tunnel like a hole in the centre. There were wires and tubes and buttons all over the equipment. Obviously, it was some sort of scanner. He sat there while the two men wheeled it in. They placed it right in the centre of the room and laid out all the plugs properly and attached it to a special power supply unit. Then the medic brought on two screens and attached those to the actual equipment. There was also a super printer ready to chuck out paper. It took a quarter of an hour to arrange all the bits and pieces in place before Ed switched the whole apparatus on. It started to hum, buzz and bleep all at once. There were lights and screens all booting up and at this stage the medic left. Frenkel went to boil the kettle. He was feeling quite anxious and had to carry out menial tasks to calm his nerves that were already quite shot!

'I just have to calibrate everything,' said Ed. 'It will be ready in a minute. These monsters don't really like to be moved.'

Frenkel just waited patiently. He was trying to get a few things straight in his mind. He had much to do. He felt really tired and worn out. He had had a bad time last night after Susan's confession. Although reading the conversation and sending it to Ed was not a problem in itself, it was a massive task for his weak body. By normal human standards, he was an exceptionally fit man. It was his deformed brain that was the problem. His whole body shook after the long transmission last night. There was a feeling of acute nausea and his heart raced, scarcely able to pump the blood round his body fast enough to feed his brain with oxygen. He had to spend a good fifteen minutes to calm his body, and then he had a shower and relaxed in front of the TV. The whole experience was tiring and this morning, he was still suffering still. He just let Ed go about his business without asking too many questions.

'Right! All ready. This is a mobile scanner. I should have asked you first, but I took the liberty to assume that you would not mind. We should validate that it is working properly but we just don't have the time. I'd like to scan your whole body and especially your brain. I want to see what sort of blood supply you have to the brain. I also want to look at your organs. Is that OK?'

'I guess,' said Frenkel.

'All you have to do is pop onto this bed.' Frenkel obeyed. Ed then clicked a number of buttons and then turned to one of the screens and punched in some commands. The buzzing sound changed slightly, and Ed quickly ran to the light switch and turned it to dim. Then he ran back and placed his hands on the grey block at Frenkel's feet. The whole apparatus started to make a loud humming noise. Ed moved the block very slowly upwards towards Frenkel's torso. As he did so an image began to appear on the monitor. He could see the image of legs appearing. Frenkel could also see it. He saw the outline of his legs, but also the muscles, the veins and even some of the larger capillaries. In fact, the entire network of vessels and blood supply to and from the legs. The equipment was then passed over his groin area. Again, the blood supply was phenomenal. His vital parts were in good order, for all the good they were to him!

Ed then moved the block further up Frenkel's body and studied the kidneys. They were amazing! They were large compared to a normal person though the other organs in that regions were fine. The stomach was normal in size and Ed could see his subject had not had breakfast that morning. The spleen was also very large, and Ed wondered whether this meant Frenkel's antibody levels might be elevated. Certainly, this was the case in the lab animals that had been through the Corridor. He thought he would run over to the lab later with Frenkel's blood and carry out some tests. He moved the scanner towards the chest and was shocked. He expected something different, but not this. The heart was TWICE the size that it should have been, and the lungs were totally filling up the thorax. They were pushing down on the diaphragm and outwards towards the ribs. Frenkel must be in pain! It was the heart that stunned Ed. Not only was it huge, but with time, there were extra arteries taking a larger volume of blood away from the heart and on the other side huge number of extra veins pumping blood back into the heart. The whole thing looked like a mishmash of veins, arteries and capillaries going everywhere. The heart was increased in size to cope with the demands of the deformed body. Nothing very wrong in the neck areas. But the brain! Now that was the next shock. It was a wonder that Frenkel's body did not explode. Even greater wonder that he was still alive. The pressure in his head alone would be phenomenal. Ed went to the other screen and re-programmed it to look at brain activity. He then went back to Frenkel's head. The picture showed the brain in different colours. Yellow was the least active and red was the most. Almost the entire brain was showing red patches, indicating that a huge part of the brain was functioning and being used. Ed could not believe what he was looking at. He appreciated the lapses of concentration that Frenkel exhibited and the anxiety attacks. The brain was too powerful to believe. Frenkel's attacks were when the brain was over-functioning and threatening the rest of the body. He could not really be sure how long the body could withstand this. He told Frenkel to get off the bed so that he could pack the equipment away. Frenkel went to sit down.

'Anthony, do you feel pain?' asked Ed as he packed the apparatus away. 'Yes.'

'How frequently?'

'All the time.'

'Where do you feel pain?'

'Mainly my chest. And my head. I have a headache all the time. It just gets more intense at times.'

Ed then stood in front of Frenkel and looked at him for a while. 'How do you sleep? What position?'

'On my back, but, sometimes on my side. But it's painful in any other position other than the back.'

'Does this hurt?' said Ed as he laid his hands on Frenkel's abdomen and gently putting pressure on it.

'Yes. You must know it does.'

'Can I touch your head?'

'If you must.'

Ed placed his hands on Frenkel's temple. 'What about this?'

'Yes. That hurts too.'

'What about sudden movements?'

'I try not to make any. Sometimes, when I am tired, I can feel faint. But I do make sure I get 18 hours sleep.' Then Frenkel sat down and looked at the floor. He looked quite sad in that moment.

'Your body is exceptionally fit, Anthony. How many hours do you spend in the gym?'

'About two hours a day. It releases tension.'

'That leave 4 hours.'

'I spend much of those cooking, eating, reading, and *watching*. And… occasionally looking after Little Tony,' he said the last bit with a bit of grin.

Ed smiled with a dirty little sound that only men can do when they talk about their little members. Then he sat down and looked at Frenkel with a seriousness. 'It's a struggle, isn't it?'

'Pretty much.'

'Anthony, your body will not be able to maintain this for long.'

'I know. But I have to hold on a little longer. I have things to do. When I've finished, I can let go.' There were little beads appearing on the side of this face. The veins were visible and very blue.

'I'm sorry to have to put you through all that. I'll leave now. You get some rest.' Ed left.

Ed was in his room. It was late evening. Frenkel seemed too exhausted when he left him, so he decided not to visit him that day again. He went to the laboratory and analysed some of Frenkel's samples. He did not have time to look at the result. In fact, he himself was quite tired. He had not slept properly for days. He decided to get an early night. He was generally pottering about in his flat when the doorbell rang. He had been a bit of a recluse of late and could not think who would be visiting at this time. He opened the door and stepped back in surprise.

'Can I come in?' It was Susan. Ed stood there. He had a mind to send her away. He was not in the mood for a confrontation. He did not move to let her in. He was too tired to show anger, but his face was stern. 'I don't want to fight.'

'You reading minds as well? That's good,' he said with a small grin. It was not by any means a truce, but he stepped back.

'Well, that's why I'm here.' She moved into the flat and sat down. 'You have to tell me what he can do.'

'Fuck off, Susan.' This was not said in anger. He just almost whispered it under his breath. 'You have a nerve coming here with that!'

'You have to tell me. There is a reason.'

'Look, just go away. I'm tired.'

'Did you know your flat is bugged?' she persisted. 'Did you know they have been listening to you for 5 years?'

'What the fuck are you talking about?'

'They think that I don't know. But I do. All our flats, all the people working on this project have bugs. They listen to *everyone*. Did you know that? They have been watching you and Frenkel.'

'I know that! But how do you know about my flat? Where is the bug?' he began looking round like he'd be able to spot it.

'How the hell do I know! How did you know about Project 19? You came into my room this morning. But the conversation didn't happen until last night. You didn't visit Frenkel so how did you know?' There was a pause where Ed made no attempt to look at her. 'He must be able to talk to you telepathically. I know he visits his wife and mother. What can he do? The Corporation has been listening to everything! It means Frenkel must have contacted you before 7.00am the next morning. Tell me what he is capable of.'

'They can hear us now.'

'I don't give a shit!' she raised her voice here. 'They can listen all they like! I'm done with them. They have already contacted the President. They never monitored the Professor this much and that's why he was able to get away with all that crap and have his own agenda. They know you are up to something.'

'Why are you telling me all this. They know you're telling me,' then he looked around the room at imaginary eyes, 'don't you!'

'Oh, for God's Sake!' she yelled. She fumbled in her bag and brought out a pen and notepad and started scribbling something on it, threw it across the table and stormed out of the room. Ed waited for a bit to see if she would come back. In a way, he wanted her to. But she did not. He then walked over to the paper and looked at it. It was an untidy scrawl. But he could see clearly what it said. *The Professor died in the cubicle of Frenkel's room.*

He was puzzled. He already knew that. He sat down with the note in his hands. What did she mean? The Professor died of heart failure in the cubicle. He was found slumped over the panels. Edward had learnt that recently. Frenkel, from what he can remember from the notes had been in the gym for an hour before the Professor was found. There was no camera in the Cubicle to show what happened, but he had been there an hour before he was found. What has this got to do with Frenkel? Something else that he was unsure about suddenly came to his mind. *When I'm finished, I can let go.* Frenkel's words. What did he mean? What did Frenkel have to finish? The man was a virtual prisoner. He has nothing to do, but try and keep fit, eat and watch!

Ed then began to think very hard. From the notes, Frenkel had an intense dislike of both Susan and the Professor. This was obviously because he knew what they were up to. He was uncooperative and distant. If he reads her right, what Susan was saying seemed too wild to be true. He looked at his watch. It was 9.45pm. Then he realised, they were watching him here as well! Of course, she said all the flats including hers have been bugged. How was he supposed to call Frenkel? How would Frenkel know that he wanted to communicate? He needed to reach out his mind, but he was too disturbed to focus properly. He needed to get a message through to Frenkel. He thought for a while and then jumped up and started punching in some numbers on his videophone. They could listen all they like. He had work to do. The videophone flickered into action and he found himself facing the guard stationed outside Frenkel's flat. He was obviously the night guard on duty. Ed had not seen him before.

'Hi'.

'Good evening, Mr Hamilton'. These guards were good. They knew everyone! 'Did you get my message?'

'No, Sir. What message would that be?'

'Oh bother! He forgot to tell you?'

'Sir?'

'I left a message on the videophone for the other guard to take a message into Frenkel about 9.00pm.'

'No. He goes off duty at 7.00pm. He did not give any message to me.'

'It must still be recorded on the videophone.'

'No Sir, this videophone does not have a recording facility. All conversation here is to be carried out live. Your message would have been lost.'

'Oh, I'm sorry. I did not realise.' He was lying through his back teeth now.

'Look, I'm carrying out a set of experiments with the subject. It involves sending him a series of weird words to see if he can unscramble the message. He should have received a couple of words at 9.00pm. Can you give him the message?' He was expecting a doubtful look but nothing. The guard immediately agreed. 'Brick wall. Tell him Brick Wall.'

'Just that?'

'Yes. If he's smart, he will work it all out!'

The guard grinned. 'Do I tell him the message is from you?'

'He is expecting it already. But just tell him I am sorry it has come late.'

'Sure, Mr Hamilton. Leave it to me. Goodnight Sir.'

'Yeah, be seeing you, and thanks.'

The guard clicked the videophone off and then went about the long routine of opening the door. When he reached the cubicle inside, he found the flat empty. He then went to the panel in front and clicked the one in the bedroom. He could not see Frenkel, but the heat sensor told him that he was lying on the bed. The guard turned the sound on and gently called him.

'Sir. Sir! I'm afraid I have to wake you, Sir.' He paused but saw no movement. He then tried again but this time louder and Frenkel suddenly jerked himself awake and let out a small cry.

'Shit! Who's that?'

'Sir, it's me. The guard outside your door. I have a message from Mr Hamilton. He said he is sorry that the message is late.'

Frenkel did not know what was going on but he did not let on. He played along. 'Oh right.'

'Well, are you ready, Sir?'

'Ready?'

'For the message?'

'Oh yes! Of course. What is it?'

'Brick Wall.' Frenkel said nothing. He understood. 'That's it. Good luck, Sir.'

'With what?'

'With the unscrambling!'

'Oh yeah. Thanks. Goodnight.'

'Goodnight, Sir.' The guard then clicked off all the buttons and left the cubicle. Frenkel got up and went into this bathroom. He washed the sweat off his face and dried up. Then he waited. His heart was pumping away with the awakening and he was waiting for it to calm down. He laid back down. They could listen but not watch. He lay down for a full ten minutes before engaging his brain. Then he started his journey. He reached the door of his bedroom, through it and into the living room. Then he effortlessly moved into the cubicle area and out. He briefly observed the guard that he had just spoken to before being on his way. He made his way from corridor to corridor, down lifts, downstairs and actually walked his mind from the Corporation to Ed's flat. He could reach Ed without wandering around the place, but this was the only way he kept in touch with the outside world. The only way he could keep himself sane. If he was able, he would have walked to Ed's flat so that was what his mind was now doing. It took a good ten minutes for him to make this journey by thought. He entered Ed's flat and found the man lying on his couch. He then reached Ed and joined minds, and immediately felt the hostility there. He knew what this was all about, and he said nothing at this stage. Ed knew immediately that Frenkel was in his head. For a minute he forgot where he was.

'I know you're here Frenkel!'

For God's sake don't talk I can read you!

Ed was a little unsure what to do now. Does he let Frenkel read his questions or does he actually ask them?

What is it, Edward?

At first Ed could not think of the word and several thoughts all came into his head at once. He thought about Susan and being watched and about the Corridor. Then somewhere in there was a question about the Professor.

Edward, you have to help me here. You have to unscramble your mind! Focus.

What happened to the Professor?

He was killing me! He was taking samples unwillingly. Constantly keeping me in check with drugs. Day after day after day. He was killing me! I have things to do here and I have little time left. I had to try and get you involved in the Professor's work. On that day, I was exercising. I knew he was coming to get more cells off me. But this time I knew he was going to keep me sedated and intended to do it throughout his experiments. The whole time! I may not have been able to destroy any of his work. He would have succeeded in producing either a baby or a clone. I was meant to cause him mild pain in his head and disorientation. That is all. I did not know he had a heart condition. I was acting in self-defence. I did not mean to kill him.

Ed felt a shock of anger piercing his body. He knew Frenkel was not lying. He felt anger with the Professor. His mentor, his hero. The man that took him out of obscurity and a life of aimless drifting, a man who seemed to care for his welfare and gave meaning to his existence, a man so considerate and yet one who could treat another like an animal.

What do you mean you had to get me involved? You said before that you had work to do. What the hell does that mean?

I'll tell you everything. There is a purpose to everything. But not now. I am tired, I have to go.

No, you bloody don't. You talk now!

Ed could feel Frenkel becoming distant. There was a weird feeling inside his head and Ed remembered. When Frenkel said he was tired, he meant it! Ed began to see images not from his memory. He saw people, places, faces, ghouls, dead animals and along with this he also heard a huge barrage of sounds, he could hear small bits of conversation and the off words and sighs. This collection of sights and sounds eventually ended up causing Ed pain. He held his head and moved on his side crouching his legs up at the same time, so he was in the foetal position. He tried to channel his thoughts, but it was useless. His mind was a drop in the ocean! He stood no chance. Frenkel must be in agony! In a moment, blank! All thoughts, sights and sounds were gone. All was dark and quiet. He waited for a minute to adjust. Frenkel was gone.

CHAPTER 12

Lucas's office was dimly lit. Perez was at the controls and he, along with Rodrigues, Lucas and the President now sat staring at the screen. They were watching Ed's flat. It was a recording of a couple of days ago. Ed was lying on his couch very still with his eyes closed.

'Now, I'm going to put the recording of Frenkel alongside this one,' said Perez. 'This is exactly the same time.' The screen flickered and Ed's room was squashed up and appeared on the left-hand side and the space on the right-hand side now showed Frenkel's room. It was the living room and Frenkel was sitting on his sofa with his head rested back and his eyes closed.

'I suppose these men are not asleep,' said the President, still sporting dark glasses. 'No sir. Watch.' Perez set both footages for the same time. Then he paused the footage. 'At this date and time, Susan Preston was with us. The conversation you have already heard. Perez then set the tape for the conversation. 'Look what happens. I shall start the tape of Susan talking. Just watch the screen.' He turned on the tape.

Rodrigues: *Implantation? Procreate in the normal way? Womb?*
Susan: *Sorry?*
Rodrigues: *You said, 'Procreate in the normal way' In the normal way? Implantation?* Pause. *Miss Preston, in the normal way means. well, there had to be a female. Where was he going to implant these cells? Who was he going to implant the embryos into?*

There was a very short pause during which time Perez made a sigh to the President to watch the screen. Susan's voice was heard shouting out: *Me! Me! I was the female.* Before she had completed the rest of the sentence, Ed was seen on the screen to suddenly leap up from his couch and kick the coffee table next to him while shouting *Bitch! Bitch! Sodding bitch!* A few seconds after this, Frenkel suddenly jerked up on the sofa and held his head. He gave out a small cry as Ed finished the last sentence on the tape. Perez then stopped the audio tape and the video footage.

'From that footage, both Frenkel and Hamilton had a strong reaction to something at the same time as Susan's revelation. Frenkel does not say anything but Edward clearly refers to a female in his abuse and then the last comment is referring to someone as 'Judas'. Now watch this footage. This was the next day. Susan visited Ed late in the evening in his room.' Perez played the footage. The whole conversation was watched by the scrutinising eye of the President. He did not interrupt or make a comment at this stage. He just watched the whole scene. They then watched closely while Susan wrote something on a piece of paper, threw it on the table and left the room. They watched Ed as he read the note and walked around the flat pondering. They saw him pick up the phone and start talking to the guard. They heard the conversation only from Ed's side. The guard could not be heard. They heard Ed giving the guard the message for Frenkel. Then Perez stopped the footage and turned on the sound to Frenkel's room as the guard went in to give him the message. There was no video footage since Frenkel was in his bedroom and there were no cameras in there. They just heard the conversation.

'At this stage, the guard goes back out and Frenkel stays in his room. He walks around a bit and washes his face. Then he lay back down on his bed. About fifteen minutes later, Ed is back on that couch.' Perez fast forwarded and resumed playing. They watched as Ed lay there. Eventually, after what seemed an age, they heard him say *I know you're there Frenkel!* Perez stopped the footage. He walked over to the light switch and turned it up. Then he went back to his chair and sat there. They all were waiting for the President. Eventually, he spoke, quietly and clearly.

'Hamilton and Frenkel can communicate!' He then paused. Lost for words. They were all looking to him for guidance and here he was. Lost. How the hell did they let the Professor get away with all this. How could he have not realised what Frenkel was really all about? Why did Frenkel trust Ed after a couple of days when he did not let the Professor near him? This was a situation that was getting totally out of control and the President was a worried man. There was mutiny also from Miss Preston. The most worrying aspect was that Frenkel and Ed were communicating in a way that could not be monitored. Even if you could see them communicating, there was no way of knowing what was being said. There was something happening and the powerful men at the top could not control it. The Corporation trusted a man who abused the trust that they had in him. The Corporation let the Professor have a totally free hand on the basis of that trust. The situation as it stood was brought on by the Corporation not having full control of the Professor. The President was always a man who looked forward. Always to the future. Now it seemed difficult to see where they could go from here. He could not remove Ed's access to Frenkel since Frenkel did not trust anyone else. From an earlier footage that he was sent a few days ago, he knew that Ed used his mind to help Frenkel control his. Frenkel was too important to lose now. In an ideal world, Frenkel would already have learnt how to survive in the outside world and would have become to superhero, working for the good of peace and mankind, taking out the bad guys and generally being wonderful. His powers could put Superman to shame. However, this was the real world. In this world, Frenkel was a prisoner and at the moment, Ed was the only man who could control him. They had no option but to let this relationship take its course. The only real problem was Susan Preston who had already expressed her wish to leave the Corporation. This was a problem nobody had foreseen. However, all was not lost. She had great respect for her father who was involved with the logistics behind building the Corporation. He also knew the truth behind the Corporation. He would surely be able to talk to his daughter. They could not and would not tolerate anybody leaving the Corporation. It was too important to allow people to further their careers elsewhere. They were so sure that the top team would not want to leave such a prestigious position within the company that they had not thought out what they would do if someone wanted to leave. Yes, thought the President. Susan Preston had to be controlled. He father would understand.

'Gentlemen, we only made one mistake. That was to trust the Professor. Now we have to live with it. I have a few private calls to make so if you would all please allow me the privacy of this room and the videophone, I shall not be long. We will meet here again in an hour.

Anthony Frenkel was a tired man. His body was not going to be able to take the pressure for much longer. Every day the pain was greater, and he had to work harder to maintain control. He almost had achieved everything he had to, but a major chunk was still left. He had to talk to Ed in way that could not be monitored. He knew that his room was bugged. They could go into the gym. There was no visual there and he could use mind conversation. He could not use mind control all the time because it took too much out of him. He had to stage the conversation. He knew that at some stage, he would have to leave the flat. He would have to talk to Ed without being monitored and his best bet was outside the flat. He was now building up his strength so that he could do that. After their last conversation, he had to beg Ed to give him at least a day to recover. However, the President was here at the Corporation and they were planning to close the net around Ed's freedom. He had to talk to Ed soon. He had to tell Ed everything today. Tomorrow, Ed had to act. He was relaxing his brain when he heard the door of his flat open. He knew it was Ed. He opened his eyes as Ed quietly walked in.

'Morning,' said Ed.

'Well, it's a bit late for morning!'

'Yeah. I had a couple of things to prepare for the animals.' He paused for a while very conscious of the fact that they were being heard all the time. 'I hear the President is back in town!'

'Yes. I guess this town too big for the both of you!' said Frenkel.

'Well. I suppose,' said Ed as he sat down on the sofa. 'You're looking tired. Are you all right?'

'Just tired. I thought a change of scenery might do me some good.'

'Change of scenery? How do you mean?'

'You asked me last week if I wanted to visit your lab. Does that offer still stand?'

Ed was thrown at this. He did not know if Frenkel was joking or deadly serious. From the look of the man's face, those huge dark, burning eyes, Ed could see that he was deadly serious. 'Are you really ready?'

'Not yet. But give me another half an hour and I'm willing to give it a go.'

'Alright. We'll see you do. But I don't want to push you is that understood?'

'Yes, Doc.'

They sat there for a while. Then Ed began to tell Frenkel in detail the results of all the tests that he had carried out. Frenkel had huge amounts of IgG antibody just like the animals but the antigen linked to it was still a mystery. His blood count showed a huge white cell count, but the proportion of granulocytes, lymphocytes and monocytes were normal. No abnormal morphology was detected either. Everything in the blood film looked normal, but just increased. The chemistry samples were normal as were the swabs taken from his mouth, nose and ears. The only thing that Ed could say that Frenkel's body was under considerable stress. That they both already knew. Ed was prattling along in this fashion for a while before Frenkel interrupted him.

'Do you believe in God?'

Ed was stunned by the question. 'Well. I don't think so.'

'But you believe in the Soul.'

'Yes. We all have a Soul. That is what governs us.'

'Do you really think that the Soul can be found in the body?'

'Well, maybe. I don't know. Maybe it is. Maybe whatever it is that makes us what we are is not the spirit, maybe it is a small, tiny part of our body that we have not discovered yet.'

'You know, 'said Frenkel almost in a whisper, 'our lives, all our lives have a purpose. Everything that has happened, everything that is going to happen. It is all meant to be. My father was meant to die young; I was meant to meet my wife; you were destined to come and work for the Corporation. It all had to happen. We do not have to be important. Even a tramp out in the streets has a purpose. Something that we do today can affect someone else years from now. Sometimes even hundreds of years later. All our lives are inter-linked. Some have many hundreds of links. Some people not so many. But everything that happens has a further cause. Cause and causality. The laws of being.'

'Anthony, I lost you with your first sentence! Are you OK?'

'You have to listen. Have you never thought about the purpose of us being here? Do you think that there is no aim in life? God put us here for a purpose. Every single one of us has something to contribute towards mankind's survival. Something you do today may affect someone in ten years' time that you have never even met. The guy who builds a road but builds it badly is responsible when a girl a few years later trips on the uneven surface and breaks her leg. You affect many lives but over half of them will be people you have never met.'

'So, do you believe that even disasters are meant to happen?'

'Yes. This is difficult for you if you do not believe in God. But sometimes, something awful has to happen for something good to come out of it. Take relationships. Plenty of people have terrible relationships that they wish they had never experienced. I was in an awful situation with a woman. She was almost a nut. We had a terrible row and it all ended up badly. There was a court case where she accused me of anything she could. I would have done anything to wish her out of existence. But it was during the court case that I met Jennifer. I had just had a terrible time in the witness stand and afterwards, I had to run out to be sick. In order to make a dash for the men's, I knock down a woman in the corridor. I could not hang around because I would have vomited all over her! So, I carried on and ran into the mens. When I came out, she was there ready to read me my rights! She stood there wagging her finger at me and yelling. Then she stopped and realised I was unwell.' He paused with the memory. A small smile crossed his lips. His eyes looked sad. 'That was Jennifer. She was a juror. That was my Jennifer. How could I have wished that I had not gone through all that? I would never have met Jennifer.'

'What about now? You cannot possibly be happy about your life now?'

'I never said I was happy. No. I said it was meant to be.'

'So, you do not wish that you had never been on that expedition? One phone call changed your life. Would you not change that?'

'No. It was meant to be. You were meant to meet the Professor, and I was meant to find the Devil's Corridor. I was meant to go through and come back a freak. This ability I have been given that I used to hate so much has been given to me by God. I was always meant to have it. It is for a purpose. I have a duty to perform.'

'Anthony, have you been e-mailing the happy clappy people?'

Frenkel smiled. He looked at the time. He got up, took a couple of deep breaths and then went to the door of his flat. He then turned round to Ed. 'I could sure use your help now.'

Ed got up. He walked over to the door and looked Frenkel full in the face. 'Are you sure about this?'

'It has to be done.'

They then opened the door and Frenkel hesitated for a very long time before he held Ed's arm. Ed led him gently out. Frenkel was unsure and scared. He knew this had to be done. He had to talk to Edward in total privacy. They managed to walk to the cubicle and Frenkel began to shake.

'Look, Anthony, I don't think you are ready.'

'Let's go!' he said through gritted teeth.

The guard outside must have been watching because the door hissed open before they got to it. Frenkel was shaking and sweating. Every step was a huge effort, and he could feel his head becoming lighter. Slowly, they made their way out. The guard offered to help.

'Just make sure that nobody disturbs us. We will be sitting in the rest area. Please do not let anyone come without warning. Call me from outside first. Any sudden movements by anyone could be dangerous for all concerned.' The guard nodded at Ed. He then left them alone to make their progress down the corridor. The rest area was about 35 feet away straight ahead of them. As he came out of the cubicle, Frenkel's body was hugging the wall just outside the door. He was scared beyond belief. Ed was shocked. He was like a child learning to walk again. It seemed an age before Ed managed to pull him by the arm and face towards the rest room. When he tried to pull

Frenkel away from the wall altogether, Frenkel clung to him, like a baby, clinging with fright to its mother. He had his whole-body weight on Ed. He eventually managed to take a step by himself. He held onto Ed almost the whole time. The second step came soon enough and eventually, they made slow but steady progress. Frenkel stopped a couple of times and looked like he was going to pass out. It took a full fifteen minutes. When the door of the rest area came, Frenkel leapt at it. He stood there with his head buried in the glass, his breath causing condensation. Ed opened the door and the two men fell in.

Frenkel was heaving. Almost hyperventilating. He threw himself on the sofa there and tried to catch his breath. Ed sat opposite him and watched him. Frenkel was still out of breath when he spoke.

'Did you never wonder why the Professor liked you so much?' he said between breaths. 'Did you never... wonder why he insisted on you coming to Santiago? Why you? Did you never wonder?'

'Don't tell me. It was destiny!'

'Well not entirely. I have just today to tell you this, so pay attention. You have to act tomorrow. The President will come for you tomorrow.'

'What do you mean come for me?'

'He has had orders from his superiors to get you away from me. Tomorrow is the end one way or another.'

'Anthony, what.'

'Just listen, Ed! It was me! You were always destined to meet the Professor, but you would never have been asked to accompany him here without my interference. I have been monitoring you for years. Well before the Professor got his hands on me. I was crap at it to begin with and that is when you had that little problem with blackouts. That was me losing control. I apologise.'

'Hey, this is all weird!' gasped Ed. 'I don't...'

'I had to make sure that he brought you with him. I made him think that you were vital to his work. I was cooped up for about six months before they chose the Professor to take care of me. By the time he came, he kept me drugged up for so long that I was unable to make further contact with you. But it was also crucial that we met at the right time, on the right day. Too early or too soon would have been a disaster.' He paused but Ed did not say anything. He just stared at Frenkel with his mouth dropped. 'I guided you and am vital to your life. In the same way you are vital to life as we know it today.' Ed glanced at the door. He wanted to make sure there was no chance of someone overhearing this conversation.

'OK. So, you guided me here. What for?'

'There is something that we both have to do. It affects all our lives. Everyone living today. If we do not do this, then we will be wiped out. There will be another world, another possibility, another outcome. But the world today will not exist.'

'Something we do now will… do what? Cause another world war and wipe everything out?'

'Not so simple. It has to do with the Devil's Corridor. The time is not now. The time is… in the past. Something we do now will affect the past.'

'I'm sorry Anthony. I've lost you.'

'How well do you know your history?'

'Well, so so.'

'Remember that famous king of yours. The one that apparently gave up his throne for love! Remember? During World War II?'

'Oh yes! Edward the eighth, I think. Yes, that American woman.'

'Wallis Simpson,' said Frenkel.

'What about them?'

'Well, she won the King's heart, so the story goes and for love, he abdicated. Well, the truth of it is that he was a strong ally of Hitler's. He had no intention of giving up the throne, but he was a security hazard. He was dangerous. England could not have had a King whose sympathies lay with the Reich. British intelligence had to come up with something other than assassination. Wallis was the key. It was better to have the history books tell the world it was a forbidden love than the truth, which was that the King was a Nazi. They used Wallis to force Edward out. He abdicated unwillingly and she was the official reason.'

'You would have made a fantastic history teacher! What's all this got to do with us?' Frenkel paused and stared at Ed. His next few words were crucial. He could not fail.

'What do you think would have happened if Wallis Simpson was not at hand?'

'He would not have abdicated,' said Ed.

'And? What do you think would have happened?'

'Well, surely intelligence would have found another way to get rid of him.'

'Not enough time. Remember what I said. Timing is everything. Everything! They would have needed time. I know! I have seen! I have seen the alternative to today's world. I have seen! They would have been too late. Hitler would have had an invitation through the front door and there would have been no turning back.'

'So?'

'So, unless we interfere, that is exactly what would happen. Unless we do something now, Wallis Simpson of the past would meet a self-made millionaire who would promise her more than the King of England. She would be wooed away, leaving the King free to socialise with Hitler. There would be no abdication!'

'But it has *not* happened. We are here.'

'It will not happen because of what *we* are going to do.'

'I still don't get it!'

'Edward don't be a thickie! There are two possibilities. Either she meets someone else or she doesn't.'

'But she didn't, and we are proof.'

Frenkel paused. 'She did not meet him because *someone* interfered. About 50 years before the abdication, *someone* stopped the millionaire tycoon from being born. That line was stopped and so there was no millionaire. No wooing. No coronation. No Hitler.'

'Who? How?'

'The who is... *you*. The how I cannot tell you.'

Ed looked at him. 'What the fuck are you talking about! What the hell are...'

'Listen! Ed! Listen. The interference is *you!* You have to go through Ed. You have to go through Devil's Corridor. All this was meant to be. Me, you, the Professor. It all fits into place. Without it all, we would never have been born as we are today.'

'Me! How?'

'You have to go through tomorrow. You will travel back in time and you will change the course of history. You must! You have no choice! This is your destiny!'

'Screw destiny! I'm not doing it. I don't believe you.'

'But you will. You will prevent the millionaire from being born.'

'But I don't know who he is!'

'You do not have to. You will do it by your actions alone. Unwittingly, you will have prevented a disaster! You have to believe me! Think rationally!'

'Rationally? What the hell is rational about all this?'

'Edward, go home. Rest. Wait. At 10.30pm, prepare to communicate with me. I will show you something that will change your mind. It should persuade you to make this journey. If it does not, then I will make you go. Against your will. But that is a last resort. I hope you will understand.'

'Anthony, we are friends.'

'And it is as a friend that I speak to you today. I have struggled to keep myself alive for five years just so that I can perform this task of sending you through. After this, I will have done God's will. I can die in peace.'

'Die?'

'I would have willingly given up my life several times up to now. But I cannot. Not until my work is finished. Remember, you will come back. And I will be here.'

They sat in silence for ages. There seemed little to say. Frenkel was exhausted. He could barely sit up by himself. He whispered to Edward. 'I am tired. I have to regenerate myself so I can talk to you later. You have to get me back to my room.'

CHAPTER 13

Edward Hamilton was in turmoil. He did not fully understand anything. All that he believed in, all that he expected out of life was shattered. He felt like a child. An innocent child, calling out for some guidance, for some comfort, for a helping hand. If his mother were alive, he would have been talking to her. If ever he needed her, he needed her now. There were tears in his eyes as he walked back to his flat. He did not believe in the Professor. He knew that. But now he was expected to believe that it was not his talent that had attracted the Professor, it was Anthony Frenkel. Frenkel had guided his career from about five years ago. Frenkel had been watching him all that time. He had caused the death of the Professor paving the way for him to meet Frenkel. He had spied on people within and outside the Corporation. Looking at it from that point of view, Anthony Frenkel was a murdering pervert. It could also be true that he was a lunatic. A pathological liar. Making up stories and using his vivid imagination to wind Ed up and to make him risk his life for the sake of entertainment. The story he had just told Ed was hugely far-fetched and beyond belief. If this was the truth, then Ed would have been a happy man. He would just think of Frenkel as a twisted madman who should be controlled at all costs. An animal who deserved to be locked behind that window. A man who deserved to be isolated. However, Ed was here beating his head and crying like a child. This was not because Anthony Frenkel was a lunatic. It was because Anthony Frenkel was a genuine man. What frightened Ed more than anything else was the fact that he knew it was no lie. It was not a far-fetched fable. It was true. It was reality. He did not want to believe it, but he had to. He knew that Frenkel was not suffering inside just to use his energy playing practical jokes! It was for real. Someone does have to make that journey to prevent a huge disaster. The end of the world as it existed today. His tears stung his face as he opened the door of this flat and threw himself onto his couch. He called out to his mother again and again as if he was summoning her spirit. He did not want it to be him, but this was his destiny. Frenkel was not lying. Suddenly he saw Nicole. That sweet little innocent face from his past. All those years, he had never thought of her. Never even thought of her name. She was nothing to him. Now her face appeared to him. Pure, sweet, precious. The image of a summers' day came to him. Lying in Hyde Park under a tree. Smelling the grass, seeing the pale blue sky above him and squinting slightly as the sun flickered through the trees. He was with someone. He could not remember who. Suddenly, it was dark and the noise he heard was familiar. Where was he? Yes, that's right. Chinatown, London. Night-time. All he could smell was food. Noodles. Fish. All those Oriental faces. The waitress trying to take his order without knowing a single word in English. Now he was in Hawaii. The only holiday he remembered having with his mother. He was very young, and Hawaii meant stunning scenery, lovely girls and Steve 'book him Danno' McGarrett. He could almost feel the hot sun baking his delicate skin and his mother struggling to keep the sun-tan lotion on him. That was the life he wanted to go back to. He could not believe that that part of his life meant nothing. That he was destined to risk his life saving the world. He was not a hero. He was Edward Hamilton. He was his mother's son. That was all he wanted to be. Saving the world only happened in macho action novels to people such as James Bond and Indiana Jones. He was Edward Hamilton. A drifter and an idler who happened to be in the right place at the right time. Just happened to meet the right people. Just destined to meet Anthony Frenkel. His head was truly aching now and this time, it was not Frenkel. No. this was a pain from deep within him. He missed his mother like never before. Here he was, forty years old, alone and confused. Totally lost in his old wilderness. He needed her. He needed her to stroke his head, to whisper reassuring words and to wipe his tears away. Tears of a child. He begged her soul to come to him. To watch him. To help him. To guide him. He closed his eyes as he lay there and thought of her face. Her scent. Her smile. His tears ceased and he slowly became calm, his breathing became regular. Was he falling asleep?

Eddie my baby! Go to sleep my angel. Mummy's here. Mummy will always be with you! Sleep my precious little boy!

He awoke suddenly. Jerked himself up and looked wildly about him. His flat was dark, but he was totally calm. The panic that he felt was gone. His heart was calm, and he knew she was with him. He was not alone. He looked at the time. He had been sleeping for hours. It was almost time to prepare himself for Frenkel. He knew what he had to do. He accepted his fate. His destiny. His mother was with him. It was going to be fine. He lay down on the couch. Waiting. He opened the channels of his mind, the passage of his brain. He waited. He was at peace with himself. All was silent and calm.

Hello Edward.

It was Frenkel.

I hope you are well.

Ed was a little unsure how to respond.

Just focus your mind to what you want to say. I will pick up the thought.

How are you? Do you have the energy for this?

I'm fine. Yes, I do have the energy.

Oh my God! You heard me!

Yeah. A little trick I picked up somewhere!

Look Anthony I have been thinking…

No, I have limited time. I have to send you this. Just relax and close your mind to everything.

Ed did as he was told. He sat back and totally cleared his mind. He was already very calm. He waited. Eventually he began to see an image. Faint at first, but slowly it became clearer. It was a moving image. Like one of those old projections from an old projector. He saw a street. It was a sunny day in the middle of a street. He thought it looked like London, but he could not be sure. At first there were no people. But then he began to notice them. Happy smiling faces. Clean, smart people. Walking, talking on street corners, women with numerous children running around. They carried shopping baskets and seemed busy enough going about their normal chores. What was it that was not right? Something strange about these perfect people. All the houses looked the same. Yes, that was it. The houses looked the same, but so did the people. Inbreeding? It did not look like the past. It seemed more like the present. He then saw another street. This time, he recognised Westminster. The Houses of Parliament. The Thames. The tourists. Another lovely summer's day. But here too. Something was wrong. It all seemed to be lacking something. What was it? Blonde hair! Everywhere!

There are no Afro-Caribbean, Asians or mixed breeds.

That was Frenkel. Yes! He was right. They were all white. White, blonde with blue eyes! Like 'The Children of the Damned'! What was going on? No! This could not be the perfect Aryan race. Could it? Look! There! In the distance. He could see a black face! There *were* black people. Thank God for that. Let's move. We have to see that person to be sure. Closer! Closer! Yes, look. That is a black person. Indeed, it was. A face showing pain, suffering, torture. The man was badly dressed and looked at Ed with imploring, tearful eyes. A white, blonde woman was screaming abuse at him and suddenly a whip appeared from nowhere. She began to whip him. The pain must have pierced his very soul, but the man looked at her in defiance. This must be the past. It cannot be the future. It cannot be. Ed looked around. Where was his London? His London was a cosmopolitan metropolis. He could see no other people except blonde, blue eyed clones! Where? Where were they? The image dissolved. He was somewhere else. He was in a factory, cold, dark and damp. It was full of blacks, Asians, Indians, Chinese and other nationalities. There were some white people there, but they seemed to act strangely. Maybe they were mentally deficient. Ed could not tell, but they certainly were not like the healthy, fresh faced, bouncy, blonde little perfections he had just seen. All the individuals wore overalls. They all seemed to be cleaners. This seemed to be some sort of base. There were road sweepers, window cleaners, rubbish collectors. They all received instructions from here and were being given their orders by men who were white, but swarthy looking. Ed was beginning to get the picture. The black workforce was being governed by the slightly imperfect white. But before he could take too much in here, the image changed again. Now he was in some hospital. Or was it? Some clinical area. White walls. White furniture. He was led to a door labelled 'STERILISATION CLINIC'. He looked in. There they were! On one side sat the women. On the other side the men. This had to be wrong. This could not happen. It could not be his London.

This is the future. This will happen.

It was Frenkel's voice.

The only ones who can breed are the strong ones, the workers. This is 2056. Now you will travel ahead to 2103.

The image again changed and now Ed was outside a room. It was an official building swarming with armed soldiers. Not much had changed that much considering it was well into the future. The firearms and computers were very advanced but all else seemed unchanged. In front of him was a heavily guarded door.

Behind this door is the world summit of the major first world countries.

Ed was frightened. This was the group of people responsible for running the world. This world. He had no time to prepare himself. The door was flung open and he looked in. The sight sent a chill down his spine. He was frozen as he stared.

There they were.

All sitting there, talking, wagging their fingers, talking in foreign tongues. All of them white, dark hair, small dark moustaches and a stern, mad look about them. Some of them were very old with wrinkles and grey hair. Others were very young with moustaches not quite growing properly yet. But there were the ones in the middle. Ed knew that face! They all seemed individual but looking closely, they actually looked related! Or were they? No! They seemed to be… different version of the same man! They sent a deathly warning to any hesitation which Ed may have mad. Each one had a name tag on their jackets: England, America, South America, Africa, China, Australia. How many of them were there? How many? God, if only he could count. What have they done? Oh my God! My God! Please help. They suddenly all turned round and stared at him. Stared at him with identical eyes! He could see the madness. The evil that lurked behind their eyes. His eyes watered and the scream grew as it travelled from the lungs to the mouth. OH MY GOD, THEY CLONED HIM! He saw all the images, all those faces, dying people, starving, being shot, babies being throttled at birth, suffering human faces, all the images flashing in his mind, flickering and changing by the second! His mind was being filled with images far beyond his understanding. Stop! Stop! He was trying to get a message to Frenkel, for God's sake stop!

He screamed continuously until all went black.

Frenkel had been crouched up on his sofa for the whole night. His hair had gone slightly white and he looked at least five years older than he did on the day before. His heart had been pounding all night, but the body was in agony. He had struggled to maintain his sanity while sending Ed those chilling images. But they were not just images. They were reality of a future that would exist, and he could feel Ed's doubt. He could read Ed's heart. He knew that Ed wanted to believe him, but how does he explain that what he was looking at *was* the future if nobody interfered. He felt the pain in Ed's head, and he felt the confusion. His aching body was writhing all night and it was just now he settled in the foetal position and slept. His job was almost done. He now had to guide Ed down that path of terror. It was about 8.00am when he heard the door of his flat click. It was Ed. Ed also looked older and in pain. He had a task to perform and Ed had hoped all night that it was insanity that was driving Frenkel. However, he knew that it was not. In front of him was the most level-headed man he had ever met. He was not a liar and he was not mad. For the first time in his life Ed prayed. There was a guiding force and it had guided him to Anthony Frenkel. Maybe there was a Divine being. He hoped that he had enough courage to do what he needed to. He walked into the flat and looked at the wreckage in front of him. Anthony Frenkel opened his sleepy, tired eyes. They still sparkled. They had life in them yet.

'Anthony…' he whispered gently. 'Are you OK?'

'Yeah. What about you?'

'When will they come for me?'

'Well, you have half an hour head start.'

'I will need you.'

'I'm here Edward.'

'Please, don't leave me! Don't leave me even for a second.'

'I'll be with you. When you get back, I will still be here.' He sat up and faced Ed. 'Will you be with me on the other side?' asked Ed.

'No, I cannot do that! But I will be with you here and when you get back.'

'They can hear us.'

'Does not matter. You have half an hour.'

'Anthony. What am I looking for? Who? I don't know how to go about things. Do I have a name?'

'You don't need one. It will all happen naturally.'

'Now?'

'Yes. Edward, now.' Frenkel then raised himself from the sofa. 'Edward, you know I told you a couple of days ago that sometimes, in order to have something good, you must experience the bad. Sometimes, something good comes out of real tragedy.'

'Will I die? Am I coming back?' His voice was shaking.

'Relax! Yes, you will be back. *We all came back!* But remember, out of tragedy, real human tragedy, the world will survive as it is today. Just have Faith. There is a God. And you will also find the soul!'

They both stood opposite one another. 'Help me Anthony! Do not leave me!' Frenkel reached out and held him by the shoulders.

'I'm here. Go Edward! You have 30 minutes before they get to this room.'

'They will not hurt you, will they?'

'No, I'll be fine.'

'Stay with me Anthony. Give me courage.'

'I will do, if you need it, but I think you will not.'

'How do I get past security?'

'I will take care of that. Just go!'

They looked at each other. Time was short. They took a minute to remember the others face. They were both crying, silent tears running down their faces. They were grieving for each other and for what was about to happen. In the short time that they had known one another, they had lived a whole lifetime worth of trust, understanding and friendship. There could not have been two men on Earth who were closer in mind and soul than Anthony Frenkel and Edward Hamilton. They hugged each other as if for the last time. Frenkel grieved for the man who would not be the same when he came back, and Ed grieved for the man whom he thought would die before he returned. With the tears still streaming down their faces, they parted. Ed went to the door and looked back.

'Thanks Anthony. Please hang in there. Do not leave me!'

'See you soon Edward. You can't get rid of me that quickly!' Then he watched as Ed made a swift exit. As soon as he was gone, Anthony Frenkel sank to his knees and crouched on the floor, holding his wet face in his hands and wailing like a child.

As he left the cubicle and ran down the Corridor, Ed met Susan Preston. He stopped dead in front of her. Her face, worn and tired, looked shocked to see him. He did not ask any questions, but she felt a need to explain her presence.

'I have to see Frenkel. I have to apologies for...'

Ed did not listen. He bent down, kissed her cheek and whispered in her ear, 'stay with him. Look after him for me.' Then without looking back, he dashed off, leaving the puzzled Susan Preston standing in the Corridor.

Edward Hamilton was well prepared. He had all his passes with him and ran through the corridors of the building at full speed. There was no time to think. He also knew that Frenkel was with him. He could feel him in his head but this time, Frenkel's presence was welcomed. The tears stilled rolled down his cheeks as he dashed through the 7th floor. Eventually, tired and out of breath, he came up to the guards outside the door. Both of them were sitting at their stations but both were staring straight ahead. There was no expression in those eyes, and they did not move a muscle. There was not time to examine them, but Edward was sure that this was Frenkel's handiwork. The guards could not see him.

'Thanks, mate!' he said out loud, referring to Frenkel.

When he reached the door, his head suddenly felt a piercing pain. Frenkel was overworking that brain of his. It was just a few seconds, before the door clicked and hissed open. Ed ran in and went straight for the control panel in front of him.

The President, Lucas and Perez were on their way to Frenkel's room. They reached the cubicle inside and saw Frenkel on the floor crouched into a ball, holding his head with Susan bent over him, holding his back. Just as they got inside his flat, the red light on the panel in the cubicle area went off. It started to flash red and the alarm, loud and deafening reached their ears. They stared at Frenkel. He raised his head and looked at the President, smiling.

'Too late, Reuben! He's going through!'

Ed started to punch some data on the terminals and struggled to remember the codes. He was sweating profusely and started to panic. He gave himself a few seconds and started to recite the codes aloud in a bid to calm himself down. He tried to steady his breathing. Panic was setting in and he was frightened beyond belief. What do I do? Mummy! Please help. Suddenly, without him having done anything, the codes began to appear on the screen in front of him. Frenkel was helping him. He just hoped to God that Frenkel was not killing himself by doing this. The codes were in and the inner door, the one that led to the Blue Haze, hissed open. Immediately, Ed could feel the chill as the temperature of the icy Corridor reached him. Now, it was up to him. He took a deep breath and slowly walked into the chamber. The cave was as it had been when Frenkel had gone through five years before. The musty smell reached his nostrils, and the chill penetrated his entire body. He went up to the Corridor and stared at the brilliant Blue Haze. It shone off his face and his tears glistened like sparkling blue topaz beads. He waited. This was it. No going back! He tried to remember those horrific images he had the previous night. The real outcome of the world. He tried. He tried to justify what he was doing now.

Anthony, are you there? Don't leave me!

Edward, I am here. I am with you, Remember, out of tragedy comes something good! Go! This is your destiny. I will be here when you come back!

Before he could hesitate, he heard the door outside swing open and there he saw the President. *The eyes!* Oh God! He saw the eyes! There were no dark glasses, the President was looking at him in horror with his naked eyes! From his peripheral vision, he could see the guards raising their firearms to aim at him. Frenkel's voice screamed at him.

EDWARD! GO, GO, GO. GO NOW EDWARD! GO, GO, GO. JUMP!

And he did.

CHAPTER 14

Darkness engulfed him. He was in total darkness and panic set in rapidly. Space was restricted. His arms and legs were not free. He felt like he was cocooned in a small area with no light. He could barely breath and he started to gasp for air. No air! He began clawing in front of him at unseen things, trying to push himself out of this small space. But where? Which direction did he want to be in? Where did he want to go? Oh God! No, the pain. His whole body was suddenly overpowered by pain! There were sounds in his head and suddenly flashing images began to enter his head. He could not *see* anything with the eyes, but the images came and went in the dozens. Faces, eyes, objects, memories from the past, of times gone by. He was trying to scream but could not breath. He felt like his body was being pushed forward by unseen forces, moving slowly and painfully. His heart was pounding inside his chest and his head felt like it was going to explode. Please God, help me through this one. Please God! Save my Soul! The images continued. Whose memories, were they? Certainly not his. He was pushing, almost clawing his way out and all the time, he was in pain and unable to breath. It seemed an eternity. What on Earth was this?

Now he could feel a burning sensation all over his body and he sounded like a person trying to scream but was not heard because they were gagged. His ears were in pain and he felt like his hair was on fire! His body was now passing through a slippery area and he could feel the stench suffocating him. God Almighty! He was being born! Or was he? Was this a giant womb about to spew him out into another world? Natural reflex action caused him to struggle like an animal, fighting for survival. He had to get out! This thing was going to kill him! Push! Push! *Push!* His head was filled with faces, Vienna, a tiger, a child suckling, a dead body, a beggar, a cat, trees, sea, a woman crying, China, an angel, computers, fireworks, his mother, Frenkel, noodles, salad, birds, oh God, he was going to *die!* Breathe! Push! Push! Push! *PUSH!*

CHAPTER 15

He fell. Fell heavily onto a hard, wet surface. The scream that left his throat sounded like a wounded animal. His body burned and his nostrils picked up the heavy, pungent stench of burnt hair. Or at least, he thought it was burnt hair. It could quite easily be burnt flesh! In the distance he heard a woman's scream and a man's voice. He was still moaning with pain and felt a chill as his body was wet. He yelled and screamed and writhed on the floor and it was then that he realised that it was grass! He had landed on grass! He managed to squint as he tried to focus on his surroundings. It was fairly dark, and he could just make out a woman running away and a man, looking at him with a look of terror. The man was holding his chest as he gasped for air. Edward could hear him mumbling away, as if in prayer. Still writhing on the floor, Edward held out his hand to the man. The man shrank back with a cry.

'Oh, God Almighty! Forgive me my Sins! I confess! I confess! It was an accident!' He fell back onto the bench behind him. 'Forgive me!'

'HELP!' cried Edward, still holding out his hand.

'No. You are here to judge me. You are here to take me for my Sins!'

'For Heavens' sake help me up!'

The man was shaking with fear. Just a few moments ago he had been engaged in a secret rendezvous with his mystery lady. Charming her with his cheerful banter, he was in total control. Now here he was, facing this apparition that appeared from nowhere. Small sparks appeared to be flying out from it and it howled like a wolf. It barely looked human. It was so animal like that the man decided it could not be Divine. It had to be the Devil's messenger. It certainly looked like it belonged to the Prince of Darkness.

'You are the Devil's creature!' mumbled the frightened man. 'Give me your hand you ASSHOLE!'

The man moved slowly forward and held out his arm. Edward clasped the hand and the man screamed. He shrank back even more.

'NO! You have the Fires of Hell in your flesh! Get gone spawn of Satan!' The man was now weeping like a child.

'Don't be such a drama queen!' Edward eventually got up and threw himself on the bench next to the frightened man. The man wept and moved to the other side of the bench and again started to pray. He kept asking God to forgive him for his Sin. He seemed to be preparing to die! Edward could see that his own hands were scorched, and his hair smelt like it was singed. He obviously sent an electric shock to the man's hand which made him fall back in fright. Edward examined his clothes torn, wet and burnt. He was still in pain and struggled to talk but at least he could now breathe. He was out of that tiny hole that he was in. He was trying to place himself. He seemed to be in a park. The man sitting on the bench with him was still praying. He kept referring to Edward as the Angel of Death. Yes, Edward could see why the man was so scared. Appearing out of thin air and looking like he did, Edward was sure he could pass off as the Grim Reaper. Well, a modern one anyway! Suddenly, the man fell off the bench and onto his knees, moving himself in front of Edward. His head was lowered, his eyes clenched tight and his hands clasped together at his temple. Edward looked around in embarrassment. The scene looked very suggestive and he hoped no one else was around!

'Please, please forgive me,' cried the sobbing man. 'I did not mean to Sin. It was an accident. If you have to take me, then at least let me see my wife and children for one last time! I implore you.'

Oh my God, thought Edward. He really did think that he was face to face with the Grim Reaper. Edward was in pain. He had burn marks and cuts all over his body. He was going to need help. He had to be really smart now. He would not have a second chance. He held out his hand and placed it on the head of this whimpering bag of potatoes!

'How can you justify that it was an accident?' he asked quietly, trying to play along.

'I was trying to talk to her. She kept walking away from me, not listening and threatening all the time to tell Florrie. I was trying to protect Florrie! I could not let her find out.'

'Go on!' said Edward, taking his hand away and waiting.

'I was trying to stop her but ended up hitting her. She fell and cracked her head open! It was an accident.'

Edward paused as the man cried with shame. 'Rise. Take me to your home.' Edward said this with assertion, but he was still weak inside. He had to act like the Angel of Death if he was going to be convincing. 'Give me a hand. Take me to the place where you live.'

The man reluctantly helped Edward. He helped him walk out of the park and climb into a coach. Edward was almost sleeping as they rode. He vaguely saw a path leading up to a huge house. He opened his eyes as he realised that the coach was stopping here. The man got off first and said something to the coachman. They both then came round and helped him off the coach and walked him up to the house. The coachman then left them as they entered the house.

The maid staggered back on seeing Edward. She looked stunned and the man had to talk sternly to her before she snapped out and helped the injured man to the living room. Edward vaguely heard the man instruct the maid to call the doctor. Oh no! What was he going to do? He slumped on the sofa as the man went out. Then he could hear people moving about him, making him comfortable, bringing him hot drinks, blankets and food. He must have dozed for a few minutes. When he awoke, the man was sitting on a sofa opposite him. He seemed calmer than before and now; Edward could see the seeds of doubt on his face.

'Who are you?' the man asked him.

'So, you don't think that I am the Angel of Death?' chuckled Edward.

'The Angel of Death brings death to others, not look half dead himself!' The man was very wary of Edward. Edward could see the paleness of the skin, the spots of sweat on the forehead, the shaking hands and the nervous disposition. If Edward was not mistaken, this man was under the influence of narcotics. And if Edward remembered correctly. The man sitting opposite him was a murderer.

'What is your name?' Edward asked.

'James Maybrick. This is my home. Battlecrease. I live here with my wife and two children. You will remain as my guest as long as you have to in order to recover your strength and then you will leave!'

'Oh, but you forget, Mr Maybrick. I am here on a mission.'

'What mission? You are a vagabond falsely entering my house! I should turn you out right now!'

'Have you forgotten from where I came?'

James Maybrick stared at his unwelcomed guest! In the coach, he had managed to convince himself that it was a powerful illusion brought on by a stronger dose of Strychnine. He thought that he had imagined the scream which they both heard long before they saw anything. At the time he thought that someone somewhere was being butchered alive, but he could see no one. His lady friend also looked and could see nothing. A few seconds elapsed before suddenly a huge blue light just appeared right in front of their eyes, out of thin air. The ground shook and the light made them both shield their eyes as the man suddenly dropped onto the floor, literally from nowhere. His lady friend ran off and left him to his fate. All the guilt that he had been supressing came back to him. He instantly thought that this was Divine retribution for his Sins. He was begging for mercy and would have done anything that this creature had asked him to do out of shear fright. However, in the coach, he brought himself back to reality and he decided he was letting his guilt get the better of him. This was no Grim Reaper, and it did not appear out of nowhere. It was a vagabond, and it was the sight of this vermin that made her runaway. Now, this creature was making him think again.

'Who are you?' persisted Maybrick. "Where did you come from?'

'You dare to question ME!' yelled Edward. 'Just remember, I am not of this World. I am here to Judge you. If I think your actions were justified, I will spare you! But I have to judge you first. You will do all my bidding. And remember, I know ALL about you!'

Maybrick suddenly rose from the sofa and started to sport the frightened look again. 'So, you did appear from the air?'

At that moment, the door was opened, and a woman walked into the room. From her manner she was obviously mistress of the house. The one that wore the trousers, thought Edward. It was then that Edward noticed the attire. The long dress, the hair. His host was well attired in a suit with a waistcoat and a chain with a watch. Was this in the past? What century? Maybrick immediately moved towards her and kissed her outstretched hand.

'My dear, I hope you have passed a pleasant evening at the opera. I have brought home a guest.'

'A guest or a street dweller?' she replied rather rudely.

'Now, now, dear Florrie. My friend has entered upon hard times. You must be kinder.' Edward then rose unsteadily from the chair and held out his hand. 'Mrs Maybrick, please forgive the intrusion to your home. I'm afraid I have been the subject of muggers.'

'Muggers?' she looked at him puzzled.

'Er… yes. Thieves took all my money and left me half dead in the gutter. Hence my appearance. If it were not for your husband, I would surely have died.'

'What is your name?'

'Edward Hamilton, at your service.'

'Mr Hamilton. It will be a long time before you are at anybody's service. Please forgive my rudeness earlier.'

'It's already forgotten.'

'Where are you from? Yours accent is not local.' Edward was stumped. Before he could try and guess where 'local' was, the maid announced that the doctor that arrived.

'Well, I shall leave you to the Doctor, Mr Hamilton.' And then she left. A few seconds after that, the Doctor walked in and shook hands with Maybrick. They then exchanged a few pleasantries. What kind of accent is that? Edward knew that he should know, but his head was blank. Maybrick repeated the story about being attacked and robbed.

'So, 'said the Doctor. 'Seems like you have suffered in the hands of the petty criminals!' He looked at Edward as if waiting for a reply. Edward was too scared to reply. He had no idea what condition his body was in and what the Doctor would find. Then it suddenly dawned on him. *Where was he?* In all the commotion and his dramatic entry onto the scene, he had totally forgotten what had happened to him. There was no laboratory, no Frenkel, no President. He was in another building altogether! Suddenly, his head went mad with excitement! He quickly looked around the room. The patterned wallpaper, the silver ornaments and the furniture would all be described as antique by experts in the year 2007. He looked at these two men. Their clothes! Oh my God, he thought. They look like they walked off the set of a Sherlock Holmes movie! Their hair, their moustaches, even their faces were those belonging to another world! *Judas Priest! He had travelled back in time!* He looked wildly at the two men and suddenly shot up from the sofa. He ran to the window and looked out, as if that was going to tell him anything. He swung around just as the Doctor was asking him if he was alright and looked around for a calendar, the time, the year. Anything.

'What is the time? Where am I?' he said to both men. 'It's late in the evening,' replied the Doctor.

'No, I mean, the *time of year? What time is it? What year?*'

Both men glanced at one another and Maybrick especially looked worried. He certainly did not need a lunatic on his hands. He remembered his ill-judged confession.

'Mr Hamilton,' said the Doctor, 'I think you had better sit down and let me look at you.'

Edward ran about the room like a wild cat picking up things and putting them down, looking at pictures, ornaments, goodness knows what he was looking for. He then ran to Maybrick and yanked him towards him by the collar yelling, 'What is the bloody time period? Where am I?'

'July! It is summer.'

'Summer of what bloody *year?*' Edward was almost hysterical 'Where is this house? What country?'

'Mr Hamilton.' This was the Doctor, talking very calmly and steadily, and all the time wondering if the local asylum would let in a severe case this time in the night. 'We are in the house of James Maybrick, and this is Liverpool. The season is summer in the month of July. Now please sit down.'

'*WHAT BLOODY YEAR!*' retorted Edward.

'July 1888,' answered Maybrick.

Edward stopped dead in his tracks. He stood totally still and looked like a terrible statue. There was a long pause from the other two men as they watched him.

'1888? The year 1888! July? 1888!' He suddenly laughed and ran about the room as if delighted. He jumped about and yelled *'Yes! I made it. I made it! Shit! I made it!* Frenkel, if you can hear me, I made it. It's 1888! I'm in Liverpool!' He just caught the Doctor from the corner of his eye quietly talking to Maybrick. Their tones were suspicious. He suddenly realised. Eighteen eighty-eight! They still had workhouses and asylums! He had to pull himself together. He must have sounded like a real nutter! He had to remember he was here on a mission and getting himself certified was not part of his plan. He immediately calmed down and walked over to the two men.

'No, Doctor, I am not insane!' he said, though he still had the slight glint in his eye. 'I have suffered much and am confused. Please forgive my slight lapse.'

'Mr Hamilton, if you sat down and let me examine you, I will be the judge of your health.'

'OK, sorry Doctor.'

'Well, I shall leave you gentlemen to your business,' said Maybrick as he left the room.

James Maybrick was a troubled man. He had been a troubled man before that lunatic in his front room even materialised in front of his eyes that evening. On the face of it, he was a happily married middle aged man with two children. He had a successful cotton trade business and a high standard of living. That was the image those close to him saw. However, inside, James Maybrick was slowly dying. He only wished that his body would realise that the brain was in turmoil and that it should really give in now. He knew his wife; his beloved Florence was unhappy. She had been lacking in her duty towards him as a devoted wife. He wondered whether she knew about his infidelities. That would explain things. She had moved out into one of the other bedrooms and never missed an opportunity to mock him. His eldest, James had been weakened by Scarlet Fever the previous year and he suspected that his youngest, Gladys, was being neglected by the children's nurse, Alice. He did not want to interfere in these things, Alice was recommended to him his brother. His health was poor. It was not helped by years of self-inflicted torture that he had been administering himself. It had been five months since they moved to this house and he thought the added responsibility of running a big household and have a new house to decorate would change Florrie. However, things were worse than ever before. He was too sick to travel and so his brother was preparing to go to America to sort out that end of his business. All these things he could have coped with. He could have let things sort themselves out and survive best he could. But not now. He could no longer just exist as he had been before. He had fallen from grace heavily and had raised his hand to the one thing that remained sacred to him. Life itself! He had forfeited all his rights to being a decent human being. He had blood on his hands and now he must pay. He would have been able to live with that blood as well, almost blocking the horror from his memory. He had done so already for the last four months and every day that passed made his crime lighter on his shoulders. Until now. Until today. Until that visit to the park. Now his Judge was here. In his house. Watching him. Ready to pass sentence. Whatever was in his living room with the family Doctor, Maybrick was certain that it was not of this World. It knew his sins. Who was this person? Every time he believed that he was the Angel of Death, the man acted a bit insane and seemed to have no idea what was going on. Maybrick could not get the image out of his head of that wall of blue. A bright blue light, and a man falling out of it. Heaven knows what it was that rested in his house and what Sins it knew. Maybrick sat there in his study, drinking. He held his head in his hands and tried to steady his nerves. He eventually heard the door open and the Doctor walked in. He came and sat on the chair opposite Maybrick. He began to speak almost immediately.

'James, where did you find this man?'

'Well… in the street. He was hurt.' Maybrick had to tread warily. The creature knew about his Sin. He had to protect it. 'Well, actually, I know him.'

'*What?*' The Doctor was astonished. 'Why did Florence not mention that. She said you had brought home a vagabond scrounging for lodgings!'

'Well, he does give that impression. No. He is an old friend from my younger days. I met him by chance and now he is in need.'

'But he speaks in a strange tongue. What accent is that?'

'He has travelled all over the World. He has picked up many tongues!'

'James. Be careful. His injuries are alien to me. I cannot tell you how any of them can be explained. The open wounds are not made by sharp tools, the burn marks show no signs of coming into direct contact with fire or steam. He is calm and normal one minute and totally delirious the next. He is unable or unwilling to explain his condition.'

'Don't worry Richard, he is a friend. I will look after him.'

'I shall be back tomorrow to see him.' Maybrick did not want the Doctor to come back and see the creature again, but he said nothing for fear of arousing suspicion.

'I will see you tomorrow. Let him sleep now.'

'Call me if you need me for anything.'

'I will.'

Then the doctor left. He left Maybrick to deal with the creature. His horror at having this person spend the night under his roof was already tormenting him. He could not even rely on Florence. She was sure to have retired already to her own room. He slowly walked towards the living room. He had to face the music one way or another. He walked in slowly and found that the creature had fallen asleep of the sofa where he sat. A brief moment of pity passed into Maybrick's head, but it did not last long. This was an unknown entity. He had to tread carefully. He slowly walked out of the room. Florence had given the orders to have a room prepared for the guest and Maybrick instructed the manservant to wake the guest and to help him to bed. Maybrick retired for the night relieved at not having to face the creature.

CHAPTER 16

Edward Hamilton dreamt of his mother. She was holding him in her arms and stroking his head. Running her fingers through his hair. *My little boy!* He heard her voice over and over again. It was a warm dream, and he was happy. He slept like a log all night and when he awoke, the morning sun was flickering through the drawn curtains in his room. He squinted and sat up in bed. He glanced round and immediately panic set in. This was not his room! Where was he? It was not his bed, not his clothes. Good Lord! Where was he? He ran to the window and looked out and saw, not the mountains of Santiago, but a very English looking garden. He ran around the room looking for his clothes. Then he saw his burnt clothes on the chair next to the bed. Yes! Now he remembered. His clothes! Oh yes! It all came back to him. He was in England. He could not remember where, but he remembered that he was home. Wow! This was fantastic. He wished he could still communicate with Frenkel so he could describe everything to him. He decided to start a record of his experiences as soon as possible. Why England? He was in Argentina and yet he crossed the ocean and ended up on a totally different continent. How come he ended up here? Did it have anything to do with him being born in England? Surely it could not be coincident. He tried to remember the passage here. That tiny space that he was travelling in. He still could not think what it was and how he was cut and scorched. There were lapses in his memory, but he remembered every word that passed between him and Frenkel on that last morning. He was on a mission and he needed lodging and help. He had to make friends with Maybrick. He vaguely remembered that Maybrick mentioned two children. He did not mention the sex. Were they two boys or a boy and a girl? But then he remembered that Frenkel said he had to *prevent* someone from being born. Prevent? Did that mean he had to prevent conception? Whose pregnancy was he preventing? Maybe the caustic Mrs Maybrick was pregnant. If she was, how was he going to prevent the baby from being born? All these thoughts raged in his head as he tried to find clothes to wear. He had no idea how to go about things. He should have questioned Frenkel more and found out exactly how he was going to do what he had to do. He was getting nervous just thinking of it. How long did he have before he was whisked back, or rather, forward to his own time? Was it hours, days, weeks? Would he know exactly when that was going to happen? How was he going to live here? He needed Maybrick on his side. He did not want to be the dreaded Angel of Death. He could not quite explain how he came to be here, but he intended to gain his trust. If that did not work, then he would have to resort to blackmailing him. Right now, he had to explore. He had to find out exactly where he was. He had much to learn. Learn about the place. The people and the customs. This was a time zone that he could only have read about in books and seen in films. To actually be here was amazing to him. He was going to work straight away!

When he came downstairs, he had no idea what he would find. The manservant who had helped him the previous night guided him into the breakfast room.

He saw her there. She immediately rose and met him by the door. She then directed him to his chair and a plate of breakfast was placed in front of him. She smiled at him and made him feel welcomed. She was a petit woman, light brown to blonde hair and twinkling eyes. He had trouble remembering who she was. He had seen her face, but it was some minutes before he remembered that she was Mrs Maybrick. He also knew that she did not like him. Her attitude towards him last night was rude, even if he had been a down and out. And although she was polite this morning, he knew that she did not like him. She smiled and engaged in small talk, but she was only tolerating him. He made no attempt to win her over since he figured that she would go along with her husband. It was Maybrick who had to be won over. He ate and listened to her but said very little. He still could not remember where in England he was. He could not properly remember what date it was. And, as of yet, he had no history about himself because he had not thought about it yet. He needed more information about the life there as it was before he gave himself a false family and life. He did not feel all that well. The bruises and burn marks were still hurting him and his whole body still ached. He could not remember why he had forgotten certain things. He knew that the Doctor and Maybrick had told him the exact date, but he could not accurately re-call it. He knew it was eighteen hundred and something or other. The breakfast was nice, but he began to feel nauseous and felt like he was going to embarrass himself at the breakfast table. He must have looked ill since Mrs Maybrick called over the servant and ordered the guest to be taken back to his bedroom. Edward fell into semi consciousness and vaguely helped while a couple of people struggled to get him back. He then lay on the bed and wondered why he felt so sick. He could barely raise his head off the pillow although he could hear all the time. He was aware that there was movement in his room, and he knew exactly what was said. The servants were under the impression that Mr Maybrick had taken leave of his senses and taken pity on this miserable wretch. If he had so much money to waste on scum like him, why could they not have an increase in their wages? Yes, he heard all that. But he could not move or talk. Then he could feel someone prodding him. His chest, his eyes, his mouth and his nose were all prodded and Edward hoped it was the doctor. He now felt chilly and could also feel his body shivering. If he was not mistaken, he was suffering from a severe form of the common cold. After all, the germs in this time period were alien to him. His immune system must have had a shock! Oh my God, germs from Sherlock Holmes' period! What do we do? He just lay and listened as the doctor who was talking to Maybrick confirmed what he had already diagnosed himself. What did not occur to him was that although in his own time zone, this was a minor ailment treatable with appropriate drugs where sufferers would still be expected to turn up for a full day's work, here, in eighteen hundred and something or other, this was a critical sickness. Some of the crucial drugs had not even been invented yet and basically, old fashioned nursing was available but at the end of the day, his immune system had to deal with it alone. He could do nothing else. He had fever and sickness and on occasion he was quite delirious. He knew that he was being nursed and that Maybrick often came to see him. He never remembered the lady of the house pitching up, but he did have a vague recollection of a young boy. He had no idea how many days he was sick. His dreams were vivid and disturbing. He always saw his mother. She was always soothing him and stroking his hair and calling him loving name. He also saw Frenkel. He kept remembering that last conversation he had with Frenkel. *I'll be here when you come back. Out of tragedy comes something good.* There were many other images in his head, including those of the future horror awaiting the world if he did not succeed here. He only hoped he was not talking during these attacks. He was sure the doctor would have him certified and locked away in some nut house given half the chance. He knew Maybrick would not stop him from doing that. If he was certified, then there was no way that anybody would believe him if he spilled the beans on Maybrick's crime. He had to recover. He had to have a strong immune system. He had to recover! His only comfort was that both Frenkel and his mother were with him in his dreams.

The Maybrick family doctor had no idea what was keeping this strange man alive. He had been in a delirious fever now for five days and nights, constantly boiling, sweating and restless. He was not being fed and administering water was difficult. The man was feverish and desperately ill. Two nurses were constantly by his side, wetting the forehead, chest, arms and legs. He was sweating so much that at one stage, the bedsheets had to be changed twice a day while the sick man slept on the sofa. With no food or water for five days and a temperature soaring, this man should have expired. Some of his cuts and burns had also turned septic and the doctor was concerned that maybe he had total blood poisoning which was sure to kill him. All this time, the doctor was trying to pry as much information out of Maybrick as possible about who this man was. Maybrick was willing to pay for all the costs and seemed to protect the man so the doctor assumed that they must be quite close. Whatever the situation was, the doctor was coming to see Edward twice a day. They were wondering that maybe arrangements should be made to find his relatives since it did not seem likely that he would wake up at all. On the sixth day, the doctor walked into the bedroom for his early call and was shocked to find the patient sitting up, still looking very, very ill, but at least conscious! The doctor rushed in and immediately started to ask him questions, but he soon realised that his patient could not talk. He understood what was being said to him, but the voice was not there. However, this was a good sign, and the Doctor raised a glass of water to Edward's mouth and gently wetted the lips. The doctor began to tell him about the weather, the household, his own children, anything just to keep Edward's attention. He offered some food to the patient but thought that it was probably better to leave it until Edward himself wanted to eat. He was just relieved that the patient was recovering. He stayed there for half an hour and then went to the breakfast room to find Maybrick.

When James Maybrick heard the news, all the hope he had built over the last few days with the expected death of the creature, drained out of him.

CHAPTER 17

For six days, Florence Maybrick had been angry. She wanted this man out of her house. She was angry that she had no say in things. It was her house. She was the woman of the house. Deep down though, she was angry with her husband. It had nothing to do with bringing home strange men. She was angry because she was unhappy. She had found out that her husband had a mistress. She always suspected that he had been unfaithful but now she heard rumours about there being illegitimate children. She had insisted on moving out into another bedroom and he did not argue at all. He just accepted the situation with no discussion at all. She was too afraid to delve deeper into their problem because she herself had been no angel. Her father died when she was young, and it was always her mother who looked after her welfare. She herself was strong willed and always did what she wanted. She met James Maybrick on the SS Baltic, sailing from New York to Liverpool in March 1880. She was a hot blooded eighteen-year-old. Always wilful, always doing things her way. Heaven knows what the attraction was. There he was, middle aged, overweight, addicted to drugs, alone. He told her no lies, no smart lines, no poetic language. She saw him as rich and at that time, exciting. She could want for nothing being married to such a man. So, she allowed herself to be swept off her feet. Her mother cried when Florence told her that she had accepted Maybrick's marriage proposal. She had always wanted a wealthy husband for her baby, but she could not see a happy alliance between two people separated by so many years. If the girl's father had been alive, he would have guided her. But as her lenient mother, she had no influence. Florence was truly happy when she married James Maybrick the year after they had met. A year after that, their son was born. The years went by. They had spent many months travelling between Virginia, USA and Liverpool. James' business was doing well, and his brother helped him from time to time. However, as their lives progressed, Florence began to see the disadvantages of marrying a man much older than herself. She was still young and hot blooded while James was old, tired and unadventurous. She had fooled herself into believing that she could love him. His idea of a good time was a book and an early night. He did not like to go out much, never wanted to accept invitations and always reluctantly agreed to Florence's demands for social activities at their own home. It was only human nature that Florence Maybrick took a massive gamble with her own dignity as a woman living in that period. She allowed her weak heart to be wooed again. A heart that had already been given in marriage. She offered it and allowed it to be taken. She may love James Maybrick as someone does a father or a brother. But she would never be *in love* with him. Not the way she was now. The passionate woman inside gave in to young romance. Now she lived in hatred and fear. Hatred for herself in making a choice based on financial security, hatred for James for being so old, and fear that one day he would find out that not only had her affections for him died, but that they had been given to another right under his very nose. She could not bear to hurt him like that. However, now that she had found out about his mistress, she could hardly be angry. She knew the anger she felt was at herself more than her husband. Two years after her son was born, she gave birth to a girl. She had two children whom she loved more than anything in the world and she knew that she had to stay with James. If they ever lived apart, he would never allow her to take them. She had to stay. She could never let him find out about her lover. They had recently moved into this lovely house and to all the world, she was the mistress here. She had too much to lose if he ever found out. So, she tried to look and be innocent. She tried to act like the injured party, to make him think that their separate bedrooms were about his infidelities. She was angry with herself, not with Edward Hamilton. But his presence in her house did not help at all.

'Good, now he can leave!' was her response to Maybrick when he told her that the sick man had woken up.

'Florrie, he is a friend. I would appreciate it if you were kind to him.'

'I will. When he moves out!'

'He was to stay for the entire season, bunny.'

'Oh yes? And when exactly where you going to tell me that? I am the lady of the house! Should you not consult me?'

'Well, he came earlier than I expected,' Maybrick pleaded. He had no idea how long the creature wanted to stay. But he had to make his presence as normal as possible. 'It seems a bit rude to ask him to leave now. His illness is just unfortunate. Please Florrie.'

'So where did he come from? We've been married eight years and you have never mentioned him before.'

'He is a friend from school whom I have not met for years. You can hardly have expected me to mention all those I have met in my life! Please, Florence! Be reasonable! He is a friend. I don't have many of those and some affection would be welcomed!' He was trying not to lose his temper, but his words were coming out between gritted teeth. 'Look, I don't make many demands! But I am demanding that you obey me on this! He is staying as my guest! Is that clear?'

She tried to glare at him, but in the end, it was fruitless. She had to capitulate. Her affirmation came only in the form of her storming off into the breakfast room. James Maybrick now had to do that which he thought he would be saved from. He had to talk to his guest. He had to show human concern for the creature. The only thing that made his task easier for him was that the man had been sick. If he was sick, then he must be of *this* world, not the next. He was human. If a bit strange. But one thing was clear. This man was not here to judge him. He was mortal.

Edward was in a total daze. He knew the doctor was delighted. He was chatting and jumping about which meant Edward must have come back from the brink! Just how much on the brink had he been? He was at first unable to talk. His head was still swimming around. The light was too much for him and he spent quite some time sleeping. He was wondering how long he had been sick. Back in the laboratory, the animals came back within a few days. How long did he have before he was whisked away? He tried to think about Frenkel. He wanted to talk to him. He wondered if Frenkel could *see* him. He felt totally lost out here. He had forgotten what time period he was in but one thing that he did remember was that he had to make friends with Maybrick. He had to make Maybrick keep him here. He knew this and tried to devise a plan in his sick head. He was mentally exhausted. The doctor came back several times to see him and was the last person he saw that day. He slept soundly at night with the maids still keeping a watch over him.

He awoke with the sound of clattering cutlery. It was bright. The light of the morning sun was again flickering in his weary eyes. He squinted and vaguely saw the figure of a man putting a tray down on the table. He knew who this was, but the name did not come immediately. He had to struggle to remember where he was and who this was. By the time Maybrick sat down near the bed, Edward had regained full memory.

'Mr. Hamilton, how are you?'

'Please, call me Edward, or Ed, but never Ted.'

'Who are you?' said Maybrick, seating himself on a chair. 'Oh, please not that again!'

'You came into this house as the Angel of Death and have remained here for eight days under my roof. I think…'

'EIGHT DAYS! Shit! Shit! Bloody hell! Why haven't I gone back?'

'Mr Hamilton! Can you please refrain from such language!' Maybrick was angry. He stared at this crazed person in front of him. Edward was speechless. He tried to think how long it should have taken. Did the return process not work? Why had he not gone back? Was he stuck here forever? Maybe he had jumped to another time zone but Maybrick is the man he saw in the park. What the hell was happening? Panic set in and he tried to get up but was swooning. He fell back onto the pillow. FRENKEL. FRENKEL! PLEASE HELP ME! Maybrick instantly ran to him and tried to calm him down. Maybe it was not such a good idea to provoke him, thought Maybrick. The man was still quite ill. He needed to regain strength. It also seemed that he had trouble re- calling things. The man kept asking him again and again what year it was, what time. Edward then lay back. Maybe, one day back at the laboratory was not the same as one day here. But then how many days made up one day back in him own time? He should have asked Frenkel that! He should have asked him how many days he was away. Shit! Why did he not ask that? Call himself a scientist! He looked into Maybrick's face. This stranger was the only hope he had. He had to make him a friend. He lay back onto his pillow and collected himself.

'So. Eight days!' he said calmly. 'How sick was I?'

'Sick enough for the doctor to ask me to contact your family,' replied Maybrick, equally calmly.

'Family? I have none.'

'None? No mother, father, brother?'

'Well. no. I was an only child. My parents have died.' He hated lying.

'Obviously from the shock of knowing that their son and heir was the Grim Reaper in disguise!' added Maybrick sarcastically.

'Oh!' Edward was embarrassed. 'Look. I am sorry about that, but I was frightened.'

'YOU were frightened? How do you think we felt?'

'Who was your lady friend? I'm sure it was not Mrs Maybrick.'

'Who are you?' insisted Maybrick angrily.

'I am Dr. Edward Hamilton. I was born in London and I specialise in physiology. I study anatomy. I developed drugs which can cause temporary amnesia. I had no one to test it on since animals cannot tell you if they have lost their memory! I found out by accident its capabilities when I tried it on myself!' He paused to see Maybrick's face. He carried on when the other man refused to comment. 'It took me some time to figure out that it was causing me to lose my memory in short bursts. I had by that time been on the drug for ages and had become quite dependant. I have to have it, but I lose my memory. It was to begin with just short-term memory. But after repeated use, it has become long term. I can remember many things but my past I have trouble with. It is likely that I do have siblings but that I have forgotten them. I am sure that my parents are dead. I do know that I used to live in London. And I have all my medical knowledge. That has not left me.' He looked into Maybrick's astonished face. He was hoping that this farce had been accepted.

'Mr Hamilton, I think that your sickness has contributed to your mental health.'

'No! I am telling the truth! My name is Dr Edward Hamilton. I am a doctor and a physiologist. There are advances I have made in the field of science that doctors today are totally ignorant of! You have to believe me.'

'So, you have created this drug which causes you to lose your memory?'

'It slowly destroys the neuron activity in the brain and slows down the synapses. I don't know whether the effects are permanent or not. I need more of the drug.'

'How did you make the drug?' asked Maybrick, looking as if he was beginning to believe.

'Mice. Rats. It exists in their brain and gut area. In fact, we all have this drug in small doses but when extracted in large amounts and concentrated, it has a potent effect. In order to extract it, you have to.'

'Dr Hamilton, you are wasting your breath. I am not a medical man and would not understand anything you may explain to me.'

'Look. I am telling the truth. Think of the park. Do you really think that I fell out of thin air? Can that be possible? You are a rational man. Is that possible?'

Maybrick cocked his head to one side. "What exactly are you saying?'

'The bench you were sitting on. How long had you been sitting there?'

'No more than twenty minutes.' Maybrick was looking well puzzled.

'The drug takes ten minutes to take effect. Just sniffing in the air is enough.'

'What are you talking about?' Maybrick launched himself forward towards the bed and looked like he was going to grab the sick man by the throat. But he stopped himself just by the side of the bed. 'Tell me! What are you saying?'

'The pair of you did not see me fall out of thin air. You were under the influence of that drug. I left some deposits of it on that park bench. I was monitoring you from a distance. I wanted to see what effect it had on you. I cannot take it anymore. The drug has been wrecking my brain, so I needed to see what effects it had on others. I was watching you from behind. You both experienced temporary loss of memory. You saw me walking towards you and we chatted for about five minutes about the weather. Then suddenly your lady friend screamed and ran off and you accused me of being the Angel of Death! I am sorry for using you in such a way.'

'You blaggard! Scoundrel! How dare you use us! What damage has been done to my brain?'

'Well, from the sudden reaction that you had, I would say that your brain has already been damaged by something or another. I would guess that you are also dependant on something.'

Maybrick gritted his teeth and started to pace up and down the room. He did not believe a word of all this but then how else would he explain the incident in the park? How else would he explain the knowledge that Hamilton had? The reference to his dependency was made without any medical examination. Maybrick was scared. What was he going to do with this man? And what exactly did this man want? Surely, he could remember where his home was! He must have some memory, if not, wish to go home! Before he could say anything at all Edward spoke.

'Look. Do you really think that I could make up such a yarn as this if it was not true? How did I appear out of thin air? My story sounds so stupid that it has to be true. If I told a medical man what I have told you, would I not be locked away in a nut house? Yes, I would. So why do I risk telling you this? It is true! I had a massive blackout recently and cannot remember exactly where I came from. And I cannot explain why I was so sick but that was no hoax! I was sick!'

'Hoax?' Maybrick looked puzzled.

'Look, you have to give me shelter.' Edward pleaded with Maybrick. He thought his story was ludicrous, but it was the only one that he could come up with that would explain the events in the park, his obvious memory difficulty which he had been experiencing and also, hopefully, help provide him with a few things that he really wanted. Like a few mice!

Maybrick was about to leave the room, obviously not too convinced with this fairy tale. Edward had no choice. No choice at all. He had to play his best, and yet his most detested card.

'What was her name?' he called out to Maybrick.

'That is none of your business! You cannot use her to blackmail me! Florence already knows about her!'

'Oh no! Not her. I meant the other one. The *accident.* What was her name?' Maybrick's eyes flashed with anger.

'You are my official guest. Just stay out of my way!' And then he walked out.

CHAPTER 18

Edward's recovery was just as sudden as the onset of his sickness. He was sure that his immune system had received a massive shock. The germs, bacteria and viruses of this time zone obviously differed a great deal to that of his own time zone. His body was responding in the best way that it knew. It takes about seven days for the immune system to mount a response to an unknown antigen and there probably was a collection of unknown antigens that his system had to deal with. He began to eat and slowly strength came back to him. The doctor and the maids looking after him were his only visitors. All the time he kept thinking about his mammoth task. How does he go about putting things right? He was confused. It was now ten days after he had arrived here and there was no sign that he was going to be whisked away soon. He began to doubt Frenkel. What if he had made the whole thing up? There was no world to save. There was no lover for Wallis other than the King. It was all a huge hoax concocted by the bored and bitter Frenkel. The seeds of doubt began to grow like a carefully nurtured plant. It grew and lived and looked like it was about to stay. Edward wanted to go back. He was alone and frightened here. Here, now, he could not even feel the presence of his mother. He was totally secluded. He concentrated on recovering. He ate the food placed in front of him and took the medicine that the doctor had prescribed. He made friends with the doctor and charmed some of the staff waiting on him. He began to move about the room and take gentle exercise. It was not long now before he would have to go outside. Outside into the unknown world. Like a foreign substance existing on unknown ground. He would have to leave the safety of his room. He began to realise how Frenkel must have felt for all those years, cooped up in one room, too frightened to venture out into the unknown. He braced himself and decided to take the plunge on the third morning after regaining consciousness. He had breakfast in his bed as usual and then asked one of the maids to accompany him in the garden. He also got one of the other maids to send a message to Mr Maybrick to inform him of his intention to take a stroll. After all, he was a guest, and he did not want to do anything without letting his host know what he was up to.

His stomach was turning, and he walked like an invalid. The air smelt different to him. He could feel the unknown. Almost smell the possible danger that lay for him outside. The people around him, the doctor, the maids, the manservant, Maybrick, they all came from a time that was not his and he could tell almost by their faces that they belonged here, but he did not. Their mannerisms and language were different. Their English that they spoke was totally different. It seemed almost too polite. There was no crudeness or rough words. He was almost frightened to swear openly in public. The fashion of the day was totally alien to him. The long coats and the hats worn by the men were definitely strange. It also seemed to be the fashion to keep facial hair. Moustaches seemed to be all the rage here. He was never used to pomp and ceremony and felt awkward in the presence of the servants, no matter how helpful they were. All these things he had to overcome. He had to act like he was a doctor of the day. A clever inventor of drugs and medical procedure or whatever. He had to fit in. In order to do that, he had to take his first stroll. He expected it to be a disaster. He expected to suffer much in the same way as Frenkel had done when he left his room for the first time, clinging to Edward as though he were a child.

However, all these anxieties were ill founded. He took the first few steps into the sunny garden, took in a whole lung full of air and seemed to be instantly intoxicated! The air! Wow! Fresh, clean, grassy smell. The sun shone brightly and the warmth of it engulfed him and gently ate away at his chills. The blanket covering him seemed unnecessary and he quickly handed it back to the maid. He walked gently all over the place with the little maid following him. He soaked up the flowers, the trees, the grass, the blue sky! Oh heaven! If there was such a thing. He walked to a bench and sat down, motioning the little maid to sit next to him. She was a little unsure. Sit on the bench with a nobleman? But she obeyed him and sat next to him still clutching the blanket. He rested his head back and closed his eyes. A silly grin on his face. He could get used to this, he thought. Yes. Frenkel must have it all wrong. There was no world to save. A world as beautiful and as resilient as this was always going to survive. It had special regeneration powers. Like Dr Who!

The maid sat next to him and watched him as he rested. At one stage she was certain that he was asleep, but she dared not wake him. She just sat there and wondered how long she was expected to sit there, keeping this man company. She was about to doze off herself when she saw Mr Maybrick walking towards them. She was immediately on her guard with an explanation ready as to why she was sitting there with Mr Hamilton. Maybrick walked up to them and looked at the little maid, still clutching the blanket. She immediately rose.

'Sir. He asked me to come walk with him and then he fell asleep,' she said defensively.

'It's aright Annie. Is he well? Did he struggle?'

'No Sir. He seemed excited but he got tired very quickly.'

'You may go.' Maybrick then gently sat down next to the sleeping man and watched him. His head was full of fears about how he should progress from here. He could not let this man loose since he knew too much. Truth of the matter was that Maybrick himself had been suffering the effects of narcotics. He knew what it was like to lose control of everything. He had no control over his own mind. Slowly but surely, his memory was also going. He had headaches and memory blackouts. He never knew what he did during these blackouts. He never knew whether he was awake or asleep. It frightened him and the way that Hamilton had described his own illness was very accurate. Maybe he was telling the truth. Maybrick tried to keep in mind that this was a sick man and he gained nothing by such a silly story. He sat and waited.

Edward eventually stirred and his head jerked to one side, waking him up. He looked round and was surprised. He sat up straight and pulled himself together.

'That's funny,' he grinned. 'I fell asleep next to beauty and woke up next to the beast!'

'Thank you, Mr Hamilton.'

'Look, whether I stay or not, can I please insist on you calling me Edward? Please.'

'Very well. But I insist on you calling me Mr Maybrick.' He said this with a slight smile which was reassuring for Edward. 'Whatever you say, Sir.'

'I take it that you are recovering well. You seem to have made good progress walking all the way here.'

'I feel so good. This is a fine place you have here. Exactly where is it?' He had hoped that Maybrick will accept his memory loss story and help him out.

'Liverpool. The house is called Battlecrease. That way is the cricket ground. Do you like cricket?'

'In my younger days, as a teenager I was a great fan of David Gower's. But I lost interest when England kept losing all the time.'

Maybrick stared at him as if the man had just spoken a foreign language. 'I'm sorry? Who's David Gower?' Edward realised his slip and started to laugh. He totally forgot himself for a second. 'What is a fan?' persisted Maybrick.

'Oh. Sorry. David Gower was a brilliant young player a few years ago but had to stop playing due to injury.'

'Did he play County cricket? Why have I not heard of him?'

'No, I think he did not make it to county cricket. I think he was a local hero in his local club,' said Edward, still trying to suppress his laughter. All this time he was thinking frantically. Liverpool! He was in Liverpool where he spent his university days. Could it all be linked? What was the possibility that of all the world, he would have landed in Liverpool?

'So, you do not remember your past?' said Maybrick quietly.

'I come from London. I am a Londoner. I do remember many things, but the memory comes and goes. I cannot explain it. You can either take my word for it or not.'

'Do not use the drug on me again.'

'I am sorry. I have no drug to use. I need to establish some equipment somewhere.' He paused before asking the next question. 'What is it that you are on?'

'What? What do you mean 'on'?'

'I mean, you are drug dependant, yes? I mentioned it before, and you did not deny it.'

'Not that it is any of your concern.'

'Fine.' Edward stayed silent. 'Strychnine.'

'*What?* Strychnine!' exclaimed Edward. 'And Arsenic.'

'Strychnine and Arsenic! Have you a death wish? They are deadly if administered wrongly!'

'I am aware of that, Mr Hamilton,' said Maybrick wearily. 'You must have severe side effects.'

'Maybe.'

'How on earth…'

'Malaria,' interrupted Maybrick. 'I travelled between America and England quite frequently. About… well it must be… about eleven or twelve years ago I contracted malaria. Quinine had no effect. Strychnine and Arsenic worked just fine.'

'Prescribed?' persisted Edward. 'Yes.'

'That is astonishing!'

'But that is common practise. Surely as a doctor you would know that.'

'Well, it's so ancient! I mean… so… well.' He had walked into another mistake.

'You are a doctor?'

'I know very little clinical medicine. I am a physiologist! I study anatomy of the human body!'

'You must have a job of some sort. What are your means?'

'I worked at the London Hospital in Whitechapel. However, erratic behaviour and an unholy alliance with a young female employee meant I had to move on!'

'So, what now?'

'Look, I just need to stay here for a while until I have my bearings. You have to understand, I had everything, money, a job and a career. It has all gone! All been destroyed by me. By my habit. You can refuse, but then you know what I will do. I hate to blackmail you like this, but I am a desperate man. I have to have help.'

'You need not resort to blackmail,' said Maybrick. 'If you are charming and polite, you are welcomed to stay. Just do not use that damned drug anymore.'

'I told you, I have none left.'

'I think it would be good idea if you went back and rested indoors. We don't want you over doing thing.' Then Maybrick rose and helped Edward back to the house and summoned a maid to help him to his room.

CHAPTER 19

Officially, Edward Hamilton was now a guest of the Maybrick family for an unspecified amount of time. He himself had expected a lot more resistance than this but it was soon obvious to him that all was not well with the Maybricks. He could not help noticing the age gap. She could easily pass off as his daughter or niece. Relations were a bit strained and this was apparent even in the presence of a third party, but they did both have their own work that kept them busy. Maybrick was not up to travelling to America to sort out that end of his business and he was busy making arrangements for his younger brother, Edwin to make the journey. Florence was planning her afternoon teas, her evening soirees and her candlelit dinners. Although she was polite to him whenever they met, she really was not too concerned about Edward. She made no attempt to talk to him or go with him round the ground or do anything expected of a hostess. She did not seem to mind him talking to the children and he did actually spend much of his afternoons playing with the children outside. They were young and at that age when one could interact with them without too many tantrums. The little girl Gladys was quiet and shy and was not too happy around the nanny, Alice. So, Edward sat with her and told her stories. He never had any contact with children in his own world. His came from a small family and since he had none of his own, he was learning new things with them now. He was enjoying himself at the same time and as each day went by, he began to develop a little routine of his own. He rose at a certain time and always had breakfast with the children. He then went for a stroll around the grounds but never ventured outside the perimeter of the house. He needed more courage for that! He then sat and read or dozed until lunchtime. In the afternoon he played with the children before having another snooze in the study with a book perched on his lap. He generally had dinner with the rest of the family but the last few days, Florence always had at least one other guest or couple for dinner.

Maybrick arranged for him to use some of his wardrobe but try as he may to really blend in, Edward always felt different. His features alone made him stand out. His dark, worn complexion and his short, dark cropped hair, minus facial hair was definitely unusual. He often found them staring at him, especially the women with Florence Maybrick being the worst offender. They probably found him exotic and attractive solely because he was different. Mrs Maybrick was almost obsessed with questions of the places he has visited. He never told her he had travelled but something about him convinced her that he was a well-travelled man. Edward back in his own time had not really travelled much as an adult at all. He remembered little from his family holidays with his parents and as an adult, most of his travelling involved work. Argentina and North America was about it. So, he had to make up stories about countries of the world that he had pretended to have visited. He became quite good at making up things as he went along, and his only problem was remembering what he had made up. In fact, remembering things in general became a problem. He would have to sit up in bed almost every morning and actively try to remember who he was and what he was doing. He remembered the Maybrick house and the dwellers in it. He remembered that in this time zone, he was in Liverpool. What he found difficult was to recall his mission here. What the purpose of his presence here was. Most of his memory was failing him where his other life was concerned. He remembered Frenkel and the Corporation, but he struggled to remember details. Frenkel's face was slowly becoming featureless and the conversations he had had were fading. He knew that time was short, but he did not have the will to try and achieve his aim. Besides, he was fast losing faith in Frenkel. The more he thought about it, the more he was convinced that Anthony Frenkel was a lunatic who had fooled everyone. He was no longer even certain about his 'powers'. Maybe it was all a hoax.

Certain things in this life made him remember things back home that he had totally forgotten. In the Maybrick household, having a bath was a major event. There were a number of servants involved with this process and having an impromptu wash was frowned upon. It had to be pre-planned and scheduled. The water was hot but not always as it should be. There were limitations on the type of soap and shampoos available. During one of these occasions, he suddenly remembered the fully automatic, adjustable and re-freshing showers he used to have at his flat that the Corporation had provided for him. The heated toilet seats and the running water with hundreds of soaps, gels and shampoos. One evening he drove himself crazy thinking about the things that he began to miss. The television, radio, electricity, mobile and videophones, fridge freezers. All these things which were taken for granted in his previous life were unheard of here. He tried to explain to Maybrick one day his vision of transport. He predicted that the world would be full of automobiles which ran on a fuel called petrol and that every working household would be able to own one. He was truly disappointed when Maybrick fell about in hysterics. The man never really showed much sense of humour and yet this amused him so much, he had tears running down his eyes and he had to leave the room. All the things which he thought about now almost drove him to the edge. He was desperately home sick even for the Corporation. There were times even Susan Preston's face would have been welcomed. However, if there was one thing he was doing well, it was making friends. He was charming and polite to all in the house and those visiting. As far as all were concerned, he was a friend of Maybrick's who had come for the entire summer and was unfortunate enough to have become ill at his guest's house. He had met two of Maybrick's brothers, Michael and Edwin and was becoming a familiar face. He could not understand how it was that a total junked up stranger could have found it so easy to establish himself in someone's house like this. He thought that Maybrick was gutless until he remembered that little blackmailing issue. He always thought about this with embarrassment. It was the only reason that Maybrick allowed him to stay at his home. Besides, Maybrick was a somewhat strict father. He showed very little affection towards his children and Edward thought that this was due more to Maybrick not having a clue how to interact with his children rather than not loving them. He was awkward around them and often he would go outside and sit and watch while Edward played with both of them. Recently, Edward noticed that Maybrick was looking unwell. It was not something concrete. Just paleness, tiredness and general raggedness which appeared on his face. He started to complain about headaches and often retired to his study mid- afternoon and was not seen by anybody again until the next morning. He spent much time away from home, mainly trying to deal with his business. Altogether, Edward thought he was strange man. Since allowing him to stay, Maybrick had never mentioned the subject of leaving the house. He did not ask any questions and generally acted like Edward was really a man whom he had known in his school days. Edward had slipped up once or twice when talking to Michael Maybrick, the elder brother. He had told him that he had been brought up in London and had never lived anywhere else. Considering that all Maybrick's education was in Liverpool, it begs the question as to how they have been school friends. But nobody seemed to have picked up on it and so Edward assumed that they generally could not care less and had just accepted his justification for being there.

One evening Maybrick entered his own study to find Edward already engrossed at the writing desk. Edward had begun his journal. He decided that his memory, being what it was, made it a necessity for him to record everything. He recorded his journey here and his purpose. He wrote as much as he could remember and also made a log of his progress in this world from a day-to-day basis. He was so engrossed in this work that he was not aware of Maybrick having entered the room. He was somewhat startled when Maybrick asked him if he wanted a sherry.

'What I could really do with is some G and T.' He saw the total blank look on Maybrick's face. He had forgotten himself again. Maybrick probably did not know what a G and T was!

Maybrick poured them both a sherry and then sat down. 'Mr Hamilton, you have a strange way of talking. You are not from this country at all are you?'

'I come from London, but I have travelled around.'

'You are a strange man. I wonder why I let you into my house at all.'

'Because you are bored with the people you have surrounding you and you want some intelligent male company.'

'You see what I mean. You have a strange way of talking,' said Maybrick. 'Your wife is a lot younger than you is she not?'

'What business is that of yours?'

'I'm just wondering what it is that you are unhappy about.'

'Unhappy?' Maybrick was astounded by Edward's directness. 'You have incredible audacity, Mr Hamilton.'

'Oh, for Heaven's sake, can you please call me Ed!'

'No. Not yet.'

'You still doubt me, don't you?'

'Wouldn't you? You are here out of blackmail.'

Edward paused. He took his pen and journal and put them away. He then relaxed back into the chair and spoke. 'What exactly happened.'

'You do not expect me to give you more blackmailing power, do you?'

'Look,' said Edward, 'you are a family man. You have children, a business, a small drug problem not to mention the few infidelities. One thing that does not fit is the murder bit. Now tell me exactly where that came into it. I already know so fill me in.'

'Fill you in?' asked Maybrick.

'Tell me what happened! Who was she? A mistress?'

Maybrick gave this question some thought. He had had a relatively bad day. There were a few complications where his business was concerned, and he had spent the day so far dealing with that. He had also found time to row with his wife and those headaches did not help much. He could have done without a huge confession now but instead of asking Edward to leave him alone. He found himself trying to find the right words to begin his explanation.

'I suppose I should start with my addiction since you have made so many references to it. I have been dependant for years and am taking doses that you would find astounding. I could seek help but then it is my only escape. I have children who are frightened of me, a wife who, due to our age difference, finds me old and boring, and a business that is running well, but needs my constant attention. The business is the only part of my life that I can control since I have family that will help with that. As you know, Edwin shall be leaving for Virginia in a few days to sort things out there. I really do not wish to give up the one thing that keeps me sane in all this.'

'But there must be side effects.' interrupted Edward. 'I suffer frequently from blankness.'

'What do you mean 'blankness'?' asked Edward.

'I mean just that. I cannot remember things. Sometimes I find it difficult remembering what I did for an afternoon or a morning. But what is odd is that I can remember almost everything in a single day except perhaps an hour here, or two hours there. When that happens, I cannot tell where I have been or what I have been doing. It is a total blankness.'

'You suffer from blackouts!'

'Call it what you will. I have already explained.' Maybrick was weary now but he felt already lighter when talking about his addiction. He had never spoken to anyone about it, not even his brothers. 'The blankness is getting worse and I think the headaches are due to that.'

'You need a brain scan. It may be a tumour or a '

'A what scan?' Maybrick was now puzzled.

'Well, you need ' Edward was thinking hard. Brain scans did not exist in this world!

'Well anyway, we will discuss that later, get on with your story.'

'It was during one of these blank periods last March that I think it happened. We had a row. She wanted to tell Florence. Tell Florence everything. She wanted to bring my whole world down.'

'So, she was a disgruntled mistress!'

'No! She was not my mistress! She was the friend of someone I have an alliance with! She was blackmailing me. She said she would tell Florence everything unless I paid her. She was a whore! She would do anything for money, and she tried to blackmail me. All I wanted was to try and explain things to her. There was a struggle and I pushed her. She fell and I could hear her scream. I then cannot remember anything! I found myself wondering around the place looking for my room.'

'Looking for your room?'

'I was on business in London. I have a room which I rent when I am there. I found myself lost and was trying to find my way back. I had no memory of anything! I remembered arguing but that was it. Next morning the news was that a woman had been killed. She had been knifed.'

'Knifed? Do you have a knife?'

'No.'

'Where you covered in blood?'

'No.'

'Then how do you know it was you?' asked Edward. 'We had had a row! I had a blank period! It all fits.'

'Fits! My arse!' Edward looked at Maybrick's face. He was not sure whether Maybrick was offended by the suggestion he had made or by his colourful language!

'Did they find fingerprints? persisted Edward, without thinking. 'Fingerprints? What the Devil are you talking about?'

Oh Shit! No fingerprints! When were they invented? Goodness, there would hardly be any forensics at all!

'Are you sure it was the same woman?'

'Of course, I am. She's was a friend of... well,'

'Of your mistress? Why do you have a problem saying 'mistress'? I mean you have admitted to having affairs.'

'Affair! Just the one. Just the one mistress! What do you think I am?' retorted Maybrick.

'Hey, calm down.' He saw Maybrick shifting uneasily in his chair and glancing at the door. 'Look, nobody can hear us! The door is thick and listening bugs have not been invented yet!'

'Listening what?

'Never mind,' said Edward. 'Just carry on.'

'Well, that is it. I cannot remember. I know only what I have read in the papers. That was in March and since then I have been living in Hell! Every knock on the door, every policeman in the street has me terrified. I haven't slept properly since it happened. How on earth can

I expect my wife to justify our existence when every time she looks at me, she is looking at a murderer!'

'Possible murderer, possible.'

'Mr Hamilton, you seem to have great faith in me.'

'It's got nothing to do with faith! Look at the evidence. You rowed. You pushed her. She fell. You cannot remember anything. She was knifed and yet you were not covered in blood. She was a prostitute. Say she fell but was not hurt! Say she got up, ran off and spent the rest of the evening *working*. Say it was someone else who attacked her. What time span are we talking about? What time did you push her and when was her predicted time of death?'

'Oh, I don't know. She was found cut up! That is all I know.' Maybrick was almost in tears.

'But you have to know! This is your life we are talking about! Do you not want to clear your name? You could be innocent?'

'But who is going to take this seriously? More to the point, how am I going to explain contact with a whore?' Maybrick was almost shouting and Edward had to motion to him to keep it down.

'Why the Devil should you care anyway?' growled Maybrick. 'If I was innocent of that crime, you would not have a handle to blackmail me!'

'I'm trying to help you, you ungrateful sod!'

The two men now stared at one another. Maybrick was confused. This crook that he had let into his house was now trying to prove his innocence. The stranger had more faith in him than he did himself. Why should he care? Why is the man so passionate about this? It was obvious that Edward Hamilton was no criminal. Sure, he did resort to blackmail, but maybe that just proves the story of him not really knowing where he belongs. Maybe he did create this drug and had lost his long-term memory. Maybe Edward Hamilton was telling the truth. Certainly, the man did have difficulty remembering things. The date was something he could not get into his head. The number of times he had to tell him exactly what year and month it was. Maybrick had got used being asked that question and just answered it every time. He had never tried to hurt or threaten anyone. He did not leave the house grounds so Maybrick knew that he never went out to take part in criminal activity. He was polite to all and although he had the most outrageous way of talking, he seemed educated. He was very good with the children and as of yet, had not seemed to notice that the lady of the house was young and attractive. He never seemed to take an interest in Florence Maybrick at all and never spoke to her unless she spoke to him first. He did not have difficulty with women because he seemed popular with the servants, male and female. Every now and again, he would go on about the future. Maybrick did not believe in such things but began to wonder whether he was psychic. He seemed obsessed with technology in the future. No, this was no criminal. That worried Maybrick even more. If the man was not there to 'rape and pillage' the household, then what was he there for?

'Okay. Let's change the conversation,' said Edward. 'I need some help from you.'

'Do you not think that perhaps I have helped you enough?'

'You do not have to help me any more than you have done. But my request is small.'

'Go ahead,' said Maybrick.

'You have a basement do you not?'

'Yes. It's small but we do have one. It is not being used for anything much.'

'Please, I need some equipment. I am wondering if you could help me.'

'What do you want,' Maybrick was on his guard now. What did the man want? 'I need a long table, some dissecting equipment and some laboratory mice.'

'Mice?'

'Or rats. I am not fussy.'

'Mr Hamilton, can you hear yourself? Do you have any idea what you have said?'

'I am a DOCTOR! I used to dissect animal all the time! Please.'

'You are going to generate that drug, aren't you? I told you not to do that. NO! You cannot have a laboratory in my basement.'

'Maybrick, you have no idea what I am going through. I will not use it on anybody. I promise.'

'But you did not ask my permission last time!' shouted Maybrick.

'No. But I promise, it is for my own personal use. Please. You must know what it is like. I am suffering! I need you to help me.' Edward was thinking how fortunate he was that James Maybrick was a drug addict. He decided now to blatantly use this weakness to get his own way. Not being in a laboratory setting was giving Edward withdrawal symptoms. He needed to relax. He wanted to carry on his search for the Soul. He knew what Maybrick was suffering and he used this. 'Look, you can evict me straight away if I do anything improper with anything, I do in the Lab. Please. You will not even know that I am down there! Please Maybrick. I am suffering here. Please!'

His pleadings just continued and became louder. He sounded desperate. Maybrick knew that he would give in. If he did not give in today, then maybe tomorrow, or the day after. He could evict him now, but he thought that would be dangerous.

'What *exactly* do you need, Mr Hamilton?'

CHAPTER 20

In many ways, the presence of a third person in the house made things easier for Florence Maybrick. He helped ease the tension between her and James. The most advantageous part of it was that he was very good with the children. Her son aged four had been poorly in the last year with Scarlet Fever and he needed exercise and building up. He was not one of those children always running around and jumping over things. Florence wanted him to be more active and it was just good timing that Edward Hamilton was on hand and that he did not mind spending time with him. The boy had started to enjoy the outdoors and was much more interactive than he had been before. As for her shy little girl, Florence made a good effort herself to bring the child out of her shell, but Gladys seemed to respond to Edward in way that Florence had not seen before. She enjoyed the quieter side of life. She like to sit and scribble or, listen to someone reading to her. Being a young child, she was not long in Edward's company before she wanted her mother. But the general effect of Edward's presence was good for the children. Florence had just accepted Edward as being James' friend. She was not too keen on entertaining him. He seemed to do that himself, but she eased the pressure on James about him staying the whole season. Florence had noticed that James' health had been suffering more than usual. He kept complaining about headaches and was not away from home as often as he used to be.

It was the latter part of July and garden party season. Florence always had her fair share of events, despite James' reluctance. She was waiting until such time that Edward had totally recovered and could meet the guests. The chosen day was blessed with glorious sunshine and all had gone to plan. The servants and the lady of the house were running around preparing things and amongst all that activity was James. He was dreading the event but had accepted that it was taking place. He just swanned around in a world of his own. Edward just wondered around and watched. This was the life! Lovely house, lovely weather, lovely wife and children! Edward was beginning to envy all this. He took a long stroll around the garden and generally prepared himself. Maybrick had given him some clothes which were then accordingly altered to fit him. The days in the garden during these summer months had given Edward the most wonderful tan and he was looking fit and healthy. He took in the air and enjoyed the atmosphere as the guests began to arrive one by one. He revelled in the fact that most of them found him fascinating! He noticed many of the women could not take their eyes off him! He had made no attempt at all to grow facial hair or to look like the men around him. In fact, the truth was, Edward found it hard to remember that he was not from this age. Each day that went by resulted in his memory fading. He had his academic abilities, but he had begun to forget about the Corporation. He had already forgotten Susan and the President. Frenkel was just a blur and he could not remember exactly what was so important about him. When he really tried, he remembered that he was not of this time, but he could not remember how much from the future he was. He should have been worried, but he had forgotten the main purpose of him being here. He was blending into his surrounding and was happy with things as they were. Right now, he was blending in with the Maybrick's guests. There were children all over the place and the food was artistically displayed on the tables. He spoke to Michael Maybrick for a while but recently, Michael had started to ask questions about Edward's past. Edward found it uncomfortable talking to him, so he avoided a long discussion on anything. He had already slipped up a couple of times when talking to Michael and he did not want to make too many mistakes. He then went and spoke to Edwin Maybrick. In a couple of days, Edwin would be off to America. The Maybrick children were eventually allowed into the garden and they immediately made a bee line for Edward, which made both Mrs and Mr Maybrick a little jealous. It was normal for children when faced with a crowd of strangers to seek one of their parents. Edward was delighted to see them and immediately planted himself at a table and sat down with them, ready to entertain. He was well aware that many of the guests were intrigued by his presence. Hardly anybody spoke to him much.

Eventually, Maybrick walked up to him with another man. Edward knew that he was about to be introduced to a doctor. The man looked like a doctor. Or was Edward just stereotyping him? Alice, the children's nanny immediately appeared out of nowhere and whisked them away.

'Edward,' said Maybrick putting his arm on Edward's shoulder. 'I want you to meet my friend, Nathaniel Grey. Doctor Nathaniel Grey. Nathaniel, this is the fellow I was telling you about. Edward Hamilton. Also, a Doctor.'

The two men shook hands and exchanged pleasantries. There was some polite chatter and then Maybrick made a move to leave the two men together.

'So, Dr Hamilton.'

'Please, call me Edward,' interrupted Edward in the vain hope that someone may actually listen to him.

'Edward. James tells me that you are staying here for the entire season.'

'Yes. I am an idle dog and have nothing else to do!' The doctor paused for a few seconds as if surprised, but then suddenly burst out in laughter.

'James also tells me that you wish to set up some equipment in his basement! That is quite extra ordinary. What do you hope to do?'

'I study anatomy. I was extracting some steroids from animals and I would like to carry out some small experiments.'

'Fascinating! Shall I just call you Victor?' Edward was frowning now. He looked at the Doctor quizzically. 'As in Victor Frankenstein?' The Doctor was laughing. Great, thought Edward, at last someone with a sense of humour. They both laughed together, and Edward felt at ease.

'I'm afraid I haven't quite mastered the art of making monsters out of dead human parts! But I do know how to clone a human!'

'Clone? What do you mean?'

'I mean… well, there is a way that you could, in theory, make a human without the normal human reproductive process.'

Then Nathaniel laughed. 'James warned me you had a strange way of speaking! What kind of a doctor are you?'

'I am physiologist. Academic. What about you?'

'I am a General Practitioner.'

'You are from London?'

'Yes. I have my own practise. I used to work for a friend of my father's. You may have heard of him. Sir William Gull?' Nathaniel waited for a response.

'I'm sorry,' said Edward in embarrassment. 'You must think me ignorant.'

'Not at all. I was just showing off! How can I help you set up a laboratory in James's basement?'

'Well, all I really need is a Bunsen burner, some dissecting equipment, ether and… of course, mice. Maybe an old microscope. Is that too difficult? Have Microscopes been invented yet?'

'Well of course they have! You are a strange fellow.! Do you need the mice to be alive?'

'No. Not really.'

'Well, let's see.' Nathaniel then started to think. He eventually spoke up. 'I think I should be able to send you most the equipment that you want. That will not be a problem but there will be a financial side to the mice. Also, the equipment I send may not be too brilliant.'

'Fine. That should be fine. I shall arrange the finance through James.' Edward seemed delighted. Nathaniel Grey was one of first people he had met who had not treated him like a freak. He spoke to him like he was a real person.

'Have you ever been to London?' asked Nathaniel. 'I was born there.'

'So, you spent your childhood in Liverpool?'

'Yes.' Edward remembered just in time that he was supposed to be Maybrick's school friend. He decided not to elaborate too much on his background. He was not aware of what Maybrick had told the doctor.

'What about your work. Do you have a career?'

'It is on temporary hold. In fact, I have got myself in a tricky situation. I am here as a guest but am not in employment. I shall have to look for something.'

'But why are you in that situation? You are young and educated.'

'Well. Yes. But also, dependant on certain substances. The bane of my life!' Edward decided to stick to that story, hoping that sympathy would be enough to get him through.

'So, you have much in common with our friend James!' Nathaniel obviously was a very good friend. Even the Maybrick brothers were not aware of James' addiction.

'Well, I have no job! So, I suppose I am running on charity!'

'Look. I have known James for many years. He is one of my closest friends. I think I can trust you.' Nathaniel Grey was a very astute man and was good at separating the rot from the rest. He was taking a gamble now. 'I have connections. How about you come to London. I have a banker friend that I could recommend you to.'

Edward was stunned at the suggestion. 'What exactly are you suggesting?'

'Well. You need capital, yes?'

'Well, yes! But what happens if I can't pay?'

'We'll think about that when the time comes! You can't let something as small as that get the way of pleasure!'

Edward chuckled 'You know, you would have been a huge success during Thatcher's boom and bust era!'

'Boom and bust?'

Edward's smile faded. Boom and bust? Thatcher? That was a memory which suddenly burst into his head. Why did he say that? Who was Thatcher? The term boom and bust was so familiar! He suddenly realised that he did not know what he was talking about! Nathaniel immediately noticed the change and asked him if he was fine.

'Kind of. I… struggle with my…'

'I'm sorry. I am prying now.'

'No that is OK.'

Just at that stage two women came up to the doctor full of smiles and cheers and from their reaction and conversation, Edward guessed that the doctor was a bachelor! There was a lot of that going on. Women looking and giggling. The whole point of these events for women is to find out which people have money, which have no money, and which have no money but do have good connections. The richest single men had to endure swarms of people and hardly said a few words to anybody before being whisked away to talk to someone else. Of course, not everyone who wanted could talk to these eligible men. Those who were not so luck had to make do with fairly rich. Edward observed again. He watched the young ladies, guided by their beady eyed mothers. Among the men there was much talk about the politics of the day. Edward was constantly in fear that someone may come up to him and start talking about the politics of the day, or some other topical conversation and he would have no idea what he was talking about. He did notice that the only person looking stiff and uncomfortable was James Maybrick. He walked around introducing people and generally making sure that all was well with the catering and the drinks. But generally, he looked as if he wanted all these people to go away. He sat on a table by himself. Edward walked up to him and sat down.

'Hey, thanks. That doctor fellow is fab! I liked him.'

'Good.'

'What's the matter? Are you OK?'

'I have a slight problem in that my house has been invaded by gold-diggers and would-be wives and so-called gentlemen. Nobody is here without a purpose. Except for Nathaniel. He is a capital fellow.'

'But social activity is important! You are a businessman, and you have to do things like this. It certainly has brought out the sunshine in your wife,' said Edward glancing at the radiant Mrs Maybrick. 'She does not normally smile, does she?'

'One can only smile if given something to smile about,' said Maybrick also looking at his wife. She was talking to a family friend Alfred Brierly.

'What on earth threw the two of you together? I mean, you must have had something in common.'

'Yes. Money. I had it and she wanted it.'

'Oh come! That cannot be it.'

'It sounds shallow. But women these days rule their lives solely on marrying well. Why else would a young eighteen-year-old American marry a forty something cotton merchant!'

'Well, I can't see that she proposed to you!'

'No. I suppose I did. She was so beautiful and charming. Funny how the thought of money brings out the charm! I was lonely. We met on a ship. SS Baltic. Her mother was horrified! She cried nonstop at the wedding!'

While James was prattling on like this, Edward could not help noticing that Florence Maybrick had that look in her eye. That glint, that tiny sparkle which not many men ever saw. She was not just radiant; she was glowing with affection. Edward was no expert but to him, Florence Maybrick was in love. That look was only visible when women in love were looking at their heroes. Her passion, her adoration and her attention were there, naked, on her face, in her eye for all to see. There could not be a woman present here that did not notice that Florence was in love with the man she was now looking at! Seeing that Florence and James were about five tables and twenty people away from one another, the object of her affection was not Maybrick. Well, thought Edward. She's a dark horse. He looked at the young man she was looking at. Smart, elegant and probably rich. Edward immediately looked at Maybrick and found that even though he frequently glanced in that direction, it was possible that Maybrick was not aware of this. It was quite possible that Maybrick was the only man there who could not have noticed this. Edward himself figured it out in seconds. How could it be that Maybrick could not see it! Flirting openly with this man and Maybrick was blind to it! They were now accompanied by the other two Maybrick brothers.

'James,' said Edwin. 'I am to leave tomorrow but it will be early, and I have to visit someone now. I will not see you again after today. I shall be in constant contact.' The two men discussed final arrangements and then embraced before the younger man took his leave.

'Michael, could you not please find a way to tell these people to go home?' said a tired Maybrick.

'James! As social as ever! You are on top form today!' mocked Michael.

'Yes well, this is more your scene is it not?'

'Look at Florence, James. Do you not think she looks ravishing! It is good for her to circulate!' Edward wondered whether Michael was not trying to attract James' attention to Florence's indiscretion. He was a nasty piece of work!

'Michael,' interrupted Edward, 'your brother has never mentioned your profession. I think you are a singer, yes?'

'A what!' exclaimed Michael. 'Mr Hamilton, there is a difference between a singer and a musician! A singer describes the crude rantings of a down and out in a pub somewhere. A musician is someone who is learned and accomplished enough to be performing at the court of Queen Victoria herself!'

'Queen Victoria! Of course!' Edward had again forgotten where he was! Yes. Queen Victoria! The monarch of the day! Good Lord! His reaction was such that Michael Maybrick thought he was being mocked.

'Mr Hamilton. You are bordering on the rude!'

'I apologise, Sir. That was not my intention.' James Maybrick made no attempt to join this conversation.

'You have performed for the Queen! That is fantastic.'

'I happen to be a good friend! I often liaise with Eddie.'

'Eddie?' asked Edward.

Michael was getting a little annoyed. 'The Duke of Clarence! Do you not know anything!'

'I am sorry again. What it is to be on first name terms with royalty!' added Edward sarcastically. He decided he did not like Michael Maybrick at all.

'I suppose that makes you famous,' added Edward.

'I am in demand! I am giving concerts to the most accomplished and may even be going abroad. I am amazed that you have not heard of me!' Michael Maybrick obviously was a stranger to modesty.

'So, you are a popstar! Like Kylie Minogue!'

'What the Devil are you talking about!' shouted Michael angrily, while Edward again tried to remember where exactly that name and memory came from? Kylie Minogue. Who on earth was she?

'Michael, please remember you are in public!' said James.

'I NEVER forget I am in public. I am always in public. My life centres around projecting my image! This man you call your *guest* is an imbecile!'

'That is enough!' rasped James. 'He is my guest, and you shall treat him so.'

'Mr Maybrick,' said Edward. 'I am sorry. My language is different from yours, being less well educated than yourself. Please accept my apologies.'

'What is a damned popstar?' shouted Michael.

'It's a slang term used to describe a popular performer. I suppose it's not a widely used term!'

'Popstar? Popular performer? Well, I suppose that is not so insulting. Popular you say?' He seemed to be pacified by that one word. He kept repeating it to himself.

Edward had been entertained enough for one day. He had watched the lovely Mrs Maybrick wearing her heart on her sleeve, watched the aloof Mr Maybrick trying to appear invisible, accepted an offer of financial help from a total stranger and managed to annoy the narcissistic Michael Maybrick! He was almost constantly chuckling to himself for the rest of the day. Now he walked off and found a bench to doze off on. He had some odd glances from people who thought it was rather bad mannered to sleep on a bench like a vagabond. But Mrs Maybrick was beyond noticing and Mr Maybrick was beyond care. So, Edward slept.

CHAPTER 21

Nathaniel Grey had started to accomplish his task. He had been briefed by Maybrick to make friends with Edward and to try and get close to him. Maybrick had asked him to find out exactly who Edward was and where he was from. Maybrick had told him the whole truth about how he had met Edward and under what circumstances he was staying in the house, except that the unfortunate prostitute was not dead, but merely assaulted. They were friends but Maybrick could not confess to the murder. He knew that Nathaniel would be repulsed by that. So, Nathaniel Grey went to work. He found Edward a pleasant enough chap with a strange way of talking. He was not meant to offer any financial aid, but he thought that the one way to get close to someone and gain their trust was to offer help when that person was in need. Edward Hamilton admitted he was in need and the doctor decided to provide him with help. In order to truly find out who this man was, he and Maybrick would have to cover the loan themselves. He had made that clear to Maybrick.

Within a few days of the garden party, the basement in Maybrick's house was cleared and Nathaniel had sent a Bunsen burner, a distilling flask with holder and a well-used dissecting set. But the piece of equipment that sent him into hysterics was the 'state of the art' microscope. Edward was sure he had seen it at the Science Museum in 1984! He had also included a small collection of scientific literature. Edward was overcome with excitement. A laboratory! In the basement! This was fantastic. He could explore the mammalian body again! From deep, dark recesses of his mind he remembered his search for the Soul! Yes! The Soul. It must be something that can be seen with the naked eye! Maybe it was an organ. Of all the things that his brain had forgotten, he remembered his obsession with the Soul! He was going to carry on his work. He spent hour upon hour setting things up and updating his journal. During this time, he was even taking his meals in the basement and saved Florence from having to see him! She was relieved at this. She had not failed to notice that since the garden party, he always looked at her with a mocking smile. He knew! He must be the Devil himself! He knew that which her husband was thankfully too blind to see. She did not think at all that she had been blatantly obvious in her reaction, but Edward knew. Yes, Florence was glad that Edward had found a knew interest in the basement!

Within a few days, the mice began to arrive! He was on cloud nine! He started his work. He had forgotten how relaxing this was! This was the only part of his former life which he had still retained in this world, although by now, he had totally forgotten his origin. He knew not from where he came and really started to believe that he had taken drugs which affected his mind. He began to believe that he was of this time period. He kept having flashes during which time he would suddenly remember a face, a word, a saying. Some things took him away entirely and for a brief moment, he remembered everything only to forget it a few seconds later. He was in turmoil as far as his head was concerned but he was happy to exist as he had been. Maybrick had come to protect him like he really was a friend. He spent all his waking hours looking for the Soul! The animals could not come fast enough for him. At first, every cut he made was just to explore and examine every specimen properly. He would come across necrosis, tumours, inflammation, organ failure. All sorts of things and he would study these animals for hours. The microscope was the pride and joy of all his apparatus. It was one of these old-fashioned ones for which you needed an external light source. Edward studied one animal for hours. It had leukaemia and the cell morphology fascinated him. Suddenly all his academic knowledge came back to him and he remembered leukaemia. In a flash he remembered Juhi. Lovely, swarthy, exotic Juhi. Her face suddenly flashed in his mind and a pain hit him. He dropped what he was doing and fell to the floor. Lovely Juhi. He had hidden her deep, deep at the back of his mind.

A memory too painful for him to think of. Her face, her name, her scent, he spent month after month learning how to eradicate her from his mind. Every little memory had to be forgotten. The walks in the park, the dinners, the nights in, the romancing and finally, the big day. He even remembered the date which never came. The big day that never was. The one true love of his life. Acute Myeloid Leukaemia. The cells proliferated and swamped her bone marrow. They totally overwhelmed her and spilled into her circulation. They infected every nook and cranny. They eventually killed some of her major organs. It devoured her and eventually, wrung out her very life, her very Soul. He even remembered the ceremony her parents had of releasing her Soul from her earthly remains. Yes. The Hindus believed in the Soul. The Soul reborn! Recycled! Now he remembered his fascination with the Soul. He was looking for Juhi. His lovely Juhi. Hour after hour he sought that which he knew was almost impossible.

Edward Hamilton's memory was not the only thing to leave him. His sanity seemed to be withering as well.

One evening, he sat there in the basement, exhausted. He had been working for hours and Nathaniel had sent some more laboratory equipment. He had spent ages cleaning it and setting it up. Now he was weary and closed up for the day. He was on his way to his room when Maybrick jumped out of his study and asked him in for a port. He accepted.

'Do you not think you are working too hard?' said Maybrick. 'If I could keep awake 24 hours a day, I would!'

'You obviously find your work fascinating. Have you managed to extract the drug?'

'What drug?' Edward had forgotten. He tried hard to recall which drug he was meant to be extracting.

'The one that makes you forget!'

'Oh no! No, I have not. But I am working on it. I do not have all the equipment I need for it. But I will get there in the end.'

'I have a proposal for you. Nathaniel, as you know, lives in London. I think I have already mentioned that I have accommodation in London.'

'Yes. You have.'

'Well, I visit usually at the end of each month and stay for about one or two weeks. I was wondering whether you would like to come with me.'

Edward hesitated. The idea was interesting, but he was not sure. He wanted to visit London but also wanted to carry on his work here. His hesitation was noticed by Maybrick.

'You were born there. Surely you would like to visit.'

'Yes, but I am so busy.'

'Nathaniel has sent you a lot of equipment. It would be nice if you personally accepted his invitation to call on him. Also, I think there is a little matter of that financial help that he offered you.'

'Oh yes! I had forgotten about that.' Edward began to think.

'Look,' said Maybrick, 'I am in Whitechapel between July 25th and 11th August. If you would like to come, let me know and I can make the arrangements.' He rose as if to go when Edward suddenly shot out from his seat.

'*Whitechapel?* WHITECHAPEL!' Suddenly, a whole host of images and memories stormed his mind. There was a man and woman and some school friends. Yes! He remembered his childhood in Whitechapel. In an instant he remembered that it was a totally different time zone! Yes! Whitechapel had been his childhood home! He also remembered his University years. Nicole flashed across his face although he could not think of her name! The Professor! Yes. His face came to him. He must go there. This was a clue to his past. His home!

'I'll come.'

Maybrick stood there looking at him. 'Maybe it will be good for you to get away from here. London is your home. You may remember things. I shall make the arrangement. We shall take the train on the 25th which is the day after tomorrow.'

The next day and night were troublesome for Edward. In a short space of time, a whole collection of images from his past had come to him. Some of these had already faded but now he could remember where he came from. He had no preparations to make. Maybrick handled everything for him down to his luggage which the servants organised. Edward did not have to think about anything!

The journey was uneventful. Maybrick slept most of the time. He was looking unwell again and Edward was wondering whether he should get Nathaniel Grey to examine James. He must see to that. On arriving in London, they continued their journey in a Hanson coach. When Maybrick described his accommodation as a room, he was not joking. It really was just a room which was attached to a house. The room had an entrance of its own but was actually part of the house it was attached to. The entrance gave Maybrick privacy. The rest of the house was also let out. Maybrick told him that the landlord owned other properties in the area but did not actually live there himself. It was basic. A bed, a sofa, table and chair. A small sink at the far end. It was clean and well placed. Maybrick had arranged for an extra mattress to be laid out there for Edward. They dined out for the first night at Maybrick's club and did not meet anyone. They then retired and slept soundly until morning.

Edward was woken early the next morning by Maybrick. At first, the sight of the room was a bit of a shock. Maybrick had to explain to him where they were. They rose, dressed and then went. The first stop was for breakfast which again, they had at Maybrick's club. One or two men came over to briefly talk to Maybrick, but Edward spent most of the time trying to find things that may be familiar to him. So far, nothing triggered his memory. Maybrick had connections here with his business. This was a vital link to his cotton business and he actually had work to do. After breakfast, they walked. It was a fine bright summer's morning but being very early, there was a cool chilly breeze in the air. They walked briskly to the docks. Most of this area was mainly docks. Busy, bustling even at this time of the morning. There were shipments here from all over the world. Mahogany from Cuba and Honduras, wood from Burma, tea and spices from the Asian countries, tobacco and cotton from America, coal mainly from Newcastle. The place was teaming with people and at its busiest was a huge collection of noise. There was plenty of manual work here for those with enough stamina and these men stood here now, at this early hour to queue for work. They were tired looking men, obviously they had already put in a good day's work the previous day, and with minimal sleep wherever they could find a comfortable bed for the night and probably with empty stomach's these men stood here for work. Edward was informed by Maybrick that the work here was allocated on a day-to-day basis. It was rare for labourers to be taken on permanently. They had to queue every morning to see what work they could do. If any. The queue was long, and the men looked weary and miserable. Edward asked what the wage was but Maybrick made no answer. The question was answered by his silence. Maybrick knew that these men earned barely enough to buy themselves a basic meal for the day, and if they were lucky, they had enough left over for a bed. That was their day, their life. Day to day, hand to mouth. They came up to a point where Maybrick left Edward behind and he himself went to talk to some other men. Edward watched him as he went. A well-dressed man, well- groomed and obviously with means, talking to other well dressed and well-groomed men, also with considerable means. Extreme poverty alongside affluence. Neither one able to exist without the other. Maybrick eventually came to Edward and explained that he would be some time. He wanted to know if Edward would be OK by himself for a while. Edward could not wait to stroll around and see what he could soak up. Maybrick's concern was unfounded. They arranged to meet up again at docks in an hours' time.

Edward turned around and started walking the way that he had come. He passed the line of dockers, still waiting to be allocated jobs. He now noticed their dirty faces, their torn shirts and some of them stood there barely with their shoes covering their feet. Were these family men or those on the edge of non-existence? Some of them were lucky. They had already been given jobs to do, but for every man who was given work, at least three others were joining the queue. Edward felt awkward. His own attire and well-groomed appearance were out of place here. He walked as fast as he could to try and get out of this dock area. The pungent smell of tobacco and spices was getting right up his nose!

He turned down many streets and noticed that generally things were waking up. He also noticed the number of people littered all over the pavement. Suddenly an image rushed into his head of a cold, wet and miserable morning outside Warren Street station being attacked by a vagrant begging for money. But here, the vagrancy seemed extreme. Some of them had an ounce of grey matter left in their heads and used their dwelling to accost passers-by like himself and to try and entice them with home-made trinkets and jewellery or cloths. But generally, they were just there. Waking up to another day of need. The noise of the dockers was fading as he walked only to be replaced by another noise that he could not place. He followed it and found himself standing outside a slaughterhouse. Well, he guessed that was what it was. There were pigs and cattle he could see being led there by weary men. There were men coming out every now and again with their aprons covered in blood. Right next to this hellish building was a warehouse sort of place. Edward peered in and was shocked at the sight. Scores of women and children, some of them really very young, heads down making sacks. The sort that potatoes used to come in. Their faces were also dirty and tired. There was no laughter in the children, no time to play. Just following the actions of their mothers. This has to be illegal surely, thought Edward. What he was unaware of was that these women with their dirty little offspring were the fortunate ones since they earned a few shillings doing their task, and they were indoors, in the shelter. They would at least have some money for some mouldy bread and maybe even some soup. Edward moved away from this area and continued to walk. The early morning market was already in full swing. Edward walked past another small building which was full of women shelling peas. One little child popped a pea into her mouth only to be beaten by her angry mother. How much money could they earn shelling peas? The market was full of pungent smells. Fish and meat mainly. The noise was tremendous. All along the streets there were shops and buildings offering menial, manual work. Sewing here, peeling there, lifting there, mending and packing at another place. In all these places one could see women and children. There were a few men around the place, but Edward assumed that the strongest were back at the docks, waiting for heavy work. This must end soon thought Edward. There must come a street eventually that was free from such need.

The entire area that he was in was full of work of the lowest kind and people of the same type. The houses in the area seemed full of people, all crammed inside. Being a warm day the children who were not working were pouring out into the street, running around and grabbing every opportunity to steal. All this was happening right under his very nose! And not a policeman in sight. Somehow, even the thought of capture and arrest seemed cruel. These people had so little, how could you take petty crime away from them? Crazy, thought Edward, crazy. A far cry from the garden parties at Battlecrease. The wants and needs of the Maybrick household seemed trivial compared to the needs he saw in these people.

He came from here. He had memories of his childhood. He tried hard to find something here linked to his younger days but nothing. All this poverty and deprivation, he could not remember seeing it before. As the day started, the undesirables disappeared. The market was in full swing and the workhouses and slaughterhouses were busy, but those with nowhere to go could not be seen.

Edward met up with Maybrick at the assigned time and place and the rest of the day was taken up with lunch, more walking and a rest back at Maybrick's club. For a busy businessman, Maybrick tended to keep himself very much to himself. He spoke to few and even then, never pleasantries and small talk. It was always business and straight to the point. Edward just followed him. He felt protected when he was with Maybrick. When the evening came, they prepared to dine with Nathaniel Grey. Edward was relieved when Maybrick told him he had arranged a coach.

CHAPTER 22

I t was very late into the evening. The meal was settling in their stomachs, being washed down by port. And plenty of it. It blended in well with the wine that had accompanied the food. Now, they sat around a cheerful fire. The hot day had given rise to a fine night, but the chill was beginning to set in. The men laughed aloud and spoke in loud tones. They were comfortable with one another and anyone listening to them could have believed that they had known each other for years. No one could have guessed that one was a successful doctor who spent his evenings talking to 'daughters of the night', the other a successful merchant hooked on strychnine and the third came from over one hundred years in the future and was now hooked on searching for the human Soul.

Edward saw a side of Maybrick that he had not seen yet. A relaxed and happy man. Laughing, enjoying himself and totally at his ease with the company around him. At the same time, Edward was aware that these two men really were very good friends. From their conversation it was obvious to Edward that they wanted to find out more about his background. They did not ask anything direct, but their mode of questioning certainly had him on his guard. Having said this, he was not angry. He really like Nathaniel and was interested in listening to his going on about the politics of the day. Edward was learning a lot. Although he was happy now, he had not forgotten the misery he had seen earlier in the day. He could still remember the faces of some of the dockers, and the little girl severely reprimanded for popping a pea into her mouth. He could not remember seeing such poverty ever in his life. There must have been times when his eyes wondered off to some other place, for Nathaniel made a comment.

'Edward, you seem a little troubled. Is anything the matter?'

'No… well. You know…' he seemed lost.

'What is the matter?'

'You know how it is,' interrupted Maybrick, 'we all accept that poverty exists and are unaffected until we are exposed to it!'

'Poverty?' exclaimed Nathaniel. 'What on earth are you talking about?' Edward was embarrassed. 'It's nothing really. I just found it all a bit difficult.'

'What difficult?' Nathaniel persisted.

'How can you not be concerned?' asked Edward. 'There are people out there who are struggling to find their next meal!'

Nathaniel screwed up his eyes and stared very hard at Edward. 'There will always be poverty. There will always be people who do not have things. That is nothing new.'

'I have never seen it concentrated in such a small area.'

'But you are a traveller! You claim to have visited many exotic and *poor* countries!' mocked Nathaniel. 'Surely poverty in other countries is much worse than what you see in London.'

'Well maybe that is what I cannot understand. This is England! We are a first world country! We have a democracy, wealth, a well-equipped army! We have conquered many! We bloody well won two world wars! Granted we would not have won the second world war without America, but we played a huge part in world peace!'

There was a short pause. 'World wars?' after a long silence, Maybrick had been compelled to question Edward. Then Edward remembered, the World Wars had not happened yet!

'Well, you know what I am saying,' Edward hoped that they would just assume he was prattling on with alcohol running through his veins!

'What was that about America?' asked Maybrick. Edward declined to answer. 'You know Edward, sometimes you talk as if you are not with the rest of us!'

Edward laughed out loud. 'Finally! You did it finally!' he shouted at Maybrick. 'Did what?'

'You finally called me EDWARD!' And he laughed heartily, hoping that the men had been diverted enough to start another topic of conversation.

'Poverty and the poor are nothing new and will always exist. The facts surrounding the riots last year in Trafalgar Square surely could not have escaped your memory,' said Nathaniel.

'Riots?' questioned Edward.

'Mr Hamilton,' said Nathaniel, 'where on earth are you from? How can you not know about the events of last year?'

'Nathan, Edward's memory is not what it should be,' said a protective Maybrick. 'Well, let me fill you in. Unemployment, prostitution, poverty, scarcity of food, starvation and a very cold winter resulted in the most violent riots in London for years. The whole country was on the side of the rioters. Men, women and children should not have to endure such extreme conditions. Have you ever been through the East End at night? You should. That is the real picture of how these people live. Overcrowded houses, families, quite large ones, existing in one room, giving rise to bad sanitation and incest. Offspring being born with severe defects due to being inbred. Can you imagine, being born to parents who are related by blood? A child surviving beyond its first year is lucky! But this is reality! Life as it exists. We cannot ignore it. It is existing. We can try to help it. But we cannot stop living ourselves because of it!' Nathaniel Grey's voice was full of emotion as he concluded his speech. 'You shall come with me, Edward. I believe James is otherwise occupied tomorrow evening. I shall take you to the heart of poverty.'

'I do not think that is necessary,' said Edward.

'We have to face up to reality!' exclaimed Nathaniel. 'You have to face up to this. You cannot pretend that it does not exist! The Soul! You said you wanted to find the Soul! It does not exist among those who are not in need! They have no need for the Soul! They have wealth! The real Soul you will find among the needy! You want to find the Soul? You will, in the slums of the East End.'

Twenty-four hours later, they were in the slums. Nathaniel seemed to know the area and its inhabitants fairly well. They sat in a pub. Edward had memories of pubs coming into his head. They were very similar to the scene he saw now. The place was full of men, labourers they looked like. Some had meals with their beer and others just sat talking or drinking. The atmosphere was quite social and as the hours wore on, rowdiness set in. There were women here as well, but something told Edward that these were not the wives and girlfriends of the men. Some sat in groups of women, some sat with the men folk. Edward felt comfortable here. Nathaniel seemed to know the owner and some of the people who sat around them. There were no airs and graces around him. At one stage, one woman came over to him with an ailment. Nathaniel immediately took her to a quiet spot and Edward could see him peering down her throat. He wrote down something on a piece of paper and gave it to her. She looked as pleased as punch and thanked him many times. He was from a different world to these people, but now, at this time, he was part of their world. He mixed in and blended with these surroundings and he seemed to command a certain amount of respect from these people. Edward was sure that Nathaniel regularly helped those in particular need with small amounts of money. They had been there about an hour, talking, chatting and generally becoming very merry. Eventually Nathaniel called over a woman. Emma.

'Emma my dear, meet my friend Edward.'

She sat down with them. Her clothes, although fairly clean, were a mishmash of colours and seemed like she was wearing layer upon layer of clothes. Her ginger hair was long and tangled but put up in a tight bun at the back of the head. Her face was clean, but she had teeth missing and she looked very pale and freckled. The most striking part of her was her eyes, clear light blue. Under different circumstances, this could have been a lovely young girl sitting opposite him, but all Edward saws was a dishevelled looking woman who from a distance looked much older than she really was. She sat there chatting away and being generally pleasant. She seemed to know Nathaniel really well.

'Emma, what did you eat today?' asked Nathaniel like an adult would to a child.

'Well, sir, I was lucky today,' she said. 'I had enough left from the day gone and I 'ad a bun!'

'Did you have enough for some butter on that bun?'

'No, sir. Just the bun.'

'And what time were you working until last night?' She hesitated and looked nervously to Edward. 'It's all right, Emma. This is a friend.'

'Why all the questions?' she asked slightly aggressively.

'I am studying the current diet of people generally. People like yourself. You only rarely get a full meal. I am trying to study the effect it has on your body.'

Emma looked at him and seemed to be pacified by this. 'Oh. Well, I was out until… maybe 3.00am.'

'And you had lodgings?' asked Nathaniel.

'Yeah! Business is good in this weather. I had some left as I say already.'

'Are you fixed for lodgings tonight?' said Nathaniel digging into the pocket of his jacket.

'Yes, sir.'

'Well buy yourself a meal with this then, Emma,' he said bringing out some coins. 'No, sir. That is charity. I work for my living!' she said proudly.

'This is not charity. It is a gift.' She took the money and thanked him before taking her leave.

'What was that all about?' asked Edward.

'I'm showing you real life. Real life which exists in real places. Emma was born in Surrey. Her family moved to London in order to find work. She was one of eight children. Her father lost his job due to an accident which left him crippled. Unable to work, they had to move into one room. The eldest at that time was twelve and the youngest was 3 months. They lived in that room together. Lived there, ate there and washed there. When the youngest was eight months old, it died. The family had no money for a decent burial and the child remained with them in that room for three weeks before it was removed and cremated. I paid for the cremation. Heaven knows how long the dead child would have remained there if someone did not help them. They all carried on sleeping, eating and living in that room with their dead child tucked away in one corner of the room. All other family goings on happened in that one room, father, mother and all those children. Children learn only from those around them. Exposed to the harsh realities of such an existence, the children become adults at tender ages. Emma was the second eldest and at fourteen years of age, she gave birth to a child. It had been fathered by her elder brother. With her mother also pregnant, her father was desperate to cope with the extra mouths to feed. Emma strongly hinted that she thought her mother was 'working' so to speak when all the children and her father were asleep. She suspected that her father knew but turned a blind eye. It was likely that the child her mother was carrying was not his. Whatever the situation, the invalid father turned his eldest two out of the house. Disgust at the incest was given as the reason. But Emma could not bring herself to say a bad word against her father. She knew it was a bad existence, but her father had no choice. She does not know the whereabouts of her brother as he abandoned her and their unholy offspring. Fate was kind to her. The child conceived from such a forbidden alliance died through being inbred. Now she 'works' in the only way she knows how. To her, success is finding a bed for the night and some sort of a meal. She is still too proud to accept from charity. But she is rare. There are those who would not have such pride and would demand from you whether you wanted to give or not. There is a current estimation that one in nine women in this part of London are prostitutes like Emma. That is just the women. Those in the very poor category are dying faster than the statistics can count.'

'But there are state benefits! Cheap council accommodation! Dole money!' exclaimed Edward.

'Which world are you in now, Edward?' said Nathaniel calmly.

Edward froze! *Which world?* Then he remembered! He remembered where he was from! He had forgotten all that. For a split second the Corporation leapt into his mind and he remembered that he was in interloper from a different century! A different Millennia!

'But there must be something that the government can do!'

'In order to alleviate the situation, the men in Parliament have to recognise that the situation exists! Public unrest goes unnoticed unless the public protest.'

'So that was what those riots where about that you mentioned last night.'

'Well, there has to be more of the same in order to make people understand.'

'You seem to be in favour of unrest.'

'I do not see another way of making those in power understand,' said Nathaniel. 'But a doctor such as yourself. You have studied these people; you socialise among them. Have you no influence?'

'All my wondering around this area and shoulder rubbing with the poor have given me the reputation as a professional man who prefers the company of whores.'

'Emma surely has to be an extreme case.'

'You see that woman there. Slightly plump. She is in the same 'profession' as Emma. Dor, they call her. Dor was married with children. Her husband had a reputable job, and they had a reasonable life. As is normal with these people, they had many children. All would have been fine. The children would not have been great philosophers or doctors, they would have found jobs in the manual sense, but their father died. Dor was left with some money which soon ran out. All she had was hungry mouths to feed and no income. There is not much available by way of help. The Church is no place for comfort either. The Reverend Barnett at St Jude's does not believe in hand outs. He says that handouts do not help. In the long run, people become used to the hand outs and come to rely on them. They make no attempt to get themselves out of their mess. I suppose he does have a point. But few can get themselves out of a bad situation. Some kind of help is necessary.'

Edward listened with intent and he saw the doctors face as he spoke. It was clear what role this doctor played for the people here.

'Tell me,' said Edward. 'What sort of a role did you play in the riots of last year?'

He expected an angry reaction but there was none. The doctor answered straight away. 'Every riot has its *silent* protesters! Those that do not get involved but say things to the right people.'

'Just *say* or provide capital?' asked Edward.

'Well, let us say, assist in any way they can!' There was a short pause and then Nathaniel rose.

'Where are we going?' asked Edward.

'It's a beautiful evening. A stroll would be nice!'

'No! I don't want to.' Edward was frightened.

'You have to face the demons that haunt you, Edward. You have to be able to face reality and look at sickness in the face. You have to accept life the way it is. The Soul is here! I will take you.'

It was indeed a lovely night. There was a cool breeze which was refreshing after the mugginess of the scorching hot day. The clouds were heavy, and Edward was sure that the heavens could crackle with thunder. They strolled along the streets which were still busy in these small hours. Nathaniel seemed to know exactly where to go. The streets became darker and darker and the alleys narrower. The area they came to seemed residential, but the front doors of many houses were open. Peering inside, some had faint lighting in the corridors and others were in complete darkness. Every now and again, they came up to a house where he could see faint movement in the corridors. His eyes were accustomed to the dark and most of the time, the movement were two figures, some scurrying away deeper into the darkness and others not even bothering to do that. From dark corners he could hear giggling or sounds of a carnal nature. He was certain that many of these were 'daughters of the night'. Women who had no choice and had swapped their dignity in return for a meal or a bed. From nowhere came the lyrics of a song, crashing into his head:

He drinks to the health,
Of the whores of Amsterdam
Who've given their bodies,
To a thousand other men.

Yes, they bargain their virtue,
Their goodness all gone,
For a few dirty coins,
When they just can't go on.

Throws his nose to the sky,
In sin of above,
And he pisses like I cry,
On the unfaithful love.

He heard these lyrics in his head as tears swelled up in his eyes. He felt like a voyeur, peering into the lives of these people. He had no business to spy on them like this and he was upset. He tried to get Nathaniel to leave but the doctor had other things on his mind. At one of these houses, Nathaniel walked through the front door and into the dark corridor. He went upstairs and Edward followed. Nathaniel came up to a door and slowly opened it. He looked in and waited for his eyes to become fully accustomed. Then he asked Edward to look in. Edward saw nothing at first but then he could see dark bundles littered all over the floor. Some were big bundles and others were small ones. Edward quickly counted at least ten bundles. There was a rancid stench in the house. It was a mixture of food and urine.

He turned and walked away.

CHAPTER 23

The rest of Edward's visit was just a vague blur to him. The pubs and drinking houses in the area served up a particularly unusual kind of gin. Maybrick had spent the next few evenings away from his room and although Edward did not ask, he knew that Maybrick was visiting his mistress. There was one night which Edward spent with Nathaniel Grey, but he had found courage from somewhere to walk the streets by himself. Night after night he, like Nathaniel, studied and watched these people. He talked to them and associated himself with the lowest kind in order to find out why they lived like they did. His brain suffered from questions and the effects of gin. All these people were born, innocent into the world. All these women. What made them so desperate as to live like this? Surely there had to be a better way. His dreams were full of images and memories which were painful to him. His mother. Juhi's dead face. Squaller. He normally woke up in the morning far more exhausted than he should have been. Maybrick was in a world of his own and left Edward by himself most of the time. On one occasion, Edward became friendly with Parry, a middle aged docker. Parry was born to a prostitute. He had lived a life of struggling which he found easy since he knew no better. His mother died when he was young, and he always managed to find enough day to day work to keep him going. But working the hard life outdoors was having its effect. He told Edward that the last winter was very cold and things workwise were very bad. His body had taken a bashing over the years and now he was old, tired and weak. The dock work was too much for him and some days he had to choose whether he would spend what little he had on food or a bed. That evening Edward slept in one of the workhouses. Rows and rows of beds in a long room, with the bedpans spreading urine cologne all over the room and the rats creating their own blend of scuttling and scratching noises. Every so often, he could hear the Emma's of the world earning their few shillings in order to buy breakfast the next morning. Then there were the begging's of those without money, hoping for a bit of charity with the janitor. But here, like everywhere else, no pay, no bed. He knew he would have been lynched if anyone knew that he already had a free bed which stood empty. On the night before they were due to catch the train back, Edward walked the streets all night. He spoke to Agnes. Agnes was looking for a room for the night. It was only a few coins, but Edward was all out of money. He had spent his last few coins on gin. He took up her offer of walking together. He was in too much of a daze to see where she was leading him. The streets became darker and eventually, she led him to the back of a house. She reached her hand above the fence of the back yard and swung the lock. The door opened and they went into someone's' courtyard. Agnes immediately stood up against a wall and started fumbling around, lifting all her many layers of clothes up. She expected him to take charge at some stage, but he just stood there, confused. She waited a little longer but then her patience wore out. She shouted at him to 'get on with it' and that was when Edward sobered up. He tried to catch her eyes in the darkness and explain that she had it all wrong. That was not what he wanted. He wanted to help her but not like that. Agnes did not want to hear him. She was angry. In him she saw the promise of a bed for the night and now she had been robbed of that. He was a crook this man and she laid into him. She started shouting and punching him. The blows stung his face, and he could see the windows open and people with candles looking out to see what was going on. One of these people knew in the darkness that this was Agnes. They must have given her permission to use the back yard. They called out to her and asked if she was in trouble and she yelled backed that she was being robbed by a crook. There was nothing for it, he had to run. He sobered up in an instance and made a dash for it. He was too quick for Agnes and he ran before people could see him. He must have wondered around for ages and it was quite light before he made it back to the room, all bruised with blood dribbling down his chin.

He slept through most of the journey back to Liverpool.

The next couple of days after getting back to Liverpool Edward spent locked up in the basement. He found comfort in these dead animals and he convinced himself that the Soul was there to find. He ate very little and slept even less. Personal hygiene was a thing of the past and he started to look untidy and dirty. The facial hair began to grow out of control and his clothes were dirty and becoming ragged. He did not eat with the family at all and on one occasion when little James knocked on the door begging him to come play with him, Edward shouted at the boy to go away. He went out on one occasion to stock up on gin. When he was in London, he had successfully arranged a loan through Maybrick. If he wanted cash, he had only to ask for it. As it was, the only real finance that he had was the money for his equipment and animal material. That was all he did. Maybrick tried on several occasions to talk to him but he found himself talking to a different man to the one he had so easily let into his house for the first time almost a month ago. What concerned Maybrick was that this may be a form of sickness that was going to affect Edward's mind and that Edward may tell someone else about Maybrick's sin. Maybrick had become too closely attached to this man just to let him go and he would have had to answer to Nathaniel about what had happened to him. He was concerned that Edward was making himself sick. Florence had one of her tiresome dinners and there was a question as to what to do with Edward. He knew Florence wanted him out of the house. She did not witness Edward sleeping on the garden bench during the summer party, but she had heard all about it with disgust! She was burning with shame and would die if he embarrassed her during this meal. It was a smaller occasion with just a few people including Alfred Brierly. She wanted everything to be perfect. When the day came, she personally saw to it that a bath had been prepared for Edward. She took a bold step and actually went inside his bedroom. At first, she gasped. She thought he was sick. He was slumped over a small table in his room next to the window. It looked as if he had been sitting there looking out of the window and had just fallen asleep. What she was shocked at most was his appearance. He was filthy. She started to clear up some of the mess surrounding him on the table and he suddenly woke up and grabbed her by the wrist. She was shocked by the physical contact. He pulled her face close to his and she immediately protested.

'What do you want?' he hissed. 'Why are you sneaking around here?' His eyes were wide open, and his face was curled up in a crude grin. 'Is it not improper for you to be here?'

'I have guests coming today and I want you to have a wash and to be groomed before you come down.'

'So. You want me to have a wash and a groom, do you? Are you offering?'

'Sir, you are most improper!'

'No, madam, it is you who are improper. Is Master Brierly coming to dinner?' he sneered.

'He is not Master Brierly!' she retorted.

'Oh, but I bet he is when you are together!' Before he could say anything else, he felt his cheek stinging from her slap. She then stormed out of the room and sent in two manservants to help him bath and dress.

He knows! She was in tatters. Her whole world was thrown into acute danger. The man in her house was mad. She thought he was strange when he arrived but now, she was convinced that he was insane. The animals, the hours in the basement, the lack of food. He was totally changed from the man she had first met. And she did not like him very much then. She loathed him now. She wanted him out of her house this instance. It crossed her mind that it might be better if Edward did not appear at the dinner. But if he did, he ran the risk of embarrassing himself and James. That alone may convince James to ask him to leave. Yes! She wanted him to make a complete fool of himself. After all, everyone knew that he was James' friend. He was nothing to do with her. She asked for progress reports as to how he was looking. Most of the guests, which included Michael Maybrick, had now gathered in the living room. Edward should have been there, and Florence was furrowing her brow and looking very unsettled. Even the masterful Brierly could not make her radiant this evening. She kept glancing nervously at the door the whole time and did not engage in chatter with anyone. Most of her guests knew that something was wrong with her.

Eventually, the door swung open and all eyes immediately turned to him. He stood there, clean, well groomed, well dressed and handsome with his tanned skin and his short dark cropped hair, but there remained in his expression something very animal like. He had a sneered grin on his face and a look of arrogance that the old Edward Hamilton would have been shocked with. He looked at Florence and she immediately weakened under his glare. Her heart was pounding, and her legs were going to give way had Brierly not been holding her up. Lady Cuthbert's daughters instantly let the devil into their heads and allowed themselves to fall in love with him. They saw the raw, uneducated, unrefined man in front of them and would have instantly thrown good breeding, finishing school and a good financial background away for the sake of this man. Total animal!

Edward Hamilton glided into the room and took up a glass of champagne. He tasted it with a look of disgust and asked the servant for gin. There was a gasp from the guests in his vicinity. Gin! He thought he heard a faint sound from the delightful Florence. He turned to look at her but caught Alfred Brierly's face instead. Brierly was no coward but in Edward's face he saw pure hatred. A look of such intense hate that Brierly shrank back himself and took his eyes away. Edward waited for his gin and then moved to one corner of the room and remained there, looking at those he was going to dine with and thinking of those who had to struggle all day to find a meal of stale bread and beer. In everything he saw, his mind was taken back to London. In the young Cuthbert girls, he saw Emma. In Lady Cuthbert he saw Agnes. In Doctor Braithwaite he saw Parry. In Brierly he saw the pimp and in Florence he saw the whore! His rational thought had left him, and his head was swimming with all these thoughts which drove him mad. His reason existed no longer, and he held the affluence such as that in the Maybrick household responsible for the deprivation he had seen among the poor. He decided that these people were the real vermin of society and should be treated so. If he had put himself through one of those mobile scanners which he had in his own century he would have noticed an abnormally high blood supply to an overactive brain. He may even have noticed vast synapse damage which was causing his erratic behaviour. All rational thought had been abandoned and he really believed that the Soul existed only in those in need. These people here had no need of the Soul. They had materialistic possessions and all they craved was more money at the expense of others. They would all rot in nothingness when they died. It was the people in need who bared their Souls so that the world could see who they really were. How they really lived. Fighting for life, fighting to live. Facing death each day that they were alive.

It was plain that the Edward Hamilton who stood here in 1888 at the home of James Maybrick was not the same man who had worked at the Corporation in 2007 and who had made friends with Frenkel. He looked the same, walked the same and to a certain extent talked the same, but it was as if the man had received to brain transplant where his new brain belonged to a mixed up, confused and bitter junky. He saw everything differently and no amount of explanation was going to change his mind. His desire to find the Soul lingering in the human body became an obsession. He soon began to lose control of himself altogether and his conscience seemed to have left him at this very moment in time. He roamed the room slowly, taking in what was being said, looking people full in the face and staring at them until they turned away. He had power over them, and he loved it. He looked longingly at the Cuthbert sisters. Yes! They were begging for it! Pity he was not so much of a bastard otherwise he would have taken up the opportunity to mentally scar them for life! The small one with the tiny waist could not take her eyes off him. It was being noticed by her mother who scolded her, but she kept staring. He walked over to the girl who looked like she was going to faint! He stopped right in front of her and bent his face down close to hers and gently with his finger, stroked her cheek. He heard the whispering from the other guests and smiled while still staring into the girl's eyes. At one stage it looked like he was going to bend down and kiss her when she was suddenly yanked away by her livid mother. He smiled and resumed his wondering knowing that Florence was totally agitated. He was going to make her pay for parading him around like this.

Florence was almost physically sick! This man was wrecking her life! She should have left him in the basement. Wherever he went, she followed him to see what he was doing, who he was talking to. That incident with the Cuthbert girl was just too much and Florence's brow could not frown anymore. She decided that it was better if the man sat so she told the servants that the meal would be brought forward, much to their annoyance. She announced dinner early. The guests made their way to the dining room. Florence rushed ahead instead of being escorted since she had remembered that she had placed one of the Cuthbert sisters next to Edward and that did not seem like a good idea. She rushed ahead to change the seating order. It was highly irregular, but she seated Edward in between James and Michael. Her gamble seemed to pay off. Edward was certainly more subdued when he sat down on the table. The only shocking thing he did there was to ask for gin instead of taking some wine. The meal was a rather subdued event in itself due to Edward's behaviour beforehand. Lady Cuthbert was still shocked, and Edward laughed out loud at the thought that what upset her most was her daughter's reaction, not his behaviour. Florence's tearful face made Brierly angry and he took every opportunity to glare at Edward, though he did make sure that Edward was not looking at him at the time. Doctor Braithwaite was a charming fellow who could see no fault in anyone, and the undertones of the evening seemed to pass him by. The other Cuthbert sister was upset because it was her sister whose cheek was stroked by Edward rather than hers. Maybrick had a splitting headache and was beyond care what happened at Florence's tiresome dinner. The only person who seemed happy was Michael Maybrick. Edward watched him closely. Michael seemed to be having a great time at Florence's expense and Edward wondered whether he liked his sister-in-law at all. Maybe it was her association with Brierly that Michael objected to. James Maybrick as usual was oblivious to this and seemed beyond care anyway. The muted conversation struggled to build up momentum and but at least Florence was relaxing a bit more. She thought the worst was over and she began to take her eyes off Edward and actually talk to Alfred. Things were relaxing a little more when the doctor asked James how his recent visit to London had been.

'London! You did not tell me you were going to London, James!' said Lady Cuthbert.

'Oh, come now mama,' interrupted her eldest daughter, 'you know that Mr Maybrick visits London every month.'

'Don't correct me my dear, you know my memory is not what it used to be,' she said pompously.

'Does that mean you have forgotten already that I touched you daughter's cheek?' asked Edward. The girl in question giggled much to her mother's dismay.

'Be quiet Charlotte!' shouted Lady Cuthbert.

'Now, Lady Cuthbert,' said Michael Maybrick. 'There is no need to overreact to that. Do you not see that the gentleman is entertained by your response alone?'

'I see no gentleman! A gentleman would have apologised.'

'Lady Cuthbert,' said Edward wearing a serious face. 'I am most truly sorry. I was rude and deserve your anger.' He waited for her response and saw that she had been shallow enough so as to be pacified with that insincere apology. He could have killed someone, and this woman would have forgiven him as long as he apologised!

'Well,' said the doctor, who seemed to have missed that entire chunk of conversation, 'you did not say how the trip was. Has London come out with any great new fashions that we should know about?'

'No. You still have the rich and you still have the poor,' said Maybrick. Edward was surprised by that remark. In all the time that they had spent in London, Maybrick never mentioned the poor, never gave them anything and never even seemed to notice them as they walked through the streets so his mentioning them now was surprising.

'Nonsense!' ejaculated Lady Cuthbert. 'I have had many seasons in London. My first coming out was in London. I have seen no poverty. The poor are a law unto themselves.'

'By that you mean that they are not poor?' said Edward.

'No. By that I mean that they do nothing to help themselves.'

'And how do you suggest they do that? asked Edward quietly.

'Work!' she retorted. 'They are lazy. They do not want to work. They want to live off the Church!'

'You make sweeping comments about the way that they live and yet you claim never to have encountered the poor on your many visits to London.'

'Mr Hamilton, you do not need to have visited France to know that they speak a different language and eat garlic and frogs' legs!'

'The poor are not a foreign entity. They belong here and are part of your existence!' he said. The Cuthbert girls were split. Do they swear allegiance to their mother or the dashing rogue with the strange way of talking? It seems loyalty was suffering from the effects of rampaging hormones! Florence could see Michael Maybrick's face looking at her and smiling. She had many enemies at this table, and she wondered what possessed her to bring them together like this. Lady Cuthbert paused and there seemed to be a moment when she may have given up, so Michael Maybrick helped fuel the fire.

'Certainly, of all the places in London that you may want to visit, Lady Cuthbert, Whitechapel would not be desirable. The kind of life that exists there would be incomprehensible to you.'

'But they have the docks, the trade. That is where the jobs are! People just don't want to work,' she continued.

'Well, the population of that part of London is huge! There are many children to one couple. Disease and sickness are widespread.' This was the doctor, who had for a short time, come out of his little bubble to talk about real life. 'My medical training was in the London Hospital. I had to come into contact with these poor souls every day. Sometimes, coming into hospital was a Godsend! It meant shelter, a bed and food.'

'Oh, come now, Dr Braithwaite. You give them far too much sympathy and they take advantage of it. Every man can help themselves. They can work if they want to.'

'And what do you do if you husband died leaving you with children and NO money! What would you do?' asked Edward quietly.

'My husband was a shrewd man! He worked hard and made sure we were provided for even when he passed on.'

'Your husband was a merchant like Maybrick here, yes?' persisted Edward. 'What if your husband was a manual docker? By the time he was 35 years old, his body was battered by a hard life and he could no longer do heavy work. The work that paid. What if he died and left you, a docker's wife with children and barely a roof over your head? What would you do?'

'That is totally obscene! It's an unfair comparison!' she said angrily.

'I'll tell you what you would have done! You would spend the days looking for something to feed the children and you would have spent the nights selling your body!' There was a huge gasp of horror from the females around the table and even the Cuthbert sisters were shocked! Alfred Brierly could stand it no more. He had never seen Florence look so aged!

'That is enough!' He then addressed Maybrick. 'How can you let this filth onto your dinner table?'

'That's alright, Alfred' said a frail Florence. She could not let this thing get out of hand. Brierly was angry but he backed down.

'Why is everyone so shocked at what I say? You do not doubt that prostitutes exist! Given certain cruel and difficult circumstances, we would all prostitute ourselves in order to survive!'

'It's filth! Nobody has to sink so low!' shouted Lady Cuthbert.

'Mr Hamilton,' said Florence being brave. 'Nobody doubts that the whores of our society exist. But we do not want to talk about them over the dinner table.'

There it was! The golden moment that he had been waiting for. The devil really rose and swelled up in his veins. Now there was nothing stop him!

'Mrs Maybrick!' he sneered. 'You have it all wrong! It's not the women who have fallen on hard times and have landed heavily at the bottom of the lowest pit and are forced to sell their bodies who should be seen as the whores of our society! No!' He paused slightly and she knew the blow was coming. 'It's the women who spin a deadly web of deceit waiting for a rich suitor to become ensnared, only to marry them and then practice unfaithful passion with others who are the *real WHORES* of our society!'

He remembered nothing of the commotion that he left behind as he exited the room except for the sobbing of Florence and the Cuthbert's angrily taking their leave.

CHAPTER 24

'That is ENOUGH!' wailed Florence, choking through her tears. 'I want that man out of my house! Do you hear me, James? OUT, OUT, OUT!'

She was totally inconsolable and Maybrick did not even try to soothe her. He just listened as she paced her room up and down, crying and beating her fists against the air. It was many hours after the disastrous meal and Maybrick was hoping that this would put an end to her overzealous socialising. He thought it was rather odd for young Brierly to challenge the mad Edward to a duel! He wondered what possessed him to do so.

'I am serious, James! I do not want to have to see him again. I can't believe you just sat there and let him humiliate me like that. You did not even try to defend my honour!' she sobbed.

'My dear,' he said calmly, 'I did not think it was your honour that he was questioning.' She paused when he said this. She knew exactly what Edward was questioning but her husband still showed signs of dimness quite uncharacteristic of him. She did not want to give him any ideas. 'I will never be able to look at the Cuthbert's in the face again!'

'I think that is probably for the best!'

'But they have good business connections. They are important,' she continued.

'If you mean *my* business, then you can rest assured that I can cope without the Lady Cuthbert's help. As we have no son of matrimonial age, the young Cuthbert girls cannot be of any use to us. I am sure we will survive if we never see them again. '

'Oh James!' she screamed. 'You have no social ambition!'

'No. You have enough for both of us. That is why you are so devastated. It will be your downfall Florrie.' He sat still at Florence's writing desk.

'Look, over a month ago you brought a total stranger to this house and let him do whatever he liked! You do not question anything he does, for all I know, you could be financially supporting him. You say you are childhood friends, but you never share a single conversation about the time you grew up together! This man is odd, James. Very odd. He is different. When is he going to leave?'

The tears had not stopped flowing down her face, making her eyes swell up. Her face was red and blotchy, and it looked as if she was going to cry all night! He had to pacify her.

'Florrie. There is something that I have not told you.' He wanted to tell her that Edward will be asked to leave, but Maybrick had a coward inside him and that coward came to the forefront. He knew he should try and control Edward. He knew that it was wrong to let Edward live in this house forever and let him use blackmail in the way he had been doing. He had to settle things with Edward for once and for all. But during the last few days, Edward showed signs of aggression that Maybrick was frightened of. Edward did not exhibit the normal personality that he had a month ago. Something was making him ill and Maybrick could not tell him to go just yet.

'Well, what is it?' she said, bringing herself to a halt from her pacing.

'Edward is sick. He has a brain sickness and nobody else to help him through it. He cannot help what he is becoming.'

'Oh James! You expect me to have sympathy with him!'

'You know that this is not the same man who came here a month ago! He is sick.'

'Is he dying?' she asked in a very cold manner.

'I do not know.'

'What is he sick from?'

'Brain sickness. Richard did examine him and tell me, but I forgotten the name.'

'So, I have to accept that he will stay here and make my life hell! If he loves the whores of London so much why does he not go and stay, there!'

Maybrick suddenly stopped and stared at her. Of course! She was right! He had a room there which he kept all the time! The rent had been paid in advance for the next four months! Why did he not think of it before! He was delighted at this solution.

'Look, Florrie. I will wait until tomorrow and then talk to him. I will tell him to leave. I promise.' He looked at his wife's face. Only eight years ago, this was the face that stirred his passion. Young, innocent and daring. Now, it was old, with worry lines and blotches! Much older than it should look. 'Don't worry. I will sort it out.'

Edward was angry. He had to find a way of slowing down. He was tired, weak and confused. He slept in his basement and woke up sprawled across his work top. His neck was aching, and his eyes were stinging. If he was not mistaken, he had a hangover. The gin was still circulating in his blood! He wanted to be sick and knew that he was better off taking in the morning air. Instead, he had four rats left. He decided that his search for the soul was more important than taking a stroll and running the risk of an encounter with Florence Maybrick. He got to work. He was convinced that he would find the answer. It was important. He believed that the soul only existed in some people and that the innocent were more likely to have one! This obsession was generally taking over his mind. He was slowly going mad and not even realising how ridiculous he looked. When Maybrick came down to see him, he had the small intestines in one hand and with the other, he was digging away to find a kidney. He stank of formaldehyde and looked quite insane. He had unsuccessfully destroyed all the corpses of the animals he had, and he was mad. He expected to have found what he was looking for. He was angry and when he saw Maybrick standing at the top of the stairs, he remembered Mrs Maybrick. He immediately threw the bits in his hands at Maybrick and then proceeded to trash the place. The glassware crashed to the floor and smashed into thousands of pieces. The Bunsen burner went flying and it was just as well that it was not lit at the time. The papers and books that he had accumulated also flew all over the basement. His anger had to have an outlet and Maybrick just stood and watched him, cool as ice. When Edward stopped, he sat on one of his chairs and heaved. He was hyperventilating and felt faint and unwell. Suddenly, a pain numbed his brain. He could feel a pounding which filled his head and he held it in his hands as if to try and hold it still. He was unaware that Maybrick had come down the stairs and was right next to him asking questions. His eyes were shut, and he screamed in agony. Within half an hour, he had that fever again and by late afternoon, he was totally bedridden. He vaguely had some memory of the Maybrick family doctor attending him. Again, his only visitors were Maybrick and little James. He ate little and he was aware of their concerns over his health.

The Maybrick family doctor announced that Edward was suffering from the same fever that he had before and like before, there was a question as to what had caused him to become sick so suddenly. Also, the doctor examined that patient twice a day and was convinced that anyone else could not have survived this but remembering how Edward came back from the brink of death last time he was making no predictions. The sick man was again nursed night and day. On the ninth day after falling ill, Edward sat up in bed. His recovery just as quick as the onset of his illness and again the doctor was baffled at this sickness. He had no idea what it was and what made it go away so suddenly. Within a couple of days, Edward decided that he was well enough and that he should again join Maybrick on his monthly business trip. Maybrick was a little worried considering the effect that the visit had on Edward the last time, but he had a greater evil at home in the form of Florence. Getting Edward away from here was for the best.

Four days after recovering from his second bout of fever, Edward was again in the East End of London and once again underwent a huge personality change.

Edward once again felt at home. This was where the Soul was! He felt he could relate to the people here. He was left on his own again only this time Maybrick had told Nathaniel to keep a closer eye on Edward. This time, instead of Nathaniel taking Edward for a stroll, Edward took Nathaniel. Edward wanted Nathaniel to meet his friends. He introduced him to Parry and to Simon. They both told Nathaniel their tales of woe and although they were good men fallen on hard times, they were not too proud to accept charity off strangers and were hoping that Nathaniel would dig into his pockets. It was some of the women that Edward introduced to Nathaniel who seemed reluctant and unsure of this stranger. Nathaniel soon poured out his charm and the others tended to relax a little more. Parry was on a high. He had found a friend who worked in a funeral parlour and there was manual work to be done. Parry was overjoyed because the work was permanent until further notice and he had never had a permanent job ever in his life. He had spent every penny he had on buying beer for all his friends. At the end of the evening, he was left penniless and still in search for a bed for the night. Simon was a jolly man. Large, round, red and noisy. It seemed amazing that this man could have been living on the poverty line with a beer gut quite that large. He was on the breadline but was so incredibly happy and you would find it hard to believe that this man had everything and lost everything. A business, a family, children. All gone because of bad planning, women and alcohol. The very things surrounding him now in the drinking house. He had working women coming up to him all evening thinking he was a potential customer loaded with money. He loved the attention and laughed out loud at every opportunity. Late in the evening they were joined by Sidney who was a friend of Nora, one of the women sitting at their table. Sidney had looked pretty rough and one of his eyes was red and badly swollen. He had a wound to his lip and small amounts of fresh blood could still be seen. He looked well annoyed. He was a sailor. His ship was docking temporarily, and he was a well-known figure in these parts. He would visit every time his ship came in. He was a working man with money and Edward was puzzled as to why he looked so rough. Nathaniel on the other hand was not surprised at all. He guessed what had happened. He was accurate in his assessment of Sidney's situation.

'Sid! What 'appened to you?' cried Nora.

'Stupid hag!' he said. 'I don't know 'ow I could a been so daft! I should 'o known!'

'What happened?' repeated Nathaniel.

'Not more than two hours here and I meet this lass. Kind 'o old. Trusting face.'

'Oh no, Sid. Don't say you fell for that!' wailed Nora in a thick cockney accent.

'I did na think! I've been away too long!' he said dabbing his sore lip with his bare fingers.

'I don't understand,' said Edward, who noticed that all the others on the table seemed to know what happened without Sidney explaining anything.

'Like Sidney says,' explained Nathaniel, 'it's an old trick. Foreigners fall for it all the time. Sidney here was a touch careless for he should have been looking out for it!' He said this with a smile and a gentle wink at the unfortunate man. 'Women slightly less honest than your average women, pick up sailors or men whom they know would have money. They entertain the men and often lead them down secluded alleys or corridors where the unfortunate man is surprised by a gang of men who rob him. The lady in question looks distressed and screams a lot and when the man has been robbed, she stays and offers comfort and sympathy so that the man does not suspect that she was part of the deception. The locals in the area know of this kind of theft but those from foreign parts are not aware and are easily fooled. Am I right Sidney?'

''Cept the last bit. She gave no sympafy. Just stood and hoo'ed with laughter!'

'Well, it's all character building,' smiled Nathaniel. They laughed at Sidney's expense which seemed cruel, but under the circumstances, they could have done nothing else. The man had lost his weeks wages and his pride and lamenting with him would not pick up his spirits. He always had the option of returning early to his ship so a bed for the night was not a problem. Nathaniel bought him a beer and soon, Simon's overpowering jolliness had cheered up Sidney considerably. Rose, one of Nora's friends offered to give Sidney sympathy of a different kind which embarrassed none except Edward.

'You know,' he said quietly to Nathaniel while the others carried on their laughter, 'there seems to be more happiness in this sad little place among these needy people that there ever has been in the Maybrick household, a household that has everything that they could want.'

'That is because people who have everything forget how to appreciate it,' said Nathaniel. 'They take it for granted. They forget where it all came from. They forget the basic purpose in life. They build other needs which to them are important but to the real world are trivial. There are two sorts of need. The need of the physical body, and the needs of the Soul. Here in this place, the body needs and struggles to find the basic things for survival like food and shelter. The Soul does not get a look in. In the wealthy, the body always has things. There is no question of food and shelter not being given. The body is never in need and the focus of that individual turns to the inner self. The inner person. The Soul.'

'No! That is where you are wrong!' exclaimed Edward who had established himself as an expert of the subject of the Soul. 'Here is where the SOUL is! Here!' He hit his fist on the table as he said this, and the others stopped talking and listened. 'The Maybrick's have no SOUL! They are too busy with their garden parties and dinners to think of their inner self. The Soul lies here! These people have a Soul.'

'We all have a Soul, Edward,' said Nathaniel gently. 'No!' shouted Edward.

'Let me get this straight,' said Nathaniel. 'If I understand what you are saying, people who have no money have a Soul and people who are wealthy do not.'

'Yes!'

'Nonsense!' Nathaniel saw the fire in Edward's eyes and decided to dig deeper to draw out the flames and look right into them. 'All have Souls! What differs is the way people exhibit them. Some hide their Soul deep inside and never let it out. Some show theirs in public.'

'I tell you the Soul does not exist in all! I know, I have searched for it!'

'Searched for it? What the Devil do you mean?' asked Nathaniel, really intrigued now.

'I fink Eddie's 'ad enough,' concluded Nora as she rose to go. She left the seat which was then quickly filled up by other women who saw a hot meal and possibly breakfast in the form of Nathaniel Grey. Sharp suit, good manners! Yes, he could be a good catch.

'I can prove it. I can find the Soul. It exists as an organ!' said Edward with a twisted look on his face.

Nathaniel roared with laughter. Maybrick was right, he thought, their friend certainly was showing the early signs of madness. It was the sudden hot temper which concerned Nathaniel the most. Edward was a gentle man, and this anger was not right.

'I suppose you have found this organ!'

'No. But I am close! I know it's a matter of time. I will find it. I know I will.'

'So that is what is happening to the mice and rats that I am sending you?'

'Yes.'

'I thought you were trying to extract a drug of some kind which makes you lose your memory! Or was James mistaken!' teased Nathaniel. Edward had forgotten what he had told James. He had to find the Soul, and, in his head, this is all he remembered.

'Don't mock me, Doctor!' hissed Edward. 'I know more than you ever will.'

'I do not doubt that. But the human anatomy has been extensively studied and nobody has ever found an organ to represent the Soul.'

'Ow 'ave you looked for it then?' asked Sidney.

'Well. How does one see anything?' said Nathaniel. 'By looking inside!'

'What! Inside dead people?' gasped Rose.

'No! Well yes! Sort of.' Nathaniel felt he had to explain. 'Anatomy means the study of the internal biology of animals and humans. The animals are specially bred for the purpose. Human anatomy is helped by the study of dead humans, but we wait for them to die first!'

Betty, the toothless women who up until now had been staring greedily at Nathaniel suddenly stopped with a frown on her face. She turned to Edward and said, 'There ain't no Soul in dead people, is there? 'Ow do you 'pect to find it then?'

'No!' shouted Edward. 'I haven't been looking at dead people! I look at mice and rats!'

'There ain't no Soul in them animals niever!' yelled back Rose and the others nodded and grunted in her favour.

Edward suddenly froze in thought. Of course! Hell! Why did he not think of that himself! Animals do not have a Soul. Only those who can think and can reason have a Soul! No! How did he expect to find a Soul among the rats and mice that Nathaniel had been sent him? He felt really daft now looking at all these people sat around him. He was meant to be a doctor and an expert in his profession, and he was being taught logic by a prostitute whose intellect would be successfully challenged by a dog performing tricks! A whore showed herself to be more intelligent than him! He was livid and he clenched his fists and stormed out of the drinking house in a fit of rage. Nathaniel rose as well and ran after him. The night air was warm but there was a heavily charged atmosphere. Thunder was imminent. A few spatters hit Nathaniel's face while the odd flashing light appeared in the darkness, followed by the gentle rumbling from the skies. He could see a dark figure running away and turn a corner but by the time he reached and turned the corner himself, he was alone. He could not see Edward or hear his footsteps. He stood there looking anxious with rain falling on his face.

CHAPTER 25

Stupid! Stupid man! Edward roamed the wet streets totally dejected. How could he have been so daft. All those wasted hours, days, weeks. Was its years? Had he been searching for the Soul for years? Such a waste of time and him, a scientist, a learned man unable to figure it out himself. He had not been as humiliated as this since... since Frenkel! He stopped in his tracks as his head was bombarded with memories! Yes! He remembered! A face! Frenkel. Anthony Frenkel. *Don't call me Tony.* That was Frenkel's voice in his head. How could he have forgotten him. The Corporation came back. The Corridor. The deceit. Yes! His head ached with this onslaught of thoughts and he had to lean against a wall for support. A man walking past him asked him if he needed help. He waved the stranger away. He was too frightened that he might forget everything again if he was distracted. He wanted to remember everything. The Professor. The cloning experiments. They were going to clone Frenkel. The powers that Frenkel had. It all came back. He was not meant to be here! This was eighteen hundred and something or another and he was not meant to be here spying on these people. He was from another world, may as well call it another planet. How he had survived here he had no idea. Maybrick was incredibly stupid and gullible to let a total stranger into his house. Set up a laboratory in his basement! He began to control the images entering his head and the initial shock of his memory returning was passing. He began to walk in the general direction of Maybrick's room. He had to lie down. The Corridor! The animals. He could not remember the names, but he could see them. *They all came back.* Why was he still here! Why had he not returned. A sudden panic attack hit him. Was he stuck here forever?

Frenkel came back mad. So did his animals. But he was not mad. Whatever sickness had affected their brains he was thankful that it had not affect his. He remembered many things and by the time that he reached the room, he was soaked. He peeled off his wet coat and threw himself on the bed. Try as he may he was missing huge chunks of events. Was this a dream? It seemed so real but now that he was concentrating, he realised how daft it all sounded. Travelled through *time!* That was ridiculous! He was dreaming. This was fantasy that had momentarily crept into his tired and gin-soaked mind. There was no mission! Two thousand and seven indeed!

He rested and let his mind wonder over to Betty. She made him angry. She was not meant to have two brain cells to rub together and yet she could plainly see that which he could not. She was right. He had not found the Soul because animals do not have one! Humans did. The shame of it! Why did he not think of it before? The more he thought about Betty's face the more annoyed he became. He tried to forget her.

The solution to his problem was impossible. He had to try and look at humans. *Body snatchers!* He sat up in bed. Sweat dripping off his forehead. Who said that? That voice! He remembered that story. Unscrupulous men selling dead bodies to a medical man. Was it fact or fiction? At first the idea seemed sickening. But then he began to think. What did it matter to those who were dead? They were not going to suffer. They were already dead and if their bodies could be used to further scientific knowledge then it must be good. A small number would lend themselves for the good of many. Suddenly another voice came into his head: *The needs of the many outweigh the needs of the few, or the one!* A face appeared. Tortured, in pain. Funny hair, pointy ears! Who was he? *The needs of the many outweigh the needs of the few, or the one!* Yes! Spock was right. For every scientific discovery, there were those who suffered. What harm could be done if a person was already dead. Then the tormenting face of Betty taunted him. *The Soul leaves after death Stoopid!* She was right again the Bitch! The Soul leaves. Or does it remain until holy prayers are said to release it. Which religion was it that believed that the Soul had to be given permission to leave the body? He pulled himself off the bed and began rapidly pacing the room. No wonder he had been so unsuccessful! He needed to look at humans! He tried to avoid the obvious, but in the end the conclusion he came to was that he needed to look at those on the brink of death! He needed to find someone who was dying, and he needed to be ready at the point of death to look for the Soul as it left the body! Yes! That was his answer. He was sure of it. Betty's voice came back into his head: *Glad to be of help, lover!* How does he do this? This was worse than the body snatchers. He wanted his specimens to be alive but on the brink of death! He had to choose the right specimen. Those in need! They were the ones in whom a Soul could be found! He had to be careful. He needed to be right. Let's recap! He needed a human who was in need, but who was also on the brink of death where the time of death was known so that Edward could be ready to do his work. That does not sound so impossible! No! That was feasible! All he had to do was find an ill person and wait. Maybe he could visit the hospitals and see if the doctors let him keep the dying company. He could say that he was helping them through their transition from this world to the next! He could say that he was studying them. But who would let him do that? Apart from Nathaniel, he had no other connections. He certainly would not risk telling Nathaniel. He may take the idea as his own and publish it himself in a leading scientific journal before Edward got his act together! He would have all the resources and the specimens he could want! He would find the Soul and get all the credit! No! Edward could not risk getting help from a thieving medical man. He had to find another way. He thought better when he was still and calm, so he planted himself on the sofa. The only sofa in the room and he relaxed his mind.

He thought back to his limiting factors. He had people in need. He was surrounded by them! London was full of them! He needed one on the brink of death. He needed to be ready at the point of death to do his work. Yes! Point of death. Brink of death. Edge of death. Transition from this world to the next. That was the limiting factor. He could deal with all the rest, but this was his limiting step. How should he overcome this obstacle? He laid his head back on the sofa and closed his eyes. Think! Don't sleep! Think. Just before his mind faded, he heard Frenkel's voice: *Out of great sorrow and human tragedy comes good.*

An hour later he jumped up angrily from the sofa, cursing himself for falling asleep. He had no time for sleep! He had to find a solution! He started pacing up and down the room again. It was very late in the morning. He looked around for the time but there was no clock in the room, and he had no watch. His time here was important. Maybrick always kept him up to date but he was obviously entertaining his mistress. Edward thought of Nathaniel. He had to talk to him. He put on his wet coat and grabbed his bag before leaving. The bag contained his journal and medical notes along with some equipment. Maybe he could make Nathaniel a partner in his study. He would make it a condition that Nathaniel was not to publish anything on his own. Yes! He was on the brink of a marvellous discovery and Nathaniel Grey would be honoured to join him on it. He left the room.

At first, he walked briskly and straight in the direction of Nathaniel's house. But then he lost his bearing and he found himself wondering around without recognising any of the streets or the buildings. It was a clear night. The ground was wet and the air fresh. The thunder and rain had come and gone while he slept. He struggled to find something familiar and was relieved when he stumbled across Whitechapel Underground station. Now he knew where he was. His head was full of ideas about his limiting factor, what he was going to say to Nathaniel and how he was so close to finding the answer to the universe. As far as he was concerned, total logic had been restored and he was not even angry at Betty for momentarily being a bit more intelligent than himself. He was still wondering around when he saw two figures on the Whitechapel Road. It was two women. There were no other people around, but it was not quiet. The sound from the slaughterhouses could still be heard as they were in full swing. He slowed down. One woman was coaxing and pulling the other one. She wanted her friend to go with her, but the second women were leaning unsteadily on the wall. She appeared to be drunk.

'I can get my doss money, don't you worry!' said the plump woman. 'It's late Polly! Come back with me.'

'I made enough money for *four* beds! I can get one more! I'll see you in 'alf 'our!' She then pulled herself away and staggered off. The other woman appeared to have given in. Edward stood there staring at the staggering women who was now approaching his direction. In her drunken state she looked oblivious to things around her, but she slowed down in front of him and stared. She noticed him just standing there.

'Wha' you starin' at?' she slurred.

'Nothing. I was just wondering…' he remembered Agnes. Talking to a women out on a mission like this had landed him into trouble then and it could do so again. He tried to move away from her.

'You lookin' for sumfing?'

'No.' He tried to walk past her but she grabbed his sleeve. 'Wha's your name?'

'Edward. And I really have to get somewhere.'

'If you ain't lookin' for it then I'll be please e'nuff wiv a cup 'o tea.' He looked at her face. Greyish brown hair and front teeth missing. Years of torment and suffering and drinking. She looked middle-aged. He decided to have pity on this poor wretch.

'Look, how much do you need for a doss house?' She was shocked. 'Wha'?'

'Buying you a cup of tea would still not give you a bed for the night. You would still be in need. If I buy tea for you, I may as well give you the money for a bed. How much?'

'No,' she said. 'I can't take for nuffing.'

'Don't let your stupid pride get in the way!' he said sternly. 'Where is the doss house?' She pointed and they walked along, her staggering about and him holding her by the arm. She started nattering and in a short space of time, her prolific ramblings had told him that she was married at twelve years old and had a huge gang of children. Her husband was something to do with the printing business. She referred to him several times as bastard because on their separation he had stopped all financial support towards her.

'You had the children?'

'No. 'Ow could I?'

'But he would have had to support you then.' She made no reply. She was crying now.

'He chucks me ou'. I was drinkin'
'eavy.'

'Did you have a job?'

She was coy on this subject and he learned that she did have a decent job as a maid, but she stuck to it for a few weeks before leaving after stealing some articles. He just looked at her stunned. This was certainly a woman who willingly put herself in this situation. She had a husband with a job, living accommodation and children and she threw it all away on alcohol. Even the job she had she messed up. A real loser by choice. She wept as they walked.

'You had everything, and you threw it away,' he said gently. 'Yeah, don't rub i' in! I know I was stoopid!'

'I did not say you were stupid. Just unfortunate.'

She was really crying and staggering now. She told him to leave her alone and stuff his charity. She would get a bed for the night without his help. He ran after her and apologised. He did not mean to hurt her feelings. She turned her ugly face towards him.

'I know I screwed up! I knows it. I wish I were dead!'

That was it! The solution! It was staring him in the face. In the form of this toothless creature who was wishing herself dead. He saw it now. The means. Someone in need. Someone who was wishing death. She wanted to be gone from this harsh world and she was forced to live like this, hand to mouth, whoring her way through the night so that she could sleep and eat in the day. She was sick of her wasted life and wanted to be gone. *The needs of the many.* She would kill herself if she had the courage. *Outweigh the needs of the few.* He would be doing her a favour. *Or the one.* He would be helping her. He would be answering her prayers. *The needs of the many.* She had no life. No love. No one to mourn her. *Out of real tragedy.* If she died in the gutter, her life would have been totally wasted. No point in life or in death. This way, his way, he would be freeing her from this hellish life. He would free her Soul so that it would go to another recipient. *Comes good.* He would free her. He would give meaning to her death! Her life would not have been totally wasted. *Something good to come out of something bad.* He would give her life meaning. He had the POWER to give her life meaning. *The needs of the many!* He looked into her drunken, blotchy, tearful face and he knew that this was his solution. He dug into his bag. Along with his journal and notes was the tool he was looking for. He gripped it for the sake of science. For the sake of mankind. For the progress of the human race. She was a going to be his first martyr. He would make sure that he would mention the fact that she helped him in his study. He would acknowledge her when the study was written up and published in the leading journal of the day. Yes! She would have her name down in history! The whoring life that she had lived, empty, loveless and worthless was now given meaning! He would give it meaning. *The needs of the many.* 'I wish I were dead!' She wailed again. It was her last wish. Her last breath! Her wish had been granted. For the good of mankind! Seconds after she had said this, the blade entered her throat. He hesitated as he held her from behind. A brief moment of uncertainty entered his head. He brought the blade out, but this was a passing thing. He quickly dug the sharp point back in to her throat and pulled it all the way across. *Outweigh the needs of the few.* Free! Free! *Or the one!*

Now his experiment began! He proceeded to explore. He dug and rummaged and invaded the body which should have housed this women's Soul. He was dead certain that he would find it. There was too much darkness and he cursed and swore at the fact that he had to carry out the most important experiment that mankind has ever known as a vicious vagabond searching for money! Like a pauper! Like a street urchin! He worked and dug and waited! Waited to see if he could spot anything. The Soul must have been here! He could see nothing, and he heard some of the men from the slaughterhouses finishing for the morning! Shit! Shit! Shit! He had failed! This experiment had failed! He had to abandon it. He made sure that he had his journal. He had to make proper notes. Although she was not positively successful towards his experiment, she would still be acknowledged. He was only upset that he did not ask her name! The sound of someone coming suddenly made him flee. He hid the tool and his bag inside his cloak and fled. Fifteen minutes later, he was in Maybrick's room. A few more minutes later he could hear the policemen's whistles going off.

CHAPTER 26

Edward was elated! He had found the perfect specimen farm. He did not have to breed the specimens, to feed them, to bring them up, or monitor them. His source was unlimited. Unlimited access to those in need. His problem of finding one that was close to death was also solved. He had to create this part himself. That was no longer the limiting factor in his great experiment. The limiting factor was that he had to find someone who *wanted* to be freed from this world. He could not possibly bring about a death situation unless the person donating their body to science was willing. To do that without permission would be immoral! That would be sin! Murder! No. He had to scour the streets looking for someone who actually wanted to die. By declaring themselves unhappy in this world they were helping mankind in the future! He could see the toothless woman now, looking down on him from wherever she was, thanking him for sending her to a better place. A better existence from the one she had on Earth. He felt elated. He had helped her and she in return had helped him. God bless her and guide her Soul!

In the next few days, he roamed the streets at night and slept during the day. On two of the occasions, he met up with Nathaniel. He was going to ask Nathaniel for help with specimens but now that he had come to a solution by himself, he did not need Nathaniel. He could carry out his work safe in the knowledge that nobody would steal his work. He trusted Nathaniel but such a fantastic breakthrough in the science world may tempt an honest man to steal! He dined with Nathaniel and acted normal. He was aware that Nathaniel's attitude towards himself was different. The doctor was very cautious of what he said and seemed to be holding out on Edward. He was talking to Edward as if he were a patient. It made Edward want to chuckle. He was still on a high and found everything amusing. He was totally unaware that the medical man he was talking to was seriously concerned about the mood swings of his mysterious friend. Kind and gentle one minute, angry and violent the next. What worried Nathaniel even more was that he was given the task of finding out who this man was and where he came from. An awful lot of money had been invested on Edward by James and Nathaniel, but they still knew nothing. Edward was still a stranger and he was getting weirder and weirder by the day. Nathaniel was concerned about Edward's sanity. He had tried to tell Maybrick this. But the evening that the two of them met, Maybrick was terribly ill. He had another headache and Nathaniel had to visit him at the home of the woman he was with in order to treat him. Nathaniel thought it was unwise to burden him further with Edward, so he decided to see him another day when his health was better.

Edward had one more night before they had to go back. It was a warm August night, and he had a good feeling. It was days since his last experiment but as a good scientist he knew that patience was everything! Rush an experiment with sloppiness or short cuts and it never works! So, he waited with patience. On this night he roamed about not hoping to find a great deal. He had talked to many women and men but had not found the ideal candidate who wanted to be released into the next world. The first one was willing to part with details of her life and told him everything in a couple of minutes. But now after days on end he had found no one else so willing. He decided to change his tactics. He decided to formulate a questionnaire in his head. The correct answers to the questions would deem the candidate eligible to enter the trial. He thought for hours about what to ask and what the ideal answers should be. He thought he had it all set and, on this night, he was going to select his candidate based on the questions that he had thought up. He had asked the first question a number of times to about five different people and was somewhat disheartened when they all answered wrongly! Their answer meant that they had to be disqualified from the selection. He could not possibly ask them the other questions because their first answer had made their suitability null and void. He was beginning to think that he had asked the wrong questions when his sixth candidate turned out to be real gem.

She was middle aged, ugly and also toothless. But this one also sported a black eye. He began to ask questions and found that she was suffering from the result of a vicious attack upon her. Thinking that it was an unsatisfied customer, or one who did not want to pay, Edward was surprised to learn that the injuries were administered by a woman. The other woman must have been a violent thing since the women he was looking at was stocky and strong looking. The row was over nothing but a piece of soap! What a sad life, thought Edward, to be fighting so viciously over a bar of soap! The woman had obviously been injured in the chest as well for she looked in pain and was crouched somewhat and looked altogether sad and pathetic.

'She was lucky, the bitch,' she said. 'Who was lucky?'

'That bitch Liza. I was already unwell, other I would 'ave beat 'er good.'

'Why do you live like this?'

'I 'ad a 'usband but we split. 'E paid me, but the bastard gone and died. Now I 'ave to live.'

Now it was time for his first question. 'Are you happy?'

'Wiv wha'?' she said, rather angrily.

'Well. Generally. With your life.'

'Wha' the bloody 'ell are all them questions for? Do I look 'appy?' she yelled at him. He took that to be no. Yes! She had answered the first question correctly. She could be a good candidate.

'Would you like to do something that would help others?'

'I'd be 'appy if I were 'elping meself!'

'But I would do that for you! If I were to help you, would you be prepared to help someone else?' He spoke gently, almost in a whisper.

She thought about this and said, 'Course I would.' Then she grinned, thinking that this was a romantic way for him to approach her and that maybe all his questions were to lead to somewhere. Whether he saw her real intentions or not, Edward saw only that she answered his question correctly.

'I am carrying out an experiment. Would you like to take part?'

'A wha'?'

'An experi… well, a test. I am testing something. I am a doctor.'

'Oh! You mus' be rich!'

'I'll be even richer when I finish my experi… test. Would you like to take part?' He was standing right over her, towering, piercing her with his eyes. She was totally under his spell and he had not even touched her.

'You want my 'elp?' Just as she said this, she noticed a woman walking close by. The woman looked her straight in the face, but Edward had his back to her. He did not even seem to notice that someone had walked by.

'Will you?' he asked again. 'Yes.'

Total elation! He had found the ideal candidate! The ideal person. She had answered all the questions correctly albeit with some coaxing and guidance! She had successfully qualified to take part in his experiment! He let her lead him into the corridor of the house they were leaning against. The front door was open as was usual. If he remembered correctly, all these houses had a huge number of people sleeping in each room. The corridor and the gardens were empty but accessible. She led him to the back. There was no need for talk. She leaned against the garden wall and he was ready. He had his tool gripped tight in his hand and he wasted no time in 'helping' her to the next world. She was an ideal candidate and she made not a sound. He held her when the initial incision was made to the throat and then laid her down. The incision had to be attempted twice since her wretched scarf she wore round her neck got in his way. He laid her down and then began his search. He was overjoyed in yet again finding a person who was sick of this world and who asked him to free her. To leave her body to the advancement of science! She willingly laid her life in his hands and she must be thanking him for it. He rid the world of another loser and brought this sad life to an end and made her a martyr. *Out of tragedy!* He was going to be justly rewarded. The medical world would hail him as a genius! As far as this second experiment went, all was well. This time he decided to take away some parts for microscope study. These included the uterus and the bladder. While he worked, he realised that she had been quite extensively bruised in the chest area. Her tissue was dark brown where the tiny blood vessels had been damaged. She must have been in considerable pain. Not now though! He had put an end to her misery! He was her Saviour! He finished and then waited. He saw no sign of what he was looking for. With a touch of disappointment, he decided to bring this experiment to an end. It was getting light and he still had to make his way through the early morning market to his room. Before he left, he noticed that some of her belongings had fallen out of her pocket and onto the floor. Some combs, pennies and small material thing. He collected them and laid them respectfully at her feet. He also noticed the rings on her fingers which were soaked in blood. He struggled to take them off. When he managed, he took a piece of leather material that was lying close by, cleaned the rings and placed them neatly at her feet. He threw away the blood-soaked material and smiled at a job well done and thanked the lady for donating her body to science.

CHAPTER 27

During this period, Edward had totally forgotten that he was not meant to be going back with Maybrick. The lovely Florence did not want to see him again. But all of his equipment was in the basement and he really had to examine those parts that he had removed from his last participant. He wanted to examine them under the microscope and boil them and remove the proteins and many other things. He was so eager that he could not control his excitement! He wanted to leave for Liverpool straight away. Maybrick had told him again that he was to stay but Edward argued with him. He would love to have stayed and carried on his work here, but he had to take stock of the results so far and to write down everything he did. It was always important to maintain the scientific notes properly, so you know exactly what you did. If he did not get them down soon, he would forget important things. He put this all pleadingly to Maybrick and even told him that Florence would not be a problem and that he would make his peace with her. The tired and ill Maybrick gave in as usual to this most impossible request. It seemed to him irrelevant what Florence objected to. He had that morning received a letter from Nathaniel. It read:

My dear James

I was going to wait until we met in person but this is urgent. I hope the illness you suffered has passed.

I must apologise since I have failed the one task that you set me. I have not been able to find out who Edward really is although I do not think that he is a criminal. It seems very uncharacteristic. to want to blackmail you. I think you do not have to worry about that little problem of yours. However, I am deeply concerned about our friend. He seems to have changed somewhat. He is irritable and aggressive as well as being extremely forgetful. One moment he could be kind and concerned about those around him and the next he is a wreck. I fear the story he has told you is correct. I do think he is a medical man and that his addiction to substances he administered to himself have made him sick. His mind is very affected and I suggest you watch over him. He may need medical attention. I am on hand if you need me.

Your very true friend
Nathaniel Grey

'What is he doing here!' yelled Florence as she looked out of the window and saw that James had brought that man back. She was livid and stamped her foot. She looked at the maid standing behind her and yelled even more. 'How can he do this to me?'

Edward was kind to her. He decided to go straight to the basement and stay there out of sight. He was sure there was going to be a scene and he wanted them just to get it over with. Maybrick left his luggage and coat with the servant and then went straight to pacify his wife. He was right. Her wrath had surpassed all his expectations.

'You have so little respect for me! How can you bring that imbecile back to my house? Do you want me to sit out this entire social season?'

'Hello, my dear. I am well, thank you. How did you pass the time?' he said as he wearily slumped on the sofa.

'Are you listening to me?' she yelled. 'I can't help but hear you.'

'I thought you were going to leave him there along with all the other filth!' She was pacing the room as she often did when she was upset. She rubbed her hands together and wiped her tears away as she paced. She was hugely disappointed. Her house was free of this man and she was planning the rest of her summer without a care in the world. No worries about things not going right or people being offended. She had spent these last ten days or so happy that the Devil had gone from her home. To find that he not only was back, but that he did not need her permission to walk freely to the basement was unbearable for her. The shock of this produced the tears but the anger was mounting.

'Florrie. Listen.'

'No! No! NO!'

'Florrie. Please, calm down.'

'DON'T TELL ME TO CALM DOWN! 'she yelled.

'Florrie...'

'Out! I want him out!' she screeched.

'FLORENCE!' His roar stopped her in her tracks. She stared at him in silence. The tears stopped. He was still master. 'For God's Sake Florence, why do you never listen?' He put his hand into his pocket and pulled out Nathaniel's letter. He waited while she read it. He hoped that this would be all the explanation that she wanted.

'He must have family of his own!' she retorted. 'You said he was a friend of yours! I was right! You did pick him up off the street! He is living off our charity!' She was about to say more when she heard someone clearing their throat at the doorway and she knew it was him! She swung round with the look of hatred in her narrow angry eyes. But even through her anger, she saw a total transformation in the man before her. He was thinner. Much thinner than before. Grey hair could be seen clearly on his once dark head and he had facial growth which was unkept and unruly to say the least. There were dark lines around his eyes and mouth and his brow was permanently furrowed. He was still well dressed but he looked like he had been roaming around for days without food or sleep.

'Mrs Maybrick. I have come back, much to your dissatisfaction, I know. But I am here only for a short time to complete some of my work. I shall go as soon as that work is finished. In the meantime, I apologise for being rude and ruining your life. I shall stay out of your way in future.'

'Mr Hamilton,' she said in an unforgiving manner, 'you had apologised on a previous occasion in much the same way and I accepted it, only to have my hospitality thrown back in my face! I cannot forgive you this time. Your crime was too great a blow to me for it to be so easily forgiven!'

'Florence' interrupted Maybrick but she was beyond reason now. 'I will not have…'

'Mrs Maybrick,' said Edward as he lost his sincere face and replaced it with his sneered look, 'the last few days must have been very pleasant for you! Pray tell us how you passed the idle hours away!' She made no reply. She watched him as he strolled into the room and sat down. 'I think a husband and wife should always be interested in how the other spends idle hours. What hobbies they took part in, what functions, what friends they saw. After such a long journey, I am sure James would prefer you to sit down and fill him with dainty stories of your recent chores and recreation.' He paused to let her answer but carried on when he was met with silence. 'I don't know about James, but I met many people. Parry, Simon, Ethel, and of course, Nathaniel. Who did you see?'

'Now look here, Hamilton!' interrupted an annoyed Maybrick. 'Why do you harass her so? If you are going to carry on like this, I suggest you go back to London!'

'It's fine, James. Mr Hamilton was only teasing,' she said coldly. 'Of course, he may stay!' She then took her leave of them and hoped that the illness was severe enough to remove the vermin from her house in a coffin!

When they were alone, Maybrick turned to Edward. 'What was all that about?'

'What?'

'All those questions! What point where you trying to make?'

'None. I was trying to be social.' Maybrick said no more but the seeds of doubt had been planted. Maybrick fell into thought and spoke no more.

Once more events just plodded along in the Maybrick household as they had been before. Nobody could have guessed that residing in the house was a double murderer who was totally insane. What made Edward even more dangerous was that he had no idea what he had done. In all other respects, he was totally normal. He held normal conversations with Maybrick and still played with the children although he did spend much of his time in his basement. Although Florence had held a dinner or two, Edward did not attend. He occasionally went and joined Maybrick late in the evening for some port or sherry. Edward noticed that Maybrick was looking more and more unwell. He complained all the time about headaches and pains in his stomach. He had increased his dose of strychnine, much to Edward's horror. The man was sure to kill himself with an overdose if he was careless.

Edward spent much time working but he decided that it was a disadvantage to him not to know the general news of the day. He remembered nothing about the Corporation. However, he knew that his knowledge of the politics and history of the day was limited and constantly caused him trouble. He spent some time reading. Newspapers, old and new, books and recent history. Queen Victoria was indeed the monarch and had been so most of her life and there were people alive who did not know any other monarch. It was always Queen Victoria. Since the death of Prince Albert, the Queen had advisors. Lord Melbourne and Benjamin Disraeli were two such advisors and certain literature of the day suggested that the Queen was not too clever as a figure herself and needed guidance all the time when it came to running the country. Somewhere from his memory Edward remembered bleak, dark stories penned by Dickens. Suffering, poverty and need. Dicken's England was a sad and cruel place if one did not have money. However, the research that Edward had done suggested that this version of events was one sided. There were those who were very rich. Some of these rich people in their stately Manors had consciences. They were concerned enough about the poor to change voting rights and to abolish the Corn Law which, however the Government described it, was a cruel tax on food. Politicians realised that they could not remain wealthy without the support of the poor. During Queen Victoria's reign there was an increase in the middle class. These were people who were hard working, innovative and clever. They saw what had to be done and they learnt quickly. Designers, builders, industrialists, they were all there and England was transformed in a way that could only be described as the Victorian

Renaissance! England began to show off their talent. Prince Albert played a part in all this showing off. The Great Exhibition in 1851 was his special project. The literature of the day gave him the credit. How much it was a truly Albert idea remains a point of debate. Whoever thought of it, Prince Albert ran away with credit. The one major blot on the landscape was the Crimean War in 1854 where England joined forces with France against the Russians, who were in conflict with Turkey. The conflict was seen to be a success but the actual cost in terms of human life made it questionable. Figures such as Florence Nightingale took the attention away from the political questions being asked. The plight of the wounded soldiers acted as a smokescreen. On the whole the war was seen to strengthen the British position on the world map. While Edward was reading this little section in a history book designed for school pupils, he remembered a vague reference to the Boar War. When on Earth was that? He did not know anything about this war except that it involved South Africa and it was meant to be in Victoria's era. Or was it? He tried to think but his head ached too much. He went on to other things. He learnt that Victoria, or the monarchy for that matter was not too popular among the people. There was poverty, sickness and instability in England at the start of the Victorian reign. Now, however, the Queen was regarded as a pillar of strength. The Empress. During her reign, there had been changes on the home front in employment, education and health. Laws were brought in preventing child labour. All children of a certain age were expected to attend school on a regular basis. The Salvation Army was born in this era. Religion once again became the focal point in all family life, rich and poor. Public executions were forbidden although they were still carried out in private. The Victorians came to respect their Queen. There was still poverty and unemployment not to mention the hordes of orphaned children to be seen at this time. There were still riots. But the revolution predicted by many never happened. Edward had read somewhere that Evolution and not Revolution paved the way for British success at home. While Edward read and learnt, he still could not help thinking that before she patted herself on the back, Victoria should take a stroll down the streets of Whitechapel just to remind herself that she still had much to do.

This was Edward's life here in Liverpool. He read, learnt and planned his great experiment. One evening, Edward decided to go and visit Maybrick. He wanted to go back alone to London. On entering the study, he found that Maybrick had guests. One was Michael Maybrick and the other was man whom Edward did not recognise.

'Ah, Edward!' said Maybrick who looked unusually cheerful. 'Come in. I do not think that you have met Paul Gerrard-Smith.' The two men shook hands. 'Paul this is my friend Edward Hamilton.'

'Edward,' said Michael Maybrick as Edward sat down and accepted a port from Maybrick. 'You look rather ill if you don't mind me saying.'

'Oh, just too much work I think.'

'What do you do?' asked Paul Gerrard-Smith. 'I am a scientist.'

'Oh fantastic! What are you working on at the moment?'

'The study of cells. Anatomy is my field.'

'So, you know my insides better than I do!' They all laughed. It turned out that Paul Gerrard-Smith worked for Scotland Yard and was a close friend of Michael Maybrick's.

'So, you are a policeman,' said Edward.

'No. I am actually a forensic scientist. But I am not fully trained yet. I still have two more years to go.'

'I suppose the training is long.'

'Yes, but there is a lot to learn. It's the gruesome side of things that are a bit difficult to deal with. It takes many years to get over that. Some in the profession say that you either become totally heartless, or depressed!'

'Do you know anything about the latest murders in London? Have you had anything to do with them?' asked Michael

'What you mean the prostitutes?'

'Yes. What's the latest on them?'

'Yes, well. These crimes are most bizarre and has had even the most hardened forensic scientists becoming nauseous!'

'Are they as gruesome as rumours would have you believe?' asked Michael.

'Much more!' Gerrard-Smith's face took on a sombre look as he obviously thought about the crimes.

'Well!' persisted Michael. 'Tell us what you can.'

'It's no more than the papers have already described. The women were butchered!

The second one more than the first. It is still puzzling how this monster ever got away without being noticed! He must have been covered in blood. He must have been a madman. An animal.'

'Do they have any leads?'

He paused before he spoke. 'Gentlemen, you realise everything that I say about this is in strict confidence!' They all nodded. 'They think that the man known as Leather Apron may have been involved. He is still being questioned. They found a piece of blood-soaked leather at the scene of the second crime.'

'But surely, he would not want to leave such a blatant clue as that except if he wanted to get caught!' said Maybrick.

'What about fingerprints?' said Edward, who had not realised which crimes they were talking about.

'Finger what!' exclaimed Gerrard-Smith.

'Fingerprints. Surely you must know whether the killer left any or not,' said Edward, wondering why it was that they all looked at him in a puzzled manner.

'Oh yes,' said Maybrick, mockingly. 'Edward has mentioned these before! He seems to be under the impression that people have… what was it again?' he said looking towards Edward.

At that very stage, Edward realised that he had made a mistake. He remembered he was not of this time period. He had no idea when fingerprints came to be discovered. Was the detection of fingerprints even invented yet?

'Well. Every human has a print, the pattern on their skin at the tips of the fingers which is unique. We leave these prints on almost everything that we touch. With special techniques, one can take fingerprints and link them with the individual that they belong to.' He was met with three stunned faces. Eventually, there was a huge roar of laughter from Michael Maybrick. The others smiled as if in agreement, but Gerrard- Smith seemed less willing to mock Edward entirely.

'Fingerprints?' he said slowly.

'You must know that everyone has a different pattern on the tips of their fingers,' said Edward.

'Yes. So, what you are trying to say is that when we touch something, the imprint of pattern on the skin is left behind. Fascinating! Where have you picked this up from?'

'Pardon?' said Edward stupidly.

'You must have seen this technique in action somewhere.'

'No. Well, not exactly. Not here,' was the confusing answer. 'Well. I mean I have not actually seen it anywhere. It is … my own theory!' he lied. 'I figured that it is possible. Only I do not have the resources to test this out.'

'Fascinating! 'repeated Gerrard-Smith. 'Would you be annoyed if I put this theory to my superiors?'

'No! Of course not!'

'We will of course credit you with any discovery we may make! Are you willing to work with us?' said Gerrard-Smith. Edward was at a total loss. His mind had gone blank and he struggled to find an answer. He looked to Maybrick like a lost child would to its parent.

'Well, to be honest Paul, Edward has been told to take things easy for a while. It may not be too good for him to get involved with anything too taxing. I am sure you understand,' said Maybrick.

'Of course! I only hope that he is right about the… finger… prints!'

'I think you will find that I am,' said Edward in a cocky manner.

'Let's get back to the crimes!' said Michael Maybrick who was getting bored with the fingerprint theory.

'Well. What more do you want to know?' said Gerrard-Smith, knowing that he was breaching his employment conditions.

'How badly mutilated were the women?' said Michael. 'Was he artistic or just a butcher?'

'The Yard would like to believe that it was just someone thrashing and slashing about with a knife. But I think the horror of it is that this animal is a well-educated man. The method of opening the bodies up shows that he had a certain amount of medical knowledge. He knew how to make the incisions, how to remove the first and second layers of the skin and how to find the major organs.'

All this while, Edward sat there totally oblivious. He thought what a terrible crime it was and wondered what kind of crazy lunatic would do that to another human being. At least what he had done was not as cold blooded as all this. He had freed tortured Souls from those who wanted to leave this Earth. He had helped them to a better place in return for the use of their bodies. He was totally calm and relaxed, sipping his port.

'The strange thing is that on the second victim, the uterus and bladder were missing. The freak had removed them totally from the corpse and the forensics could not find them anywhere,' said Gerrard-Smith.

Edward froze. He suddenly felt like a knife had penetrated deep into his heart. He could feel his temperature rising as he realised what crimes they were talking about. *Uterus and bladder?* Surely Gerrard-Smith could not be referring to *his* work. Nobody was meant to know about that! He was about to say something when he realised that he himself thought that they were talking about some madman. He stared at Gerrard- Smith in disbelief. This could not be right! His work was not that of a madman! He was *not* mad. This was his research. He was angry now. How could they be so stupid that they could not see that! They were the stupid ones. He was performing a well needed task. He was helping those women. They needed his help. They were desperate. They had willingly donated their bodies to science! If they only knew how much information, he had managed to get from that uterus and bladder. He was sure that if they knew what the nature of his study was and exactly how the women had agreed to donate their bodies, then they would understand. But he felt now was not the time to do this. He had to wait until he had carried out more research.

'You don't understand,' he said quietly. He spoke almost as if to himself. He had by this stage walked over to the window and was staring out. 'But now is not the time.'

'What? Are you alright, Edward?' asked Maybrick. 'You seem to have turned a funny colour.'

'It's all been misunderstood!' said Edward still staring out the window. He was fighting an incredible urge to enlighten them all so they could congratulate him on his genius.

'My dear fellow,' interrupted Gerrard-Smith, 'there is not much that can be misunderstood about a crime like this. The man has to be mad.' Edward was biting his lip. He wanted to tell them. He was wondering maybe now was the time!

'Sure, it all seems to be gruesome. But there may be a reason,' said Edward.

'A reason!' shouted Gerrard-Smith. 'What reason can there possibly be for ripping a human being open? I cannot think of one even in the weirdest of dreams! The Ripper is a madman!' He then paused. 'Mr Hamilton, if I was not mistaken, I would say that maybe you know something about him!' Working at Scotland Yard had definitely given him a suspicious nature.

'The *ripper?*' Edward whispered. 'You called him... *Ripper.*'

'So?' said a puzzled Gerrard-Smith.

'Ripper!' Memories came flooding back. He started pacing up and down the room.

'Edward, I think you had better rest.'

The penny dropped. Edward's brain was racing. Ripper. Whitechapel. East End.

Eighteen hundred and something or another! Oh God, no! NO!

'Jack!' said Edward. 'Oh my God! No! No! NO! Jack the Ripper!' He was swooning now as he paced the room.

'Jack?' repeated Michael Maybrick. 'Who the Devil is Jack!'

'Mr Hamilton. Do you know the identity of the Whitechapel Murderer?' asked Gerrard-Smith in a stern manner.

'How many!' Edward was thinking aloud now. 'How many were there?' He was sweating now and paced madly. He was shocked! He remembered the name. Jack the Ripper! Jack the Ripper! Oh God! He realised where he was. At first, he was confused. The name 'Yorkshire Ripper' came to mind. He remembered reading about Jack the Ripper when he was a teenager. It fascinated him and he had even become a member of a Ripper Club! Now he realised what he had become! That book that he had read. He was reading about himself! The Hollywood film that he had seen. It was about himself! The mystery surrounding this series of crimes, it was all centred around him! All these years! The years of speculation, the theories, the possible suspects! It was him they were trying to identify! He was sickened! He did not want to be Jack the Ripper! He was a scientist, and his work was misconstrued! Over a hundred years later, a different millennium altogether and they had totally misunderstood it all! It was not a gruesome series of murders! It was an experiment! There was a lump in his throat at how society had managed to get it all wrong! How had they totally misjudged this? Jack the Ripper was a good guy!

'Edward, I shall call someone to take you to your room,' said Maybrick.

'How many were there?' said Edward suddenly. The question was not directed to anyone. He knew that there were more. How many? Four? Five? Six? He thought hard to try and find the answer to that. He had to know how many there were. How many would he have to enlist on to the study before he found the answer! Before the servant came to take him back to his room, he was stopped by Gerrard-Smith.

'Mr Hamilton, why did you call him Jack? What do you know?'

'Nothing,' smiled a mad looking Edward. 'Jack the Ripper. Has a good ring to it, don't you think?' He then disappeared out the door.

'Jack the Ripper!' exclaimed Michael Maybrick. 'What an extraordinary description! I think that should become your nickname for the lunatic.'

'Jack the Ripper,' repeated Gerrard-Smith. 'Well let's hope that he stopped at two.'

Edward Hamilton was a tortured Soul. *He* was Jack the Ripper! Eighteen hundred and something or another, Whitechapel. The East End of London. Why did he not think of it before! He was Jack the Ripper. There were tears running down his cheeks, but these were not tears of shame or guilt. These were for his misunderstood study. They had it all wrong! His work was seriously at risk from not being understood at all! What he had done were no crimes, they should not be looked upon as such. However, he remembered much about the way in which history saw these crimes. The sensationalism surrounding them was sickening! They had not understood anything. He decided that this was an advantage for him. He could not remember how he came to be here, but he did know that it was not his time zone. He knew that without his interference the crimes would always be seen as those performed by a crazed lunatic. He would not let that happen. He would make sure that when he revealed himself to the world, he would explain exactly what he had done. He would hold meetings and seminars and debates. The world would understand that Jack the Ripper was not a butcher, but a great scientist who had discovered the Soul! He found it fascinating that he was linked to the most infamous serial killer of them all. Uncanny. The crimes had fascinated him as a young boy. But to grow up and find that you had been reading about yourself! It was brilliant! He loved this time travel business! It was great! All he had to do was show everyone their mistake! He was upset at first, but now, he realised that his work must go on. He had to carry on and keep filling in his journal with meticulous detail. As he wondered off into sleep, the name *Jack the Ripper* kept coming into his head.

Edward Hamilton was Jack the Ripper. A man born in the 1960's had travelled back in time from 2007 to the year eighteen hundred and something or another and had become the infamous Jack the Ripper!

CHAPTER 28

Edward spent much of the next few days keeping his journal up to date. He had much to put in there. At first, it was meant to be purely a scientific piece of work but as the time went on the journal took on a very personal note. His anger was obvious in his writing. His dislike of all things affluent and especially Florence Maybrick. Once or twice, he had a doubt as to whether or not he should put all the details in. On one occasion he started to read some of his earlier entries and found that it all sounded fairly ludicrous. Appearing from nowhere in the park and claiming to have come from the 21st century just did not give his journal any credibility. He decided that the time travel part was never going to help his cause. It was not important where he came from. What was important was what he was going to discover. He decided the best thing that he could do was amend the front part of his diary. Ripping apart the first 40 odd pages made it look like a well-worn but damaged part of someone's journal rather than the fantasy rantings of a lunatic. He also made other amends and decided to leave out his own identity. It would not be too smart to leave his identity open since anyone could prematurely find the document and on reading his journal could identify him as the Whitechapel Murderer and he would have to bring his study to a premature end. All the time that he was here in Liverpool he was itching to get back to London. His work was being severely delayed. He expressed his wish to return to London alone but Maybrick seemed to be blocking him. He could not understand. It was originally Maybrick's own idea that he should stay in London in the room he had but now he seemed to have changed his mind.

He insisted that the two of them should wait until the end of the month and go together.

'Look,' said Maybrick one evening towards the end of September. 'I have arranged for us to go to London together in a couple of days' times, but we cannot spend too long there. I have some things to do but they will not take all that long.'

'Why can't I just stay there? You don't need me here. Mrs Maybrick would be delighted.' Edward was a touch annoyed. He was of late being treated like a child. Maybrick was always asking if he was feeling well. All his movements were always monitored and at every opportunity. The family doctor was asked to take a look at him. He did not remember being sick. The idea of being chaperoned to London was distasteful to him. All he wanted was to be left alone to do his work. Of course, financially, Maybrick was still helping him and it did not seem like he was going to pay back that loan he had borrowed from Nathaniel. To a certain extent he had to do what Maybrick told him to.

'Edward. It is plain to everyone who knows you that you do suffer from loss of memory. It is long term and at a moment's notice you forget where you are or who you are talking to. You seem to forget everyday casual things and if left in London for any length of time on your own, you will run into problems. You need someone with you.'

'I have Nathaniel there.'

'As a matter of fact, it is Nathaniel who has advised me to accompany you.'

'Shit!' The word came out and he knew as soon as he had said it that it was taken to be offensive. He had to be so careful with his speech but that was a momentary lack of concentration.

'Edward! You have the language of a sewer rat! Please control yourself!'

'Well, I'm sick to death of being treated like a child! Why do I have to tell you where I am going all the time! I know what I am doing, and I have many friends. I don't need you!' He was angry but all the time, he was aware of the fact that he was biting the hand that fed him. He beat his fists in the air in frustration and turned away towards the window. He then immediately turned around and faced Maybrick while pouring out his apologies for his behaviour. Maybrick had not moved a muscle. He began to understand what Nathaniel was talking about in his letter. The mood swings, the anger, the confusion. Together with the loss of memory Maybrick was convinced that he could not let Edward alone in the streets of London. Edward knew that to row with this man now was foolish. He still needed his equipment and needed to keep his base here. It certainly would not all fit into that room in Whitechapel. What is more, the room was totally insecure and open to anyone. At least here, he could move freely in and out knowing that the things in his basement would be safe.

'I'm sorry,' he said in a dejected manner. 'I am under a great deal of stress! I know things have not been that easy for you. I really do appreciate all your help. I tend to lose my temper every now and again! I'll do whatever you say.'

'I think you could do with a rest. All those hours in the basement. You hardly eat, you don't sleep, and you look a mess!'

'Thanks! I'll consider that a compliment!'

Two days later they were in Whitechapel again. Maybrick had made things so difficult for Edward that the latter found it hard to get away. They spent an evening with Nathaniel and the next couple of days dining somewhere. In the day, Edward scoured the streets. The workhouses, the begging corners, street sellers and the hungry. They were all potential participants for his experiment. With children he had decided to draw the line. There was every chance that they would be able to live a decent life as an adult. Also, one of the entry requirements was that you were willing to give up rights to life. Edward decided children would not know what it was to lose your life. He did however decide that if he came across one that was in a real bad way and begged to take part in his work, then he would accept them. After all, his aim was to help these people as well as be helped by them!

On one of his daytime visits, he was alone. Maybrick had to leave him to his own devices and he decided to take a stroll. It was a hot sunny day. He had totally misjudged his ability to walk long distances. He was quite a long way away from his room. He suddenly became very tired and lethargic. He felt like he was going to faint in the heat. He had to sit down somewhere and in desperation, he jumped on a bus. He had not travelled in anything other than a coach. On this visit, Michael Maybrick had given his brother access to the coach that was actually one of those discarded by the Duke of Clarence! A fact that Michael Maybrick could not resist from broadcasting to everyone. Maybrick was using this coach and also allowed Edward to use it when it was available. Edward moved through the bus to look for a seat. The bus was crowded but he was lucky since a seat right near him became available. He sat and relaxed and almost dozed off among the noise. When he awoke, he realised that he did not actually recognise where he was. In panic, he suddenly jumped up and moved towards the exit. The bus was still moving as it approached the bus stop. He was moving and pushing past people when he stumbled and made a grab for one of the seats. As he did so, his hand rested on the arms of another passenger. As soon as he did this, he felt a sensation in his head. It was not pain. Just a faint tingling which he was sure he had experienced before. He looked at the face of the man whose arm he was clutching, and he was suddenly filled with terror! The man had a long, pale, pasty face and his eyes, clear blue, frightened eyes, stared at him in terror! There were huge dark hollows in which his eyes were set, and the man had perspiration running down the side of his face. Edward had never met this man, but he *knew* who he was. Edward saw that the man's terror had a reason. The stranger knew! He knew who Edward was. The tingling in Edward's head increased and he immediately saw that his identity was known to this man! Their brains were connecting! He had to get away! The bus had slowed considerably but had not stopped. Edward saw the man looking round him as if to warn others. Edward had no choice. He had to make a dash for it. He took his hand off the man's arm and immediately the tingling in his head disappeared. In an instance, Edward jumped off the bus and landed heavily on his feet almost losing his footing. He staggered along and ran as fast as his legs would take him. On looking back, he was horrified to see that the bus had stopped, and the thin, pale man had also got out and was following him. The stranger eventually found a constable and was pointing towards Edward. Edward's heart was pulsating erratically, but his head was crystal clear. He looked ahead and saw someone getting off a coach. Before the driver took off, Edward jumped into it and shouted for the driver to go! He breathed a sigh of relief when he found that he had managed to get away. They were not following him. He sat back and breathed! That was close! He had no idea who the stranger was, but he knew that their minds connected on physical contact and that the other could read him!

Robert Lees was distraught! He stood there on the pavement looking at the coach. His wife was by his side and the constable was asking question after question, but he was not listening. The pain and the images in his head were subsiding! He stared at the coach as it moved away from them, getting smaller and smaller. He watched it, knowing that in it, sat the most wanted man in London. He was tortured for months to come as he lay in the darkness and saw the eyes of the Whitechapel Murderer looking back at him!

CHAPTER 29

S o far with his two participants he had not found what he was looking for. The Soul was a well-hidden feature! He decided that maybe he would be luckier if he went in deeper. He also wanted to even out the bodies he had by sex. He was actually looking for a male candidate. Although he came across many men during his time here, he never actually heard one so distressed with his lot that he craved death. This was still an important requirement, though by the third night, he was thinking of reviewing the limits. It seemed more difficult than he thought to find people willing to give their lives. He talked and talked and searched but he was not lucky. His frustration was growing. He had actually intended to have a participant for every night that he was here! Then he could have gone back to Liverpool and spent the rest of the month analysing his data and forming a theory. The only downside to finding a male candidate was that they would be stronger than the females and so it would be more difficult to handle. He eventually became so desperate that he decided to take whichever sex came first. Ideally, he still wanted to find someone who did actually want to die. When its came to publishing his data, the scientists of the day would ask what his criteria for selection was and he had to be honest. He could not lie about his selection conditions. It could invalidate all his data!

Maybrick was also hampering his experiment. He was like a parent keeping close watch on an unruly child. It was not until the fourth evening that Maybrick's personal needs outweighed those of Edward's and he decided to make his visit to his lady friend. Usually, he would not be back until late, if at all but on this occasion, he was careful to be back by 11.00pm only to find on entering the room that

Edward was not there. Maybrick's first instinct was to leave him to it but on reflection, he decided that Edward's sanity was seriously in question and he had to go and look for him. Maybrick had to follow him and bring him back.

On this occasion he had use of Michael's coach. Michael had just been given another coach discarded by the Duke of Clarence, or Eddie, as Michael referred to him. Michael also supplied Maybrick with a driver but at night all the driving had to be done by Maybrick himself. He took this coach and scoured the area for a couple of hours hoping to find Edward. He tried all the drinking houses and the social gatherings around street corners. At a quarter to one in the morning, he was tired and in need of sleep. He had earlier left the coach nearby and had started to make his way into the tiny roads by foot, but now he thought it was time to give up. For all he knew Edward could be back in the room already. He was fighting a losing battle here, so he started to make his way back the way he had come. The lights from the windows of nearby buildings were still bright as people went to bed rather late in this part of town! However, some of the smaller roads had no lighting at all and Maybrick found himself in total darkness for as much as fifteen to twenty steps. He was feeling uncomfortable and decided to quicken his step, his gait being heard as it echoed in the darkness. He turned into Berner's Street and was immediately aware of someone shuffling about there. He peered into the darkness but could not make out what was going on. He walked slowly in the direction of the noise hoping that his eyes would soon become accustomed to the night. He could hear some noise in the distance but as he moved forward, he heard faint footsteps, almost scuttering about the place. There was definitely someone there who seemed to be moving about at the same spot but not actually going anywhere! A sudden shiver ran through him and he decided to turn around and walk away, which was just what he was about to do when suddenly, the footsteps started and Maybrick could hear them moving. Moving steadily and with speed! Moving oh Lord! They were moving towards him! He froze on the spot as he watched. He had to use all his effort to keep his bladder from emptying! He was rooted to the spot in fear. From the darkness he saw a shadow appearing. He could just make out a huge shadowy thing on the floor and his heart started thumping away! What on Earth had he disturbed! He started to walk backwards, but very slowly as his fear still gripped him! Out from the shadows emerged a figure and Maybrick gave out a small cry.

'Who are you?' he shouted, his voice shaking.

The figure stopped in it tracks. The two were fairly close now and within another second, the man came out of the darkness.

'Maybrick?' It was Edward's voice! 'Edward! What the Devil are you doing!'

'Maybrick!' shouted Edward, who had the knife in his hand at the ready. 'I could ask you the same thing! Are you following me? What the hell are you doing here?'

Maybrick was looking past Edward at the bundle on the floor. Edward caught his gaze and then took him away by the arm in the opposite direction. He had already hidden the knife and his hands.

'What are doing?' asked Maybrick, suspiciously. 'Who is that?'

'Some drunk. He'll be fine in the morning.' He almost dragged Maybrick away. 'Don't you think we ought to put him somewhere safe?'

'Don't worry, the constable will be passing this way soon. He will deal with it.'

They moved away from that street where Maybrick led them to his coach. Edward seemed on edge and was glancing back all the time. He seemed shifty and worried. Maybrick took control of the coach after Edward got in. They drove away.

Edward was hugely agitated. He had to abandon that experiment and was annoyed at the total waste of material. He had not even started yet. He had only got as far as extinguishing life. He had kept to her side of the bargain which was to end her mortal existence on this Earth, but he had got nothing out of it himself. He had heard footsteps soon after the initial slitting of the throat. Now he was in panic! They were to leave the next day and so far, he had no more data! He had to strike now! He had to make a second attempt. He had two problems. Maybrick was one. He had to find a way to ditch him! Selecting someone appropriate was another. It had taken him four days to find that last one. Four days of searching to find someone who gave him all the right answers to his qualifying questions! And even then, he had to help that last one out with some of the answers! How was he going to find another one so soon? Drastic action was needed and for that, he had to act immediately. He had no idea where Maybrick was taking him. He poked his head out of the window and started banging on the side hoping that Maybrick would be able to hear him. Maybrick drove on for a few yards and then stopped in a busy street which had the remnants of the drinking house filtering out after a long night. Edward got out and was insisting that Maybrick went home and just let him be. Maybrick on the other hand was adamant that they were going together. They were arguing like this for a few seconds when they were approached by a 'daughter of the night', old looking though she was. She came up to them and kindly offered her hospitality to Edward. Maybrick began to tell her to be on her way when Edward saw his chance. He immediately linked her by the arm and put on a bit of charm. He then made out as if he was interested. He told her to get in the coach. When she sat inside, he went to Maybrick.

'Look. I am a man, right?' he said to an annoyed Maybrick. 'You have your needs, I have mine. I don't question your needs. And you cannot prevent me from attending to mine,' he said with a certain glint in his eye. Maybrick looked at him but then conceded that the man had been there for almost two months and had shown no interest in women up until now. It was refreshing that there was something about him that was normal. He showed a healthy interest in women. Maybrick could not stop him. He agreed to drop them off anywhere they wanted.

In the time that Maybrick was taking them somewhere quiet, Edward tried to make some sense out of the woman sitting, or rather slumping in front of him. He understood from her terrible speech that she had just been released from the prison where she was sobering up. They let her out when she was sober enough to be let out which surprised Edward since by his estimation, she was totally plastered and would have needed at least a week to properly sober up. He looked at her and constantly pushed her away from him as she leaned on his shoulder. He had a great deal of sympathy for these people but this one repulsed him to a certain extent. He could not explain why she was any different from the others, but he wanted to get rid of her as soon as possible. She was rabbiting on about her children and husband and it did not seem to Edward that she looked all that dejected with her life. It was impossible to use his normal questionnaire on her simply because he had no time and also because she was totally drunk. She would not be able to answer the questions truthfully. He was desperate. He decided to take the unprecedented step of deciding for her! After all, she was pissed, stupid and penniless. The only kind of shelter she was likely to get was in the prison, sobering up, she had a pathetic life which was bearable because she was intoxicated all the time. Her life had no meaning now. If she were sober and able to think for herself, she would have realised her futile situation and would have gladly helped the progress of mankind by donating her battered and abused body! Edward was certain about this. For all these good reasons, Edward decided that he would answer all the qualifying questions himself and make the decision for this unfortunate Soul. By the time Maybrick dropped them off, Edward was already peering inside his bag for all the equipment. The two of them walked or rather she staggered, and he held her up, a short distance in a quiet and dark part of the road. He was a little unsure where to go. The place that he was in was open and exposed them both. He wanted to find a dark passage somewhere but before he could think what he wanted; the hag next to him fell to the floor. She lay there singing and laughing, a shrill, mad, drunken laugh which annoyed him. He was trying to pull her up thinking that the people living in the area may hear them. The night was hot, and many had their windows open. Eventually, he was so desperate to shut her up that he knelt down, and, in a flash, he passed the sharp edge swiftly across her throat. He could not see exactly what he was doing and the tool he held felt as if it passed across the nose, or was it the ear? That certainly did the trick, he thought. It had shut her up instantly! No more shall she sing, or rather wail like a demented cow! He had the least amount of affection for this one. He proceeded with his work with a certain amount of contempt! The slashes were very irregular and jagged. He had not bothered to move the clothes out of the way and when she was open, he unceremoniously dug out her insides and threw them to one side. He was annoyed because the location was not by choice and he could barely see what he was doing. He managed to get about her corpse by feeling his way round. He knew where everything was and generally moved around by feeling his way into the body. He found it impossible to work like this and decided after a few minutes to abandon the wretch! He was livid and he angrily tore her eyelids away! Damned! Damned! What a waste of resources! He should have taken her somewhere else! He could not see anything! The Soul could have been staring him in the face and he would not have been able to see it! He cleared up around himself and kicked the body before angrily stomping off, his cloak covering his blood-soaked hands and arms. Bitch! It was all wrong! She was all wrong. He did not choose her! He did not get her to answer the questions! He was in a rush and he picked the wrong specimen! He was forced to take her! Now he was no further in his study than he was that morning! Two failed attempts! TWO! What a waste of time! And tomorrow they were off! He was desperate to have another go. He walked off and began to search for someone else when he suddenly heard footsteps in front of him! He looked up and saw a constable walking towards him. He had a concerned look on his face, and he was staring very intently at Edward. Edward noticed that as he walked towards him the constable was looking to see if he could see Edward's arms and hands. He was looking and trying to peer inside the cloak! Edward's hands were totally soaked in blood! Edward tensed himself up, seeing in the next few seconds, his great experiment coming to an end! No! He could not have that. He had to act. Suddenly, the constable seemed to Edward to be the perfect specimen! Yes! Someone normal! Edward was ready for him!

'Sir. Can you tell me from which direction you are coming?'

'Why? Is there a problem Constable?'

For some reason, the constable was very suspicious of Edward. 'Sir, I am going to have to ask you to accompany me.' He reached out his arm towards Edward, who in return had clenched his bloody fists tight and was ready to lash out. Before anything else happened, they heard another constable's whistle. This time, it came from the direction that Edward had just come from. There was a faint voice in the distance saying that there was another one!

'Another one? Good God! Heaven forgive him!' said the constable. He was reluctant to let Edward go but he eventually left.

Damned! Why? Why did he let that perfect specimen walk away! He would have been perfect! His anger was now growing! He had had a disastrous day! It was a total failure, and he would have to explain all these failed attempts in his journal. He stomped away! He had to find somewhere to wash his hands. He found a puddle in the street and suspiciously bent down to wash his hands. On digging into his pocket for a napkin he felt something warm. He pulled it out! He found himself staring down at part of a kidney! Wow! He had no idea that he had managed to salvage this! Brilliant! He smiled. The night was not such a total failure after all!

CHAPTER 30

E dward travelled back to Liverpool with Maybrick, totally oblivious to the panic and confusion he had left behind him. London, on the whole, was in the grip of Ripper fever. The police were inundated with hundreds of letters telling them how to tackle the situation. There were people advising them how to entrap this killer. Using 'respectable' women as decoys, using dummies around street corners stained with red dye so that the assailant would be marked and easy to trace. There were suggestions that the women of the night could be given weapons for their safety so that they could try and maim their attacker. The Church had also become involved saying that it was lawless society that had led to these killings. Others were concerned that it was an act of God to remove the whoring that went on in London. It was right that somebody had the sense to remove this filth from the street so that they could be clean for God-fearing people to walk on.

Along with this came hundreds of hoax letters from people claiming to be the Ripper. Why any normal adult would want to claim to be an infamous, cold-blooded killer is anybody's guess. These letters hampered the police not just by the fact that there was a huge amount of sorting out to do among all the information collected, but because they wrongly believed some of these to be true. They were beginning to build up a picture of the sort of man they thought could do something like this. The suggestions ranged from a demented doctor to a qualified butcher. There were even rumours going round that Royalty was involved and Queen Victoria's court were trying to keep it under wraps. Prince Albert Victor, the Duke of Clarence and Avondale, was the eldest son of the Prince of Wales, Edward.

Grandson of Queen Victoria. It was rumoured that a Hansom coach was seen with an outline of the Royal Crest on it. There were concerns about the Duke's wild ways. Other theories were that it was a crazed midwife, unable to have children herself was venting her fury on the whores on London. Another that it was an escaped lunatic and the most common perception that it was a doctor. The way that the bodies had been dissected was not random slashing, but more like a surgeon carrying out an autopsy. It did not look like the police were very popular at this this stage. Around Whitechapel and in areas like Hyde Park, gatherings began. The public gathered to voice their unhappiness at the police. Their concerns about the rumours that it was either the royal physician or a member of the royal family. Social unrest was brewing, and the police were taunted in the media and in the public.

Hundreds of policemen were drafted in from other areas such as Essex, to patrol the streets at night in larger numbers. No one at the time could have imagined that over a hundred years later, the mystery would still be raging on.

With all the chaos, and all the theories, nobody could have guessed that Jack the Ripper was actually a scientist from the year 2007, who had travelled back in time, become insane, and proceeded to carry out a huge experiment where he was looking to release the Soul from certain unfortunate people!

Edward Hamilton was quietly sleeping his way to Liverpool. In his mind, the World would thank him for his efforts. Total Oblivion! One who was not oblivious to anything that happened that night was James Maybrick. Up until tonight, there was doubt in his mind. He had heard the early morning news and had been horrified to learn that there were two more victims last night. Two! He knew Edward was walking away from one bundle. Was it really a drunk? He then saw him in the company of a woman just a few minutes later. He looked at the face of the man sleeping in the carriage opposite him and it did not look like the face of a crazed killer. But then what did the face a crazed killer look like? It was a calm and peaceful face, conscience clear from any atrocity. Surely any man that could have ripped a Human Being open like a laboratory rat could not be normal!

Edward had many problems but Maybrick could not imagine that he could have done something so horrendous, and then manage to calmly sleep afterwards. He tried to examine Edward's person to see if he could see anything that gave him away. Edward also seemed totally oblivious to anything the next day when the story broke out in the streets. People were standing around on street corners talking as were the gentlemen at Maybrick's breakfast club. The first editions of the newspaper's solidified the rumours. Surely the actual murderer would want to listen to the rumours and the read the newspaper stories and see the effect that his grisly crimes had on society. But with Edward, there was nothing. He treated it all with indifference. Maybrick was no psychologist but this action was not normal. He found it hard to believe that this man was Jack the Ripper.

The next day on their journey away from London, Maybrick felt ashamed of himself for even suspecting Edward. Edward seemed to genuinely care about the poor and the needy. He had a bond with the people of Whitechapel. There is no way, thought Maybrick. It was impossible that Edward was the Whitechapel Murderer.

The next few days saw Edward engrossed in the basement. Every now and again he came out and took a stroll in the garden to get some fresh air. He still ate very little and drank a lot of gin. He was at peace with his own conscience to such an extent that Maybrick totally forgot his thoughts about a crazed killer. The Maybrick household on the other hand was definitely not at peace with itself! Again, it was Florence Maybrick, but the source of her trouble was not Edwards. James Maybrick had returned home and was surprised to find that Michael was there. He had not been expecting him. The social scene in London was in full swing and Maybrick was sure there was some event that Michael was performing at. He was in demand this year as his popularity had increased due to his high connections! Although Maybrick could not tell what the problem was, he felt a certain amount of tension between Florence and Michael. They had never really got on very well, but the atmosphere now was very thick. Maybrick tried to question Florence but she was ignoring him. All his questions were going unacknowledged, and he knew something was up. Of course, he never could have guessed that his brother was harassing Florence about her lover. Michael had something over her, and she felt very much on edge. Even her appearance had changed. She began to look haggard and run down due to not being able to sleep or eat properly. What would she do if James found out? What would happen to her and her babies?

James Maybrick had been blind to the antics of his wife for a very long time, however, certain comments from his brother were beginning to stick in his mind. He had not forgotten that grilling that Edward gave Florence when they returned from the last London trip. It was unusual, out of place questioning that suddenly took all the fire out of her to such an extent that she allowed Edward to stay. Maybrick began to wonder if there was anything about Florence's life at home that he did not know about. Surely, she would not be doing anything unbecoming of a wife. Not Florence. Not his Florence. He knew that his wife was aware that he himself had a mistress, but could she really be hitting back with a lover? His brain was in a mess thinking about who it could possibly be. He knew no one except your Brierly who called on her frequently but surely, a man of such breeding would not risk his reputation on a married woman? And then there was age. Brierly was a young man and the thought of him with an older married woman was distasteful to Maybrick, though he himself in his younger days had entertained an older woman or two. Although he actively put the horrible thought to one side, the bitterness between his wife and his brother was increasing. Florence was definitely looking ill and spent much of the time in her room and on a couple of occasions actually took to her bed with a headache. She rarely dined with them of late.

As if this was not enough for Maybrick's sick head to think about, Michael Maybrick was making his brother's life even more miserable. Michael Maybrick was an artist! A great performer! He never wasted a moment in informing those who did not know that he had royal connections. He dined often with the Duke of Clarence and Queen Victoria had invited him to the Palace to perform at some of her social events. This is how he was able to move around London in an ex-royal coach where the crest has been removed. James' cotton business was successful, and the family had land, money and a good reputation. Being in among the thick of the London gossip and very often actually being the subject of this gossip. Michael was currently in the grip of Ripper fever as well and he had not forgotten Edward's strange behaviour when the murders were mentioned. He also knew that Maybrick spent a large part of each month in Whitechapel. He knew about the room. Further independent investigations had told him that James was in Whitechapel for each of the dates when the murders took place. He also suspected that James' mistress was a prostitute. James certainly had connections there and coupled with the fact that James was ill and sickly all the time and the fact that his anger was increasing, Michael believed that James had something to do with the events. Michael had connections with Scotland Yard, and he had information that was not open to the public. For instance, he knew that the police were considering involvement by two people, at least on the night of the double event. There was a narrow time span between the first victim being found and the second. Considering that the second victim was found some distance away, actually in the City of London, the investigators thought that the killer had attacked his first victim, was disturbed, and ran off, found another victim some distance away, and then had exactly five minutes to perform his grisly task before the second body was discovered. The experts concluded that it would have taken a medical man with great experience and knowledge at least ten minutes to have ripped a body apart to such an extent. Even if it was learned man, considering that the light was appalling the whole procedure had to be carried out in very dim light, and the killer must have been hampered by this, thus slowing him down. The second body was still warm when it was discovered, and the blood marks and the position of the body suggested that the murders had not been carried out elsewhere. The killer actually worked on the body where it was found, so was not mutilated somewhere else and then dumped afterwards. The investigators had come to the conclusion that the only logical way for both crimes to have been carried out by the same hand, which they thought they were, is if the killer had travelled to the second location by coach. This is where the two-man theory had come into it. The Duke of Clarence was receiving this information in finite detail from

Scotland Yard and the same details were now in the head of Michael Maybrick. Who had two very strong suspects for the crimes?

Michael Maybrick decided to carry out his own investigation and if it meant exposing his own brother, then so be it! The frightening thing was that shock and revulsion at the crime was not his motive. Michael Maybrick's motive lay solely in his reputation. He was a man of wealth and influence and a member of his family turning out to be a killer was not good for his career. He could not be associated with such scandal. He cared little for anyone else, least of all his troubled brother. He had to find out the truth and then deal with it himself.

His investigation included snooping around his brother's study. There must be some evidence lying around which could help him. He found this difficult since James was always around and the fear of being caught red-handed meant that his searched were always hampered. He decided to help James sleep by adding pills to his food. This was easily administered in his drink. The idea was always to be on hand to make him a drink. When he was sure that James was in deep slumber, he spent time rummaging around through the study. He was on occasion caught by Florence but that did not bother him at all. She would not threaten him. Not with all the information he had against her. She just watched him with her cold deceitful eyes. He was somewhat irritated that he had found nothing to suggest anything among James' paperwork. He knew not what he expected. Surely his brother could not be daft enough to leave something lying around the study. A few days later, he saw Edward, sick and pale, taking some air in the garden. That was it! The basement. If Edward was the accomplice, then there must be something in the basement. He made his way down there and was annoyed to find the place locked. He kicked the door in anger, and then shot off to find Florence. She would have the key and she would not dare stand in his way. She did not.

He was shocked! The place looked like a mortuary. It was all clean and organised, but the dark grey walls and floor gave it a slightly gothic feel. What was shocking was the jars. Hundreds of small jars. Small, round, square, large, coloured, clear. All filled with grotesque animal tissues. He could see rats, intestines, eyes, internal organs. Not being a medical man, he had no idea what these organs were or even if they were human or animal. The smell! Heavens! He has to overcome the stench. The table in the middle of the room had some equipment on it along with animal remains. He walked to the table and looked at the tissue on the table. Goodness! Was that a heart? Or a kidney? What was it? The bottles all housed animal parts, and he could not take his eyes off the butchered little bodies all submerged in liquid of some sort. What he was not sure of was who was responsible for all this. Was it James or Edward? He never really paid much attention to Edward or how he spent his days, and he had no idea how much his brother had spent on the basement. Truth is Michael Maybrick only ever took an interest in himself and would never notice anything unless it affected him directly. He knew very little about the workings of the Maybrick household. Except, of course, Florence Maybrick. Yes, he knew all about her and made it his business to know what she did. However, this basement stuff was shocking, and he did not know what to make of it. He was conscience of the fact that he should not be here at all and Edward may be back very soon, so he left.

Back in the study, he sat and watched his brother sleeping on the couch. Michael Maybrick was not moved by much, but he was still shaking from the experience he had just now. He was trying to calm his mind so he could think. Bottles! Filled with dead animals all cut up, probably by James and Edward. They were both in Whitechapel at the time of the murders and they were both eccentric. They both had access to the basement. They were both intoxicated most of the times. Jack the Ripper. Even the name was coined by Edward. And now everyone was using it. The media, the police, the public. The police were even getting letters signed by Jack the Ripper. This was strange, somebody in this house had been cutting up animals and for all he knew, was cutting up human parts too. It was too much of a coincidence. Michael's investigations had a long way to go but he was convinced he was on the right track.

When James woke up, he was still quite groggy and tired, and he wondered what had made him fall asleep so heavily in the middle of the day. He woke well past the normal time the evening supper was served. Obviously, no one tried to wake him. He was grateful really as he had no appetite. Food was something to be enjoyed but it was a long time since he remembered enjoying anything let alone food. His head throbbed and he felt as if he had given himself a stronger dose of strychnine. He wandered around the study and had no intention of leaving it in fear of running either into his wife, or brother. Both would have been an unwelcomed situation. He wondered why Michael was still hanging around here. He did not mind his brother coming and staying but there was normally a purpose to the visit, which right ow seems a mystery. At this moment, Michael walked in.

'James, how odd of you to sleep so heavily in the middle of the day!' Heavy lunch?'

'No. I don't know. I just slept.'

'Are you hungry? I'll get Adam to fix something for you.'

'No that will not be necessary.'

'You ought to see a doctor, James. You have been looking sick these days.' This sentence was delivered with a certain amount of indifference by Michael. 'Come to think of it, so does that lodger friend of yours. He does not look too good either. He looks half dead! I wonder what the two of you get up to during your visits to London. I must come and join you one of these days.'

The warning alarm went off in Maybrick's head. Michael obviously suspected something, and it was very uncharacteristic of him to wonder what James had been doing in London. He was normally never concerned. His head ached and he was unable to focus very well.

'What do you want?'

'What?' exclaimed Michael, slightly unprepared for James' direct approach.

'You are not normally concerned with what I do, Michael. You normally do not care about what anybody does, or how they look, or if they are well. Your whole world revolves around yourself yet here you are concerned about what I have been doing in London! Like you really care!'

'Steady on, that's a bit aggressive is it not?' retorted Michael. 'You still have not said what it is that you want,' persisted James.

'What I want is to know what is going on. You and that person in the basement.'

'I think you forget; this is my house! I am entitled to do as I please in my own house and can have whomever I want living in the basement, or anywhere else in my house!'

'Why so angry, James. You don't normally talk to me like this.'

'You do not normally interfere in my business! It has not escaped my notice that Florence has been disturbed by your visit.'

'It is not my visit that is disturbing your wife!' Michael laughed when he said this. 'What are you implying!' shouted James.

'Look. It was an innocent comment, James. You seem to be spending a lot of time in London and I was just wondering what you get up to?'

'I have business. I do not know what else you want me to say.'

'What? Business in Whitechapel?'

'Well, that is where my room is!'

'How are your headaches? The blackouts? Getting worse?'

'Oh, for God's sake Michael, just say what is on your mind! Your questions are getting rather cumbersome!'

'Fine!' shouted Michael. 'Who the hell is Hamilton? What are all those dead animals in the basement? Does he practice here and then perform for real on the whores of London?'

Maybrick sat frozen in his chair. That was it! He suspected Edward, or even both of them.

'You had better leave!' shouted James. 'I shall not be spoken to like this in my own house!'

'They think it was two men, James. The yard. A coach. I lent you my coach. What did you use it for?'

You had better STOP!' yelled James. All the thoughts about Edward that he thought he had dealt with had come back. Oh Lord! Did he provide shelter for the Whitechapel Murderer? If Michael could suspect him, then the police could.

'Answer me! Who is Edward Hamilton?'

'There are hundreds of suspects! Edward is a scientist, and he is bound to have dead animals in the basement. I've been visiting London for years. I cannot believe you could suspect your own brother!'

'Every killer is someone's brother!'

'So! That is what you think! Why don't you call your friends at the yard?'

'You had better get rid of Hamilton, James. He will bring you down!'

'Answer my question!' roared James, 'if you think you have the Murderer then call the police. What is stopping you?'

Michael stopped. The conversation had gotten out of hand. He did not want his brother to know what he was thinking and the suspicions that he had. It was better to keep his cards close to his chest. Now, both, James and Edward would be on their guard. There was little doubt in his mind that he knew the identity of the killer and all he had to do was deal with it so that he could preserve the family names. His name. He needed more evidence and to do that he needed to prevent a row with James. 'Look James, I'm sorry. I am out of my depth. I cannot go to the Yard simply because I know nothing. I am afraid there is little else that the society in London is talking about and I suppose I have been caught up in the intrigue.'

'What exactly are you up to Michael? One minute you are practically accusing me of being the Whitechapel Murderer, and on the other hand you are telling me you are out of your depth. What are you up do?'

'You are so paranoid'.

'Paranoid! So, would you be if you were being accused of being a cold-blooded killer by members of your own family!' He slumped down on the sofa again. 'If you have nothing else to say, then leave!'

'Let me fix you a drink, James.' He walked over to the drink cabinet and mixed a cocktail. Maybrick accepted it and he calmed himself down. They said very little in the remaining time. They just sat. Michael watched James, very closely. A few moments later they were joined by Edward. Edward gave Michael a long stare which made the latter man very uncomfortable. It was almost as if Edward knew Michael had been in the basement. He was careful not to touch anything. Michael rose to make Edward a drink and he fumbled around in his pocket to see if he could find any of the substance he used for James' port. Although Edward was staring at him intensely,

Michael still found an opportunity to put the substance in Edward's drink. All done!

'You seem very illusive these days, Edward. You do not take your meals with us anymore.'

'Is that a question?'

'Well, I suppose, yes.' Michael was certain these two were so jumpy. There was definitely something going on.

'Well, Hamilton,' persisted Michael. 'there must be a number of things to do and discover in London? Always something to reveal?' He looked at James and saw these dark eyes staring back at him.

'Yes, there is plenty to do in London,' said Edward.

Michael waited a little longer before taking his leave. He was satisfied with his day's work and it was important that he sorted things out. It was worth missing the social season in London as long a huge, shocking scandal was avoided.

The next two days saw both Maybrick and Edward terribly sick. They were both unable to get out of bed and the doctor was constantly as hand. They suffered stomach cramps and fever. Maybrick knew the symptoms! He had lived with them for years. He knew exactly what it was. The only thing was he thought he must have overdosed as his ailment was worse than most days. He had no idea that Edward was sick, and that Michael had taken total charge of the sick men in the house. Michael had taken all James' meals up by himself and he also took charge of all medicines that the doctor had left both men. He also administered medicines to both men. After many years of dependency to Strychnine, Maybrick's body was used to the symptoms and he recovered in a few days. It was Edward who was critically ill, and he was out for days. Michael was trying to keep both men at bay with illness for as long as it took for his younger brother, Edwin, to tie up loose ends in America and come home. He needed help if he was going to deal with this without attracting attention. His only problem was to convince Edwin that the situation was grave enough for this to come home. His other problem was James was very suspicious of the round the clock care his brother was giving. James at first though he must have overdosed himself. However, him becoming sick again after an initial recovery, he knew his 'attentive' brother was up to something. It was an acute illness that came only when Michael had visited. James was heartbroken! He loved his brother, but it seemed this very same brother was slowly poisoning him. Surely his brother was not trying to kill him. What were Michael's intention? James has no contact with anyone, not even the servants. Why was his brother trying to keep him sedated? All his visits to Florence had been chaperoned by Michael. The pair had no privacy at all, and poor Florence was under a lot of strain and she was very concerned about James, who was very sick.

However, there came a time when Michael had been called away and this could not be avoided. He was away for three days and it was during this time that Maybrick not only recovered but realised that Edward had also been sick. He also learned that the doctor was mystified and could not understand why neither man was recovering at all. All three men were in Edward's room discussing the events. Maybrick concluded that Michael could only have administered the drug in his drink and decided to be very careful of his brother when he returned.

On the day Michael returned, James met him at the door, much to the surprise of his brother. 'Michael! You seem surprised to see me! Are you not happy that I have recovered in your absence?'

'Of course!' Great news,' however, anyone could have seen the frown that Michael wore when he uttered these words.

'Come, tell me about your visit.' They went into the study. 'How is Hamilton?'

'Also recovering. He is sitting up in bed.'

'You have both made a remarkable recovery!' said Michael, with a stunned expression.

'Yes, we have, especially seeing that the doctor had no idea what was wrong with either of us!'

'Food poisoning was it not?'

'Maybe,' said James.

'Well, what else could it be? You both being sick like that?'

'Well, the main thing this is that it is over. Can I fix you a drink,' said James, with a twinkle in his eye!

'Of course,' said Michael, who was very much on edge. 'So, what took you away?' asked James.

'Should you not be resting? I mean, you should take it easy. You may overdo it.'

'I'm fine.'

'Well,' said Michael, 'I for one am tired. I shall retire and check in on Hamilton.'

'No that will not be necessary. He is being cared for. It was very thoughtful of you to take care of us while we were sick, but I am sure the servants can handle it from here.'

'It was the least I could do.'

From that point on, it was a struggle for Michael to get near Edward. He spent a lot of time with his brother but was never given an opportunity to administer anything without being seen. James has got into the habit of going into the kitchen and taking his food himself, much to the annoyance of the servants. He was careful what he ate and drank and never shared anything with Michael. He was still very weak, but Edward's recovery was very slow. It was mainly Florence who attended to Edward. As much as she disliked Edward, she disliked Michael was even more. He just wanted Michael to go away.

One evening, James walked into his study and found Michael writing a letter. He had never known Michael to write letters and he almost laughed out loud when he saw him. He asked no questions but just sat with the same book that he had been attempting to read for the last year! He hardly ever read a full paragraph. His mind was always so full. This book was the only thing that remained constant in his life. Constant and unread! He stared at it now and wondered who Michael was writing to. Who was fortunate enough to be the receiver of the only letter that Michael Maybrick ever wrote? Michael finished the letter, sealed it and left the room. Maybrick knew he was putting it in the box next to the door, where the Adam would take it to the Post Office in the village. Maybrick waited up to an hour but his brother never returned. He looked at his book. Then the fireplace. And then his book again. He never felt so alone in all his life. The only person he felt he could trust was Edward Hamilton. A man with no traceable identity, no family, no history. Florence was right. He was a vagabond who had been living under his roof, free of charge and slightly insane. Yet this man was the only person he could rely on. His only problem was that he suspected Edward of something insanely hideous that Maybrick could not even think of the evidence before him. He decided that if Edward was guilty then he was far more dangerous than anybody could have expected a vicious murderer to be. The whole world expected the Whitechapel Murderer to be evil, wicked, cruel, cold-blooded and insane. The thought that he was caring, warm-hearted, thoughtful and educated scientist sent a shiver down his back. Edward suffered from Amnesia. This totally normal man was performing a totally abnormal act and it is possible Edward had no idea what he was actually doing. Clearly, if Edward was guilty, he could not understand the true nature of his crime. This made him far more insane than any crazed butcher! Far more dangerous than any advocate that Lucifer could have sent. Maybrick was at a loss of what to do. Maybrick had to be the older brother than Edward needed. The man had no family of his own. He had to do the right thing. Maybrick had to tell the police himself and make sure that Edward was well taken care of. However, before he could do that, he had to find more evidence of Edward's guilt. He was still following his own gut instinct with very little concrete evidence. He had to try and find out.

He passed a whole hour in such thoughts before he made a move. He made a quick search of all the rooms downstairs and decided that Michael must have retired for the night. He could see the light from Michael's room. He could either wait until the light went out or he could move now. His impatience was getting the better of him. He moved quietly towards the door and laid both hands on the box next to the door. He emptied the contents and quickly took them to his study.

He locked the door. Heaven knows why he did that. He then sat at his desk and looked at the three letters in front of him. One was in Adam's writing, who wrote to his mother every week. The next was in Florence's writing. Maybrick froze when he saw the receiver's name. Alfred Brierly. What! Why was she writing to him? His body went numb as he realised that which he had failed to notice for so long. It could be that deep inside, he always knew but did not want to accept it. Better to pretend it was impossible rather than to face the truth. He wanted to read the letter but decided that was not his purpose. Was he a strong man for not looking at the letter, or a weak one in denial? He put down the letter from his wife to her lover and picked up Michael's letter. It was addressed to his brother, Edwin. Edwin was in America. Maybe this letter was to do with business? He felt a bit guilty opening it. But then he remembered that Michael had almost certainly been poisoning him and Edward and he must have had a motive. He tore the seal and read the letter very quickly. Then he had to read it again, slower this time as he took in every word.

Dear Edwin,

Time is short and I am not good at writing, so I will come to the point. I do not know how much home news you receive, but it seems like someone has taken it unto himself to rid the streets of vermin whores. While this seems to be a good thing in some ways, the problem for our family is that the culprit is not only crazed, but among us. I am with James and I think his involvement with Hamilton is dangerous. For certain reasons of family honour, I cannot go to the police and I fear, if I am right, then we will have to deal with this privately by ourselves. We cannot let this get out. All depends on how we protect ourselves.

Please see if you could tie up business at your end and make your way back to Liverpool as soon as possible. I will need your help in dealing with this.

MM

James sat back and buried his head in his hands. Home was no longer refuge for him. There was danger here and the most important part was his brother aiming to deal with this without the police. What did that even mean? Maybrick himself was going to the police and he was going to make sure Edward was well cared for. If he could prove Edward was insane, he could escape the death penalty. But not involving the police meant Michael intended to do something illegal. What was Michael intending to do? Maybrick would have liked to believe that his brother cared for him enough to protect him while trying to solve the problem. But his own inner being was telling him that Michael had a much more sinister plan. Maybe, Michael's plan was to poison both men and blame Maybrick's depression after finding out his wife's infidelity as the reason. Nobody would care about Edward's life. He was a nobody. Michael could even try and frame Florence, saying that she poisoned her husband so that she could be with her lover. The possibilities were endless. He had to remember what his brother was. A man who solely cared just for himself. He never loved any one and he never went anywhere unless there was a financial gain for himself. He was not doing this to save the whores of London, he was doing this so that no one would know that he was the brother of Jack the Ripper! The scandal alone would kill him! Maybrick was tempted to go to the police and claim to be the killer just to see his brother's face!

No. James Maybrick's real enemy was right here, in this house. The real danger was Michael. James had to get out. He had to leave as soon as possible. He had to take the sick Edward with him and get out. He had to go to Scotland Yard and turn Edward in for his own protection. He had to make the journey without telling anybody. Edward was seen on his feet earlier so he knew he could walk. He had to get Edward out.

He was about to open the letter Florence had written to her lover when he heard footsteps rushing down the stairs. Somebody had stopped outside his study. He watched in terror while the handle turned but the door did not open. Then started the wild thumping and shouting. Maybrick, startled, dropped the envelops. He thought it was Michael behind the door, but through his panic, he realised the voices belonged to Adam and the servant girls.

He rushed to the door and opened it. The two started to yell at him and from the corner of his eye, he saw Michael was standing at the top of the stairs. Maybrick panicked as he looked at the box. Did

Michael know the letters are not in there? 'Please calm down Adam,' he said sternly. 'What is the matter?'

'Sir! He has gone. He was here in the morning, but he did not take any of this medicine. He is not anywhere to be found.'

'Oh, for God's Sake, who are you talking about?'

'Mr Hamilton, Sir. His bed is empty and his clothes are gone.'

Maybrick rushed upstairs in panic. He rushed past Michael and went into Edward's room where he found Florence.

'James, what is happening? I heard screaming.'

Maybrick looked at the bed. There was a note on the pillow. Maybrick walked to the bed and picked up ad read the note.

My Dear James,

I have been nothing but trouble for you.

I have decided to free you of any obligation.

Sorry about the loan but I hope to pay you as soon as my experiment bear's fruit.

I know you will not believe me but watch yourself. You are not safe as long as your brother remains in this house. Take care.

Edward.

'No!' exclaimed Maybrick. He crumpled up the paper and threw it across the room. His actions caused panic among those in the room and Florence ran to the note, uncrumpled it and began reading. He saw the servants shouting and frantically running around. Then he thought of Michael. He looked at the door. Where was Michael? He ran downstairs and into the study. Where was the letter? Where was Michael's letter? He ran to his desk and started fumbling about looking for the letter. The door slammed shut and there stood Michael.

'Looking for this?' Michael was locking the door with one hand and was holding up the letter with the other. Maybrick's head was spinning. He could not see properly. He saw his brother slowly walking towards him.

'Intercepting my mail? What on Earth for?' He moved closer to the desk. He had a menacing look on his face. 'Now look here, Jimmy boy! I have worked too hard to risk it all now. Your little hobby could cost me my career. And I will not let anybody do that. Not even you.'

Maybrick just about caught the silver glint of the needle just before the feeling the scratch. He tried to scream and call out to Florence, but too late. There was a hand over it. Then, darkness. The Strychnine had taken over.

CHAPTER 31

Edward Hamilton sat in the carriage shivering. He was truly sick. But he knew that he had to get away! He was under increasing threat from Michael Maybrick who seemed to look at him if he knew something. He knew that Michael had been into the basement. He had seen him. He knew that Michael's presence in the house was a fishing expedition where he would not leave until he had caught his fish! He had to get out, but he could not involve Maybrick. He still had the key to Maybrick's room, and he had his notes and tools. He had to operate on his own. No doubt he felt that Michael would come after him but at least he had a head start. He felt that he was close to his final experiment! He was almost there! He had to change strategy, but he had to think about that at another time. He had to get to London. He hoped that Maybrick would understand why he left.

As soon as he reached London, he went to see Nathaniel but found him out. The woman answering the door did not know when he was coming back so Edward had no choice but to wearily make his way to Maybrick's room. He lay on the bed and closed his eyes. In an instant he was in another world. He could see his mother's face. She was looking down on him and smiling. She was stroking his face. *My little boy! My lovely little Eddie!* He heard her voice almost as if she were right next to him. He could almost smell her perfume! He was yearning for her now in his slumber. He wanted to go back to that time. He wanted to be a little boy again. He wanted to snuggle up to his mother's chest and allow himself to be cradled like a babe in arms. The next face to come to him was that of Frenkel. He remembered Frenkel's face although he knew not who this man was. He was disturbed by this face and he became restless in his sleep. His head was thrashing from side to side and he tossed and turned while his brain was struggling to place this face. He calmed down a little when he saw Juhi. Beautiful large, dark eyes and lovely long black hair! He saw the sun shining onto her hair and she was laughing and teasing him. They were lying on the grass in Regent's Park feeding the bold squirrels. He dreamt of the Corporation. The President. The Professor. He lay there and dreamt of his former life. In his dreams, he was Edward Hamilton, the scientist in the year 2007!

At some point in his sleep, he could hear banging! It was persistent and getting louder all the time. He was trying to rouse himself. He was still sleeping but something in his subconscious told him that the noise was not in his dreams! His ears were actually hearing it. The sound was external. He tried to escape his dreams. He kept hearing his own voice urging him to get up! Then he heard a voice! It was not his own. It was also external. He struggled to wake up. Nathaniel? Why was Nathaniel yelling! Heaven knows how long it took him, but he eventually woke himself up. He lay on the bed and tried to call out but not much sound was coming out.

'Nathaniel?' It was barely a whisper which escaped his lips. He moved an arm, but the body was in pain. He was wet and cold with it. His head throbbed and his stomach was aching. He felt like someone was wringing his stomach like one would a soaking wet cloth!

'Nathaniel!' It was louder this time. The knocking stopped. God no! Don't go! I'm here! The words all rushed into his head, but he could not say them. He looked at the chair next to the bed. Desperation made him launch his body towards the chair. He fell onto the floor making an awful racket as he hit the ground. He lay there for a few seconds and to his relief the thumping on the door began again.

'Edward! Are you in there? Open the door!'

'Nathaniel!'

Nathaniel made a couple of failed attempts at opening the door, but it was far more solid than he had anticipated. He waited. Eventually the lock clicked, and the handle turned slowly. He pushed it slightly and was almost in the room before the sick figure in front of him collapsed onto him. He managed to hold him up and to drag him back to the bed. Edward did not say anything. He knew Nathaniel would look after him. He fell back asleep.

It took a good two days to nurse Edward back to health. When Edward woke up on the third day there was a woman by his bedside. As soon as she saw that he had woken up, she opened the door of the room and called out. A young boy came to the door. She gave him some coins and he ran off. She came back to Edward. She did not smile but just told him that he had been sick, she was the nurse instructed by Dr Grey to look after him and that the doctor would be here soon. She then proceeded to feed him. His stomach was still in pain and he felt weak but at least his own mind seemed to have come back, and he had the power of thought. He remembered Maybrick. He was surprised that Maybrick had not followed him to London or at least sent him a message. Maybe he was just glad to have got him out of his hair! He had something small to eat and then he rested a little more. In a short time, Nathaniel arrived, and he immediately thanked and paid the nurse before dismissing her.

'Edward! Thank God you have recovered.'

'I've been nothing but trouble for you and Maybrick. Why on Earth should you be glad that I have recovered!'

'My dear fellow! That is a strange remark to make. You are in trouble yourself. We could not abandon you when you are most in need!'

'Most in need! I don't need anything! I have almost finished my experiment! I shall be hailed then! But do not press me on the subject! I want it to be a surprise!'

'Fine,' said Nathaniel, thinking that there had been no improvement to the man's erratic speech and general behaviour. He had sent several messages to Maybrick and was surprised to find that none of them had been answered. He then got a brief message from Michael Maybrick saying that his brother was very sick and was totally bed ridden and unable to receive visitors. There was something in this cold, undetailed account of the sickness which sent the alarm bells ringing in Nathaniel's head. Something was wrong. He had hoped to find the answers now from Edward.

'I have been trying to get in touch with James. He should not have let you travel by yourself. You were too sick.'

'Steady on! It's not his fault. I did not tell him that I was leaving. He had some problems of his own to sort out, so I left. I left him a message telling him I was going back to London.'

'But he is sick himself! Was he sick when you left him?'

Edward looked up suddenly. 'Sick?' He thought back. They had both been sick. He knew that. But Maybrick at one stage seemed to have totally recovered. He was sure that Maybrick was not sick that day that he left for London. He was certain of that. He also thought that his own illness was caused by a stimulant. He did not feel that his body was sick, he felt like it was reacting to something which had been given. When he was sick, he remembered only one face. One face was there, watching him every time he opened his sick eyes. Michael Maybrick. Cold, indifferent and evil.

'Nathaniel. I don't think James is safe. You have to see him. You have to get Michael out of the house!'

'Michael! What on Earth are you talking about.'

'I do not know what is going on. Michael had been staying at Battlecrease, but his presence was not wanted by Florence or James. He was there when both of us were ill.'

'Edward! I have to stop you there! Michael is James' brother! Be careful what you say.'

'I'm telling you,' yelled Edward, 'Michael was up to something. He was snooping around all my work, in the study, in James' desk! He was controlling Florence too! I do not know what he was up to but we both fell ill at the same time and were attended entirely by Michael. And funnily enough, James began to recover while Michael was away for a few days! The evidence was there! James was well when I left the house! How could he suddenly be bedridden? I was drugged, Nathaniel! And I think James is too.'

'But why? It all has to be for a reason!'

Edward paused, trying to find the words. Then he chuckled. The chuckle grew into a laugh. He was laughing almost hysterically before he could speak again. 'Because he thinks that we are Jack the Ripper! He thinks James and I murder prostitutes!' He fell about now. Nathaniel did not laugh. He was shocked. Stunned. He sat back in his chair and thought very hard. He knew that no matter how ridiculous it sounded; Jack the Ripper had to be somebody. Somebody's friend, husband, father, brother. He had to be a real person. A living person who lived among them and who lived in a normal way. Nathaniel did not believe that it was true, but he could not dismiss it either. If Michael Maybrick thought that his brother was involved in such an atrocity, then his actions would make sense. Nathaniel had known Michael many years but had tolerated him because of James. He did not like the man and thought that he was too selfish and self-centred to be a good man to know. He would have a good reason for thinking what he did and if he did think that James was a killer, then Michael would not stand by and watch while the huge scandal descended upon his life. Upon his career. He would do anything to protect himself. Nathaniel knew this. It was a tricky situation. Nathaniel knew that if Edward was telling the truth, then James was in very real danger. He had to try and send a message to Florence. He had to make sure that James was safe. He had to try and find a way to take Michael away from Liverpool. However, his immediate problem was Edward. As far as he was concerned, Edward had been drugged. He was recovering now but still very sick. Treating this part of Edward's illness Nathaniel himself could do. But he was concerned about Edward's mental situation. The man seemed totally sane. There seemed to be no indication that he was mad. But from what Nathaniel could remember it was those who appeared totally normal on the outside who were the maddest. The ones that are truly a danger to themselves and to others. He decided that he had to take Edward to another doctor friend of his. Someone who could mentally evaluate Edward and advise on how to treat him.

'You need to eat and get plenty of rest, but I need to monitor you,' said Nathaniel. 'That's not necessary! There's no one here to poison me. I'll be fine in a couple of days.'

'Yes, well we cannot be sure of that. And you do need to eat. I cannot provide you with a person all the time. You will have to come to my house.'

'No!' Edward panicked. If he were couped up under strict observation, how on Earth could he finish his experiment. He was too close to give up and too far involved to tell Nathaniel about it. He wanted to finish the whole thing on his own! He wanted all the glory of single handedly finding the Soul. He could not stay with Nathaniel. 'No! I cannot stay with you! I have things to do.'

'What things?' asked Nathaniel, who was used to the sudden panic attacks.

'I have my experiment to finish. For goodness sake, don't ask me to tell you what it is, I want to tell you all about it when it is finished. I am almost at the end now. But I have to get on with it.'

'All the same you have to eat! You will come and spend tonight with me. I have someone I want you to meet tomorrow. I will not take no for an answer!'

Edward gave in. He did not want to arouse suspicion. He just decided to eat, sleep and think about things tomorrow. He had to change his strategy a little but was too exhausted to think about tactics now. He had to wait until he was alert. He quietly said no more but let Nathaniel take him to his house.

The evening was taken up by having a meal and then relaxing in front of the fire. The cool November night chill had set in and Edward was almost constantly shivering. He noticed that Nathaniel said very little but stared at him for long periods of time. He could not tell why, but the doctor seemed quiet and withdrawn. He spoke little and spent most of the time in deep thought. He wrote some letters, but they seemed brief. Edward sat and decided to nap but he was disturbed. It was a month since his last experiment, and he felt that he was forgetting much of what he had learnt from the work that he had so far carried out. Certain details escaped him. He had been ill at Maybrick's house for so long he thought that the sickness had confused his brain. He could not remember anything about experiments one and two. He wanted to read what he had done so far and suddenly panicked. His notes! Where were they? His notes! His journal. His tools. He could not remember whether he had taken his Journal. He remembered fingering his journal and examining his tools during his journey to London so they must be in his room.

He relaxed a little. At least they were in his room. All he had to do was collect them tomorrow. He tried hard to remember exactly what he had done. The last experiment was carried out on the last day of September. Today was the eighth of November. He needed to get working soon!

He gave much thought to his work so far. There were many things hampering his work. Bad light to begin with. Most of the time he had to operate in badly lit streets, and he could not see what he was doing. The other thing was time. He was constantly rushed, constantly on guard just in case he was seen. He could not work in those conditions. He had to have good light and plenty of time. He was thinking hard about how to get round this, and he came to the conclusion, that he needed to take the next participant to his room. It was quiet, well-lit and totally private. He could take as long as he needed. He was close to the conclusion of his work and he was sure that after the next one, he could announce to the public the nature of his work. He need not fear that anybody would find the remains since he would be hailed as a hero. A man who found the Soul and at the same time freed all those tortured people. He would be a hero. They would even help him clean the room. He would be too busy giving interviews to the paper and signing on to write the papers and attend scientific meetings. He would be too busy to clean up! They would do that for him. Then he could pay back the debt that he owed to Nathaniel's banker friend. He had it all worked out. One more! One more experiment and life for him would change drastically!

Just one more experiment and the whole world would be altered!

CHAPTER 32

E dward woke up very late the next day. Nathaniel was attending to his patients. The servants had been given orders to monitor Edward and to make sure that he drank all his tonics and medicines as instructed. What Edward did not know was that they were also given instructions to call Nathaniel if Edward attempted to leave the house on his own. Nathaniel was very disturbed by Edward. Edward made many references to his experiment. What experiment? Certainly not laboratory based. What was he up to? He said that the experiment had almost come to an end. It was a sick mind that accused the wrong person of a terrible crime, but Nathaniel could not get his mind off the subject. There were too many references which led to something sinister. Whatever it was, Nathaniel was sure that Edward was not aware of what he was doing. Nathaniel had contacted his doctor friend and they were expected to visit in the evening. He had to keep watch on Edward until then.

Edward was recovering very well. He was strolling around the garden under the watchful eye of the nurse. She was the same one whose face he had woken up to. He grinned at her knowing that she was unlikely to smile back! She was even more unlikely to let her guard slip. He would be wasting time there! He gave in. His work could not begin until after dark anyway. He would find a way to get round Nathaniel. He spent some of the time writing to Maybrick. He was sure that Michael would be intercepting all letters in the entire Maybrick household, so he did not put anything in it suggesting where about in London he was. It was a polite but very general letter. After that, Edward napped a little and waited for Nathaniel who eventually arrived late in the afternoon.

They left immediately. Their journey took them to the West End. Edward wondered why all his time here he had never ventured as far as this. He kept himself close to Maybrick's room. He was fascinated by the West End. In his mind he suddenly had memories of this area. He remembered spending a good few hour in the book shops around Tottenham Court Road. He remembered spending a huge amount of money in Foyle's before crossing the road and doing the same in the bookstore on the other side of the road. He remembered Oxford Street, hot, crowded and expensive. His favourite place was the Embankment. He used to walk along there towards the Houses of Parliament on many a long, warm summer's nights. There was a bar near the Royal Festival Hall which he always used to go to with Juhi. She was scared of heights and he had spent months trying to convince her to get on the London Eye! He managed after two years of trying. As they came up to Soho, he remembered an Asian arts and crafts shop from which he had bought some embroidered Indian bedsheets and a huge wood carved elephant. That Chinese restaurant. God! What was its name? It was on the tip of his tongue! That one that had a reputation for having rude waiters and waitresses. He could never understand why it was so popular. All those people regularly going there to be insulted and badly treated! It all came to him as they passed steadily through London. When his work was finished, he would have time to explore this part of London! Time and money. He tried hard to remember what happened to Juhi. But his memory seemed to fail him there. He also wondered why he had images of shops, restaurants and streets which he could not see now. It all looked so different from the images in his head. He was mentally exhausted now and wanted to nap but just as he was dropping off, they arrived at a quiet residential area. All the houses looked huge and well maintained. This was definitely a far cry from the poverty of the East End. All this material affluence which he saw here. He remembered what his experiment was all about! Free the Souls of the miserable! Yes. These people here had no need for the Soul. Evolution saw to it that they were born without. They had no need for them! They climbed out of the hired coach and Edward waited while Nathaniel paid the driver. Then Nathaniel turned towards Edward and directed him to the house they were standing in front of. The servants had been expecting them and they were immediately shown in.

They entered the well-lit and richly decorated room. The owner was a tall, middle-aged, handsome man who greeted Nathaniel very affectionately. They were obviously very close friends. They looked of similar age, so Edward assumed that they had been to school together.

'Hello Ralph!' said Nathaniel. 'It has been a long time!'

'Too long. How are things?'

'Well. I see Jennifer had abandoned you!'

'Yes,' said Ralph. 'She is staying with her sister. My sister-in-law has been blessed with a little babe who is driving them all mad! Jen has gone to offer advise!'

'Goodness, Alice has a baby! I was not even aware that she had got married!'

'Yes well. You let her down terribly Nathan. But time is a good healer. She met and married a banker.'

'There you go! I always told her she would meet someone else!'

'Meeting and marrying someone else is one thing. Still carrying a torch for someone is a different matter,' said Ralph. 'I do not think that she is over you!'

'Over me! There was never anything to get over!' Nathaniel then noticed Edward standing there looking at them.

'Goodness! Where are my manners! Ralph, let me introduce you to Edward Hamilton. Edward, this is Ralph, a great friend of mine and an excellent doctor. We studied medicine together!'

'Hello,' said Ralph shaking Edward's hand. 'I am sorry. Nathaniel and I have not seen each other for a long time!'

'No apologies needed.' They all sat down. 'So,' said Edward looking to Nathaniel. 'Who is Alice!'

'Oh!' groaned Nathaniel. 'That is not important!'

'Sounded important,' grinned Edward. 'A little romance was it?'

'Well, not really,' said Ralph. 'It was a romance that never was! The lady in question was besotted with Nathan here. Could not imagine why. The age gap was huge! Most men would have jumped and grabbed the opportunity with both hands, but not Nathan. He thought it would be a mistake.'

Nathaniel did not say anything, but Edward saw the look in his eye. He was a little upset and Ralph also noticed it. They suddenly went quiet. Nathaniel saw Edward's puzzled face.

'A young girl, a child almost and a middle-aged widower. Not a good idea.' Edward then realised. Nathaniel was not a bachelor. He had been married. He was a widower. Another thing that he was neglecting of late. He was so wrapped up in his own affairs that he had little time for other people's lives. Nathaniel had helped him. And he did not even know that the man had had a wife.

'I am sorry, Nathaniel. I did not know.' Edward was truly sorry, and it showed on his face. The moment was broken by the servant announcing that dinner was about to be served. They then went and dined together. It was a fabulous meal and the first really good meal that Edward had eaten for ages. The three of them sat and talked for a while after the meal before Ralph decided to focus more on Edward.

'Edward, Nathan tells me that you are a scientist.'

'Yes. My speciality is the human body.'

'Where did you study?'

'London.'

'So where did you meet James Maybrick?'

'At school.'

'Was any of your childhood education in Liverpool?' Edward paused. 'I guess it must have been.'

'If you and Maybrick were school friends, how do you explain the difference in age?' said Ralph.

'Well, I guess he was…' He could not remember what he was supposed to say on the subject of his childhood. He could not really remember where he came from at all.

'Do you have trouble re-calling your childhood?'

'What the hell are all these questions?' yelled Edward.

'Relax, Edward. We are trying to help.' Ralph's questioning was gentle. 'What are you up to?' said Edward to Nathaniel. 'Why did you bring me here?'

'Edward. You have not been able to recollect anything about yourself. Ralph can help you. That is why I have brought you here. You do not have to cooperate, but it may help if you did.'

'Help! You want to know about my work don't you!' he shouted. He rose from the chair and towered over both men. 'You want to know about my experiment so that you can steal my idea, steal my data! I won't let you. I have almost finished, and you are going to get none of the credit! I thought better of you Nathaniel!'

'No. You are wrong!' said Ralph in a stern voice. 'We could not care less about your experiment and your work. Sit down, Mr Hamilton.' His voice was severe and to Nathaniel's amazement, Edward sat back down on his chair and stopped ranting. Ralph walked over to a desk and removed something from the top drawer but kept it well hidden, out of view.

'Edward. Your brain is erratic. You have to calm down. You can either help me or I can give you something to help you relax.'

'Give me what? I don't want to be drugged.'

'Do you not want to find out who you are?' said Ralph as walked behind Edward. Edward was wary of him but something in the man's voice frightened him. He spoke in a steady, monotonous voice which seemed to pierce the eardrums even though he did not speak loudly. Ralph put both his hands-on Edward's shoulders from behind while still clutching the syringe.

'Just listen. Try and block out all other thoughts. Lay your head back. That's right.

Now close the eyes. Do not open them again until I have said so. Just relax but try not to fall asleep.' He paused for a few seconds. 'Just close your eyes and relax.' Ralph was now speaking into Edward's ear in a low whisper. 'Just breathe. Relax your legs. Relax the arms. Your shoulders are stiff. Gently let them relax. Clear the mind.' He paused for a few second. 'What can you hear?'

'Your voice.'

'What are you thinking of?'

'Nothing.'

'Nothing? No thoughts at all?' said Ralph.

'No.' Edward looked asleep. He was very still, and Ralph had no way of knowing whether the man was playing along or if he was truly hypnotised. He walked over to his desk again and took out some smelling salts. He quickly passed it under Edward's nose a couple of times and there was no reaction. He then held the bottle right under Edward's nose for at least thirty second or so. He knew that Edward was breathing but there was no reaction. He had Edward under control. He then rolled up Edward's sleeve and prepared his arm for the injection.

'What is that?' whispered Nathaniel looking worried.

'A short-lasting calming drug which should prevent him from waking himself out of hypnosis.'

'I've never heard of such a drug!'

'No. I developed it myself.'

'Is it safe?'

'I think so. It only lasts a short time. He'll be fine.' Ralph injected the drug into Edward's inner wrist. Edward did not move at all. He looked asleep. Ralph then waited a minute or so before sitting back down on his sofa. He started the questions very quietly as if he was just chatting.

'Anyway, Edward, tell me where you were born?'

'London. Whitechapel.'

'Who were your parents?'

'Phyllis and John Hamilton.'

'Have you any brothers and sisters.'

'A brother who died when he was six years old. My sister is living in Cardiff.'

'Where was your medical education?'

'Liverpool.'

'What was your first job?'

'Charing Cross Hospital.'

'Which hospital?'

'Charing Cross.'

'Where is that?'

'Hammersmith.'

Ralph looked at Nathaniel who just raised and shrugged his shoulders. As far as they were concerned, there was no such thing as Charing Cross Hospital and even if there was, they would have assumed that it was in Charing Cross and not Hammersmith.

'What was your next job?'

'The study of mammalian behaviour during severe trauma and stress.'

'Where was that?'

'Kennedy Institute based at St Thomas' Hospital.'

'Have you any publications?'

'Yes.'

'If I were to look up your publications, I would be able to do so under your name?'

'Of course, you would! You can find me on the net.'

'On what?'

'On the net, the net. Between 1991 and 2007. There are about twenty as a first author and several as second and third.'

The two men listening were confused now. To them all this was a foreign language. 'Can you explain what the net is?' asked Ralph.

'What! Where have you been the last 20 years!' Edward was totally out. His head was pushed back, and his eyes were closed but he spoke totally naturally as if he were awake.

'Why did you say 1991 to 2007?'

'That is when my papers were published.'

Ralph thought a long time before he asked his next question. 'Edward, what year were you born?'

'1965.'

'Impossible!' cried Nathaniel but Ralph quickly waved a hand to keep Nathaniel quiet. He could not risk Edward waking up. Putting him back in a hypnotic state would be difficult. He had to think very hard before he asked his next series of questions. It was obvious that Edward was totally confused but under a hypnotic state the mind is meant to tell the truth.

'Edward, you were born in 1965?'

'Yes. I think the Rolling Stones were number one. They could get no satisfaction!' He laughed.

'What else happened in 1965?'

'Winston Churchill died.'

'Can I ask who that was?'

'Winston Churchill! Ridiculous question! Ever heard of World War Two?'

'Edward, I am asking the questions remember!'

'Well ask sensible ones.' Nathaniel was amazed how naturally calm Edward was and how his own true personality was still showing even under this state.

'I assume if there was a World War Two, then there must have been a World War one.'

'Well done, Einstein!'

'My history is a little limited. Can you tell be what years these wars took place?' said Ralph gently.

'World War one was 1914 to 1918, or was it 1919? And World War two was 1939 to 1945. Hitler started it! He invaded Poland!' Edward then chuckled as his subconscious thought of the lanky figure of Basil Fawlty.

'Edward, do you know what year it is at the moment?'

'Well, it's 2007.'

'What if I told you that the year is 1888?'

Edward stopped smiling. He waited and thought before speaking. 'I cannot talk about that.'

'Why not?'

'Because my job relies on secrecy. I have not finished my work. I cannot talk about it.'

'What is your job?'

'I work for the Blue Haze Corporation.'

'What does it do?' asked Ralph.

Edward again hesitated. He was troubled. 'If you don't know that then I cannot tell you.'

'What does the Corporation deal with?'

'I cannot tell you.'

'Let us go back to 2007.'

'Fine.'

'Who is the Monarch?'

'Queen Elizabeth.'

'Queen Elizabeth?'

'What?' squirmed Nathaniel. 'Queen Victoria you mean.'

'No dummy! Queen Elizabeth II.'

'Who was her father?' Ralph was almost whispering now. He was worried about waking Edward.

'George V, I think.'

'What is the Government of the day?'

'Labour.' The two men again looked puzzled. Labour? Who on Earth was Labour? 'How did you get a job with the Blue Haze Corporation?'

'The Professor, the bastard! He took me with him when he was head hunted.'

'That is not a very favourable way to refer to him. Did you not want the job?'

'The job was great. But he lied to me. Lied to me about the details. He lied right up to his death.'

'How did he die?'

'Frenkel killed him. It was self-defence.'

'Who is Frenkel?'

'Frenkel is the guy who discovered the Corridor by accident. He fell into it and came back a few days later. He had special abilities.' In his hypnotic state Edward was powerless. He told the truth since that was what was expected of him. He stalled at direct questions about the Corporation, but indirect ones were fine.

'What is the Corridor?'

'A Time Corridor! It throws you back to a different time zone.'

The two men were stunned. They sat back and stared at Edward who was still sitting there calmly with his head resting on the sofa. There was a long pause, but Edward did not say anything else. He just waited for the next question. That was where Ralph was stuck. What should the next question be? One wrong move and the entire session would have to be abandoned. Ralph knew that Edward would not speak unless asked to. He just sat and thought. Under hypnosis a man was supposed to talk truthfully.

Edward believed his own story to such an extent that it became real to him in his subconscious. This is what Ralph thought. The man was so confused in his own head that he actually believed that he was born a hundred years or so in the future and had travelled back in time. He believed this ridiculous scenario. Ralph had to find out what Edward's experiment was all about.

'Did you volunteer to pass through the Corridor?' he asked finally.

'Well. I had thought about it but in the end, I had no option. I had to go. Frenkel had explained it all to me.'

'Explained what?'

'Frenkel had seen! The World would have been different. Hitler would have won. We needed to go back in time and change things.'

'Change what?'

'That business tycoon. He should never have been born. I had to come here to change that. I had to change history. I had to stop him being born or else Wallace would not marry Edward the Eighth.'

'How were you going to stop him being born?'

'I don't know. I don't know. I don't know who he is.' Edward was getting agitated now. He was thrashing about in the sofa and was sweating. He was uncomfortable. Ralph knew that he was about to bring himself out of the trance and so he threw the next question out rapidly hoping that Edward would answer.

'Do you know anything about the Whitechapel Killer?'

Open! The eyes were open! He woke himself up. He stared at the two men in front of him and had no idea what had just taken place. He did not know that he had been in a trance, but he knew that something was wrong just by their expressions. Both men were looking at him as if he had a tree growing out of his head.

'What's going on? What have you done?' he asked.

'Relax, Edward. We have done nothing! I do have to discuss things with Nathan. Some business that we have to talk about. We'll be back soon. Just relax and help yourself to more port if you want. They got up and left. Very rude thought Edward. He then looked down at his left wrist, which felt a bit sore on the inside. He saw a small red dot which looked like a pimple. It itched but on closer inspection Edward thought he could see a small hole. Was it an insect bit? Were there any insects around at this time of year to cause something like this? It was November. Or maybe it was a flea bite. Plenty of fleas around in Whitechapel! He then looked around the room. He could see nothing suspicious on the desk or the side tables. Maybe he was being a bit silly. What on Earth did he think that Nathaniel had allowed Ralph to do? He decided that Ralph was probably a decent chap but that he did not like him much. He spoke too much like a doctor and on this occasion, he acted like he was still on duty. That is what he was worried about. Ralph acted like he had a job to carry out. All those questions about his childhood with Maybrick. Heaven knows why it would interest him unless he had been asked by Nathaniel or Maybrick to find out. He walked over to Ralph's desk and started to look around in the drawers. He found nothing out of place. He stood and thought for a while. Then he remembered that Ralph had taken something out of the writing desk. He walked over to it and opened the writing flap. There it was! Right in front of his eyes! The syringe. He was upset. Upset with Nathaniel. He really trusted Nathaniel and thought he was a really good friend. He not only looked upon him as a friend but was going to tell him about his great experiment! His life's great work! The pinnacle of his professional existence! Thank God he found this out in time. He could no longer trust either men. He could not trust Nathaniel and therefore he had to assume that he could not trust Maybrick either! He had been conned again! He suddenly thought of the Professor! Yes! That face came in his mind from nowhere and with it flooded images of the Corporation. He thought about it all at once and a shiver ran through him. If Ralph had drugged him, exactly what information did he manage to get? Did he know about the Corporation? Did he know about his fantastic experiment? Is that what they were discussing right now? How to get his notes off him and then to finish the experiment themselves to public acclaim! He was angry now. He put the syringe in his pocket. He would try and find out what the drug was that Ralph used. He was about to think what to do next when he felt something in his head. He felt a tingling! He knew that feeling. He had felt it before! He tried to think. He held his head in his hand and frowned. Then it came to him. The bus! He felt it on the bus that time when he saw that sick looking pale man! He looked towards the window. He walked over and peered outside. He saw nothing at first but then he saw slight movement. On the opposite side of the road. He could see shadows. There were at least four of them standing there looking at the house. Edward had no idea who three of them were but the fourth one he knew! He could not see any of their faces since it was too dark, but he knew! Their brains were connecting again and this time there was no need for physical contact. No! This time the man had been actively looking for him and had found him! He had to leave! He was under threat from those inside the house and now, from those outside as well. He had to leave! He quietly but swiftly moved out of the room into the corridor, trying not to let the floors creak too much. He could hear voices from the room next door. He put his ear to the door and the heard faint conversation. The words 'insane' and 'subconscious' he heard. He stood for a while and could make out some sentences.

'Well, if he is, then we have to tell the Police.' He could not make out which one said this. He thought it was Nathaniel.

'They will have him committed. His mind is totally unstable. He is mad!"

'We will make sure that he is well cared for. I shall see to that,' said Nathaniel. That was it! His cue. Time to look for the back door!

Across the road from Ralph's house the four men were whispering and looking intently at the house.

'He's in there!' This was Robert Lees.

'Are you sure?' This was Inspector Abberline, the man in charge of the Whitechapel Murders.

'Look!' said Lees, who was very nervous and as white as a sheet, 'you asked me to help and yet you don't believe me!'

'Look, Mr Lees, it's not that we do not believe you,' said Abberline. 'It's just that before we go barging in accusing people of anything, we do like to be sure.'

'I'm telling you!' shouted Lees, 'In there is your *Jack the Ripper* or whatever else you want to call him!'

'Well, we cannot move until we find out who the house belongs to. We have to wait for George to get back to us.'

'Well can I go? You do not need me now.'

'Please Mr Lees, can you wait just a few more minutes,' said the Inspector. 'What for?'

'I want you to tell me if this is the same man you came across on the bus in Shepherd's Bush.'

'I already know it is! You still do not believe in my ability do you!'

'Please Mr Lees, calm yourself.' Abberline was ready to send the man home just to stop him whinging when he heard footsteps. George was coming back.

'Well?' said Abberline totally ignoring the fact that George was breathless.

'A doctor,' said George. Abberline stared at him. 'Do you have a name?'

George looked round towards the other officers and to Robert Lees. Then he came up to Abberline's arm and pulled him away slightly and whispered the name in his ear. The two then looked at the house. Abberline glanced at the neurotic Lees. He then turned to the men.

'Let's go. Mr Lees, you can go home.' They walked over to the house and knocked on the door. The housemaid answered the door.

'I'm Inspector Abberline. Can I please talk to the owner of the house?'

CHAPTER 33

Edward heard the doorbell ring just as he was opening the back door. He heard the two doctors coming out of the room and the maid, who had seen Edward rushing through the kitchen was running towards her master, no doubt to tell Ralph that Edward was leaving. He ran out into the darkness and the chilly air. He was blinded almost at once and found it very hard to see where he was going. There was a back garden, and he ran right at the back where he knew there had to be fence. This garden was private and belonged just to this property. He ran to the back and found to his delight that there was a wooden door in the fence. He just had to flick the lock to one side, and he was out. The four men standing outside obviously did not think that they were expected since none of them were 'covering the back'. Edward ran down one side and into another alley which eventually led him out onto the front road. He approached the main road with caution. He peered out and looked to his right where he knew Ralph's front door to be. He just caught a glimpse of the last figure entering the house. He looked across the road and saw that Robert Lees was being escorted by the police into a coach. He waited until the coach had driven off and then he made a dash for it. He ran as fast as he could. Turning down several streets he eventually stopped and caught a coach.

His brain was racing now. He had to get back to the room. There was no place which was safe now. He could not trust Nathaniel. He could not go back to Liverpool. He was not really safe in his room either. That was the first place that they would look for him. He knew it would not be long before Nathaniel would escort the police to his room, but he had a head start and all he really wanted was his bag! It had everything in it! All his notes and his special tools. If he had the bag, he could go into hiding elsewhere and still be able to operate. He knew it was just one or two more participants and he would find his answer. Something in his head told him that the Whitechapel Murderer had struck five or six times. He remembered that tiny morsel of information. It was either because he had found his answer by that time and went public, or that he was caught! Edward was convinced it was because he finally had his answer. His next participant was going to reveal her Soul! All he had to do was get his bag!

It was a long ride back. The coach dropped him off near his room and he threw some money at the driver before dashing off. He fumbled with the key before turning it and flinging the door open. He was about to run in when the sight that met him made him scream out in fright. Michael Maybrick stood there holding something in his hand. It took Edward a second to focus on what it was. His journal! Good God, it was his journal! The bastard was reading his private notes. His scientific study was known to Michael Maybrick! He was livid! On the bed he saw his tools lined up as if on parade! He *knew!* Michael Maybrick knew the details of his work!

'*You!*' whispered Michael Maybrick, in horror. He was truly frightened! He looked horrified! He was alone in the room with a crazed serial killer! 'It *was* you! You killed all those women! I thought it was James!'

'Give that back!' hissed Edward. He looked insane. His hair was wild, and his unkempt facial hair gave him a hideously distorted expression as his dark hollow eyes peered at Michael Maybrick. He spat as he talked, and his fists were already clenched as he moved slowly in the room. He kicked the door shut with a back kick.

Michael Maybrick had never been so frightened in all his life. He looked at the weapons on the bed and the entries in the journal that he had been reading were still fresh in his head. The man in front of him was not Edward Hamilton. Not the same man who had been living at Battlecrease for the last two months. Not the man who had fallen asleep at Florence's garden party. Not the same man who had insulted Florence so terribly during that dinner. No! The creature in the room with him right now was no man! Michael Maybrick had always considered himself the only divine being to have existed to date. However, now, in this tiny space, he started to pray. Now he looked for God. Whenever Michael Maybrick wanted anything, he clicked his fingers and he got it. He had dined with and performed for Royalty and politicians and that was all he needed. He never needed God before. But now. Here. In this room. He was looking at the *Devil*. The man walking slowly towards him was insane! Michael had the weapons in front of him but the stomach of a coward. He stepped backwards as the Devil suddenly launched himself towards him! Michael felt the blows connect one after the other. He was on the floor now and the stinging made him yell out. He expected to feel the sharp edge of the knife any second and was screaming out for God! He felt the warm fluid around his crotch as his bladder emptied itself. He felt some blows to the stomach and the ribs before he finally blacked out. In the years to follow, Michael Maybrick was to wish many times that he had died that night.

Edward Hamilton looked down at the crushed body. He had no time. He grabbed his knife. The other equipment on the bed stayed there. He had no time to collect all that. Among the stuff that he had left was his journal. He dashed out of the room and looked both ways. He thought he heard a coach approaching. Was it his imagination? He ran in the opposite direction. He could take no chances. He did not know whether the battered man in the room was alive or dead. He could feel the pain in his hands. They were also battered and bruised. He took a coach eventually. Tonight! He had to act tonight! They knew who he was and if Michael Maybrick was alive, then they would soon know what he had done. He did not want them to think that he was an insane killer! That was not how he wanted history to describe him. He was a hero who was going to change the world! He had to find the answer tonight! He had to be ready in the morning. He would give himself up instantly to public praise if he found the answer tonight. He thought again what he needed to make the next one a success. He needed light and total privacy. He had been planning to take the participant to his room but that was obviously out of the question now! He had to think! He did not know how long he wandered around for after he left the coach.

He was in the heart of Whitechapel and there were many people still around. He had to strike now! He would normally go into the drinking houses. That is where most of the possible candidates were. But after what had happened tonight, he was convinced that most of the police force would be looking for him and the drinking houses would be the first place that they would search. He had to do things the uncivilised way! He had to walk around the streets as if he was interested in business! Cheap and nasty! He walked up to a couple of women, but he was dissatisfied with them. He could not waste his chances. It had to be the one! He could not throw his time and effort away rushing things. He rushed the last one and she turned out to be useless! He decided to walk to the drinking house that he was most familiar with and waited outside. If he saw anything suspicious, he could make a quick dash for it. He waited and watched them filter out. He was getting really suspicious when he heard a small group coming out. Two women and a man. The man was Parry and one of the women was Ethel.

'Hey! Parry!' he called out. He ran towards the group. Parry and Ethel both greeted him warmly but asked where he had been all this time. He had not been seen in this area for near on a month.

'You look terrible, lover!' said Ethel. 'Wha' you been up to?'

'Well. This and that! You know how it is.' He looked towards the other woman. A youngish, plump girl with huge eyes. 'And you are?'

'Oh, mind me! This is Mary,' said Parry. Edward's smile suddenly dropped. He looked into her face and was instantly transported in time when as a youngster he was reading about the Whitechapel Murderer. Mary! Mary! This was her! He did not need to look for her. She had found him!

'Mary Kelly, yes?' he said quietly. She suddenly tensed up. 'Ow do you know my name?'

'Oh, we met briefly before!' he said naturally. Not a glint of uncertainty could be seen in his eyes. 'I remembered your face.'

'Oh, Eddie here has been around. A smashing fella!' said Parry.

Mary looked at Parry and Ethel and took this stranger to be someone to trust. They all walked in the same direction for a long distance before they had to split. The original plan was that Parry was to walk both women to their accommodation, but this was changed. Edward suggested that he take Mary to hers. This was agreed by Mary. They walked for some distance on their own and she chatted away happily. She told him that she actually lived in a rented room of her own which made her a better 'class' of person! Yes, thought Edward. A room. A room of her own! It was all fitting together perfectly. He was totally elated! He could not take his eyes off her! His heroine! His leading lady! She would never regret it! He did not even have to ask her any qualifying questions! He knew it was her. He remembered reading it! He remembered her name! She just came to him. It was her destiny! She will always be remembered! He would see to that. She would be his most important Martyr! He chatted happily away, and she hummed a tune some of the way.

'It's just here love. Do you want to come in for a night cap?' she said.

'No thanks! It is quite late.' That was sly! He knew she was the one and whatever he said, he was going to end up in her room. It was fate. It was meant to be! It was her destiny! He waited to see what she would say.

'No! It's not late! Just a small night cap! Just to say thank you for walking me 'ome! Come. I'll sing you a tune!'

He looked into her round face. 'Believe me, the pleasure is all mine!' he said.

On the corner of a road there was a man. He knew Mary and he started to talk to her while trying his best to get a good look at Edward. Edward thought he felt some hostility there and kept his face out of the light. She chatted to the man about something insignificant and then the man watched them until they turned out of sight towards Miller's Court.

Edward was then led up to a door.

'This is my place,' she announced brightly.

Yes, thought Edward, a better class of person! Just ideal. Well-lit and private! He could take as long as he wanted knowing that they were never going to be disturbed! He was so excited his head was spinning. By the time they entered the room, he was already adjusting the grip on the knife. She told him to take a seat. She started taking off her coat and immediately started singing. Wretched woman! Why did she have to sing! What a racket she was making. She managed the first few lines about picking a violet from her mother's grave when he launched himself at her.

He stumbled before he had a good hold of her and in that time, she managed to turn around and see the sharp edge!

'Oh God, murder!' was all she said. The last words she uttered before he grabbed her again and passed the knife swiftly across her neck. She flopped immediately. He had to pick her up clumsily and place her on the bed. Just minutes! Just minutes away from greatness, he thought. I shall find my answer tonight and be a great man! She shall be rewarded! He looked into his bag and was annoyed to find that he had left most of his tools in Maybrick's room. Well at least he was safe here. Nobody would know that he was here. He was sure that Nathaniel was looking for him and that Michael Maybrick had been found. Whether he was alive or dead made no difference. They must know that it was him. But here he was safe! He could work and then in the morning appear victorious in the eyes of the scientific world.

To work then! The fire was burning away brightly and there was a kettle burning above it. He looked around to see if he could find any tea. Great! Beverages while you work! This was the life! Why did he not think of this before! Crouching in the street in the dark. He should have thought of this before and made it a necessity on his list of requirements that the candidate had to have own accommodation and tea! He smiled to himself while he set to work. He made the first incision and saw an incredible sight. The others were all in the dark. He was unable to see very well. However, in the light, the white flesh being slit open to reveal a rich red fluid really excited him! He watched for a few seconds as the wound increased from a slit to a gap. He then made all the necessary incisions before opening the skin flaps. Oh, the luxury of being able to work in comfort like a true scientist! What a joy! He then peered into the lower abdomen and started to remove some of the organs. He removed the stomach and the intestines and unravelled them before throwing them aside. The spleen, the pancreas, the colon. There was no method at all in the way that he worked. He just cut deeper and deeper into the body, removing almost all the organs on the lower abdomen, before starting on the upper abdomen. Certain bits he threw away on the floor and other bits he kept in a neat pile to one side so that he could take them away. He was amazed at how the skin peeled away from the flesh so easily! None of the others were like this! He lost himself so much that he had no idea where he was. He peeled skin after skin after skin! Every time he peeled one area away, he immediately looked elsewhere for another! Wow! This was fantastic! It peeled away like that glue which dries on the hand and can be peeled off! He eventually became so excited that he began to peel it off with his hands! Boy! She was ripe, young Mary. Ripe as a peach! Her skin was plump and younger than the others. He peeled away and removed parts and threw bits all over the place. He cut off the breasts and placed them on the side table. He considered taking those away with him for further interrogation! He removed the nose, the eyes, the lips. Somewhere in all this there has to be a Soul! He had to find it! He removed the heart and placed it in his pocket. He was definitely taking that with him! In his excitement he had almost forgotten what the purpose of this experiment was. He began to indulge his own curiosity and he threw caution to the wind. This was fun! It was like he was a child again, taking apart his mechanical toys bit by bit and seeing if he could put them back together again, much to his father's dismay! Only this toy could not be put together again! He accidentally glimpsed the face and suddenly stopped. Oh my God! She looked nothing like she had done an hour or so ago! Her face had no eyes, nose, lips or skin! He was momentarily troubled, but he resolved the situation by taking the corner of the bedsheet and covering her face. He had to remember; this was for the good of mankind! She had offered her body to science and he was just doing his job! That was all. All scientists doubt their work every now and again! That was natural. He was working too hard. When all this was over, he planned to take a rest. He would be swimming in public adulation but would find the time to go away! He would see things differently in the morning. He was considering all the time to stop for tea but on the other hand, anticipation of success did not allow him to stop. He was getting faster and faster and was rushing frantically now. His hands were totally covered in blood and his clothes were almost totally soiled. He saw himself as the car mechanic who was always dirty, covered in oil and grease! He was a touch disappointed when after an hour and a half, he still had not found the Soul and what was more, he had run out of lovely fleshy skin to peel! There were still some areas to uncover! He felt tired but was adamant not to take a rest. He peered into the lower part of the body and began to take apart the bladder and went straight into the reproductive organs. He was thinking to himself that he would take some of these away with him for some investigation in the laboratory when he moved deeper and found the womb. Several thoughts were running through his head, all of a totally scientific nature when he suddenly removed a lump of flesh to reveal something which at first, he could not identify. Within seconds the memory cells in his brain began working fast. He froze as he stared at the small lump of tissue and at one stage thought it could have been what he was looking for but then his eyes stared widely in disbelief! Yes! He had seen this before! He had encountered it in rats! He stepped back and moaned! A sudden feeling of shock was passing through his body as the sheer horror of what he was looking at lay there in an unrecognisable body!

'Oh Lord! Oh Lord! God, no! God in Heaven help me!' he screamed in a trembling voice.

He stared at the round crouched shape. He could from his position see the clearly formed head, the little, tiny arms and the crouched legs. The tiny body!

'Oh God!' Tears were running down his face as he stepped back even further, slipping on some flesh as he moved.

He looked at the wreckage on the bed. This was Mary Kelly! This was just a few hours ago the body of a living woman! A woman. A talking, walking, living woman! No matter what her life was, what she did, what she had to endure, this had been a woman. She inspired joy in her mother's eyes when she was born! She cried when she was hungry, she smiled when she was happy. She grew and learnt and played. She had friends and lovers! She loved new hats and lovely dresses and cakes! She had danced around the streets causing mayhem and mischief with her hair flowing freely about her. She had siblings she fought with, friends she shared secrets with and lovers she shared special intimacies with! She loved days out at the seaside and summer days picking fruit at the farm for a small reward. She hated the cold and the workhouses. She loved cooking and sewing and yearned to be the mistress of a lovely huge mansion. Lady of the house! To have an important husband and a hectic social life. She wanted a son to be Prime Minster and a daughter to be a barrister's wife. She wanted to learn French and to play the piano. She knew about the realities and the dreams of life! She had known what it was to live. To breath. To laugh. To weep. To feel the sun on her face. To love. She had loved and had been loved. No matter what her life was, she smiled and sang and enjoyed what little life had to offer. And above all, she had that which all women, no matter how destitute, were entitled to. The love of a child! Mary Kelly had life within her! No matter what her life was, she was guaranteed the love of her child. No matter which men entered and left her life, no matter how hard she had to work in her immoral profession, no matter how many days she had to go without food, she would always have had the love of her child! She had life within her belly. And Edward Hamilton had taken it away!

God! What had he done! He was hyperventilating as his memory came back!

This was it! His purpose! His mission. He had found what he was here for! This was Wallace Simpson's alternative lover! The lover who would have taken her attention away from the Nazi king! This was the tycoon whom he had to prevent from being born! The tears rushed down his face. The breaths were short and rapid, and he could feel his head spinning. He felt his whole body go numb. No! God no! What had he done? He stared through his tears at the foetus and at the empty shell that was its mother. *There* lay the human Soul! Scattered in front of him in a hundred pieces! He was staring at the Soul. Mother and child!

His legs gave way, and he sank to the floor on his knees, shaking violently, still clutching the knife in one hand and holding part of a fallopian tube in the other. He was trying to breathe but his sobbing was preventing it. He had done it! He had found the Soul!

'NO! HEAVEN HELP ME! GOD! HEEEEELLLLLPPPPPP!' His scream roared through the tiny room.

Suddenly, he felt movement beneath him. His head was still spinning, and he could not see properly. The ground beneath him seemed to be shaking! He looked up and heard something from the fireplace! The whole room seemed to be shaking though nothing was rattling or moving on the table. He heard a huge rushing sound from the fireplace! The fire suddenly began to rage as if fuelled by gasoline! It roared violently and hissed and increased to twice what it was before. He could feel the heat increase and burn his face. In an instance the fire changed colour to bright orange and then to a shocking, light blue! He had seen that blue before! An intense raging blue furnace which melted the kettle and the surroundings while he watched! The Devil was coming for him! He knew what it was. Within seconds, the Blue Haze leapt out of the fireplace and seemed to fill the room. He could feel unseen forces pulling him into it! His body was pushed forward as if by a strong gush of wind. He resisted only to feel a stronger shove. Something was pushing him towards the Haze!

'No! NO! Not now! I'm not ready! Not now! GOD! NOT NOW! I can't go back!' His scream was unheard! He knew it was futile. He struggled but eventually, the searing heat scorched his hair, and he was sweating from the flames as he was sucked into the Haze. Sucked in by a huge vacuum. He screamed all the way in.

Within seconds, he disappeared, and the Haze disappeared from where it had come. The fireplace went back to normal. Edward Hamilton had left, leaving behind an empty, still, room with just the carnage of Mary Kelly and her unborn son behind.

CHAPTER 34

Darkness! Total Darkness. He had been here before. He could not breathe, and an unseen force was pushing him, pushing, propelling him forward to a place he could not see. Images! Faces! Pictures! Things came into his head. He remembered the Corporation. The President. The Professor. The lies. The deceit. His head ached with all these thoughts entering all at once. He could not breathe let alone think. Frenkel. He could see him. He saw him standing in his prison of a room. Anger. He felt anger. All those years. All those wasted years. The Professor's voice *trusts me my boy.* Bastard! He could kill him. The liar. The Corporation was a fraud. They all were. Then he saw Susan. Yes, that Bitch. He had forgotten her totally. Now here she was. Her smug face taunting him. Wasted work. Wasted five years. Five years it took then to tell him. And that Bitch knew all along. FIVE YEARS. His life wasted. He was used. They had all used him. They would all pay. The bitch. Five years. He would make her pay. He screamed while his grip tightened around the knife he still gripped in his hand. He moved forward in the darkness.

Bitch! He'll show her!

CHAPTER 35

Anthony Frenkel opened his eyes wide. He was on his sofa. He suddenly rose from the sofa and walked over to the camera in the room. He stared at it for a few seconds. His image was being watched even more closely than normal.

'He's coming back. He is coming *back!*" he said looking straight at the camera.

His image was seen by all those in the main control room. They had been staring for two days at the Corridor. Eating, sleeping and watching! The President, Lucas, Perez, Susan and Rodrigues. The whole lot of them. They were exhausted but there had been no indication of when Edward was coming back.

They did not notice that Frenkel had moved and was looking straight at the camera. When they heard him, they all moved to the screen to hear what he said. But he said nothing else. They immediately rushed to the glass division and stared at the Corridor. It gradually changed colour. From pale blue to orange and then red. They heard a rumbling sound like thunder and the atmosphere gauge changed. The temperature around the Haze rose. Yes! He was coming back! Just like Frenkel and all the animals, he was coming back. They were on the point of breaking out into joyous smiles when their ears were pierced by the most shrill, high pitched, animal like scream. It came from the Corridor and chilled them right down to their bones! They stared in horror at the Haze.

'Good Lord!' whispered Susan. 'What was that? What the hell is coming back?'

Her head suddenly felt a tingling. *Jack the Ripper!* It was Anthony Frenkel's voice!

The Devil!

The Devil himself was coming back to 2007!